<u>The Morningstar Trilogy</u>

Chasing Charlie

Chasing New York

Chasing the Morningstar

by

DJ Sherratt

Chasing the Morningstar

Morningstar

Final chapter in the Morningstar Trilogy

DJ SHERRATT

authorHOUSE

AuthorHouse™
1663 Liberty Drive
Bloomington, IN 47403
www.authorhouse.com
Phone: 833-262-8899

Published by AuthorHouse 10/08/2020

ISBN: 978-1-7283-7376-8 (sc)
ISBN: 978-1-6655-0169-9 (e)

All shadows of clouds the sun cannot hide

Like the moon cannot stop oceanic tide;

But a hidden star can still be smiling

at night's black spell on darkness, beguiling

- Munia Khan

Contents

Acknowledgements

It has been quite the journey to get to this point in time. Many challenges and major life changes along the way. Also, the love and support of so many. Thank you to all those that have waited patiently for life to quit taking priority! I hope it was worth the wait!

To all my friends who loaned me their names, whether in full or in part: Patrice, Kerry, Kirby, Bobby, Gary and Jessica to name a few. Thank you, you're the best!

To Gary, for capturing me looking relaxed and happy and natural. Love you!

To Ann, for once again, being so supportive and creative. Your incredible perspective has been the first visual impression of The Morningstar Trilogy and I so appreciate you and Kev Mac's help and love along the way!

And thank you to my soul mate, Mark.

What a team! I wouldn't be the person I am without you!

I love you,

Thank you, thank you, thank you.

-D xxxx

Prologue

Alabama 1911

As soon as she cleared the church steps she was moving fast. She had stayed too late, learning to read with the Minister's wife. When she realized it had gone dark, she made her apologies to her and ran her way out of the small church. If she stuck to the laneways, it would take her a few minutes longer, but she knew of another way; much more straightforward, she could be home a lot quicker. Her father's lecture would be loud and long, but he'd always end up being grateful for her safe return.

But, if her father knew she was taking the short cut, he'd be really angry. She may even get a whooping! As she neared the entrance to the short cut, through the long grasses, she weighed her options. Figuring she'd could be home that much sooner and her father wouldn't even know, she chose the shortcut and veered to her right, into the darkness, further. Using her hands like machetes against the tall grasses, she knocked each one aside as she moved forward. Her run had slowed only slightly, and she could see the moon above guiding her way.

But then, so could he. He waited, like a preying animal. Not a friendly presence. Actually a really sick fuck. He had an evil obsession of overpowering young girls and he'd had his eye on this one for a while. For a long while.

As she ran towards him she was completely oblivious of him being hidden. Focusing on clearing her pathway, she didn't see his foot as he stuck it out in front of her. She tripped and fell hard, knocking the wind out of her and immobilizing her, momentarily.

Just long enough for him to pounce. And, he did. The animal had caught his prey.

* * *

The father sat quietly dozing by the fire, waiting for his daughter's return. He worked very hard as a laborer on a cotton farm. He didn't own the farm, but it was his dream to own land of his own one day. Although, he and his family had been living and working on the farm since before he was born, he knew that if he was ever to realize his dream, he'd have to move from Alabama, northward. It had been on his mind for some time and would cost him some to move his family. He already had a horse and cart. There was only him, his wife and teen daughter and a few pieces of furniture that would be coming along. His older sons had lives and wives of their own and would not be coming. At least, not right away. They would stay on the farm and work through the harvest. Once he was settled and employed, he'd send for his sons and their families. He had managed to save some money but, he'd need more to make sure they could make the journey. He hoped to have the money together by September, four months away. It would be best to travel north before winter.

When he awoke he realized it was much later into the evening. The house was quiet, but exactly as he left it. The fire, now low and barely giving off any warmth told him all he needed to know. She hadn't come home.

Realizing this, he immediately became alert, jumping to his feet and calling out to his wife. As he grabbed his jacket near the door he told his wife to get her shoes on and run across the field to their sons' homes to come join him. He then grabbed his shotgun, made sure it was loaded and headed out to the barn. Before his sons joined him, he wanted to get torches to make their search easier.

He tried hard not to think the worst. Very hard. In fact, he couldn't help but feel anger towards his daughter for not listening to him. He had told her numerous times to never be out after dark, that it was dangerous. He had told her.

They began their search walking towards the church. She had been there and would have walked along the roadway to make it home. The father and two sons searched the laneway, along its edge and into the brush, but when they came to the shortcut she had actually taken, the walked right past it without a thought, heading to the church.

* * *

Once he was on top of her, his dirty hand covered her mouth. She tried biting down on his hand, but he pressed too firmly down and she couldn't shake his hand away. Next she tried kneeing him in his groin, but raising her knee only eased his ability to push his weight on her, and spread her legs with his own. She fought with all her might, but he was much stronger, much heavier and her small frame was easily overpowered by his over 6 foot frame. All her struggling was starting to piss him off. He pushed his weight onto the hand covering her mouth and with the other hand he punched the side of her head so hard, she immediately stopped moving.

Stupid bitch! He thought, grateful to have her limp while he began to tear away at her drawers and viciously rape her. She didn't come to during the assault, nor when he rolled off her and pulled himself up. As he stood to his full height, he could see over the tall grasses to where the laneway was. And, he could see the torches. Like the animal he was, he instinctually dropped to hide himself back in the grasses and stealthily ran off in the other direction. Those torches were nearer the church where she had come from, so he figured he had enough time to get home and thoroughly clean himself up. She had fought hard and he was scraped up from her nails. The hand he hit her with was now sore and starting to swell. He'd need to tend to his hand and get rid of his clothing. Never had a victim fought so hard. For a young girl, she had surprised him with how much she had struggled. Normally, he was able to get the job done without knocking them out, although he had done it once or twice. A sharp blow to the temple usually kept them out long enough for him rape them, but he preferred them to be awake and have a fight in them. It made it so much more satisfying.

* * *

As she lay in the grass unconscious, unaware of the brutal attack that had just taken place, her subconscious took over.

In her mind's eye she was slowly walking through the same grasses she now lay in. Except, it wasn't dark, it was a brilliant sunny day and the grasses swayed in the wind, her hand floating just at the tips end and moving them as she walked. The sunshine felt warm upon her face and she raised her head to feel its glow. Her dark skin began to feel the heat, but there were no trees around for shade. All she could see was a never ending field of tall grasses.

At some point, her eyes became focused on a small dot in the distanced. She felt as though it was moving towards her. She felt no fear as the dot became bigger, taller and more into focus. As she neared it she was able to make out the figure of a person, a woman. It was an older black woman. She didn't know who she was, but she felt as though she did. Her mind was questioning everything, but her heart was filled to overflowing.

"My child", the elderly woman said. She was older than the young girl's grandmother, but looked a little like her. She had a wrap around her head, like her mother wore in the fields. Her smile was lovely and her bright, big eyes brought a smile to the young girl's face, causing the elderly woman to smile back.

"Where am I?" the young girl asked.

"You're here with me" the elderly woman said, her arms outstretched to acknowledge the fields around them, "we're in the grasses where you lay. But not to worry, I'm here". She told the young girl. She took a moment to take in the elderly woman's words before she asked, "Am I dead?"

"No." she replied. "But, you have a very difficult journey ahead of you, which at times will be harder than what you should have to endure, but you must", she told her.

The young girl remained quiet, watching the elderly woman's face. She couldn't explain it, but deep down inside, she trusted this elderly woman.

"What should I do?" the young girl asked the woman.

"You are a very special woman. Your life is meant to be as it is. No different. You must accept your fate, but in return, you will be given an ability to help your kin. Just as I am now." She said, mysteriously. The young girl took in her words.

"We're kin?" the young girl asked

"Yes we are, my child. I am your great-grandmother. I have been watching over you since your birth. I watch over all my kin. And now, I wish to pass this gift onto you" she told her. The young girl's eyes went wide as she grasped her great-grandmother's intent.

The elderly woman came towards her and reached out her hands. The young girl instinctively took them into her own and an overwhelming feeling came over her. She closed her eyes and her head slowly fell back as her body began to vibrate with her great-grandmother's touch. Faces started to flash before her, young and old alike. Some she knew, some she didn't. Some flashes were extreme, up close views and some were distant. She saw crowds, colours and began to hear music. Her head began to spin with all the sights and sounds overtaking her, almost as if she were on a musical ride, like a carnival.

Her great-grandmother slowly released her hold as the young girl felt the sensation of floating. Their hands now apart, the young girl opened her eyes just as the great-grandmother began to fade from her vision. She could however, hear her voice.

"All that you've just seen, all those people are your kin, yet to come. It's your responsibility to guide them, whenever you feel they need it. But, you cannot overstep. Just as you can't change your destiny, you also can't change theirs. Life has so many twists and turns and everyone is meant to experience them all. Our family, and especially the family coming, are gifted in many ways and you play a very important role in all of it."

Her great-grandmother's words were surrounding her as her body floated. She felt completely loved and safe in her subconscious experience. She felt no pain, no hurt, just love. And it felt wonderful! A smile came to her face as her great grandmother's voice began to soften and drift off.

"Good will always overcome evil. In life and death, the family created through this single act of evil will bring about such wonderful things. You must believe that and stay strong! Remember, you've been gifted." She told her.

The floating sensation began to fade and the young girl began to feel the ground beneath her, some of the grasses poking into her. Suddenly, her body began to hurt and she started to feel great pain, awful pain, as though she had been ripped apart. It hurt to move, but she rolled onto her side and slowly brought her knees up to her, cradling them. Her dress had been pulled straight up to her neck and her drawers were not on her. She had no idea what had happened to them. She lay there, trying to think of anything else, except the pain she was in and how badly her head hurt. She was in this position when she began to hear voices and someone walking through the grasses. She couldn't call out, she couldn't try to catch their attention, she could only lay there and hold herself.

Within minutes, the torches were held over her and she could hear the voices of her father and brothers. They had found her and she was alive.

She was alive!

Chapter 1

WHO ARE TANYA AND REBECCAH?

Luisa Van Zeeban, secret wife and nanny of music superstar Chase Morningstar had done the unthinkable. She had managed to kidnap Chase's toddler daughter, Poppy while Chase was locked up on trial for the murder of his wife Sonya, something else Luisa was also responsible for. In fact, Luisa's criminal activities grew much worse since she became Poppy's nanny. Nothing was done without a hidden agenda and the agenda had many active items on it.

Something had snapped in Luisa's mind shortly after Sonya's murder. It was as if she felt invincible one minute and vulnerable the next. Completely in control on the one hand and losing touch with her reality on the other. There were periods of time in her day where she couldn't say for sure where she had been or what she had been up to. Almost as though she were blacking out, she'd become aware and realize she'd been out driving or doing some other activity that she was unaware she had been doing. Her reality was becoming increasingly warped and by the time Chase had secretly married her to keep her from being deported, Luisa was convinced that she and Chase were a real couple. To her, the cover of them being employer and employee was only so that people wouldn't think it was in bad taste to marry so soon after one's spouse was murdered. Otherwise, it was a real, everyday marriage.

Except, it wasn't.

They had moved to Switzerland and had been hiding out for several months when Chase was called back to the U.S. When Luisa's sick mind came to the realization that Chase would never reciprocate her feelings, she decided she'd take Poppy and run.

Luisa knew that Chase would never give up looking for his daughter if he thought she was out there. Her getaway plan had many holes in it and she had to make it up as she and Poppy travelled through Switzerland hoping to find a way of making sure no one ever came looking for her or, the child ever again. She found that answer in a restaurant in the north of Switzerland. On a dark, rainy night, she and Poppy made friends with a young mother named Tanya and her small daughter, Rebeccah who was about Poppy's age. While sharing stories and a warm meal, Luisa's psychotic mind came up with a great game plan. The only way to ensure her and Poppy wouldn't be found was to die and who better to help her do that than Tanya and Rebeccah? Luisa's mind was racing. She needed to be sure all would work out just right.

As they sat in the restaurant, she paid close attention to the weather reports, especially all the flood warnings and high, fast water cautions of the river near that area. She also paid attention to all that Tanya told her. A single mother with no financial or family supports of any kind except for a piece of property with a house on it, left to Tanya by her dead mother. All Tanya and Rebeccah's belongings in the world were stuffed into the small car sitting outside, near Luisa's Range Rover. The property was located not very far from the restaurant, but Tanya was scared to drive up the 400 foot steep hill in her overstuffed, limping car, especially on such a treacherous night.

Luisa managed to not only convince Tanya to make the trip that night, but she manipulated it so that Tanya would be driving the Range Rover and Luisa would take her car. Not allowing Tanya much chance to change her mind, she waited patiently while Tanya and Rebeccah used the bathroom one last time before leaving the restaurant. What poor Tanya didn't know was that while she was in the bathroom, Luisa routed through Tanya's handbag, took the more relevant items and switched them with some of hers and then paid the bill for the four meals, so that Tanya would not need to open her handbag again.

Tanya had no idea what Luisa was up to, but she felt in her gut that travelling up that hill in such bad weather wasn't smart, trying once more to convince Luisa that waiting would be better, but Luisa wasn't listening. She gently maneuvered Tanya into the Range Rover and got her daughter, Rebeccah buckled in tight and sent them on their way. Her plan was to follow closely behind. So much so, in fact that when they reached nearer the top, Luisa purposely drove Tanya's car into the back of the Range Rover forcing Tanya to lose control on the slick wet road, sending it over the side of the hill, plunging it down the 400 foot drop landing upside down on the banks of the flooded river that was raging that night and, is if God were on Luisa's side, a landslide came crashing down on top of the mangled Range Rover hiding it from site for weeks on end. It all worked perfectly.

Luisa got her vehicle settled and carried on up the hill. She waited patiently at the predetermined meeting spot for the young mother, Tanya and child, Rebeccah who would never show up. Once Luisa felt assured of that, she rifled through the items she'd taken from Tanya's bag. It was a wealth of information and with each piece of identification, she plunged deeper and deeper into her psychosis. When she again started the car, Luisa was no longer in charge and the fate of the little girl sleeping soundly in the backseat was in Tanya's hands. In her mind, Poppy would die and be re-born as Rebeccah.

* * *

When the child awoke, she was in a bed she had never slept in before, in a room she had never seen. It was still dark as she tried to look around the room and focus on some of the items, but she couldn't make them out. All she could see was the small amount of light coming from the window. Covered by heavy drapery she pushed it aside, looking up into the dark morning sky. The moon was far in the West, barely exposed, but she could clearly make out a small bright star. She stared at it for a moment, finding solace in its presence. On a cold dark morning, it was a welcome sign in the early morning's sky. She continued to stare at it for a while until it slowly faded from sight. She wondered, where did it go? One day, she would find out!

Feeling inquisitive, the toddler scurried out of the room. She entered a hallway which led straight into a large open kitchen and stood staring, half asleep, at the scene before her.

Papers were strewn across the table. Cards and photos were cut out and piled on top of a garbage can near the door. She had been working through the night to recreate their lives. Tanya and Rebeccah had just moved in and all their documentation had to state that. The car had been unpacked and a thorough search of the house and car had put together enough food and essentials to last them quite a while, surprisingly. In and amongst the toiletries, she had come across a hair dye for dark brown hair and a large package of red henna. She would use the hair dye on herself and then mix the henna with strong cold coffee and use it on the child's hair. If they had to go into town for anything she'd make sure they were disguised first, Tanya wasn't taking any chances.

The child moved slowly into the room towards the wooden kitchen table. It was round with four matching chairs and a small matching hutch, off to one side. The furniture, like the house, was old and needed cleaning, but it was sturdy and intact.

"Oh you're up! Come here, Rebeccah and have some breakfast." The child looked confused at the woman and pulled a face. "I'm Poppy, *not* Beccah", she said indignantly. The woman laughed.

"Oh silly you, it's not Poppy, it's Poppet." She stressed to the child, "And, you know it's just a nick name, but Rebeccah is your real name. You were named after my mother, our Grandmother, you know that. And, you're such a big girl now, we should start using your real name."

She made a face at the child, shaking her head and closed the subject with a wag of her finger. "No more nicknames. Now, come and have some breakfast." The woman busied herself while Rebeccah sat down.

"I know you're probably wondering where we are, aren't you?" Tanya asked Rebeccah, sweetly. Rebeccah nodded her head as she bit into an orange slice offered to her and rubbed her eye sleepily.

"This is our new home. We are going to live here and you and Mommy are going to be very happy here." She told Rebeccah.

"Mommy?" Rebeccah asked her. "Daddy?" She asked as well. The woman shook her head, laughing at the child.

"Silly girl, I'm your Mommy!" She emphasized. "Wee-Za was my nickname you called me, but now you must call me Mommy, okay?" The child seemed to accept this change easier than her own name change.

"Where's Daddy?" Rebeccah asked, shrugging her shoulders. At this point, her real father, Chase Morningstar was in a jail cell in the U.S., but that was not what the woman told her.

"He's gone away now, honey and he won't be back.", was all she said as she turned and continued to tidy the kitchen. From then on, Chase Morningstar ceased to exist in the child's world and slowly, but surely, the two assumed the identities of Rebeccah and Tanya.

The house they acquired was a small farm house built some 70 years previous. It had been owned by an uncle of Tanya's mother who left it to her when he died. She'd had no use for it but knew one day it might be a worthwhile piece of property, the farmland surrounding the house was often eyed by area farmers for favorable land to add to their acreage. But Tanya's mother never sold out and having read through all the legal papers found in the car, the land could now be used to rent out and become a source of income for Tanya, which she promptly advertised.

Before too long the two neighboring farmers on either side were paying Tanya monthly rent in cash for the extra acreage. This allowed Tanya and Rebeccah to live in almost seclusion only needing to travel into town for groceries or essentials whenever necessary. It also provided Tanya enough time to thoroughly brainwash the little girl into a whole new life as Rebeccah, meanwhile Poppy's death had been discovered and tragically reported, only to fade away in the media and in people's minds. For most, life went back to normal and for two years Tanya and Rebeccah lived immersed in their own little bubble, cementing the transformation completely. Gone were Luisa and Poppy. Gone, but not forgotten.

* * *

Rebeccah, now age 5, awoke in the very early morning hours. She got up and looked out her bedroom window at the morning sky and there it was. Her star. Her morning star. She watched it almost every morning. It filled her with such happiness. It twinkled bright and proud for a number of minutes, but as the sun began its ascension the star faded from sight. She watched until it had gone from sight and then climbed back into her bed with thoughts of stars in her head and quickly fell back to sleep.

* * *

Just as Rebeccah was to start school Tanya began having debilitating headaches. Believing that she needed a strong headache medication, Tanya had been to the Pharmacist in town to enquire. His name was Hans Baumgartner. Hans was a simple man who was truly the salt of the earth. Having never married, he spent his days filling prescriptions for the small town's residents and his nights listening to his music. He had looked after an elderly aunt for many years and she had left him quite an inheritance, but he had never spent her money, hoping one day to marry the girl of his dreams and start a whole new life together. As if by manifestation, Tanya walked into his shop one day. He had noticed Tanya and her young daughter a few times and fancied the young mother, but was far too shy to do anything except sell her headache medication. When she approached his counter on her third visit, he decided to find out some answers for himself.

"Still having those headaches?" he asked Tanya.

"Yes. I think they're from stress or maybe a sinus infection, I'm not too sure" she answered and smiled weakly. The truth was she didn't want to go to a doctor to find out. She didn't want anyone poking at her and perhaps realizing that she isn't who she said she is.

"I still think you should see a doctor, my dear" he told her. He was concerned for the young mother, especially seeing her in such pain.

"Thank you Mr. Baumgartner, I'll do that soon. In the meantime, can you recommend anything stronger?" she enquired. He hesitated, wanting to get her in to see his friend who was a family doctor, but he didn't want to push her. Instead, he found the strongest medication he could for her symptoms and rang her through the cash register. Seeing 5 year old Rebeccah standing beside the young mother, Hans asked "Can I give her a candy?" Tanya nodded and Hans grabbed a bag of chocolate M&M's and handed them to Rebeccah. Her green eyes lit up like the night's sky and Hans smiled wide at her reaction.

"Make sure you don't eat them before your dinner. Only when Mommy and Daddy say, alright?" he asked her. The little girl looked confused for a moment.

"No Daddy" was all she said. Tanya looked at her and then back at Hans.

"Her daddy is …dead" Tanya whispered. Tanya looked at the child and grabbed the candy and put it into her purse. "Don't hold them like that, they'll melt!" she admonished. Rebeccah's face fell and Hans felt badly for her. It was obvious that her mother was in pain, but she shouldn't be taking it out on her daughter like that, especially since in all the times he'd seen them together the child was always so lovely, so well behaved.

"Please let me know if this medication helps you. It's the strongest I have. Past that, you will have to get a prescription for a stronger pill" Hans explained.

"Thank you Mr. Baumgartner" Tanya said.

"It's Hans, actually. You can call me Hans" he smiled at Tanya.

"Tanya" she said as she held out her hand. They shook hands. For Hans, it was an electrifying moment. For Tanya it was a handshake. Before she could turn to leave, Hans was asking, "And, what is your name?" to Rebeccah. She hesitated for just a moment looking to Tanya for reassurance and then said softly, "Rebeccah". He held out his hand to the child and she shook it just as she had seen her mother.

"Well, it's very nice to make your acquaintance, Rebeccah", he said to her and smiled. She smiled back and Hans' heart melted. What a little sweetheart this child was. Her hair was almost the color of coffee with deep red tones which made her green eyes stand out immensely. She was such a striking looking child and Hans wondered if she had taken after the father, she didn't seem to favor Tanya at all.

The two thanked Hans and left the store. His plan had worked perfectly. He'd found out that there was no father in the picture. That was all he needed to know for now. The next time they met, he decided to see if he could ask her to have coffee with him. With that, he was thrilled with his progress!

The opportunity came just a few days later when Tanya entered the store. Hans was aware she was there before she found him. He had watched her enter from the mirror at the back of the store. The sight of her made his heart start to race and he noticed that she looked brighter, smiling as she walked to the back to find him at his counter.

"Well, you look better! Did the extra-strength medication work?" he asked, knowing full well they had helped judging by the smile she had.

"Oh yes, Hans!" she said happily. "They have been a huge help for me!"

"Good, will you be needing more already?" he asked wondering how often she was getting these kind of headaches if she had used up all the medication he had given to her just a few days earlier.

"No...no" she laughed. "I just wanted you to know that they did the trick and I haven't had a headache since. That's saying something, Hans" she told him. This made Hans concerned.

"Are you under a lot of stress, Tanya?" he asked her trying to diagnose what was going on with her.

"Well, let's see. I'm a single-mother to a 5 year old whose father died and left me without any kind of financial support. I live in an old house that needs repair beyond my physical or financial ability and I have no family left, making me alone in the world. I think that gives reason for some bad headaches, now and again" she answered him thoughtfully.

"Hmmm…so, stress headaches it is then" he agreed. He wondered what he could do to help her with that stress level. "It's almost lunchtime. Would you like to go for a bite to eat? Not eating properly can contribute to stress headaches" he informed her, smiling.

She was about to say no. She had kept herself basically hidden for most of the last two years in hopes that everyone would carry on with life as normal and when she and Rebeccah did emerge, no one would think anything was concerning. At times, she forgot the truth and believed the whole "Tanya and Rebeccah" story. At other times, her paranoia would cause her to act irrationally and her and Rebeccah would be house bound for days on end. School was a Godsend for Rebeccah, finally being able to socialize with other children and being able to leave the house through the week. On the weekends, it all depended on whether or not Tanya felt vulnerable or had a headache. If so, they stayed indoors.

As she pondered Hans' request, she studied him closely. He wasn't an overly handsome man, but he did have a ready smile that always reached his eyes. She liked that. He was probably 10 years older than her but he didn't look it. His hair was light brown and thin but covered his whole head. He was a clean shaven man and walked just about everywhere he went so he had a decent physique; no beer belly, or stained smoker's teeth. She liked that, too. Hans Baumgartner was possibly the very best Tanya could hope for, given her present situation. It was nice to finally have a man show some interest in her, especially after the failed attempt of her previous marriage. Feeling bitter about that, she decided that she'd take him up on his offer.

"Okay, Hans. Let's go and have some lunch, shall we?" she said to him sweetly. His smile broke across his whole face and he quickly took off the white lab coat, grabbed the shop keys and led Tanya out of the store turning to lock it up before heading up the street with Tanya walking beside him! Hans couldn't believe she had actually agreed.

"Do you come into town often?" not allowing her to respond he continued, "I come to this little corner café almost every day. They make the best meals.

9

I haven't had anything I didn't like" he said enthusiastically, as he reached the café door, opened it and made a grand gesture for her to enter first.

The café was small and packed with patrons all chatting busily as they ate their lunches. The smell was intoxicating, causing Tanya to believe every word Hans had said about the place and judging from how busy the place was, everyone agreed.

They waited for about 10 minutes before they were able to take a seat at a table nearest the front window. The quaint café felt homey and cozy and Tanya was instantly in love with the atmosphere, not something she generally cared about. However, after being in basic seclusion for almost two years, she appreciated anyplace that wasn't the small house she lived in. With no headache plaguing her and having a sudden moment of enjoyment, Tanya let her guard down and started to relax. She and Hans shared childhood stories; Hans mostly of his Aunt who raised him, Tanya lying her way through her early formative years. Hans didn't suspect a thing, he believed whatever the woman told him. He was smitten with her, very smitten. Tanya wasn't exactly smitten, but she was feeling happy for the first time in a long time.

Mistake #1.

Chapter 2

CONSPIRACY THEORY

Leena Van Zeeban had seen a lot of family tragedy in the years that followed her sister, Luisa's death. Her mother, who had battled throat cancer for many years passed within months of her daughter. Some thought it was from the grief of losing Luisa, some thought it was from the shame of what she had been accused of doing and the aftershock the family endured, as round after round of police and paparazzi invaded their privacy time and again. They rented a small house in the very southern tip of Switzerland and stayed there hidden for many months until the media interest died down. Regardless, with her mother's death, her father's mental decline began. Soon, he was unable to live and care for the beautiful house that the family had grown up in. Against her better judgement, Leena and her remaining sister Nadia put the house up for sale and put their father into a nursing home. Despite it having the latest in geriatric technology, Rainer Van Zeeban continued to decline. It was difficult to watch him fade like he had, a man whose mind was once so sharp was now completely disoriented by the simplest of things. At her last visit, he didn't recognize her and ignored her completely. The nurses tried to assure him that she was his daughter, but he would have none of it, turning his wheelchair to the wall. She left feeling lost and alone.

Her sister Nadia had married some years before and moved to Italy after the media circus surrounding Luisa's death. Her husband did not want her to be subjected to the scrutiny and Italy was where they ran to. Now, two years later, other than attending their mother's funeral and helping to sell the family home, Nadia was also gone. Leena Van Zeeban was left feeling very much alone in the world and would often travel to the north of Switzerland, to the cottage area to reminisce about a childhood gone by and a family that was no more. She rarely stopped while visiting the area, simply enjoying the drive, scenery and remembering old times.

11

It was on one particular visit back to the northern area that Leena required a drug store. She drove a little past the cabin area north through a small village. To her surprise the tiny village had a store called "Hans the Pharmacist". *Huh*, she thought, *the guy's a marketing whiz!* She approached the door, but found it locked. She tried the door three times, but it was definitely locked. Wondering why, she looked for the hours posted on the window. CLOSED OVER LUNCH. She checked her watch, 12:17 pm.

Hmmpf! She thought, *Just my luck.* She turned and walked up the street hoping to find a store or some sort of shop that may be able to help her. She came upon a café and wondered if there was anything past that point. She stopped for a moment to look and see if there was any hope of finding a store and decided she was out of luck in this tiny village. She didn't have many options; she could wait for "Hans the Pharmacist" to open or get back in her car and find another town with another shop.

Feeling frustrated she turned to find her car, catching sight of it about a block away and across the street. She got to her car, climbed in and checking the roadway first, turned the car around to make her way back towards the south. As she passed the café front window, she caught a glimpse of a woman sitting having lunch in the café. It was brief as she sped on past, but Leena audibly gasped. The woman could have been her sister, Luisa's twin, except she had darker hair, much darker. Leena was tempted to turn the car around and go back to take another look, so similar was she to her dead sister. After travelling about 5 miles, Leena's curiosity got the better of her and she once again, turned the car around and drove back to the café. As she approached the front window she slowed down to a mere crawl to get a good look, but to no avail. The dark haired twin of her sister had been replaced by a large blonde with bright red lipstick. No twin there. Shaking off an eerie feeling, Leena drove down the road and found a suitable spot to turn back around.

She passed "Hans the Pharmacist" and noticed that the store was now open. *Apparently lunch hour wasn't a hard and fast rule or necessarily between 12:00 pm – 1: 00pm*, she thought. She parked the car and went into the shop. She was impressed with the amount of things the small shop carried.

His store was very neatly organized and she quickly found what she was looking for. A plain looking gentleman with kind smiling eyes helped her at the checkout.

"Were you able to find all that you were looking for today?" he asked Leena, all the while smiling wide. *He's such a happy fellow!* She thought. She felt his smile and cheery attitude contagious and couldn't help but smile wide at him.

"Yes, thank you!" Leena said sweetly. "Are you Hans?" she found herself asking, surprised by her own interest.

"The one and only" he said proudly.

"You have an impressive store here, Hans. You carry just about everything here, don't you?" she asked being sincere in her compliment. "And, are you always in such a great mood? You must certainly love what you do!" she observed, smiling wide back at him.

He leaned forward as if to share a secret and whispered, "Just had my first date with who I hope, will be my future wife" he said winking at her. Leena's eyes went wide smiling even bigger. *What a sweet man*, she thought. *He's practically blushing!*

"Well, best of luck to you, Hans the Pharmacist. I believe she's a very lucky woman!" Leena said to him as she took her receipt and left the shop feeling a little bit brighter than she had before she walked in.

As she left his store, Hans couldn't help but feel an odd sense that she had seemed familiar to him. He stood for a moment pondering what it could be and then, shook his head to bring himself around. He was really smitten with Tanya and didn't need to be thinking about another woman who happened into his store. She was unknown to him, but Tanya wasn't, she was his reality and possibly, his future.

As Leena drove through town one more time, she again slowed past the café. Two elderly men now sat where her dead sister's doppelganger once sat, if it even was a doppelganger. Leena wasn't so sure what it was about the woman she saw that caused such a gut reaction in her, but to her it was shocking how much the unknown woman sitting having lunch in the café front looked like Luisa. She just couldn't shake it and it stayed with her the whole drive home.

Having spent the better part of her weekend in her car, Leena got home with a head full of remembrances of a time she'd rather have forgotten. Luisa was practically estranged from the family once she went to nanny for distant family in America. Never did the family think that when they said goodbye to her that day in the airport, it would be the last time they would lay eyes on her. Their reaction to finding out that she had moved back to Switzerland and had never contacted them was incredibly disappointing to her mother and father. Leena didn't really understand Luisa's problems, except to believe she had mental issues. Real mental issues. After all, who kidnaps a child? And, of a major superstar, no less? Who hires someone to kill the child's mother?

Luisa was a lost cause to Leena, but it didn't stop her from reliving those horrendous days as her weekend drew to a close. She decided to shower and get into bed early ready for her week ahead. When she climbed into bed, she reached into her bedside table and pulled out a small scrapbook. She perused slowly through the pages, reading the newspaper articles and photos that she kept in it. The last page held only one item. A business card.

Mr. Lucas Hollomby, Private Investigator.

New York, N.Y.

She held the card in her palm and drew her fingers across his embossed name. Lucas Hollomby. She had thought a lot about him over the last 2 years. It really hadn't been his fault for all the media crush and shame that was brought upon the family. He was just someone she could direct her anger at and she had been so rude. She hoped one day to correct that.

* * *

Robin Hewer booked his flight and flew into JFK airport the minute Lucas Hollomby agreed to do the interview. As the investigative reporter for the Chicago Channel 7 News, Robin thought a retrospective on the Morningstar murder and kidnapping story two years after the fact might be interesting. Lucas Hollomby was, after all, the hero of the story, breaking open the whole murder trial and proving the innocence of music superstar, Chase Morningstar with the one question he had Dana Rose ask Judge Carmichael, while he was on the stand. "Did you have an inappropriate relationship with Ms. Van Zeeban?" After that, everything fell like a house of cards and when Johann showed up at the courthouse to murder Chase and finish the job, it was Lucas Hollomby who pulled his gun and put an end to Johann's murderous attempt on Chase Morningstar's life.

But Robin had done some digging and found that Lucas had more interest in the case than just having Chase Morningstar as a client. Lucas Hollomby was intertwined in the whole story with his own childhood and it was this angle that had never been explored or examined. The police reports had told the story, but it was never released publicly.

Robin Hewer was like a dog with a bone when it came to his job and when he'd read that Lucas's father had been gunned down, execution style, by none other than Johann when Lucas was a boy, Robin wanted that part of the story told. He always managed to find a new and interesting angle to report from and he relished in having the reputation of digging deeper than any other reporter. He was going to make it big in the investigative news reporting industry. He was determined to be as respected as David Brinkley, Sam Donaldson or Hugh Downs.

Robin entered the offices of Hollomby Investigations thinking how well things had gone for Lucas since the last day of the trial. He became famous overnight and his business took off! Normally not one to have any overhead, he had to find office space, hire a secretary and reluctantly bring in 2 other investigators who took the more mundane cases off Lucas's hands. He was in such high demand that every scorned wife within a 500 miles radius came to Hollomby Investigations to catch their cheating husbands in the act. Lucas worked exclusively with high profile clients on high profile cases and Chase Morningstar had him on retainer for a 5 year term, should anything else happen requiring his expertise.

Robin approached the attractive receptionist and told her his name. She directed him to a waiting area and said Lucas would be right with him. He sat in an enormous deep brown leather chair. It occurred to him that everything in the office area was quite large, and then Lucas Hollomby walked into the waiting area and Robin understood completely why.

The man himself was large, very large; irresponsibly large. Not overweight at all, he was just a really big guy and Robin could imagine him trying to sit in a wingback or black office chair; ridiculous. So, everything was big.

Lucas stood over Robin and reached his hand out. "Lucas Hollomby, Mr. Hewer, pleasure to meet you". Robin stood his full 6'1 and still felt dwarfed. He shook Lucas's paw noticing how it literally enveloped his whole hand.

"Pleasure is all mine, Mr. Hollomby" Robin said sincerely. "I am excited about this storyline and the angle I want to take" he continued without giving up what angle that might be. They nodded at one another and Lucas led Robin to his office and shut the door. Lucas's office didn't disappoint either. A humungous desk, with a very large chair with two large chairs for clients. Lucas gestured for Robin to take a seat and sat behind his desk leaning back in his chair. Robin sat across from Lucas and opened his briefcase taking out his iPad. Robin didn't use a cameraman, finding interviewees gave up much more when it was just him and them. No crew, no cameras and no spotlight. Just a simple conversation had between two people. Nothing could be more honest, more revealing or raw. It was Robin's personal style and it worked beautifully and so, as with the man before him, Robin Hewer was in high demand for what he did. More often, if they were going to be interviewed, they wanted Robin Hewer.

Robin set the iPad up so that it was videotaping the two men. He did a test video to ensure all was good and within moments of the official introduction he was asking his first question.

"Tell me how good it felt to pull that trigger?" he asked the large man, wondering if the small boy who lost his father would answer. The question did throw Lucas for a moment and his respect for Robin grew. That's why he was the best! Lucas wanted to be completely honest but even for prime time news, it might be difficult for them to hear how gratifying is was to kill Johann. Lucas dropped his head and smiled for a moment. Robin was holding no punches. This first question set the standard for the angle the line of questioning would take.

"Anytime I pull the trigger I have to consider that it might end someone's life. It hasn't happened often in my career, I am proud to say. However, each time I did I believed in what I was doing and that the person on the other end was as equally interested, if not more in killing me." He held up his finger, smiling at Robin as he paused a moment. "However, I realize I skirted your question and I want to be fair to you and your reporting. Johann Kellerman assassinated my father when I was a young boy. He did it because my father was integral in having his father arrested and thrown in jail for most of Johann's life. He shot my dad through the eye and left my mother a widow and me without a father. Pulling the trigger that day saved the life of my friend and client Chase Morningstar and avenged the death of my father. Pulling the trigger that day felt pretty damn good" he ended with a nod of his head and a smile. Robin's interview with Lucas was brilliant. Every question asked gave Lucas pause. You could feel the emotion Lucas had for the case and when Robin asked him at the very end, "Any regrets?" Lucas, drew in his breath and held it for a moment.

"Oh" he let his breath out, "Anytime you can't give the family closure, there's regrets" he admitted. "I regret that Luisa's family had to endure such horrendous treatment afterward, it really was abusive" he said apologetically. "I regret I wasn't able to stop Johann before anyone died and I regret that it took six weeks to find the wreckage." It was as honest as he was going to be about Leena. Truth was, his biggest regret was losing any chance of a relationship with her. That was his deepest regret of all.

By the end of the interview the two men had become great, long lasting friends.

When Robin showed his Production Manager the completed piece he had put together, she was floored. It was excellent investigative journalism, worthy of an Alfred E. Murrow award for journalism excellence. With that in mind, his manager pulled a few strings, called in some favors and before he knew it Robin Hewer was presenting his investigative report on an ABC Special Report. It was riveting television, once again the country was held captive by the Morningstar tragedies.

* * *

Leena Van Zeeban sat mesmerized by what she was watching. Not two days earlier, she had been caught up in her memories of Lucas Hollomby and now she was watching him being interviewed in an investigative report on the Morningstar Tragedies. The reporter was asking about his personal connection to the case. Leena had not known of Lucas's father's murder. As he answered each question, she studied him intently. Her eyes travelled up and down the large man sitting with his legs crossed away from the screen, his left hand resting comfortably on his leg. *No wedding ring*, she noticed. She couldn't deny her feelings, especially when just his name on a business card had flooded her emotionally. Now, with him on her television screen, she felt the electricity surge again, and he wasn't even in the same room!

Her day dreaming was interrupted when the screen shot changed to the same reporter standing next to the area where Luisa's Range Rover went over the hill. Two years after the fact, the landscape had all but grown over the patch where the land slide had occurred. The mound of broken trees that stopped before the river's edge were the only remnants of it.

"This river holds the secret of where Poppy and Luisa Morningstar's bodies are. Having never been recovered, Chase Morningstar has not allowed a funeral to take place for his young daughter. He and his family had a quiet get together to honour young Poppy but Chase Morningstar has stated in several interviews that he believes his daughter's spirit is with him and he hopes she is resting comfortably in her late mother's arms".

The reporter stopped a moment, looked down towards the plunge the vehicle took over the side of the hill and then back to the camera. "But, is she?" He started walking away from the edge and towards the camera as it moved back. "There are those who believe that Luisa Morningstar did not die in that vehicle. The conspiracy theorists believe that since no bodies were ever recovered, there is no proof of death. And that makes Lucas Hollomby shake his head." The screen went back to the two men in Lucas' office.

The reporter leaned forward in his chair and asked Lucas directly, "What are your thoughts on the conspiracy theory that neither of them are dead?"

Lucas smiled and scoffed slightly, "What, like Elvis?" He tilted his head and rolled his eyes briefly before answering. "Well, I suppose that's a theory, but I saw the vehicle and the waters of that river on a night similar to the one when we believe they died. There is no way they could have survived that fall and even if by some miracle they did, where the vehicle landed, the water took everything from it. It may have been wedged in by debris, but the water tore through that vehicle. They didn't stand a chance, in my opinion, so...," he paused "I doubt the theory holds any water" he answered with a smile, shaking his head. The screen shot back to the reporter still standing near the hill. Chase's song about his beautiful daughter, "Now That You're Here" playing as the reporter begins speaking over it.

"While some have their theories, those directly involved in the case believe otherwise. They mourn for their dead family members and have carried on with their lives." He pauses. "Case Closed? This is Robin Hewer reporting for ABC News out of Chicago." As the broadcast ended Chase's video "Now That You're Here" where he sat on the piano bench, shirtless cradling his infant daughter played out and the very last scene was Poppy's little angelic face smiling in her sleep, as her daddy looked up smiling into the camera.

Leena sat motionless for a moment. So many questions went through her head. She wondered how many Swiss were tuned in. This story had disgusted the Swiss people from the beginning and they either vilified her family or ignored them completely. She was hoping that the latter would be more the case, this time. With the family home no longer in possession and the Van Zeeban's scattered across Europe or dead, Leena wasn't too concerned about any aftermath. She wondered about the conspiracy theorists. It had never occurred to her that there were people out there that felt this way. She pondered this a moment. She had to admit when she saw the woman in the café in the north, she honestly thought it was Luisa. But, how could she have managed to pull off faking her own death and if so, did she kill Poppy or is she still alive? Leena's mind went back to Lucas's answer and it played over again in her head. Weighing the odds, she decided that Lucas was right, no conspiracy at all; the river washed them away.

She knew this had broadcast previously in the U.S. and she was watching a repeat of the show, but she felt such a connection to Lucas. She was curious about how he was doing. He'd looked good, hadn't aged at all and seemed to still be the same confident, attractive, intuitive man that she recalled from two years previous. He had stated how he regretted the scrutiny her family had been put through. He regretted he couldn't bring closure. She now had her own regrets and they all had to do with Lucas.

* * *

Tanya and Hans had become quite close. Whenever she came into town they would have lunch at the café and at least three times a week he would drive out to the farm house after he closed shop for a warm home cooked meal and some quality time with Tanya and Rebeccah. Hans was extremely taken with both girls and with each visit, and each lunch shared he fell deeper and deeper in love with them.

Hans had business to attend to in the south of Switzerland and decided he wanted Tanya and Rebeccah to join him. It would be an overnight stay and a first for the threesome. When he asked Tanya to join him one night at dinner, Rebeccah jumped up and down excitedly and threw herself into Hans's arms hugging his neck tightly and breathing in his cologne. It was the first time she had hugged him and it shocked Hans. He held her tightly enjoying her affection, but she suddenly pulled away looking at him intently. She said nothing, just continued to stare and then leaned in to smell him again. Hans could see her mind pondering something, but wasn't sure what. She held herself back from him a moment longer, assessing him and then snuggled up under his chin and sat on his lap hugging into him. Hans wasn't sure what had just happened, but his heart melted for the little girl with the beautiful green eyes. She stayed there for quite some time and despite the fact that she was like a little oven, Hans refused to end such a special bonding moment between them. Rebeccah had just accepted him and he was absolutely thrilled. Now, he just needed to woo her mother into love.

Tanya didn't mind Rebeccah's affection for Hans. She was sure it was making him fall even harder for her. She liked Hans very much and the thought of being married to him didn't repulse her. If she married him it would add another layer in keeping hidden and that made her happy. She gave Hans's weekend invitation away serious thought. What could it hurt? She'd make sure their hair coloring disguises were fresh and even downplay too many outings. It would be nice to get away for a day or so, and it had been two years since Luisa and Poppy "died". No one would be expecting to see them so they wouldn't be looking. Tanya found it was easy to hide in plain sight, given parameters. She accepted his invitation and the three spent the evening talking about their trip, all the while, little Rebeccah sat curled up on Hans's lap, enjoying his smell until she eventually fell asleep, dreaming of someone strong and loving, who sang to her and smelled exactly like the cologne Hans was wearing.

* * *

Tanya packed an overnight bag for her and Rebeccah. Having not done this for a long time, she began to get excited for the trip. She wondered what the sleeping arrangements would be and if Hans would have sexual expectations of her. Perhaps, she'd start off sleeping in Rebeccah's bed and then slip into his bed in the middle of the night. Wouldn't Hans be surprised by that! Tanya decided she would most certainly do that and packed a soft see-through nightshirt to entice Hans with, although she was fairly sure he wouldn't need too much enticing. As she continued packing, Tanya started feeling a sense of happiness she hadn't felt in a very long time. It was a great feeling and Tanya allowed it to take over and started looking very forward to the trip and her plans, letting her guard down a little more.

* * *

They travelled south, stopping just a few times for bathrooms breaks. Tanya had packed up sandwiches, cut vegetables and drinks for the ride and despite Hans's insistence that he take them for a nice lunch, Tanya shot him down and offered him his favorite sandwich. Who could say no to that? The thought of stopping for lunch was gone from his mind and they travelled through to their destination. Instead of staying at a major hotel, Tanya wanted to stay at a small Bed and Breakfast nearby Hans's business dealings. Hans agreed, thinking it would be very romantic and quaint, especially if they had rooms that were adjoining. He didn't want to pressure Tanya or make her think there was any expectations, but maybe things would evolve during their trip and he wouldn't be opposed to that at all!

They checked into the B&B and got settled into their rooms. As Tanya thought, Hans expected her and Rebeccah to share one room and he would have the other and although the rooms were not adjoined, they were right next door to one another and Tanya figured a late night tryst was certainly doable! They spent the evening playing cards in the beautiful back garden of the B&B and enjoying the warm evening air. Tanya could not recall a night where she and Rebeccah had laughed as hard, while Hans told stories of his antics growing up. Anyone looking would have thought they were a natural family. When bedtime came, Rebeccah hugged and kissed Tanya good night and then came over to Hans and hugged him tightly around his neck, once again taking in his scent. It made her feel safe and secure.

"I love you, Hans" the little girl whispered into his ear. She slowly pulled back and looked at him, a serious look on her face.

Hans was stunned. He had not seen a lot of affection between mother and daughter and could not recall ever hearing them exchange "I love you's", even at bedtime. At first, he wondered what her mother must think to have heard her daughter say that, but then he couldn't help but beam with pleasure. She was such a treasure, such a sweet little girl that he couldn't help himself. "I love you too, Rebeccah" he answered back and he kissed her on the forehead. "Good night and sweet dreams, little one" he said sweetly as she hugged him once more and then ran off to the room she would share with her mother. Tanya got up to see her off to bed but hesitated by the table before she followed after Rebeccah.

"Let me get her to sleep, first" was all she said leaving Hans to wonder what she meant exactly. He decided he would wait to see what she had in mind and follow her lead. The last thing he wanted was to scare her off. He sat at the table in the backyard for another hour, nursing a vodka tonic and daydreaming of a future with Tanya and Rebeccah. By the time his drink was finished, Tanya had still not returned to the garden and Hans made his way to his room wondering if he had made a mistake in leaving it unsaid that he would like Tanya to share his room. He had settled in, going through a scenario in his mind of how he could have let Tanya know that he'd wanted her to join him in his room tonight. He was still so shy about some things. He was feeling slightly angered at himself for his lack of initiation when he heard the door next to his open and close and then heard a slight knocking on his door. With his heart beating rapidly, he remained in bed and called out quietly so as to not alert the entire B&B, "Come in".

When the door opened, Tanya stepped into the room and quickly and quietly closed the door behind her. She was wearing only a diaphanous nightshirt that hid nothing, absolutely nothing. At first, as she approached the bed slowly, Hans was too shocked to say anything. He spent the first 30 seconds with his mouth open, just staring. When he managed to make sense of what was happening, he gave Tanya a more appreciative look. Her breasts were lovely and high, nipples slightly erect and pink. Hans felt his own excitement beginning and the surge of blood leave his extremities and head straight for his penis. The weight of the sheets and duvet was even arousing to him at this point. He marveled at her slight hips, mound of soft pubic hair and how beautiful her figure was. Drinking her in with his eyes, Hans appreciated her perfect figure, thinking how hard it was to believe she'd had a baby!

She stopped short of the bed and ever so slowly removed her nightshirt, locking eyes with his. Before climbing into bed, she turned once giving Hans the full view and then climbed seductively towards him into bed on all fours. Hans was completely taken with her, her overt sexual gesture a very pleasant surprise. He threw the duvet off the bed exposing his stiff erection, his obvious delight at what he saw. She crawled before him, straddled his lap, lifted herself up and planted herself squarely on his erect penis. He gasped and instinctively thrust upwards nearly sending him over the edge. He had yearned for a strong relationship with a woman, one that encompassed all that a loving caring, respectful relationship had to offer, including a very satisfying sex life. Never did he anticipate Tanya's libido to be so strong, especially considering the shyness she had shown him. Now she was riding his erection, grinding herself into him while he groped her breasts, taking time to suck her nipples whenever they came with reach of his mouth. He hadn't had a woman in a long time, and he had never had a woman make love in this fashion. It was incredibly stimulating and before he knew it, he could feel the surge starting. The buildup was almost too much for him and his breath caught with each step towards his orgasm. With one deep thrust he exploded into Tanya, grabbing her at the waist encouraging her to ride him throughout his orgasm. As he enthusiastically thrusted into her, Tanya continued to grind herself into him, his pubic hair stimulating her with every thrust. As Hans was beginning to come back down to earth he felt Tanya's vaginal contractions and as she had her own orgasm, she cried out and sat hard atop his lap grinding harder into him. They fell into one another, Tanya's arms going around Hans' neck and he held onto her as she caught her breath. The feeling of her naked body against his was fantastic and he enjoyed holding her like that. When she recovered her breath, she sat up and leaned back looking at him, her eyes glassy and lustful, her nipples totally erect and glistening from his saliva, her hair in disarray. He liked the look on her and the fact that he made her look like that. This was a far cry from the young mother who came into his shop seeking headache medication.

"I liked that" she said as she lifted herself up off his lap and settled in beside him allowing him to cradle her body next to his.

"Mmm...." He groaned appreciatively with his eyes closed and his head back against the head board. "You're incredibly lovely, Tanya. I can't recall when I had such a powerful orgasm" he said honestly, smiling the whole time. This made Tanya smile, too. It hadn't been so bad at all. She was used to having sex with men who were older than her, but it had been quite some time since she'd had sex at all, so it was pleasantly enjoyable. She could see that she was the more experienced of the two and thought that might bode well for her in keeping Hans interested.

They slept for about an hour before Tanya woke up and slid out of Hans' bed, donned her nightshirt and slipped back into her room with Rebeccah, who was fast asleep and dreaming of music, people and places she didn't know.

* * *

The next morning as Tanya and Rebeccah slept in, Hans was up bright and early and off to meet his lawyers. Someone had made him such an incredible offer on his pharmacy and he was seriously considering it. If all went in his favor and the right offer was put before him, Hans would accept.

This was a huge decision for Hans. He'd lived in that small town and owned that shop for more than 25 years. His patrons had come to count on him having everything they could possibly need. He took pride in what he had built, but there was always greener grass. If the sale happened, he'd ask Tanya to marry him, sell her house and his property and move into a much lovelier home. He'd made up his mind; he wanted Tanya to be his wife.

* * *

When Tanya awoke, Rebeccah was sitting up out of bed looking out the window. It was dark outside and too early for her to be up.

"Come back to bed Rebeccah, it isn't time to get up yet" she scolded the child. Rebeccah looked away from the window for a moment, turned her attention back up into the sky and then reluctantly climbed back into bed beside Tanya. She let out a deep sigh and rolled over away from her mother. Tanya lay there a moment wondering what she had been doing. Unable to come up with an answer, Tanya sighed, rolled over away from Rebeccah and went to sleep.

The next time Tanya woke up, the sun had lit the room and made it bright and sunny and cheery. She woke Rebeccah and they both washed and got themselves ready for the day. They were almost finished and were ready for breakfast when Hans came bursting through the door.

"Oh no, not this time. This time we are going out for breakfast." He emphasized.

"I have something to celebrate, something very important and this just won't do" he said. He grabbed Tanya's hand and led her out of the room with Rebeccah in tow. He drove them into the city and they stopped at a large restaurant with giant windows, plants and tables. He found them a window booth and the three of them climbed in and got comfortable waiting for the waitress to come.

"Are you going to tell us what you're celebrating?" Tanya asked finding it hard not to smile and laugh along with him, his mood so infectious. As he sat across the table from her he grabbed her hands in his and kissed them, holding onto them. He looked deeply into her eyes, hoping she understood what he was communicating. She figured he was still living in the afterglow of last night's sex and she smiled at him. If she didn't know any better, she'd say he was about 4 days from telling her he loved her.

"I can't say anything just yet, but trust me, it's very exciting!" he told them.

What? That was all he could tell her? Tanya was pissed, but she didn't show it. He was paying for all of this and she could continue to smile at him as long as was needed for him to take the bait. Hans would fall in love with her by the end of their stay here, she was determined to make it happen.

They enjoyed their breakfast and fun chatter about what they were going to do that day before leaving the city. Hans wanted to buy "his girls" a pretty dress each and wasn't going to take no for an answer. His mood and generosity was so lovely it was hard not to thoroughly enjoy being out with him. They finished up their meals, drank one last leisurely coffee and left the restaurant making their way to the noisy, busy city street. Taking hold of Rebeccah's hand, Tanya went to walk over to the car when all of a sudden she heard, "Luisa!" Forgetting herself in the moment, she turned towards the call slightly before she caught herself, but it was too late, the gesture had been seen, and not only by Hans.

Mistake #2.

* * *

Leena had been in the city early that morning for two reasons. The earlier she travelled in, the better the chance of not hitting rush hour traffic. The other reason was she wanted to be in and out before it became overrun with people who might have caught last night's investigative report. She knew the chances were slim but she'd hate to be recognized and possibly called out.

She ran into the offices of her father's bank and signed a few documents pertaining to his financials. Then she ran over to the large department store and grabbed a few things. She was on her way out of the store and onto her next errand when she spotted her. Leena stopped dead in her tracks and instinctively called out, "Luisa?!" without even realizing she had. The dark haired woman across the street looked over to her for a split second, then turned her head and was hidden from sight by two city busses and a large truck. When the traffic had cleared the woman was gone. Leena looked up and down the street for a sign of her and saw no one, nothing. She played the moment back in her head, recalling everything, every detail, the way the woman moved, the shape of her face, the turn of her head when she called out *Luisa*. That was no doppelganger, she'd bet her life on it!

She looked at her watch and did a time calculation. Realizing it would probably be extremely early in the morning she shrugged her shoulders, shirked her last errand and headed straight for her car.

* * *

"Hello?" he answered, his voice like gravel, his head groggy.

"Lucas?" she asked. He sat up immediately, almost banging his head off the overhead lamp. Just the sound of her voice and his heart was racing. *What the hell time was it? Who the hell cared? Talk to her!* His mind screamed.

"Yes, it's me. I'm …It's …Lucas" he fumbled, running his hand through his hair and cringing at the fumble.

"Lucas…it's Leena Van Zeeban" she said tentatively, wondering if this hadn't been a colossal mistake. There was a small pause that seemed like an hour to each of them. When they both started to speak at once, three times in a row, they both started laughing which broke the ice.

"I am sorry for calling so early. I know you must be wondering why. But first, I wish to apologize about my behavior at our last encounter. I was angry and grieving and I had no one to …to…well, I suppose I had no one to take all of that out on. You became the scapegoat for the entire country's hatred of Luisa and our family. I am so sorry I was rude to you. You were so helpful to my family in finding the vehicle, not to mention the truth about the murder of Mr. Morningstar's wife…I just….I just feel ashamed of myself for how I treated you." She told him, sincerely. There was another moment's silence and then Lucas cleared his throat.

"Well, I …uh…understand why you felt the way you did. I only hoped one day you'd see it from a different perspective and could forgive me." He said honestly.

"Forgive you?' she said incredulously. "I should be asking for your forgiveness" she said to him.

"No need for forgiveness on this end, my dear. I regret everything you and your family endured, I really do" he told her. She smiled over the phone and shook her head, remembering the interview and his words.

"Yes, yes, I know. I saw the interview you did recently on the case. It was… hard to watch in some senses, revealing in others" she said suspiciously, which piqued his interest. She had called for a reason, what was it? He was dying to know, but didn't want to rush her in any way. He'd waited two years for this phone call and he'd be damned if he was going to chase her away.

"Oh the interview! I wasn't aware it would play over there." And, he suddenly had a horrid thought, what if she was calling because the interview had once again plunged her family into hell? He was about to ask if it had caused any fallout, but she broke in.

"Yes, it played here last night. But listen, I need to tell you something. Something very…very, well I don't know what. I don't know what to think." She said, sounding completely confused. She continued, "At first, I just thought it was a coincidence, maybe a doppelganger but, when I saw your interview and what the reporter said about conspiracy theories, well…it got me thinking. And then just now, not a half hour ago, I saw her again. Downtown. Here." She stopped speaking, letting what she said register to Lucas. When he didn't respond, she clarified her thoughts with, "I think Luisa is alive!"

* * *

Instinct took over once she realized what she had done. She bolted for the car, just as Hans raised his head to look over at a woman raising her arm, waving it their way calling, "Luisa". She was looking directly at Tanya and from his peripheral vision he saw Tanya's slight reaction before taking off, running for the car. The traffic picked up at that point blocking his view of the woman calling over their way and Hans ran towards Tanya and Rebeccah who had bolted and were already in the car. He got in quickly looking at Tanya for some sort of explanation, but she put her hand to her head, covering her eyes and put her head against the window as if she was in pain. All she told him was, "Drive, quickly, please."

Something in her voice made him take her request seriously and the car lurched forward, melting into the busy city street and lost forever for anyone who might have been watching.

Hans wasn't sure where he was to "drive" to so he asked, "Are you still up to shopping for dresses?'

"No…please, if you're done all of your business, can we just get our things from the B&B and leave? I'm starting to get one of my headaches and didn't bring any medication with me" she lied.

Hans was very concerned for Tanya's health. The headaches were really debilitating for her and he desperately wanted to get her in to see his friend, who was a doctor. She had refused him once but maybe she would be interested now with being in so much pain.

"Should we go straight to Dr. Chomiak's when we get into town?" he asked her.

Tanya knew he was just trying to be helpful, but there was no headache, really. So, there was no need to see Dr. Chomiak, really. And, if he found her out and told Hans, he might not be so understanding as to why she faked a headache. How could she ever tell him the truth? *I faked a headache to get us out of there fast because my eldest sister, Leena spotted me and called my name and I nearly gave up the whole thing.* Everything she worked so hard for, to keep her and Poppy in hiding as Tanya and Rebeccah. She decided there and then on the ride home that she would manipulate Hans to marry her and get her away from Switzerland all together. It would be the only way to guarantee that Leena would never find her. After today, Tanya needed to do all she could to stay hidden and going to see Dr. Chomiak wasn't the answer.

"No Hans" she said quietly. "I don't want to see a doctor, I just need to get home."

Mistake #3.

Chapter 3

A Dead End

"Will you marry me, Tanya?" Hans asked, on bended knee one night after dinner in Tanya's home. He and Tanya were alone as Rebeccah had gone off to bed early. It wasn't planned exactly like that, it just worked out that way, but once he realized they were alone sooner than expected, he just busted it out and threw himself down on one knee with the ring in hand. Tanya spun around from the kitchen counter truly surprised by how quickly it had come. They were home only two days from the weekend trip and he was already proposing. She knew having sex with him would probably seal the deal, but didn't expect it this quickly. The shock must have shown on her face because the smile on Hans's face slowly dropped as uncertainty began to creep in.

Tanya understood his look and quickly brought his mind to ease, "Oh... no...I mean, yes, I mean yes. Yes, I will. I will marry you!" She answered enthusiastically. He jumped up put the ring on her finger, kissed her and picked her up and spun her around. They giggled and laughed and kissed again.

"Well, I think we have a wedding to plan, my dear. Have you any idea what you want?" he asked her sweetly. She played it down completely, acting shy and demure.

"Oh Hans, I'm not a big showy person you know that. I would be happy to be married at the registry office, as soon as possible. Something short, sweet and quick" she told him. He was surprised. He understood the short and sweet, but quickly, too?

"How quick? I mean don't you want to have time to get a dress and all the trappings?' he asked her a little bewildered. Most women wanted their wedding day to be a spectacle.

"No, I don't need all that, I just want to be married to you. Neither of us has family or even extended family. I haven't made friends just because of how far I live from town and" she snuggled into him, hugging him tightly "I just want us to be married. I've waited so long to find love, why wait any longer?" she answered. The hug helped convince Hans hands down.

"Can you come into town tomorrow and we'll go to the registry office? We can apply for a license and book a date. Are you sure you want to do it this way?" giving her the opportunity to change her mind, but she shook her head in the negative.

"No Hans, I know what I want. I want to be Mrs. Tanya Baumgartner, quickly. Very, very quickly" she said as she reached up for a kiss.

"Then you will have just that my dear" Hans told her as he kissed her deeply.

The next day Hans closed his shop over the lunch hour while he and Tanya went to the registry office and applied for a marriage license. The wedding date was booked for 10 days later, the soonest they could get. They kissed as they parted, already feeling like a married couple.

Tanya was able to find a beautiful white dress that would serve well as her wedding dress, although it wasn't a wedding dress at all. Looking back, Tanya realized that she'd probably never have the kind of wedding most women dreamed of. Her wedding to Chase was never real, never once did they share a proper kiss and their marriage was never consummated. Still a bitter pill for her to swallow.

* * *

"I'm selling the business!" Hans exclaimed over dinner the next night. He had a huge smile on his face and his hands up, as if to surprise Tanya. That was an understatement!

"What?! Why?! When?! Why?!" she asked him without offering a chance to answer. Hans burst out laughing at her reaction and she swatted at him with a tea towel. "Is this the business you've been hinting at?" she asked him, completely shocked.

"Yes, the very same. I had an offer from another Pharmacist who wanted the whole shop, lock, stock and barrel." He said as he reached across the table, grabbed a piece of bread and buttered it thickly.

"I had no idea you wanted to sell. What will you do?" Tanya asked, wondering what this meant now that they were engaged and very soon to be married.

"Neither did I, my dear, until the offer was made and I knew I was in love with you!" He told her laughing. "I have been waiting for you to come along. Now, I can devote my time to us and our family. I don't need to work, I've got plenty of money! I want to retire and be a doting, loving husband for you and our children. You want more children don't you?" he asked, thinking this might have been a good question to ask before the proposal. A little bit of the cart before the horse!

"Uh…yes" she hesitated. More? She hadn't actually delivered a child and it never dawned on her that Hans may want children, especially at his age. But, if he could support them then yes, she wanted children. She smiled at him warmly, "I could give you a son!" she said excitedly!

"I'd be happy with a healthy wife and baby." He told her. "And, we don't have to live here! We could live anywhere! ANYWHERE!" he told her excitedly.

He really just wanted to spend all his time with his soon-to-be new wife and daughter. Tanya processed what he was saying. Another move, another layer. Possibly different country, another layer. Going to a place where no one knew them, having a fresh start, another layer. All these things reinforced their anonymity and without knowing it, Hans was innocently becoming an accomplice to her sins.

* * *

Rebeccah's schooling was going well. She was a very bright 5 year old and was well liked by her teachers. She paid attention in class and her teachers all agreed she was a well behaved child, but she lacked friends. It wasn't that she didn't make friends, but Rebeccah's mind worked differently than her school age counterparts. She was focused during her day, but at night her mind was filled with visions of people, places and stars. Often, she heard music in her head, although she didn't know why, or where it came from. Her mother didn't play music, at all. She barely had the TV on.

Having little to do over her lunchtime, Rebeccah would sometimes explore the school, peeking into other classes and studying the work on the chalkboards. On one such exploration, she came across a room she hadn't been in before. She had tried the door numerous times, but it had been locked. Today however, the handle turned easily and the door swung open. To her surprise, the lights were on and she could see someone sitting at a large wooden structure. They weren't moving, but their hands were placed in front of them and their body was swaying slightly, back and forth. Rebeccah entered the room, walking straight over to the person. As she got closer, she could see it was a woman. She was an elderly woman, her eyes were closed and she had a slight smile to her face. Rebeccah immediately felt as ease, standing near to her. She reached out to touch the wooden structure just as the elderly woman pushed down on one of the black and white individual little planks in front of her. The sound was mesmerizing, but what struck Rebeccah more was the wave of electric shock that went through her tiny body. The sound vibration ran from her hand, up her arm, through to her heart and then burst through every blood cell and corpuscle. Her mind's eye saw vivid colour and bursts of light through them. This was an experience like no other for the young girl and even at that age, she knew it. Her body was filled with goosebumps and she could barely contain herself.

"I wondered when you'd find us" the elderly woman said softly, smiling. Rebeccah opened her eyes and they locked onto the elderly woman's eyes. As if by instinct, Rebeccah came to sit next to the elderly woman, who moved over on the bench to make room.

"What is this?" Rebeccah asked, her hands reaching out to gently touch the individual little planks.

"It's called a piano, child" she told her. "By pushing on these keys, you can create music. Beautiful sounds. Sometimes, if you press keys together, or one after the other, you can create a melody; a song. Come, push down on each key and learn what they sound like." Rebeccah wasted no time, quickly pushing the key under her index finger. The piano responded with a deep sound, vibrating once again through her and a splash of colour in her mind. Rebeccah giggled and tried the next key. She gently went through each key until she had finished hearing and feeling the entire keyboard. That was all it took. Rebeccah was hooked!

The elderly woman encouraged her to try more than one key at once and Rebeccah obliged. Within minutes she was not only able to understand how to make the piano give complimentary sounds, she was trying to mimic some of the music she had recalled in her head. Given time, she would have been able to do it, but the impromptu lesson was cut short by a teacher entering the room.

"Rebeccah!" she called out. "What are you doing in here?"

Rebeccah turned to look at the teacher, her mouth wide open, her hands remaining on the piano's keys, not wanting to take them off.

As she spoke, she continued to play the keys, but she kept her eyes on the teacher.

"I'm sorry, but she wanted me to play with it" she explained, as her fingers danced along the keys. The teacher was about to reprimand her for being in the room, but couldn't take her eyes off what she was seeing. This 5 year old girl was playing the piano without looking at the keys. Granted, the teacher didn't recognize the music she was hearing, but she could tell the young child was playing music. There was no doubt of that.

35

"Uh, she….who?" her teacher inquired. Rebeccah was completely alone in the room and although the lights were on and the room unlocked, she had no business being in there.

Rebeccah turned her head to look to her side, but she was alone. The elderly woman was gone. Rebeccah looked back to the teacher with wide eyes, once again. Before she could speak, the teacher came closer to her and asked, "How long have you been playing?"

"She wanted me to hear what sound each key made. I've only been here for a little bit." Rebeccah explained, but the teacher was confused.

"You're alone in here, Rebeccah. But, answer my question, how long have you been playing?" she pushed. The teacher had a feeling she had just come across something quite incredulous. Could Rebeccah be gifted?

"Do you play the piano at home, Rebeccah?" She asked, directly.

"No" she answered quietly.

"No?" the teacher said amazed. "Have you ever played on a piano before?"

"No" Rebeccah answered. She hoped she wouldn't get into trouble.

"Let's see what else you can do" The teacher suggested taking a seat on the bench beside Rebeccah. She played a quick tune, only a few bars and then encouraged Rebeccah to play it, too. Rebeccah hesitated a moment, then placed her fingers on the appropriate keys, but further down the scale and then repeated the song the teacher had played. The teacher sat for a moment digesting what she'd just witnessed. It was truly rare to see a child have such raw talent, without any lessons. She saw great potential in Rebeccah and a thought came to mind.

When Tanya opened up Rebeccah's backpack that night after school, she found the following handwritten letter:

Dear Ms. Tanya Nowak,

Today I happened to find Rebeccah in a storage room playing on an old piano we keep in there. I have taught music for 13 years and have never come across a child with such raw natural talent. She was able to play back a song I played for her, completely by ear on the very first time. This is quite unusual and I encourage you to allow Rebeccah to pursue piano lessons. Given the proper tutelage, Rebeccah could go very far musically. I hope I don't over step when I say that I understand you have a difficult situation and therefore am enclosing a brochure on a foundation that helps children access music lessons, if they are not affordable to the family. I work closely with this foundation and believe that, as a single-mother you would meet the criteria. I am including a letter of reference on Rebeccah's behalf, hoping it will augment the application. Please take a moment and consider this for Rebeccah. She has a gift, I assure you.

Sincerely,

Gerta Mueller

Musical Educator

It didn't surprise her of course, she knew Rebeccah's heritage. But what was she going to do about it? Tanya held the letter in her right hand and turned over the brochure in her left. Blazoned across the top of the front was "The Morningstar Foundation". Tanya's heart stopped. *Is this a joke?* She read the letter again, making sure it was actually from the school. The letterhead was authentic. Tanya put down the letter from Ms. Mueller and opened the brochure up to its full 3 fold page size. Right in the middle was a picture of Chase and Dana Morningstar. Their story underneath explained how they came to fund music lessons for underprivileged children from all over the world. Tanya could hardly breath, the anger building in her was so overpowering. Dana and Chase looked like a happy, polished power couple. It made Tanya's stomach lurch. She tried hard to keep from vomiting. She had followed the media in the years since she had gone into hiding and knew of Chase's marriage. She had no idea about the foundation and pictured herself in Dana's place, only…it didn't fit. She considered tossing the brochure, after all, Hans could afford music lessons easily, but then a wicked thought entered her mind. *How ironic it would be that her father fund her music lessons?* Tanya felt extremely pleased with herself for thinking so deviously. The brochure included an application form and after Rebeccah went to bed that night, Tanya filled out the form, attached copies of necessary documents including Ms. Mueller's letter of reference. She would get the last laugh on Mr. Chase Morningstar. She'll have him be *thisclose* to his daughter and never know it. *Haven't you learned, Chase Morningstar? Don't fuck with me*, she thought as she licked the envelope closed.

* * *

Lucas and Robin landed at Geneva airport six days later and drove straight to Leena's apartment. Although Lucas and Robin weren't exactly convinced that Leena had seen Luisa, neither were willing to leave it alone. Lucas wanted any opportunity to travel to Switzerland and see Leena and Robin wanted any opportunity to further investigate Leena's sightings. He may not have been completely sold on this woman having seen her dead sister, but she certainly saw someone that made her think Luisa was alive. Robin was intrigued, at the very least.

When they knocked on Leena's apartment door, each had their own nervous anticipation. Leena didn't disappoint. She presented in a lovely cream colored outfit. She looked soft, beautiful, strong and confident. She was perfection in Lucas' eyes, credible in Robin's. Interesting to say the least!

Leena held back momentarily and then threw herself into Lucas' arms, as if they were long lost lovers without the public display of affection. Their hug was possibly 30 seconds too long and Robin stood in the doorway, kicking the ground slightly embarrassed. When they broke the hold they had on each other, Lucas introduced Robin to Leena. They shook hands amiably and said their salutations, then Leena led them into her apartment.

It was a pretty little apartment with all the modern conveniences modelled in a very small space. Considering her familial home, Lucas could only think she went from one end of the spectrum to the other. Where the northern home had beautiful vistas and complete privacy; a real family home, Leena's apartment looked out across a small city with little to no beautiful vistas. She had, to her credit, hung photographs on the walls of large landscape scenes that Lucas could only guess were of places in and around Switzerland, judging from what he had seen during his own travels. Her taste was excellent and her apartment spoke volumes about the woman who lived there. A bookcase filled with novels, all first editions occupied the main wall in the living room. It was larger than the TV, which wasn't normally the case these days. It was Lucas's job to observe and he spent a lot of time taking in her dwelling and its contents which wasn't lost on Leena.

"Can I get you anything?" she asked them.

"Coffee, black, please" Lucas said, staring intently at a family photo which he silently pointed out to Robin. As Leena was in the kitchen setting up the coffee maker, Robin's reporter side could hold back no longer and he started calling out his questions to her.

"Where were you when you first spotted her?" he called into the kitchen.

Amongst the clanging of cutlery and dishes, she called back, "Uh...a small town in the north. I saw her sitting in the front window of a restaurant."

"Was she with anybody?" he asked back, studying the old family photo.

"I don't actually know. Thinking back, there was probably someone sitting in the seat across, but I didn't see who they were, so I have no idea if it was a man or a woman. When I saw her in the city, I was so floored to see her I didn't take notice of who she was with or who was around. By the time she turned towards me after I called her name, traffic was moving and I lost sight of her." She told them as she came through to the living room carrying a tray of mugs, cutlery and cookies and set it down on the living room table.

"Wait...so, she turned towards you when you called her name?" Robin asked incredulously.

"Oh yes, definitely" Leena answered with confidence. Robin looked at Lucas who raised his eyebrows back at him.

"Do you think she was really capable of this? I mean, do you realize how convoluted this has to be? And, where's the child?" Robin asked rapid fire. For a moment Leena wasn't sure if he was asking her or just throwing out hypothetical questions. She waited before answering, hoping he would continue his train of thought, but he didn't.

"I'm not sure of anything anymore, Robin" she told him honestly. "I would have never thought her capable of such duplicity or evilness. But look what happened? So, I think anything is possible and after two sightings of her, I can't help but wonder if she didn't fake her own death."

"That might be getting ahead of ourselves. We need to figure out if this is her first. And with very little to go on, it'll be like finding a microorganism on the inside of the eye of a needle, in a haystack." Robin stated. The saying was lost on Leena. "Must be something in the translation" Lucas said to his friend, smacking him on the back as Leena left and then walked through with the coffee carafe.

"So, where do we get started?" asked Lucas rubbing his hands together, always anxious to begin a new investigation. "I say we head north and see what we can find" he said to Robin and Leena.

"I think you two should head north, I'll have a look around here and see what I can find. Show me exactly where you spotted her and I'll see if there are any cameras about that might have caught her." He stated. They agreed and turned on the GPS to coordinate their search. After ordering in and eating while working on their plan, the men left Leena's apartment and headed to their hotel, not far from her residence. There was a lot left unsaid between Leena and Lucas, but they were to be locked in a car for many hours in the next little while and both hoped that would give them ample opportunity for intimate conversation.

* * *

40

The next morning, Robin went straight to Leena's father's bank, where she had gone the day she saw Luisa for the second time. If there was a place that would have cameras, it would be there. After flashing his News credentials and an impromptu meeting with the bank manager, Robin was granted access to the bank's security videos. Since he knew which date Luisa was spotted on and at approximately what time, he started there. The two cameras that might have caught her each faced directly across from the bank. Robin studied both videos closely, but couldn't pick out any one individual that he thought could be her. The picture was either too grainy or too many people were together to ascertain a specific individual. He did see a number of women with children and some of them were young girls but again, nothing decisive. He thanked the bank manager and went over to the restaurant across the street and ordered a cheese omelet and a coffee. As he ate his meal, he used the table to spread out the documents he carried and made notes while he continued to go over the facts from the case. Since doing his investigative report he'd been an expert on the facts. He'd gone over these documents for hundreds of hours and there was always one thing that bothered him. The last person to see her alive was the waitress at the restaurant near the hill who had said that Luisa was with someone, another woman and child. Who were they? How would he find them? After all this time and media attention, why had the woman not come forward? Even if she had left the country, at the time, this story was making headlines worldwide and especially across Europe, surely she would have heard something of it. If this woman knew something, why had she not stepped forward? He sat finishing his coffee and wondered how he could ever figure out who the mystery woman was and then the thought occurred to him. What if Luisa was posing as this woman? The waitress said that the two women were of similar looks and age and the children were also very close in age. Robin wondered if Luisa had somehow learned this woman's story and was posing as her without her knowledge. Identity theft was so easy these days and if Luisa was good with a computer she could have taken on the woman's identity without her even knowing it. He couldn't rule it out, but again, with no idea who the mystery woman was, it was going to be damn near impossible to find anything out.

He sat looking over the photographs of the mangled Range Rover at the bottom of the ravine. *How on earth did she survive that fall?* He wondered. *HOW?!* The two questions that needed answering. When he asked them out loud to himself, they seemed to answer themselves. What if Luisa wasn't in the vehicle when it went over the hill? What if the Range Rover was empty? He pondered this for a moment until another, more sinister thought entered his head. What if the Range Rover had a *different* woman and child inside and the water took *them* away, hiding the fact forever. Robin had to admit it was very far-fetched. How could she have possibly known that the vehicle would go plunging down the ravine? How did she manage to take over her victim's identity? And what about the landslide, an incredible coincidence?

Robin's head was spinning by the time he made it back to his hotel room. *IF* Leena had actually seen Luisa twice as she claimed, how had Luisa managed to stay hidden these last two years and with a small child, too? Leena had said that the hair was darker so his natural instinct was a disguise of some sort and of course, a name change. He truly believed this was the only way to explain Leena's sightings and although he was no further ahead, it explained a lot. He was satisfied at this point that he had a feasible explanation as to why Leena had spotted her twice; whoever she had met up with at the restaurant the night of the storm was now who she was posing as.

Robin's mind wouldn't stop. How to figure out the mystery woman's name? He decided that a search of missing women and children might come up with a name. Sure, it was the microorganism on the eye of the needle he was talking about, but it was something, an angle, and Robin Hewer was always known for his angles!

* * *

Lucas and Leena left first thing in the morning with the smell of coffee and pastries making the car sugary sweet. They travelled in silence for the first five minutes enjoying their breakfast and then Leena broke the silence.

"Do you really believe Luisa is still alive?" she asked him honestly.

"I believe that you've seen someone that has made you believe she is. That's good enough for me." He answered easily.

"Why?" she asked. He knew what she wanted to hear and was ready to say it.

"Because, I believe in you. I think if you believe you've seen your supposed dead sister, I don't think that you're crazy or seeing a doppelganger, I think you know what you've seen. You wouldn't have called me otherwise" he goaded her. It paid off.

"Oh...I wouldn't say that." She answered quietly. "Hard as I tried, you're quite unforgettable, Mr. Hollomby" she teased him, smirking from using his formal name. As she watched the landscape go by from the passenger side, he was able to catch her reflection in the window and saw the smile to her lips. Suddenly he felt excited. Obviously, between her apology and her hug at the door, she had overcome her anger and had softened to him. He decided now was as good a time as any.

"So, it's been two years since we last saw one another. Has anyone significant come into your life? A serious boyfriend?" he asked her, occasionally looking at her. She noted his direct question. No head games, no bullshit, he was always about the honest truth. She truly respected that.

"No" she answered firmly. Short and sweet and to the point but, just to be sure, she added, "they never measured up to you." She turned to look at him. His heart literally skipped and he thought for a minute that he'd have to pull over, but she sensed his reaction and reached out and touched him holding his wrist as he held the steering wheel. Her touch calmed him and excited him both at the same time.

He looked at her with as much caring in his eyes as he could produce, then turned back to look at where he was going. *Shit!* He thought. *Why is it that important things are shared more often when people are moving and looking forward?*

43

"We were caught up in something that overtook everything else." He told her with as much understanding in his voice as he could muster. He let the car fall silent, and then he asked, "And now?"

She sighed a heavy sigh. "And now, I'm in a much better place emotionally, of course, but… now my life is complicated. I have my father in a nursing home here and I'm the only family he has. My sister lives in Italy and is preoccupied with her own life. My mother is gone…" she trailed off. It had been hard to put everything on hold for the past two years. She hadn't really dated, hadn't done much of anything except take care of her father's needs. "I don't know where we're to go from here." She said honestly.

"I'll do whatever it takes to make you a part of my life." He told her. "I don't care if I have to fly here every three weeks until we are able to make a permanent move. Either one of us." He told her. "I'm open to moving here. I'm open to anything, except leaving here again without having you in my life." Lucas turned to look at her, holding his gaze before turning his attention back to the road. He'd laid it all on the line as he had promised himself he would. She had to know he was serious about her and he would be damned if he was going to spend all this time with her and not let her know exactly how he felt. And now she knew.

At first, she didn't know what to say. She had longed to hear him say those very words to her and now that he had, she was too stunned to respond. Instead, she turned her body towards him and gave him the biggest smile she could, as her eyes welled up. As a tear escaped and roll down her cheek, she laughed once and covered her mouth with her hand. She looked so damned adorable Lucas just about drove off the road again. It would take everything he had to drive safely with his heart beating so rapidly. He wasn't so sure she was happy when he saw her tears, but he understood better with her laugh and beaming smile. She nodded her head to him and then reached over and kissed him on his cheek, hugging him around his neck. He kept the vehicle moving forward by sheer will because he wasn't paying any attention to the road ahead. Luckily, there was no cause for concern. He allowed her side hug to continue for a moment longer and then gently eased her back to her seat.

"I've waited so long to hear you say that. I wondered if I'd messed up any chance for us to be together" she admitted honestly to him, as she reached for a tissue to wipe her tears.

"Darlin', when I left Switzerland two years ago, you'd have found my heart in my socks. Hard as I tried, I just couldn't stop thinking of you. I reached for the phone many times, but I just didn't want to intrude and I didn't know where to begin after the beginning we'd already had." It was true, their initial meeting although electrifying, was also marred.

"Well it's not as if we can change it. It's what has brought us together again, like it or not." Leena said pragmatically. "We have to face facts, much as I hate to admit it, our relationship is because of Luisa. The sooner we accept it, the better off we'll be." She paused a moment, "Besides", she continued, "We're a team on this now so there is no avoiding it."

He felt a huge sense of relief when she said that. Now, there was no more elephant in the car. Now, everything was out in the open and they could move forward; with the investigation, with their communications, with their lives. He was so grateful for her honest, open efforts that he impulsively kissed her hand as he held it, managing to maneuver the car with fine precision up towards the small town. Mission accomplished!

* * *

With his credentials in pretty high standing where reporting was concerned, Robin Hewer was able to get in to view a database of missing women and children. It was a long shot and he knew it, but he was curious as hell to see if there were any that looked like Luisa with dark hair. It may produce a name or a lead or something. As he sat going through the photos his mind continued to imagine the many scenarios that Luisa might have used to fake her own death and perhaps Poppy's, as well. It was the only answer if he was to believe Leena's sightings were truly Luisa.

After many hours and even more coffees looking through several hundred photos of women from all across Europe, Robin had a list of about 50 names of women and a smattering of young girls. It was difficult for him to fathom that there were that many women missing. Missing, as in, their whereabouts were unknown to their loved ones. Sometimes, the job opened his eyes too much to the horror of reality but then, it was his job to show that side to the public without influencing their opinions. Giving them all the facts, good or bad and allowing them to form their own opinions. That's what a good investigative reporter did, as far as Robin Hewer was concerned and his Edward R. Murrow Award for Excellence in Investigative Reporting proved it.

With the list in hand, Robin decided he was going to drive up to the hill. He knew that Leena and Lucas were probably just there now or getting to the small town to do their own investigation and figured he'd give them a call as he drove.

"Lucas Hollomby" he answered.

"Hey Lucas its Robin. How are things?" he asked.

"Excellent thanks, Robin" Lucas said, as he put the call on speaker phone smiling wide at Leena. "How did it go with the bank manager?" he asked.

"Nothing concrete, but he gave me some great information on stale dated accounts. Said he'd contact me should an account go active or something crop up that doesn't seem right. Also, I did some digging on missing women and children today. Presuming Leena is right and she's spotted Luisa twice, I have a theory that she faked her own death and has stolen someone's identity. Which, as you know is very easily done these days. I've taken some names of missing women that Luisa could possibly disguise as." he told them, frankly. All the while, Lucas was nodding his head in agreement with everything Robin had said. The two men were definitely on the same page.

"Great thinking on the missing women. Maybe we have the name of the woman she's using already. Can you text me some of them? Perhaps when we show her picture around town and maybe throw out a few names, it'll jolt someone's memory. I know it's a long shot, but I say we try and work every angle we can until we leave" Lucas said. Robin agreed.

"I'll send you a text as soon as we're off the phone. In the meantime, I'm heading up your way to have another look at that hill. That's where all the truth lies, I believe" Robin said mysteriously.

"You know it! We'll be in touch. Perhaps we'll meet you at the hill when we're done in town." Lucas suggested. Robin looked at his watch and did his calculations.

"Yup, it might just work out, time wise. Good luck up there, let me know if you find anything" he said.

"Will do" Lucas said signing off.

With her body still turned towards Lucas and giving him her full attention she asked, "So, what's our plan of attack?" Lucas smiled. They really were going to be a great team!

* * *

Tanya arose on the day of her wedding with a splitting headache. She hadn't had one this bad for some time and it made her wonder if she should cancel the day until she felt better. But, when she thought of what was at stake and how much the extra layer of anonymity would help her to disappear, she forged onward, doing the best she could to make herself the blushing bride.

As she sat before her vanity mirror, she went through all the different things she had to be sure were in place before becoming Mrs. Hans Baumgartner.

First, The Morningstar Foundation. She had been notified by Rebeccah's teacher very quickly that The Morningstar Foundation had been in contact with her and Tanya's application had been accepted. Rebeccah's music lessons would be paid for through their organization. Knowing full well that she intended for them to be moving from the area, Tanya arranged to have all correspondence from the Foundation go through the school, and should Rebeccah change schools, the teacher would forward correspondence from the Foundation to the new school's music director. That way, there would be no mail arriving from the Foundation and causing Hans to wonder why

Tanya would need their help, when she and Hans had plenty of money to easily pay for the lessons.

Hans had been thrilled to find out Rebeccah would be taking piano lessons and that she showed a real affinity for it. Tanya lied to him, stating that her mother had left a small fund for Rebeccah to be used for schooling and she opted to use it to fund her lessons, as the piano was something her mother could play and would love for Rebeccah to now be learning. Hans didn't question it and Tanya's evil secret was safe. She kept the Morningstar Foundation brochure Mrs. Mueller sent and wrote "She's been THISCLOSE all along" across Chase's smiling face. She then hid the brochure amongst some very personal papers in a large manila envelope which she placed into a shoe box and tucked away in the very back of her closet. Her final injustice to Chase.

She also had to manipulate Hans's business dealing. Although he told many that he sold his business, he told no one that he was marrying, at Tanya's request. She also requested that their wedding day be the day he hands over the keys, if possible. Although the final sale wouldn't take place until while they were on honeymoon, Hans negotiated with the new owner to take over on their wedding day. Having been spotted down south by Leena, it was best to get directly out of the country and never return. Hans seemed open to anything as long as Tanya and Rebeccah were involved so Tanya began to work out their new life. Money wasn't a concern. With all the devious planning and lies she'd been telling lately, it was no wonder she was suffering with a massive headache. But then, it had all worked out, just like she'd planned, just like before. As she applied blush to her pale cheeks she smiled, impressed with herself. She already felt as though it would be nearly impossible for Leena to actually find her, but marrying Hans and leaving Switzerland was going the extra step to ensure they stay hidden. Hans was the key to everything.

As she finished with her blush she started applying her mascara. Raising her right eye was difficult with the headache and Luisa noticed a limpness to her lid and an almost black spot in her vision that she couldn't see through. She had experienced this once before but the medication Hans gave her eased it. Finding the medication bottle at the bottom of her handbag, she popped two into her mouth and drank them down with some water. *Life will be so much easier after today*, she thought.

* * *

Lucas steered the car into the first available open parking spot along the main roadway of the small town. He was parked just a few blocks from the café where Leena had first spotted Luisa in the front window. He got out of the car and ran around to open Leena's door, just as she was exiting. She smiled at him for his gentlemanly gesture and he held the door offering her a clear way forward. She kissed his cheek again and thanked him. Blushing, he slammed the car door, grabbed her hand in his and crossed the street on the way to the café. It was after 1:00 pm and the lunch crowd were still very present and chatty, enjoying the fare of the small eatery. Leena and Lucas entered and stood waiting for someone to come and seat them.

"You hungry?" he asked Leena, nodding his head. She laughed at him and nodded back. He motioned to the young woman walking towards him that they needed a table for two and she nodded back, motioned for them to follow her and sat them at a table at the back of the room.

The café sat about 100 people and was almost full on this day. They had decided they would enjoy their meal first and then talk to the owner. Lucas gave the café a good scrutinizing, checking over every patron for a possible fit. None worked though, none looked remotely like Luisa. As she sat opposite him, Leena watched as he studied each person intently. She knew exactly what he was doing. It was so good to look at him straight on after spending their time in the car, she enjoyed having him as her full visual and relished in his words of earlier. He wanted her. He wanted anything to do with her and she was thrilled! Lucas Hollomby wanted to be her man!

They enjoyed a very tasty meal of chicken with melted Swiss cheese and a fresh bed of greens and steamed vegetables and a glass of red wine. As they sat back while the waitress was cleaning away their table, Lucas pulled out a photo of Luisa from 5 years ago with the hair darkened. He asked the waitress if she knew the woman but the waitress just shook her head and walked away. Lucas and Leena shared a look across the table and without saying a word to one another, Lucas handed Leena the picture and she took off for the kitchen. Lucas, meanwhile, headed to the next table and began asking the patrons if they knew who the woman in the picture was and if they knew how to find her.

As Leena entered the kitchens several heads popped up to look at her. One in particular, belonged to the owner, a heavyset middle aged woman who had no time for the attractive, petite blonde who just walked into her kitchens.

"Excuse me, but I will have to ask you to leave." She told Leena immediately, not allowing Leena past the first set of shelves. Leena looked around and saw five people working away at various stages of meal preparation. All manner of smells hit her at once and she was briefly distracted from the task at hand. When she finally realized what had been said to her, she stood shocked like a caught child.

"Please, leave" she insisted of Leena, but Leena stayed right where she was. She quickly raised the photo in front of the owner's face and let her get a good hard look at the picture watching for any kind of reaction. The owner, knowing full well that she had seen this woman in her establishment at first raised a brow, but then slick as ever she kept her expressions in check. Leena thought she caught a moment of recognition on the owner's face, just like she knew she'd seen a reaction from Luisa when she called out her name, but neither were conclusive.

"I don't know this woman" the owner said, innocently enough. Leena wasn't sure if she should believe her. She paused a moment and then asked, "Are you sure? I thought I saw her in here a while ago, dining in the front window. She's my sister, I'm looking for her" Leena told the woman. Instead of looking the picture over, the owner looked at Leena thoroughly, giving her an evaluation. Of course, she had recognized the young woman who Hans Baumgartner had been having lunch with occasionally of late. She had seen them on three different occasions and thought they made a very cute couple. She had known Hans for a number of years, he was a huge supporter of her café and she wasn't about to give everything up to some woman who may or may not be the sister to this young woman, especially when she couldn't remember Hans ever having a date. She was not about to trust what this young woman said when she had seen Hans so happy. The middle-aged, heavy set owner wasn't very intuitive when it came to her patrons, wasn't very knowledgeable of the music news industry and didn't watch her TV at night, always spending her time working to keep her café running. Her efforts paid off in the great food she served, but it meant she was no help to Leena and quite irritated by her presence.

"No, no. I know nothing of her, now please. I won't ask you again, remove yourself from my kitchen!" She demanded. Leena, feeling rejected and quite intimidated by the heavy set woman, obliged and turned on her heels and left. She wasn't able to speak to anyone else, as the owner followed her out and into the main dining area. When the owner caught sight of Lucas leaning over a customer's table with a photo in his hand, she went ballistic. Before Lucas knew it, she had him by the arm securely marching him out of the door. Lucas was a large man, but this woman had no problem moving him out of her establishment. Leena was absolutely shocked, but no more than Lucas!

"What the f…" he started complaining, but the owner cut him off.

"Don't you ever come into my business and disturb my customer again!" she shouted at him. Leena was quick to follow them out and was flabbergasted at the owner's response to them trying to locate Luisa.

"Listen, I don't mean any disrespect" Lucas said, calmly holding out his hands. "We are trying to find a woman who we believe has frequented your restaurant." He tried explaining.

"You've got a name?" the owner demanded.

Lucas hesitated, then dug his phone from his pocket in hopes that Robin had texted the names of the missing woman. It was there! Lucas opened it and was taken aback by seeing the long list of names that Robin had sent. There had to be at least 50 names on there! How was Lucas to know which one to choose? As he scrolled through the names, he decided to just pick one and start there.

"Nyla Schlesinger" he blurted out. Both he and Leena watched the owner closely, but she shrugged her shoulders and made a disgusted face.

"Don't know her. Now go on." She motioned them up the street. But Lucas wasn't done.

"No wait! What about Gerta Dorn?" he asked, his face full of question. This pissed the owner off and she became very angry at them. She turned to Leena and threw an accusatory look her way.

"What game are you playing? You told me she was your sister! You don't know her name?" She shouted as she waved them away like an irritating bug and marched back into her restaurant, the door closing firmly behind her. Lucas and Leena were left standing with their mouths agape, wondering what the hell just happened.

Lucas quietly said, "Methinks she doth protest too much." Leena whipped around to look at him and then turned back towards the closed door.

"Could that be true? Do you think she knows the dark haired Luisa?" Leena asked, wondering if the owner's reaction was more over the top than just really pissed off that they had disturbed her customers.

"Possibly. It's hard to say what her reaction was really about, but it was certainly over the top. Doesn't seem to be typical behavior to me, does it to you? I don't know, are café owners in Switzerland more likely to get physical and rant and rave in the middle of the street?" he asked, half-jokingly. He'd rather not admit to her that his pride had been slightly hurt. It wasn't everyday he was marched out of anywhere by one arm and it certainly wasn't an impression he wanted lasting in Leena's mind.

Leena sensed his embarrassment from the slight blush that took to his cheeks, which only made him more endearing to her. She was a rather large woman and Swiss women with a bad temper were not to be messed with, Leena knew that for certain. She tried hard to hide her smile.

"Well, yes, I would say that you're in for trouble if you raise the anger of a Swiss female. You're best to stay on the good side of us!" she teased as she linked her arm through his and started them walking down the street.

"I have an idea. I'm going to introduce you to Hans the Pharmacist" she said as she led the way to their next stop.

* * *

The Registry Office was quiet, the only sound made was the clicking of the Registrar's office staff typing away. Tanya, Rebeccah and Hans waited patiently outside the registrar's office for their turn to marry. They were scheduled for 3:30 pm and were all three excited about the upcoming ceremony.

Rebeccah was dressed in a beautiful pink satin dress with black shiny Mary Janes, white stockings and holding a small bouquet of fresh flowers, a surprise from Hans. She may have been only six years old, but she felt incredibly grown up and was thrilled that Hans would now be living with them night and day. She truly loved Hans and hoped that one day she could call him "Daddy".

Hans had a new suit made for the occasion. He was decked out in a black jacket and pants with a crisp white silk shirt and a black silk tie. The flower in his lapel matched the smaller flowers in the bouquets carried by his girls; "his girls", something Hans reveled in saying. It had taken him a long time to find love and thankfully it came with a little girl that filled his heart with unconditional love.

His bride, Tanya wore a beautiful white silk dress, second hand at a local thrift store. It was ¾ length cocktail, A-line skirt with heavy lace over a satin bodice. She wore her hair in soft curls with a sprig of baby's breath placed just behind her right ear. Rebeccah thought she was beautiful, Hans thought she was breathtaking and Tanya thought it was the best she could do given the circumstances, in all aspects. When the door to the registrar's office opened a young couple came out smiling, kissing and full of joy, dressed in full wedding garb with a huge entourage following them. Their wedding party dwarfed the threesome and upon their exit, left them feeling small, but somehow very united; both girls held Hans's hand tightly.

"Nowak and Baumgartner marriage is next" called out the Registrar's assistant and Hans's smile spread across his face and infected his female loved ones.

"Let's go get married, ladies!" he said excitedly and he led the two into the office, as the door closed behind them.

Inside, a salt and pepper haired man sat behind a large mahogany desk with a female scribe sitting to his left hand side. He gestured for the three to walk towards him as he opened the file and looked through his glasses and then up to the three before him.

"Tanya Nowak?" he looked at Tanya and nodded; she nodded in return.

"...and Hans Baumgartner?" he looked at Hans who nodded in the affirmative. He then paused and looked at Rebeccah who stood with her large green eyes and deep dark red hair and her large beaming smile. The Registrar couldn't help but smile back.

"And, who will you be marrying today, Miss" he asked good-naturedly, not expecting an answer but Rebeccah was there for one reason.

"I'm going to marry Hans to be my Daddy" she said matter-of-factly. It made all present in the office stop and take notice. The Registrar smiled to himself and then looked to Hans.

"That's a mighty big responsibility. Are you prepared for that?" the Registrar asked, more so to Hans than to Rebeccah, but it was Rebeccah who answered.

"Yes, sir. I am prepared to be his daughter. I will listen to him and be a good girl and promise to remember his...his....um..., birthday." She answered hoping to sound as grown up as she could. The group around her all smiled at her sweet innocence but none more than Hans, her soon-to-be daddy.

"Well, I think we shouldn't keep this little lady waiting a moment longer. Do we have the proper license and documentation?" the Registrar asked his secretary.

"Yes, sir." The assistant answered.

"Then let's get started" said the Registrar smiling at Rebeccah. Tanya, seeing the attention that Rebeccah garnered, felt a pang of jealousy flow through her. Even now, even when the man she married loved her, she was upstaged by someone else, this time no less, a child. Another wedding she couldn't announce. Another bride she couldn't revel in being. Another very bitter pill.

* * *

Leena led Lucas down the street and into the small strip that housed Hans the Pharmacist's shop. As they approached Leena realized the "Hans" part of the sign had been covered over white a white sheet. Only "the Pharmacist" was revealed and Leena immediately took note. When they entered the shop she went straight to the back counter. A tall thin man in a white lab coat stood smiling wide, ready to serve their every need.

"Good day. How may I help you?" he asked eagerly.

Uncertain, Leena looked to Lucas then back to the tall man.

"We're here to speak to Hans" she told the man. He had a look of confusion for a moment and then asked, "You had an appointment?" still smiling, his broad teeth showing completely.

"Well...uh...no" Leena stuttered and the Lucas broke in.

"We would like to speak to him, please" he stated, giving his best smile.

"Well, I'm sorry, but Hans no longer owns this shop." When neither Leena nor Lucas reacted, he continued, "He no longer works here." The lean man in the white coat turned and retreated back behind a larger counter, leaving Leena and Lucas to their own summation.

"Have you seen this woman?" Leena called out after the retreating man holding up the picture she held. He didn't turn around, he didn't take any notice. Stumped by his nonchalant interest, she turned to Lucas.

"This was a waste of time" she said as she started leaving the store. Lucas's large frame turned and followed behind her. "Without a name we have nothing. Just a picture that no one seems interested in!" she stated as she pushed through the doors and stopped on the sidewalk. Lucas joined her looking equally as frustrated.

"I have to agree, our story doesn't seem credible if we don't have a name. Especially if we're dependent on appealing to them by telling them she's your sister" he said.

The two stood staring at one another as if to read each other's mind as to what to do next. Just as Lucas was about to suggest they stop in at every store and show Luisa's picture, passersby began looking oddly at the couple as they blocked the sidewalk and then some began speaking quietly and pointing at Leena. She suddenly realized that the town's people might have recognized her from the interview that aired. That alone would prevent anyone from wanting to talk about finding her dead sister and admitting that she had been seen in their town, well Leena figured that would be near suicide.

"Let's get out of here!" she said bolting for the car. Lucas caught on immediately and took off running after her. They made it to the car quickly and climbed inside.

"Don't get discouraged" Lucas told Leena. "There's definitely more to this than what's being let on here. I can't quite figure it out but someone knows something about that woman" he said pointing to the picture of Luisa, "whether or not she's Luisa... that remains to be seen. But they know of her, that I feel pretty sure of". Leena hoped he was right. It would mean the end to what seemed a very long nightmare for her; she couldn't imagine what Chase Morningstar had been going through.

"Where do we go from here, then?" asked Leena eagerly. Spurred on by Lucas's confidence, Leena wanted to try a new approach. "We need to try thinking outside the box" she said, making Lucas grin.

"Well, we could go through the names Robin sent us and see if we can match anything up", Lucas shrugged. He really was at a loss. *Some great investigator I am!*, he sat thinking. The problem was, he had nothing to confirm that the person they were chasing was truly Luisa or not. He thought of perhaps staying for a few days and walking the streets to see if they could spot her, but that wasn't very practical. Sometimes, this kind of work was just that though, impractical. It took patience for a case to come to fruition, for the person he was trailing to slip up. Perhaps a week or two staying in town would be long enough for the Luisa look-a-like to emerge.

"Let's meet up with Robin at the hill and see what he's come across." Lucas said as they drove on towards the hill.

* * *

"You may kiss your bride!" said the Registrar. Hans took Tanya's face into his hands and kissed her softly for a moment and then pressed his lips harder, more passionately for a longer sustained kiss. Tanya kissed him back. When they separated, Rebeccah's arms stretched up towards Hans and he picked her up just as she threw her arms around his neck and kissed him on the cheek.

"Now you're my daddy!" she said proudly. Hans's eyes welled up and he and Rebeccah shared another big hug. Keeping Rebeccah in his arms, he shifted her to one side, grabbed Tanya's hand with his free hand and walked his new family out of the registrar's office. It was such a lovely scene to those looking on. Little did they know that this new little family had such a sinister past and more importantly, an extremely complicated future ahead.

* * *

Lucas and Leena parked on the hillside, looking down into the ravine and the river below. The area was so dense with trees and brush that traversing it in any way, seemed daunting. Lucas was just about to call Robin, when he heard his name called out from lower down the ravine.

He looked toward the direction it came from and saw Robin a couple of hundred feet down, standing near a clearing and waving his arms.

"Lucas!" he called again as both his arms waved over his head. "I'll be right up!" he called, giving Lucas the thumbs up to which Lucas did the same back.

"Christ, the guy's relentless!" He admitted to Leena, smiling wide. "They needed to rappel themselves down there to get to the crash site and he's probably wearing flip-flops and a smoking jacket!" he laughed. Leena broke out laughing and by the time Robin reached to two of them, they were holding their sides from the laughter.

"What's so funny?" he asked as he approached the giggling couple. The sight of him made them break out laughing even harder. His hair had captured a few leaves along the way and he had scuff marks and dirt stains all over him.

"What happened to you?" Lucas managed, stifling a laugh. Robin knew right away the intrepid investigative reporter look was not what had greeted Lucas and Leena.

He had managed to walk fairly carefully down the ravine a hundred feet or so, but then he lost his footing and stumbled and rolled down for a bit before managing to stop himself. He knew it was crazy of him to try but he desperately wanted to get down to the crash site and see if anything had changed since the last time he was there.

He began laughing himself. "Oh, I tell ya" he told them with a sigh, "I've never had a case envelope me so much. It's like, we are sitting right on top of the answers here, but they haven't been revealed yet." He said sounding frustrated and tired. He had brushed himself off and straightened his hair, only after Leena motioned to him that he should do so and turned back towards the ravine and its river below. The three stood looking at it for a long moment, all lost in their own thoughts.

"The answers are all down there." Said Robin quietly, staring at the river's edge. "And, until she decides to give them up, it all remains a mystery; just a theory, perhaps". Leena and Lucas agreed, both nodding their heads. One day, the river would give up its secrets and the three of them would be ready to pounce when she did.

The drive back to Leena's apartment was contemplative for all three. Leena and Lucas both wondered to themselves how to manage their relationship from overseas, while Robin, in the lead car alone, pondered how in the world they could confirm that Luisa was either dead or alive. He would not give up until he got to the truth and he knew the truth had not yet been told. He could sense it in his gut, something wasn't quite right. Once arriving at Leena's apartment, they decided their next steps.

They would investigate the names of the missing women and children Robin had obtained and see if they could eliminate or match any of them. They surmised that if the woman was still missing then bank activity in her name should not be happening and, if the child was still missing, then they wouldn't be enrolled in school. They only had a few more days before Robin and Lucas were to fly back to home and they wanted to make the most of the time they had.

During the day, Robin would scour through database after database trying to match any one of the names on the list with someone using that name out in the real world. He made some matches, but each one was quickly ruled out as legitimate, just a coincidence.

Leena and Lucas had no luck either. School records were highly guarded so they were only able to use basic searches to try and locate any matches.

When that didn't work, they spent their days in front of the computer screen using social media to try and locate some of the women on the list. Frankly, if the police didn't have any leads, then Leena felt sure that they would do no better, but Lucas and Robin seemed determined that the answers were there, they just weren't seeing them.

At night, the three would come together at Leena's apartment comparing notes on what they had found, which so far, amounted to nothing. Once they were finished with their information exchange, Robin would say his good nights and leave the two lovebirds to explore their relationship further. It was quite obvious that they had become lovers over the course of the week and although he was happy for them, it diverted from the task at hand.

At the end of the week, they were really no further ahead. They were able to eliminate a number of the names, but they still didn't have *the* name, of anyone. Working on the theory that Luisa was alive and in hiding, they still didn't have any idea of who Luisa might be impersonating, or who the possible doppelganger was or who the woman was that Luisa met the night of the storm, and if any of these women were one and the same. Where was this mystery woman and her child? Robin pondered this over and over again until it buried deep into his cortex. This one would never leave him, not until he finished it.

With their bag checked and their flight boarding in moments, Robin said his goodbyes to Leena. She hugged him tightly.

"I'm sorry for this wild goose chase" she said apologetically and she rubbed his back as she held him. "Thank you so much for trying your hardest. It means a lot to me" she smiled at him as she separated from him. She kissed his cheek and patted his arm.

"My pleasure, Leena" he said smiling. "I always love to have something to challenge me and I do believe I've been given one hell of a challenge! I haven't closed the book on this one yet. And speaking of which" he smiled and stepped aside exposing Lucas standing there with a big grin on his face. Leena stepped into his arms and they embraced, while Robin waited. Thinking he should give them some privacy, he tapped Lucas on the shoulder and pointed his thumb over his shoulder.

"I'll go get through security. Good bye Leena, take care." Robin said, making his getaway. Lucas and Leena hugged tighter for a moment and then leaned back to look at one another. Leena had tears in her eyes.

"How is this possible that I feel this way? Really, we've known each other..." but, before she could finish her sentence Lucas interrupted her, softly placing a finger on her lips.

"..a lifetime" he ended her sentence. "I've thought about you non-stop since I left Switzerland. I'm not going to question it, I'm just going to go with it because it feels so damn good. *You* feel so damn good" he told her hugging her again. Leena nodded her head as he held her.

"I know. I know. Me too" she admitted.

"I'll call, we'll facetime, and we'll Skype. Everyday. Every single day, right?' he said emphatically, suddenly feeling caught up in the moment.

He kissed her, deeply. She melted into him, remembering their last night together and how he'd made her quiver with delight and weak with his passion. Overhead, they were calling for final boarding for his flight. Lucas gave her one last squeeze and then let her go. She walked with him as far as she could and then stood waving and watching as he walked through security and out of sight. Leena stood there for another few minutes lost in her thoughts of what had transpired over the course of the week. Regardless of what Luisa had done, she had brought this man into Leena's life and for that she would be forever grateful.

* * *

Once settled and in flight, Robin pulled his notes out of his carry sack stowed under his feet and brought down his tray. He cross referenced the notes Lucas gave him to his own. Studying them for a moment he turned to Lucas.

"Do we tell Chase anything?" Robin inquired.

"Tell him what?" Lucas asked, honestly. "We have nothing to tell him, except that Leena has spotted someone who looks like Luisa, twice. It is still case closed as far as the Swiss Police are concerned. We have no proof, even if she is in hiding. We can monitor the list of names and should any of them be found, we can eliminate them, but we don't even know if any of these names are who we're looking for." He said frustrated. "We just have to wait, and if she's out there, maybe one day she'll slip up. Maybe not go out in disguise or say the wrong thing to the wrong person. You never know" Lucas said, sighing heavily and putting his head back in his seat.

"Perhaps, but in my experience, before too long, it's your DNA that trips you up. She can go by another name and change her hair, her eyes, gain weight, whatever she needs to change her look, but she can't change her genes. She can't change the blood that runs through her body and if she is out there, in hiding, one day her own DNA will trip her up, guaranteed" Robin said emphatically, then continued.

"It's the woman she met up with on that last night that bothers me. Why hasn't she come forward? Why hasn't she been found? It's driving me crazy that we haven't found her" Robin said perplexed as he too, laid his head back in his seat and let out a heavy sigh.

The problem was, no one was looking for the young mother and child...yet.

* * *

The honeymoon began with a 4 hour long drive crossing over into Germany up towards Frankfurt. Once there, they found a lovely hotel and checked in as Mr. & Mrs. Baumgartner and child. They showed their wedding license to the Concierge and he made sure the rooms were adjoining, winking at Hans in the process. Hans blushed deeply, but smiled at the man. He was very much looking forward to the night with his beautiful bride.

Tanya, on the other hand was not. Her headache was still very bad and although she managed a bit of a sleep in the car on the way, all she really wanted to do was have a hot bath and climb into bed. She certainly didn't feel up to consummating the marriage, not tonight anyway.

Rebeccah was excited! The hotel looked fantastic, all marble and pretty. Everything shined! She looked around the main lobby, her eyes going over every item, taking it all in. She suddenly caught site of the baby grand piano that sat over in the piano bar. She let go of Tanya's hand and wandered over towards the open door of the bar. There was only a young couple inside sipping drinks and talking softly. No one was at the piano.

Turning quickly to see where her mother and daddy were still standing, she started walking towards the open door. She wouldn't go far, but she wanted to touch the keys. She darted up onto the piano bench before anyone realized and was quick to get her hands on those keys. Once she placed her hands properly as she'd been taught, the rest just fell into place. She started playing a soft classical piece that she had learned in the last few weeks with Mrs. Mueller. She hadn't learned it all as yet, but as she played it out she felt sure she could start from the beginning seamlessly and no one would be the wiser.

Rebeccah was in control of that piano and her small hands moved across the keyboard, as if they were compelled through a spiritual guide. She sat with her eyes closed playing the piece up until the point she knew and then would repeat it from the beginning again, never stopping the number. Unbeknownst to Rebeccah, the young couple and some wait staff had stopped what they were doing and were mesmerized by the tiny piano player.

Outside at the front desk, Hans and Tanya were finishing up getting registered and obtaining their room key when Tanya realized Rebeccah was no longer standing beside her. She did a double take, looking around the main lobby, scanning for the child. Hans caught Tanya's look and caught on quickly that Rebeccah was not within sight. He scanned the room twice, but then his gaze was brought back to the open piano bar. Several people were standing in its doorway speaking and pointing inside the club. Hans could hear a classical piece being played and wondered aloud.

"That couldn't be..." he let the sentence hang in the air. Hans walked towards the piano club with Tanya walking in behind. As he got closer to the open doorway he stepped between the onlookers and into the club. He could barely see Rebeccah, she was so small on the bench, but he could definitely see her diminutive feet, still clad in brand new Mary Janes. Every once in a while her head would pop up as she moved it, eyes still closed to each note she touched. She had her small audience's rapt attention and wasn't even aware they were there. This girl was in a world all her own. Hans was amazed by her talent and turned to look at Tanya with such a look of pride on his face, Tanya felt instantly angry.

"Hans, make her stop. People are taking out their phones and videotaping her. Stop them, I don't want my child all over the internet!" she whispered harshly to him. She had worked so hard to keep her in hiding and now, in one singular moment, it could all be ruined.

"Please, please!" Hans called out stepping in front of the young couple's phone and blocking their way. "Please, she's just a young girl and we aren't willing to have her exposed over the internet. Please, as her father, I won't allow it." His request was honored and the man put away his phone. Luckily, Hans had stepped in before anyone else had thought of filming her.

When Rebeccah stopped playing the applause was instant. Surprised by the sound, it jolted her eyes open and she froze for just a moment, and then just like a pro, she stood, stepped to the side of the piano bench and bowed, to which the applause grew even louder. She smiled wide, waved her small hand at them and left the piano running into the arms of Hans. He immediately picked her up and kissed her cheek.

"What a talent you have, Rebeccah!" he gushed at the little girl. "It's as if you've done this for many years! Your lessons are really coming along, I'm sure your teacher is thrilled with your progress" he told her, squeezing her tightly. Rebeccah kept her arms tight around Hans's neck, enjoying his fuss and his comforting smell. Tanya fumed and her headache increased. She didn't need Hans loving the child more than he loved her! She'd already had a marriage like that!

* * *

Once in their room, Tanya admitted to Hans that she was suffering another headache and was going to lie down. He was crushed by this news, figuring the passionate night he had planned was not going to happen, but he could tell Tanya was in pain and promptly tucked her into their marriage bed with some pain medication and a kiss on the forehead.

Instead, he and Rebeccah went back down to the piano bar, where they ate dinner and with permission from the hotel manager, Rebeccah once again sat on the piano bench and entertained the crowd and her new daddy. Hans continued to request no cameras for the privacy of his young daughter and patrons were very respectful. They knew they'd be hearing of her at some point in the next few years.

Chapter 4

THE HONEYMOON IS OVER

The Baumgartner's plan was to find a new home making sure it met all their home and school requirements. After that, the honeymoon would begin! They planned on starting in Frankfurt and then travel all over Germany for as many days or weeks as it took!

After a very productive week and despite the daily throbbing headache and illness that Tanya experienced, the new family had managed to find a beautiful little home, right in Frankfurt with a school nearby, where the music curriculum was top notch. Hans made sure of that! After seeing Rebeccah that first night on the piano, he now felt as though it was their duty to make sure the child's musical gift was well nourished! Tanya was not so impressed, but then, she knew what the others did not. Music came naturally to the child. She was a Morningstar, after all and in some ways, that caused a real resentment to grow in Tanya. Rebeccah and her mother had grown distant over the last little while and as the week progressed Hans started to see a real lack of affection between mother and daughter. It confused him because Rebeccah was such an affectionate child, but much less so with Tanya.

Hans wondered if her headaches had anything to do with it. They had certainly ruined their honeymoon nights, with her always feeling so much pain that she'd vomit and end up in bed early. They had yet to consummate the marriage and although Hans was gently patient about it, he was adamant that she get checked by a doctor before they continue with their honeymoon plans of travelling further around Germany. Tanya was reluctant to do anything and it ended up with them having their first fight, right in front of Rebeccah. When the yelling started, it was Hans that she ran to, crying. This infuriated Tanya and she flew into a rage.

"It's always been you, you, you!" she screamed, pointing at Rebeccah. "Even with *him*!" she spit at her, pointing towards the window. *Who?* Wondered Hans.

Hans was confused as to what was going on. Tanya's face was almost purple with rage and she had a strange tick to her eye. He watched as she stood rigid for a moment then her eyes rolled back into her head and she collapsed onto the floor. Rebeccah screamed and cried louder clutching Hans's legs. He managed to pry the child free and ran over to his crumpled wife. She was unconscious, but he felt a heartbeat. He ran over to the hotel phone and called the front desk imploring for an ambulance to come right away.

He then went back to Tanya and knelt beside her. He could hear Rebeccah softly crying and reached out to bring her to him. He cradled her in his arms and rocked her gently, as they both held Tanya's hand.

"It's going to be alright" he kept saying, over and over again, softly against the child's head, but in his gut he knew there was something catastrophically wrong.

* * *

"It's a brain tumor. Massive in size, I'm afraid" the doctor told Hans. Tanya had been rushed to the Emergency Department of the Frankfurt hospital and immediately went in for an MRI on her head. "We'll have to perform emergency surgery to remove it and reduce the swelling in her brain. After that we'll do a biopsy. See what we're dealing with. She may need radiation if we can't get it all" he stated rather, matter-of-factly. *Get it all? Didn't you just say it was massive in size?* Hans wondered.

He was reeling. His head was spinning. *She had been suffering headaches, but were there any other signs?* He tried remembering. But then, he thought about her mood of late, how distant Rebeccah had seemed and wondered if she'd been showing other signs all along. Signs he had missed! His heart sank at the thought of him letting her down, not being able to help her or see what was happening. After all, he'd been a pharmacist for more than 25 years, he knew a thing or two about illnesses.

"I need to be rather frank with you, we don't know what we are dealing with until we get in there. It covers a large area of her brain and could go very deep." The doctor informed Hans. He sat with his head in his hands trying hard to fight back tears.

"A brain tumor. It could kill her." It wasn't a question, more a statement. The doctor hesitated, then nodded his head.

"Yes, possibly. It's been growing for some time" the doctor told him. "It's probably progressed quickly because of her hormones. A pregnancy can flood the body with hormones that make these things grow very quickly."

Hans nodded his head in agreement and then paused, looking at the doctor confused. "Pregnancy?" he asked. The doctor nodded and then realized his mistake.

"You didn't know?" he asked, shocked by Hans's reaction. "Your wife is approximately eight weeks pregnant. You didn't know?' he asked Hans again. Hans looked at the doctor in complete disbelief. *He needn't bother answering*, thought the doctor. The look on his face said it all!

"Well, we're going to do all we can." He tried to assure Hans, patting him on the back. "However, a fetus that young…" he trailed off. Better to let the father know the risks, but no need to drill it into him. This man had received enough shocking news for one day and the doctor didn't think it was over yet.

"She isn't awake, but you can go and see her if you wish. We'll be operating as soon as we can book the OR. This surgery takes precedence so it may not be a long wait. The surgery itself will depend on what we find when we get in there. A few hours at the very least" he suggested. He stood up, smiled at Rebeccah who was sitting next to Hans on the couch in the waiting room and walked away. Hans had barely any time to digest what was happening. He wasn't sure how on earth to explain it all to the small, frightened child who sat next to him.

"Come here and sit with me for a minute, little one, I want to tell you something" he said, gently as Rebeccah climbed into his lap and snuggled up under his chin. He sat back on the couch reclining somewhat with her. He could already feel the wet of her tears, as she allowed her fears to finally release. It was as if she knew the seriousness of the situation instinctively.

"Is she going to die, Daddy?" she asked him outright.

"I don't honestly know that sweetheart. I know that the doctor's said they were going to do all they could to help her and th…." He stopped himself before saying the "baby", gulping down his own tears. He hadn't known! Had she known? If so, why hadn't she said anything? A baby! He was too afraid to get excited about it. Especially since it was the baby that was probably causing the tumor to grow! As he sat there holding his new daughter in his arms, rocking her and comforting her, he prayed that all would be alright and that soon, he would be holding his wife and another new child in his arms. His feelings were all over the place and he decided that both he and Rebeccah should see Tanya before going in for surgery.

They entered her room and were shocked to see her head shaved and many different machines whirring and buzzing around her. Hans worried about the shock of it on Rebeccah and he instinctively picked her up to hold her as she gazed on her mother.

"Where's mommy's hair?" she asked quietly, slightly scared.

"They are going to fix her head" he whispered to Rebeccah. "She can't have all her hair if they are going to fix her head, but don't worry, it grows back very quickly" he said softly to her. Rebeccah held a little tighter onto Hans as they both looked upon Tanya.

She looked as if fast asleep, of which Hans was grateful. It was a shame he couldn't speak to her prior to the surgery, to tell her how much he loved her and that they would be waiting for her as soon as she came out of the surgery and into the recovery room. Instead he leaned over kissing her on the forehead and whispered, "I love you, Mrs. Baumgartner" quietly in her ear. He then let Rebeccah do the same. They stood looking at her for a moment longer and then left the room as the nurses came in to prepare her for the surgery to come.

* * *

They had been in the waiting room for just over an hour. The doctor had said that they wouldn't really know how long it would take, but someone would be sent out periodically to inform them of how it was going. Hans had to sign numerous forms and papers, all basically stating that if anything were to go wrong, the doctors were not held responsible. He had signed them all, anything to get the doctors moving and get Tanya in for surgery. Anything to help save her life and their unborn child! The doctors had warned Hans of the severity of the tumor and the operation to remove it. There had been little time to prepare for any of it and now, as he sat in the family quiet room, he realized the enormity of the situation. He got a sinking feeling in his stomach. *What if…?* He couldn't allow himself to go there yet.

During this time, Rebeccah sat next to Hans, wondering if her mother was going to be okay. She thought back on the day and how angry her mother was when she was yelling earlier and when she fell, Rebeccah didn't understand why she had fallen. There was a couch right next to her. Why didn't she just sit down? It was Hans' reaction that made Rebeccah realize that her mommy wasn't okay.

Feeling restless in her chair, Rebeccah stood up and stretched.

"I'm going to look over at some books, okay Daddy?" Rebeccah pointed to a corner where children's books, adult novels and magazines were stacked up. Hans, raised his head from the documents.

"Yes, of course, sweetheart. Just don't go too far, okay?" He told her gently. Rebeccah nodded and headed off. She got to the long table and started looking at the books and magazine covers. The children's books looked pretty worn. She had no interest in the adult books, but the magazines had some great pictures and one in particular caught her eyes. She didn't know how to pronounce the name but, *The Cosmos* magazine had a mesmerizing picture of the stars. She studied it for a moment, not noticing the elderly woman standing next to her.

"Oh, can you read that? The Cosmos?" she asked, the sound of disbelief in her voice.

Rebeccah didn't look away from the cover, she simply answered, "No, I don't know what it says or means, I just know they're stars. I love stars."

The elderly woman smiled to herself. "The Cosmos means The Universe. Do you know what that means?" she asked the young girl.

Rebeccah thought about it for a moment, then shook her head no. The elderly woman bent forward and pointed to the cover. "The Universe is *all* the stars you ever see up in the sky and probably millions more you don't." She let that sink in for a moment and then asked her, "And, do you know what the stars are?" Again, Rebeccah shook her head.

"Stars are suns, just like our sun. Way, way far away." With that, Rebeccah finally looked up, into the eyes of the elderly woman. She knew this woman, she couldn't recall where, but she knew this woman.

"My mommy is very sick. That's why we're here. Do you know my mommy?" She asked. "Yes, I do actually" the elderly woman answered. "You're part of an amazing heritage." She told the young girl. She knew the young girl wouldn't understand, but said it anyway.

Rebeccah's attention turned back to The Cosmos cover. "I watch the stars in the morning. I used to watch from my bedroom window" she explained.

"And which star is that, my dear?" The elderly woman asked her.

"It's the only one I see in the morning. But, it only shines for a while until the sun comes up. I wonder where it goes?" she said, more out loud than to the elderly woman.

"Oh, I see. You're chasing the morning star, are you?" She couldn't help but chuckle to herself. "I've always believed if you continue chasing the morning star, you'll eventually find your way home".

Rebeccah didn't completely understand the elderly woman, but felt the need to explain. "Oh, I don't chase it, I'm still in my house, but one day I'm gonna find out where it goes." She said confidently. The elderly woman patted the girl's head lightly.

"You do just that, my dear. You do *exactly* that!" She said, with a small laugh.

Rebeccah looked at the cover a moment longer and when she looked up to smile at the elderly woman, she was gone. She spun around to search the waiting room for her, but only her daddy and another couple were in there. It confused her for a moment and she tried hard to remember where she had seen her before, but she couldn't quite place her. She made her way back to where Hans was sitting, carrying *The Cosmos* magazine with her. She was going to look through the entire magazine to see if she could spot her morning star.

Hans looked up to see Rebeccah return and was about to ask if she wanted anything to eat or drink, when the doctor came through the double doors. Hans was quite surprised to see him thinking he should be back in the operating room, overseeing the surgery, but then the dawning came over him. The doctor's face said it all. He dropped his head as he approached Hans, not able to look the man in the eye. He let out a heavy sigh shaking his head. Hans stood as the doctor approached.

"The …uh…tumor" he paused. He truly hadn't anticipated what had happened. No sooner had they begun trying to remove the tumor, Tanya had started bleeding and they couldn't get it to stop. The tumor was so deeply grown into the brain that he doubted he'd have been able to save her, regardless. "The tumor was very deep. The moment we tried any kind of extraction, she started bleeding and we couldn't stop it. I'm terribly sorry. There was nothing we could do to stop the bleed." He stopped, allowing Hans to take in what he had been told. Hans sank back down onto the couch in disbelief. He could feel the tears stinging his eyes and he fought hard to maintain composure, at least for Rebeccah's sake. Looking at the small child next to Hans, the doctor had a thought. He leaned in closer to Hans and said, "You might want to get your daughter tested. These things can be genetic." He told Hans.

Hans didn't want to engage this man any longer. He had just been given the worst news possible and needed to get Rebeccah and himself out of that environment to somewhere safe, where they could grieve and he could have the conversation he never wanted to have with her.

Gone was his new wife, in less than 10 days; the marriage still not consummated. 24 hours ago everything was fine and now, it was all gone. Gone were the hopes and dreams he had of a life in Germany with his lovely new bride and daughter. Gone. He and Rebeccah would now have to make a new life for themselves. Thankfully, he felt blessed to have the little girl that had taken to him so quickly, called him daddy the moment she could and who was now an orphan with both biological parents being dead. He thought about what the doctor had said about genetics. He turned towards her still sitting on the couch and found her looking up at him with those beautiful green eyes wondering when her mommy would be coming home. How did he tell her "never" was the answer?

He held himself in check long enough to get all necessary papers signed, returned to the hotel with Rebeccah and got her something to eat. He had to do this for Tanya. She would want him to explain as plainly as possible and answer any questions the child had. Rebeccah had stayed quiet the entire time, as if knowing that something was very wrong. She had watched her new daddy talk to the man who was supposed to fix her mommy but they didn't look happy. She felt scared and wanted to sit with Hans and smell his cologne and fall asleep on him in hopes that when she woke up, all would be okay.

"I want to talk to you about your mommy, little one" Hans said to Rebeccah, once she had finished eating. The little girl walked over to her daddy and stood before him. He took her hands in his and looked at her very seriously.

"Your mommy was very sick, you know that, right? When she fell yesterday, the doctor's told us that her head was hurting, remember? They said that they needed to help mommy by operating on her head, but it didn't …work." He said, his voice soft and gentle.

"It didn't? Mommy is still sick?" asked the little girl. "Her head isn't fixed?" She frowned at Hans, crinkling her brows together and Hans couldn't help, but well up. She was such a perfect little girl and now he had been left to care for her. How was he to be what this perfect little person needed? He felt a huge sense of responsibility to make sure that Rebeccah had as gifted a life, as he could possibly provide.

"Mommy is out of pain now. She went to sleep and didn't wake up and now she's an angel. She won't be home with us anymore. You'll find her in the heavens, in the stars." He said to her pointing upwards hoping she understood that mommy wasn't going to come home.

Rebeccah studied Hans's face closely. She registered what he had said and proved it with the huge tears that began to well up in her beautiful green eyes but she smiled slightly.

"Mommy is my star! She's my Morningstar! Now *I will* be chasing the morning star!" she said through her tears. He couldn't help but begin to cry as well. He brought Rebeccah into a hug and the two sobbed, held together for some time. No more dreams of growing old with someone, no more dreams of a house full of children. And as quickly as it began, the honeymoon was over.

Chapter 5

SPLIT DECISION

The snow was blinding! Michigan winters were usually bad, but this was ridiculous! There was no way in hell they'd have been out on the roads if it hadn't been time. Especially, on New Year's Eve 2018. The middle-aged black woman who was driving, continued to urge the heavily pregnant young black girl beside her to "breathe, breathe!" The girl was doing her best, but the contractions were incredibly painful and coming faster than before. The car pulled into the Emergency parking lot and the woman driver got out, ran around the car and pulled open the passenger side door, grabbing the elbow of the pregnant girl to steady her walk in the snow and into the emergency ward.

"Please!" she called out. "Please, my daughter needs help"!

Two nurses came running, one with a wheel chair and had the girl seated and whisked away before the mother knew what happened. The mother chased after them, going through sliding doors, deeper into the hospital than she had ever been. When the nurses stopped, her daughter was banded on her wrist, her name and incidentals were taken and she was given a room. Zone A, 1st Floor Obs #14.

"You can wait here while we get her prepped. There are forms to be filled out. I'll notify the clerk when she's ready, okay?" one nurse said to the mother. She nodded nervously. Another nurse handed her a clipboard with a small stack of forms and the mother took a seat nearby the registration desk.

It had all happened so quickly! Angel Townsend was enjoying a nice quite dinner with her pregnant daughter, Vella on New Year's Eve when suddenly, Vella grabbed her stomach and fell to her knees as her water broke. There had been no other warning signs, no early backache, nothing. Angel, thinking they could have hours to wait then realized the snow storm raging outside and a good 20 minute drive, maybe more to get to the hospital, they'd better get going. Vella's twins were not due for another 5 weeks, but apparently they had other plans. Angel's car wasn't the most reliable and her tires slid across the road precariously during the terrifying drive. Now that they were here safe and sound, her daughter in good hands, Angel took a deep breath and looked down at the first form. These were going to take a while.

* * *

Vella was groaning and gasping for breath. While a nurse got her into a hospital gown another hooked her up to a heart monitor and a baby heart monitor. They helped her into her bed and positioned the bed so she was on a 45 degree angle. Another nurse came in and started another machine up, then put a needle into Vella's arm.

"In case you need IV", the nurse said at Vella's questioning face. She nodded to the nurse and put her head back on the pillow.

"How old are you, honey?" asked a nurse in green scrubs.

Vella cleared her voice, "Eighteen" she answered. The nurse nodded and noted it on the chart.

"How many weeks along are you?" green scrubs asked.

"Thirty-five weeks, three days" Vella said proudly.

"Good girl!" the nurse said as she wrote it down.

"And, you're carrying twins?" a nurse in navy scrubs asked.

"Yes, I am" Vella said, then grimaced. Another contraction. Vella reached out to hold the railing of the bed and pull herself upward instinctively wanting to push.

"Oh, no. Now you can't go pushing yet, my dear. You have to wait a bit while we see what's going on with those twins of yours. Try hard to breathe through the contractions and do not push!" she cautioned Vella. When the contraction was over the nurse checked to see how far Vella was dilated.

"You have a bit to go yet, my dear" she told Vella. Vella groaned. She was already exhausted and the real labor had barely begun. Carrying two babies for thirty-five weeks and three days had not been easy. Especially since the father of the twins was nowhere to be found; as in, possibly dead. Vella's background wasn't that exemplary. She ran with a gang of rough kids and had done for a few years. Her mother didn't like it, but couldn't stop her. Vella had her own mind. And so, when Vella's mind decided she wanted to sleep with one of the roughest dudes in the gang, there was no stopping her. A week later he got into a fight outside a bar and roughed up some other bad ass dude. Vella's dude went home after the fight and hasn't been seen or heard from since. That was approximately 34 weeks and three days ago. Vella was fairly certain he was dead, but that wasn't going to stop her. When she found out she was pregnant, she told her mother, "I'm gonna have this and make his daddy proud". Angel wondered about that. In the area they lived, it was hard not to become just like him. Would that *really* make the dead father proud? She knew her daughter would still be loyal to the gang, no matter what. Angel had tried numerous times to talk to her about moving out of town, finding a better life, especially since she now had a baby to raise. Vella's only response was, "Good enough for me and you, good enough for it, too"

When Vella found out she was having twins, her mother seriously considered talking to her about an abortion. How on earth would they ever manage? She could see 1 baby, but not 2! Vella was not of the same mind. She thought having twins was the best news she'd ever heard. Angel wondered where Vella thought all the money would come from to feed and clothe two babies. Certainly her gang wasn't going to fork over a weekly allowance. Angel knew better than to try and change her daughter's mind. She just couldn't see a way they could manage it all. She would help Vella with the twins, but she was really too old for this shit.

And that's just what Angel was thinking as she filled out the forms. Vella's "friends" had given her some cash (which heavily smelled of weed) to help pay the medical costs, 'cause God knows, they had no medical insurance. Angel had worked very hard to raise Vella, but it wasn't like it was a career. You don't make a career out of cleaning offices. You may make a living, but it wasn't much and eventually, the neighbourhood swallowed them whole. Once Vella got in with that gang and was pregnant, Angel knew she'd never leave.

Many of the forms were for insurance. Angel put a line through the ones that didn't apply, signed her name at the bottom and walked over to the registration desk. She handed the clerk the clipboard and completed forms. The nurse looked the forms over and questioned, "No insurance coverage?"

"No", Angel responded. "I'm paying in cash". The nurses nodded her head, but her eyes didn't lie. She was judging Angel, for certain.

"We'll need some costs taken care of up front" the nurse stated. Angel opened her purse and pulled out a thick wad of cash. The smell permeated the area and the nurse smirked as Angel began counting out the cash.

Angel tried hard not to lose her cool. This is the life Vella could look forward to, being heavily judged. Angel hated it. And in the next little while, Vella would give birth to two reasons she should leave this town.

"Can I see my daughter, please?" The nurse nodded her head towards Vella's door, just across from the registration desk and said, "Yes, they've got her set up, I believe".

When Angel walked into the room, Vella's eyes lit up. It made her mother pause for a moment. Here was her little girl, her baby at eighteen years of age, ready to give birth to twins! She loved her, but a lot of the time, she didn't much like her. However, Angel had to hand it to her, Vella had done amazingly well with everything considered. She walked over to the right side of the bed and stroked her daughter's forehead. Her soft thick hair, which Vella usually spent hours straightening, had been braided back; something Vella must have done herself since being taken in the room.

"They say I'm only a few inches dilated. I need to be at least 10!" Vella complained, her head rolling back and forth on the pillow. "I've been having contractions since dinner. It's now 9:00 o'clock and I haven't had a single baby yet!"

"Babies come in their own sweet time." Green scrubs said.

"We shouldn't have left so early, Mom" Vella spat at her mother. She turn to face her with accusing eyes.

"Your water had broken, Vella. I figured the babies were on their way!" she answered back. "Besides, the storm might have stopped us if we had waited. Its better we're here now" she told her daughter, to which Vella just groaned. It was going to be a long night.

"You're not having a C-section?" Navy scrubs asked. Angel could tell the nurse did not think it was a good idea to deliver the babies naturally. Another thing Vella was dead set against.

"Nope. Ain't nobody gonna cut my babies outta me! And, the money it costs?! No way. Uh-huh!" she exclaimed shaking her head.

Two and a half hours later, Vella was now in active labor. The contractions were unbearable and Vella tended to scream as each one raged through her. She had three nurses and her mother all telling her to stop screaming, concentrate on breathing and start pushing, but Vella wouldn't stop. Any women in the birthing area, hearing Vella's screams would probably have asked to be moved. By the time the first baby was born, poor Vella was exhausted. Her baby was placed on her belly; a boy. He screamed like his mama and it made the nurses laugh. A gleeful moment for such a long night. It was December 31, 2018 at 11:47 pm. Vella continued to labor another hour before her other baby boy was born January 1, 2019 at 12:53 am. They were little in size; the first boy came in at 4 lbs, 6 ounces and the second at 4 lbs, 3 ounces. They had all fingers and toes and both were a lovely dark color. Angel was speechless! Twin boys. Identical, twin boys. Born on different days, different months and in different years. Only Vella could manage that!

It was nearly 2:30 am before everyone was settled. Angel was going to stay the night on the recliner the nurses had brought into Vella's room. The storm outside was too bad to be driving home. The twins had been taken away in separate incubators. They'd need to stay a few days in the neo-natal unit, but all in all, they were fit and healthy. With a blanket covering her and her daughter resting peacefully, Angel thought about the events of the day. Vella had shown all of them by delivering two baby boys, quite naturally! No C section necessary! She could hear her daughter snoring. All was well. *Happy New Year!* Angel thought as she drifted off into a deep sleep.

She didn't hear the beeping immediately, she actually thought it was part of a dream, but she felt the rush of air and the light come on as the door was opened and bodies filled the room. The nurses were giving instructions and information to one another lightning fast and calling out, "Code blue, code blue!"

Angel sat upright. Now there were six bodies surrounding Vella's bed and one of the nurses had come and grabbed Angel by the arm asking her to step out of the room.

"What's going on?" she asked. "What's happening?"

"We don't know yet. That's what we're trying to figure out! Please, step out of the room and let us help your daughter" she told her.

Angel was pushed back out of the room and the door closed in front of her. Another nurse came and led her to a couch near to the registration desk. Angel could see her daughter's door, but could not see what was going on inside. An overhead announcement calling "Code blue – Zone A, Floor 2, room 212" was called a number of times and Angel watched as many medical personnel ran into her daughter's room. At one point a machine was wheeled in and Angel could see Vella's bed completely surrounded. She could hear the voices, anxiously calling out instructions, but she couldn't really tell what they were saying.

She sat, still clutching the blanket she used to sleep with and held it close to her. She felt so useless. She couldn't do anything. She could feel the tears well up in her eyes. She didn't feel good about this. Not at all. Something in the pit of her stomach told her this was not good.

After a half hour, a nurse and a doctor came out of Vella's room towards her. Asking if they could speak to her, they motioned to a room just behind the registration desk. Once inside, they sat Angel down and both sat either side of her.

"I'm sorry. We did everything we could. Your daughter suffered an aortic rupture. Basically, the biggest artery in the body, bursts. Unfortunately, her symptoms were masked by the labor and delivery. There's nothing we could do. She died. We couldn't save her" the Doctor told her, sadly. Angel looked at the nurse, who slowly nodded her head. "It's true" she said. "She had an aortic rupture. Almost always fatal".

Angel could not believe them. *How could she be dead? She'd just given birth to the twins, how could she die? Not in this day and age! Women don't die from giving birth, do they?* She looked again at the nurse and doctor, who were trying hard to figure out some way to help the poor woman.

"Is there someone we could call for you? Do you have family that we could contact for you?" they asked her. She simply shook her head. No family. Only the twins, now. Only the twins.

The hospital provided as much as they could for Angel and her grandbabies. While the babies were in neo-natal, Angel made funeral arrangements. Nothing fancy. She told no one. Vella was cremated and Angel had the urn packed away in a box immediately. As she taped it up, she gave a heavy sigh. She had cried herself to sleep for the past week. She had thought long and hard about it. She had gone through everything several times over and there was only one way for her to manage and although she hated to do it, she absolutely must. She was exhausted and really was too old for this shit.

She entered the neo-natal unit where the twins were kept. The nurses had dressed them in green and blue onesies, with matching hats. Each also had a matching blanket. They were really beautiful boys. Vella would have been so proud of them. They still hadn't been named. Vella died before she could make up her mind.

Angel stood over their bassinettes and watched them closely. She knew she had to stay strong and silently asked Vella for help and guidance. A nurse came up behind her, touching her back, gently. Angel turned to look at her.

"Is it going home day for these little guys?" she asked.

"Only one." Angel told her as she turned back, not wanting to see the judgement in her eyes. Angel took a deep breath and steeled her spine.

"I can only take one with me." She stated, matter of factly. "The other will be adopted. I have no choice. I can't manage the two of them. I must move, I must get away from here and I can only manage to take one with me." Hard as she tried to hide her emotions, a single tear ran down her face. The adoption had all been arranged. She had realized it the day Vella died that she was not able to care for both boys. In Vella's honor, she wanted to keep one of the boys, but couldn't possibly manage two.

The nurse looked upon the poor woman with pity. No judgement, just absolute sorrow and pity for the horrible position she had found herself in. With no one else in her family, Angel and her newborn grandson would have a difficult enough time. Taking on raising the two boys on her own was impossible. So, she had made the gut wrenching decision to give one of them up.

But which one?

Chapter 6

NATURE VS. NURTURE

Angel found life in sunny southern California daunting. The heat! What was she thinking? Coming from a small town in Michigan, she was used to the heat of the summer, but not all the damn time! The Santa Ana winds were nice, but they fanned fires and thick smoke into the air, so breathing was tough and when it rained, landslides took out many small, peaceful towns. Don't even get her started about earthquakes! Two had occurred in the 6 years she and Tyrone had lived there.

She had packed up her poor car, her grandson and everything she could manage, running out on last month' rent, with a large unpaid hospital bill and the job she'd held for many years, leaving Michigan behind. The cash given to her to pay for Vella's medical needs was carefully stashed away. It would help her and her grandson get a new start. She was pretty certain that southern California had offices that needed cleaning and once she had a place to stay, she'd apply to any temp agency she could.

She named her grandson, Tyrone Thomas Townsend. Triple T, or "Trip" for short. It was frankly amazing to her how much her spirits lifted with every mile she put between her and the old neighborhood. She missed Vella and if she allowed herself to think about her for too long, she'd well up. *Crying wasn't going to do any good to anybody,* she'd tell herself. Angel had to be strong, strong just as Vella had been through her pregnancy and delivery. Strong like Vella.

Angel had managed to bring Tyrone out of a bad area, but for all the miles she drove, the social element didn't change that much. Far from it, in fact. She returned to cleaning offices, but this time, the company she worked for offered medical insurance, a decent wage, and flexibility with shifts. The company also provided day care, which meant Angel could drop Tyrone off and work away, knowing he was in good hands. Yet, taking all of that into consideration, unless you were extremely wealthy and part of the elite, the housing wasn't exactly the Ritz Carlton and Angel most certainly did NOT shop or live near Rodeo Drive. The apartment was on the third floor of a 7 story building. The scenery was better than last, but she could watch drug deals, prostitutes and gang members doing business in broad daylight, right from her balcony. To block it from view, she had filled the balcony with lush flowers and greenery. At least sunny California offered her that; some greenery all year round.

Tyrone did well in his surroundings. His grandmother doted on him. Her grief for Vella was absorbed by the love she felt for Tyrone. He was her everything now and she took her role as grandmother very seriously. She vowed that Vella's son would not end up being in a gang. She was teaching him his letters and numbers before he was 18 months. She read to him every night and not just nursery rhymes, she read him the classics. At 6 he'd already been through Charlotte's Web, The Velveteen Rabbit, The Story of Doctor Doolittle and many others. Tyrone was like a sponge, taking it all in. His mind would create such fantastical visions and would get lost in the journey the stories would take him on. His grandmother thought he was a gifted boy and did all she could to feed his mind. His large brown chocolate eyes could melt any heart and when he smiled, you couldn't help but smile back. His face was very expressive and his grandmother thought he'd make a great actor!

He had just started 1st grade and Angel was expecting high praise when he came home the first day. She had put him on the bus, full of hope and expectation for him to impress his teachers. As he stepped off the bus, he looked like a different child from the one she'd watched drive away, happily waving just this morning.

"What happened Trip?" she asked him, rubbing his head and guiding him towards the apartment doors. "You don't like 1st grade?"

He shrugged his shoulders. His head hanging. "It's okay, I guess." He said, sullenly.

"Doesn't seem like that to me. What didn't you like?" she asked him. Again, he shrugged his shoulders, staying quiet. As they entered the apartment building and got on the elevator, Tyrone turned facing his reflection in the elevator mirrored walls. He studied his face, intently.

"Why don't I have a mommy or a daddy" he asked his grandmother. She looked down at him, her heart saddened by his question.

"They both died, Trip", she answered him. "We've talked about this. Your dad died shortly after your mom and he began dating and your mom died just after you were born." This was how she had put it to him, when he had asked years ago. It was the simplified version, but that was all Trip needed to know. The details weren't the best. Trip then said something that made his grandmother's heart lurch.

"I wish I had a brother" he said, forlornly. Angel's eyes grew wide when she heard that. He had never before shown any interest in wanting a brother. Angel had closely monitored all of Trip's friendships and had tried desperately to keep him busy with intelligent and fun things to do at home, so he had little time to build any real friendships. *Perhaps,* Angel pondered, *he's lonely?*

Trip turned into his grandmother's knees and gave her a squeeze. "I'm glad you didn't die after I was born, Gramma" he said. She gave him a squeeze back. He tore at her heart. "So, am I sweetie-pie, so am I!" she said, smiling a little.

The conversation made Angel wonder what had happened on his 1st day. Had the kids been mean to him for being different? Surely, in this day and age, a child had all kinds of different family members to go home to. Angel decided she'd give it some time before perhaps going to his teacher.

Angel had given it a few weeks, yet Trip was no better. Actually, he had grown sullen and unhappy. Angel tried to speak with him about what was going on at school, but he wouldn't tell her, he just remained sad. When Angel finally had a chance to meet with the teacher, things started to make sense to her.

"Your grandson acts out in class!" she told Angel. "I asked him numerous times to be quiet and sit down, but he doesn't listen" the teacher complained. Angel was perplexed by this. She had never seen Trip act up, not ever. He had always been glued to whatever they were doing, constantly intrigued and involved.

The teacher went on, "Like yesterday, I was reading "Green Eggs and Ham" and he kept mimicking me and making funny voices. It's disruptive!" she whined. Angel, equally as frustrated told the teacher straight out.

"Well, Trip is a lot smarter than "Green Eggs and Ham". He read that when he was two! He's more than likely bored out of his mind!" Angel admonished. *Geezus! What kind of teacher was this?* Angel wondered.

"Listen Ms. Townsend. I have 35 six year olds who I have to teach every day. When Tyrone acts out, it causes disruption in the class. Some of these kids have never had a story read to them. They've never heard of Dr. Seuss or Green Eggs and Ham. It's great that Tyrone has an active mind, but he's being a nuisance and it needs to stop!" the teacher told her, angrily.

Angel realized right there that if she didn't do something, Trip would end up *exactly* as his father had. Dead. She could see the writing on the wall. If this school system wasn't going to acknowledge her grandson's gifted mind, then she'd have to get him into a school system that did.

And how was that supposed to happen? Angel wondered, sighing heavily.

* * *

The thirty-something black couple introduced their newborn adopted son to their family and friends with a huge celebration. The mother and father were lawyers from Chicago who ran their own firm. Mostly, Entertainment Law; contracts for television and movies. Representation for some of the biggest in the industry. They lived a busy, socially hectic life and were hoping to somehow throw a child into the mix, thinking it might force them to slow down. They had tried for 6 years to have a baby of their own, but it never happened for them. Realizing they needed to go about it a different way, they turned to their legal colleagues to advise on where to turn for adoption. They were directed to a service who were very successful in matching the child with good, decent parents. It hadn't taken long for them to be notified that a baby boy had been born whose mother passed shortly after giving birth. He was small and would need a few days to be monitored, but once given a clean bill of health, he'd be theirs to keep! Other than the fact that he had been born in Michigan during the New Year snow storm, the new parents knew nothing else about him. They flew to Michigan straight away and were picking him up from the hospital within hours of being notified.

They named him Garrett Thomas Samuels and, as far as his new parents were concerned, he was absolutely perfect! Garrett didn't know it of course, but within a week of his birth, his circumstances had greatly improved! His parents were very well off, very well educated and were in very good standing within a large and varied social circle. Little Garrett had done well!

His parents, Grant and Sondra Samuels had come from excellent families. They met on the campus of the University of Chicago and married shortly after graduation. They decided that their minds were better put to use together, rather than going out into the field and working for someone else's firm. Their families, both sides with legal backgrounds, were thrilled. Their social circle included many in the Chicago entertainment industry and Grant and Sondra soon found themselves representing their friends in the creation of legal contracts. They had been in business for nearly 10 years when they adopted Garrett and three years later, decided to take an offer they couldn't refuse. They were asked to be legal representation for the music label, KARMA! The head office was in Santa Barbara, California and after another vicious winter, the Samuels decided to move closer to KARMA!'s head office and work from home. They had set up their Chicago office quite nicely with competent personnel who had been there from shortly after they started. The "North" office, as it was now being referred to, would be on Grant and Sondra's radar, but "Sunny South" needed them more. Especially since, KARMA!'s offer included a beautiful house in a gated community, just to sweeten the deal. A signing bonus. It was common in the entertainment industry to throw in a house, especially if the project was forecast to take years and years. They needed their personnel to live somewhere, right?

Garrett was an inquisitive little boy. His large brown chocolate eyes could melt any heart and when he smiled, you couldn't help but smile back. His face was very expressive and his parents would say, *you can read his thoughts*. His parents were now much more in his life than when they lived in Chicago. They put him in a daycare, part-time which excelled in early childhood education. His time at home was spent being taught music by his mother, and the music industry and his work within it, by his father. Grant and Sondra planned to mold their son into an extremely successful man. They weren't going to tell him what to do, they were simply going to open his mind to all possibilities and let him decide where it would take him. This childhood proved a prefect nurturing environment for Garrett and he soon became quiet adept at numerous things. He could write and perform music at an early age. Although he liked the guitar, his preference was for the piano and creating pieces of music, he called "background music". At age 9, his father gave him his first phone with an excellent camera built in and he began making short movies, then setting his own pieces of music to it. He was literally *producing* his own short movies from start to finish. His parents were incredibly impressed! He really was unique; a true one off.

As far as they were concerned, there was no one like him on earth!

* * *

Angel had taken on another cleaning job to try and save enough to get Trip into a better school. She had looked into several private schools and had settled on one called "The Cascades School". It was run by a group of highly educated teachers and professors, all with an interest in bringing forth the very best in each child. They followed the philosophy of finding the child's best abilities both creatively and academically through a series of tests. Based on the outcome of those tests, they would then gear the child's schooling in whatever areas the child had shown to have proclivity in. This sounded perfect for Angel. She knew her grandson was highly gifted and he needed much more than Green Eggs and Ham to keep him off the streets. She was determined he wasn't going to be his father!

Her second job was a cleaning job once a week for a stand-up comedian in a well-off gated community. She had cleaned his father's office for a few years and he asked if she was available to clean his house. He offered excellent pay and said she could bring Trip along, if she needed to. What luck! She didn't have to pay a sitter, he could help with the cleaning and maybe get a taste for what the other life was like! It might be all the push he needed to want to live like the rich do! Angel thought it was a win-win situation and took the second job on, happily!

Upon arriving at the gate of the community, Angel was stopped by an Enforcement Officer.

"Can I ask for your name please, M'am?" he questioned.

"Angel Townsend", she answered. "I'm here to clean Mr. Gary Lee's home. I have my grandson Trip with me. He said I could bring him along. I believe its number 108", she told the officer. He nodded and checked an itinerary on his laptop. "Yup, I have you here" he confirmed. Trip watched as the officer unlocked a small metal cabinet in front of him and opened it to display many keys. They were individually hanging with a number written above. He handed her a key, had her sign the clipboard and allowed the bar up for her to drive onward. "You have to bring that back to me before being allowed out, got that?" he told her. Angel nodded in agreement. As they drove away, Angel could see Trip looking back at the gated entry.

"Pretty fancy, huh Trip?" she asked him. Trip said nothing at first. Sat in the back seat, he was mesmerized by the whole experience. He couldn't see much from his vantage point until they drove further into the community. His mind, full of questions.

"Why do they need police at the front, Gramma?" he asked. Angel smiled to herself, loving that he was taking it all in.

"They have very expensive homes, with very expensive things in their homes. A lot of people, people like in *our* neighborhood, want to steal what they have, so they have a police officer stand guard" she explained. She knew he really wasn't a police officer, but it didn't matter to explain that. Only that he understood that when you're very rich, you live like this.

The experience was life changing for Trip. The homes were a lot bigger than he had ever seen. One of them looked as big as the entire apartment building he and his Gramma lived in! The comedian wasn't stinking rich, but his wealth impressed Trip a great deal. He had a TV that was the full wall of his living room. THE FULL WALL!

Trip was convinced. Rich was the ONLY way to live! He wished he and his Gramm lived like this. He knew she worked hard and one day, he hoped to move her into a home in this community. One day!

* * *

Angel had been working the two jobs for three years. Trip, now 9 years of age had been at The Cascades School for over a year and showed a flare for the theatrics, not a surprise to his doting Gramma. He had played Fagan in the Christmas musical "Oliver Twist" and his voice and his acting were the talk of the school. A "diamond in the rough", his teacher said. Moving him to that school was the best thing Angel could have done for him. He was on his way to becoming a "someone", however, it was not how Angel envisioned it!

At public school, he had been bullied and ridiculed, one kid even tripped him continuously because of his nickname. Part of this was due to Trip's attitude at school. He may have been bored, but he acted like a little shit, know-it-all! He challenged and questioned the teachers every day. He made fun of the lessons they taught and he was quite precocious. They kids hated him, so those that could, bullied him. He had hated it, but didn't want his Gramma to know why. He had just felt so much rage and anger from it. At night, when his Gramma was asleep he'd throw things out of his bedroom window and watch them hit the street below. His water glass was hurled out one night and caught the attention of the neighbor gang of thugs, who came out to investigate. Trip studied them. They had such power, such bravado. That was who he wanted at school with him. Like a bunch of brothers who would protect him. He began going to bed without question, only to stay up late at night watching the gang and their members. He'd seen them fight, sometimes amongst themselves, sometimes with members of other gangs. Trip admired that "his" gang usually won fights and normally would disperse before any police arrived. He watched and learned all about the gang from his very own bedroom window, all unbeknownst to his Gramma. If she knew she'd kill him, then die herself! Angel had prided herself on "hiding" this from Trip, but he found it anyway. All of it.

And, if he was completely honest, it intrigued him. He was fascinated by them, the way they interacted, the things he heard them say. He could imitate one guy named "Two Tone" really well. He'd watched them intently, hiding behind the drawn curtains, his light off, so as not to draw attention. The education he got at school was nothing compared to what he was seeing on an almost nightly basis in his neighborhood!

As Trip turned 12 years old, he was losing interest at Cascades school. This made Angel frustrated and fret to no end. She was working her fingers to the bone for Trip to attend this school and at 12 years old, he wasn't interested in it anymore. She couldn't figure it out! He stayed in his room more often and rarely came out. There was no more talk of plays at school or any kind of academics. His grades remained stable, but he was a different kid.

Angel had started leaving Trip to come home alone after school. At 12 he was legally able to be on his own and he convinced his grandmother that he could manage the extra responsibility. How could she say no? Those dark chocolate brown eyes, that smile! She was assured he'd be fine, and so, she acquiesced. He was only going to be alone for an hour each day, after school. It was nothing really. She had stopped working at night after the comedian moved out and another family moved in. She now had a different home to clean 5 days a week and was able to be home for 5:00 pm each evening. She was hoping to retire in a few years, but at 62 she couldn't afford to, just yet. She also had to ensure that Trip stayed in school, got a scholarship to a fine University and made something of himself.

After an especially long week of cleaning, Angel came home feeling exhausted. As usual, Trip was nowhere in sight, but she could hear his music playing in his room.

"Trip!" she called out. "I'm home." She waited at the front door, wondering if he'd come out to greet her. Nope. More of the same.

Feeling somewhat pissed off and not wanting to deal with a pre-teen attitude, she walked straight down the hall towards his bedroom and threw open the door. Trip was shirtless, in only his jeans, going through something he hid under his bed covers and behaving strangely.

"Hey!" he shouted at her. "I don't want you coming in here, just like that!" he told her. He may have only been 12 years old, but he stood a good 5 inches taller than her and was all arms and legs. He waived his long arms at her, almost reaching her as he told her, "Get out! I told you, I don't want you coming in my room!" he yelled at her. "Not without knockin'!" he spat at her. Angel was taken aback. He had never spoken to her like that before. He'd never seemed so angry at her before. She studied him closely. He stared at her and did not back down, his nostrils flaring, his beautiful eyes, angry and as if he was looking through her. She had never seen Trip like this. She quietly turned and left his room. Something had changed.

Angel was absolutely right. Something *had* changed. Trip had become friends with a neighborhood kid named Danny, who introduced Trip to his older brother, Two Tone. *The* Two Tone and he was exactly the kind of brother Trip would have loved to have had. He was strong, smart and not afraid of anyone. Two Tone watched out for his youngest brother, Danny like a hawk. Nobody dared to do or say anything negative to Danny without the wrath of Two Tone coming down on them. There were actually 5 brothers in Two Tone and Danny's family; the 3 oldest already in jail for various crimes. Two Tone was doing as his older brothers had done, when they were on the street; protect their own. Now, with only Two Tone and Danny left at home, Two Tone took the oldest brother role and he took it very seriously.

Trip watched as Two Tone demanded respect from all others on the street and Trip knew that one day, he would love to have respect from a man like

Two Tone. Trip had started paying more attention to the way he dressed, the way he spoke, his whole persona. Then at night, when he'd stay in his room, he'd perfect the impersonation.

Maybe it would be useful one day, ya never know! He thought smugly.

* * *

Garrett Samuels got the call he'd been waiting for! An internship for six months at KARMA! Labels. He was thrilled! He had worked hard for this internship and told his parents not interfere whatsoever, he wanted to do this of his own accord.

He said nothing of his parents work with the company and simply submitted his resume through an online application. His parents didn't need to interfere.

Garrett excelled at everything he did. He had either been taught, or taught himself to do numerous things most kids his age would be envious of. He could speak 5 languages; English, Spanish, Italian, German and French. He played any keyboard beautifully, wrote his own music and created his own movies, just as a hobby. Garrett was 17 years old and he was living life to its fullest. His 6'1" tall, long lean body was perfect for all the water activities most who live by the ocean love to do. Garret was an expert surfer, diver and swimmer. His 4.0 grade average only paled in comparison to his bright, creative, unique mind, loyalty to his parents and fantastic work ethic! He had all of that *and* he was a very fine looking young man, to boot! Garrett Samuels had it all! And he was well on his way to making a real name for himself. *A real somebody!*

Garrett's parents were his greatest supporters and biggest fans. They had allowed Garrett to be exactly who he wanted and Garrett was steering the wheel of his own life. They couldn't be prouder! Before he was ready to start his internship, a small celebration was held in Garrett's honor. Grant and Sondra took Garrett to a very high end restaurant, *Carmelita Jones* for a late dinner. They left the house for 9:00 pm reservations. They ate and celebrated for 2 hours and came straight home.

As they drove to the front of their gated community, they couldn't find the Officer in his station. Grant and Garrett both got out of the car, looked into his station as best they could and called the officer's name, *"Mike! MIIIIIKE!"* with no answer. Garrett ran back near the car and took a running leap towards the large brick wall that was built to hold the even larger wrought iron gate in place. He leaped high enough to grab the very top of the wall and pulled himself up. He jumped down onto the other side and ran over to the officer's station. Mike was lying on the ground, a bullet in his head. Garrett called to his dad to "call 911", and bent down to see if Mike had a pulse. No pulse. Garrett could see the station had been rifled through and some keys lay on the ground near Mike's body. The metal key box was opened and there were only 2 keys hanging.

"Dad, tell them to hurry up! We need an ambulance and a load of cops. There's trouble!" Garrett called out, his heart racing.

* * *

Trip was reclining on the couch, enjoying a joint with Two Tone and Danny. They had been smoking weed since they woke up and at 1:00 pm, they were pretty wasted. Giggling over a TV show they watched, the three had become almost inseparable. Trip spent almost all his time at their house, going to Angel's apartment only to change, shower or sleep off a drunk. Trip didn't want her nagging at him and Angel was *really* too old for his shit!

Angel continued her house cleaning jobs and had even been referred to a few others who required her exemplary cleaning services. Her high standards, glowing accolades and years of work allowed her inside some of the most beautiful homes and these people paid very well. She made more money in the last 2 years than she'd made in the previous 5! And, now that she was no longer paying for Trip's private schooling, she was able to open up a savings account! With Trip not home much at all, she enjoyed her time alone. It gave her time to think. She'd spend time thinking about her daughter Vella and how, no matter what she had done, Vella was destined for her outcome. Nothing Angel said to her had made any difference. And now, Angel saw Trip the same way, perhaps even more so. She resented how hard she had worked to keep Trip on the straight and narrow and how quickly he tossed that all off to be friends with those kids. She had started drinking, rather heavily. She'd get home from work, eat in front of the TV and drink until she fell asleep in the recliner. Often times, she'd wake up, badly dehydrated and drag herself off to bed only to wake up the next morning to repeat it all over again. On Saturdays and Sundays, she never saw Trip. He'd usually be gone from Friday morning until Monday late. The only way she knew he was home was if his door was completely closed. If ajar slightly, he wasn't in there, if closed, KEEP OUT! Actually, the Keep Out was understood permanently. Angel daren't go near his room. She really didn't want to know, nor did she really care, anymore. She was exhausted. She felt completely spent of life. All she wanted was to do her day's work, come home and be on her own with her drink. One day, she'd have enough money saved up and she was going to get on a plane and get the hell out of California. Without Trip. One day.

Trip felt no loyalty towards Angel, at all. Once accepted by Two Tone and the gang, he didn't care about her or her feelings. She had been far too over protective, to the point of literally driving him from her arms, right in to the living room of the two young men he sat with now. He stood up to his full height of 6'1", stretched his long arms out above his head and yawned loudly.

"Fuck!" he yelled out, making the two men burst out laughing. He laughed at himself and peered through red eyes to them. He stared at Two Tone for a moment and thought, *I should show him!*

He began walking around, with his arms held to show his muscles off, just as Two Tone had done many times. He turned to Danny and said to him, "Hey Danny, go get me a fuckin' beer!" Both Two Tone and Danny broke up laughing! They had never seen Trip's impersonation and were really entertained. Trip kept it up, walking just as Two Tone did, speaking as Two Tone did. The young men were all amused.

At 17 years old, Trip was a very intimidating member of Two Tone's gang. Not just his body strength, but he was also possibly one of the smartest members. Two Tone could tell this kid had smarts that went beyond his years and Two Tone thought it best to keep him close. Any member of his rival gang could see Trip as a valuable asset, if they knew him well, so Two Tone watched over Trip as much as he did Danny. Just like a brother. His older brother. For Trip to do such a great impersonation of him, not only made him laugh, it made him proud!

"Oh, GOD!" Trip said dramatically. "I'm BORRRRRRED!" he said, throwing himself back down on the couch. "Let's do something!" he asked.

"Like what?" Two Tone asked him.

"I don't know, dude. Let's take a drive somewhere. Go see some sights!" he stated. "I need some excitement!" he told the men. Two Tone smiled at him.

"We could go looking for some things we could pawn" Two Tone suggested. This was a newer gig for this group. They had begun with small break and enters in neighborhoods across town. It brought in decent money and once in a while they really scored! Trip had taken part on just a few occasions, but for the most part, Two Tone had left him and Danny out. At the mention of this, both Trip and Danny jumped at the chance. Any opportunity to do these kinds of things with Two Tone, they were in! Two Tone began by talking about the best, most lucrative neighborhoods they could hit. Trip listened intently and then got a brilliant idea.

"These sound pretty good Two Tone, but have you ever thought about places where big money resides?" Trip asked him, rubbing his hands together. "I'm talking big money, dude!" he said emphatically. "I have a plan" he told them, smiling. "Let's go – we'll chat on the way." He clapped Two Tone on the back and went for the door.

In the car, Trip told the men how his grandmother worked in a very ritzy gated neighborhood. A new one she recently took on was especially rich. Trip was confident he knew the way the gate worked, especially after going through them over the years with his grandmother. There was usually an officer who "guarded" the gate. He had no gun, or weapon of any kind, that Trip had ever noticed. He did have the ability to alert police/fire/ambulance immediately with one direct phone. He also had his cell phone and a flash light, but that was it. If they could pull up to the gate and distract the guard, one of them could knock him out, open the lock box of keys and get into some of the homes, just through the front door! *There were a few things to work out, but with a few tweaks it could work*! Two Tone thought.

He asked Trip a number of questions and Trip took them to a couple of the communities Angel had worked at. They discussed their plot. Before long they realized, if they were to do a clean job of this, it would take proper planning. Trip suggested they access Google Earth to bring up the neighborhood and may be able to scope it out better. This proved to be invaluable to their work. Google Earth not only showed them the sizes of the homes, but also gave them a layout of the neighborhood. Once they were satisfied Google Earth had given them all it could, they began doing surveillance on one gated community after another, casually checking out the guard's station, the guard himself and their ability to do this job with a clean get away. After several days, they had decided on a specific neighborhood that looked, not only quite rich, but particularly easy to do the job on. The guard was a heavy man, short in stature and barely fit in the station. The one thing about this guy was, he kept his station open to the air, at all times. He addressed whoever was in the entering car from his station window, but his back was turned and the station door propped open. An easy mark!

Two Tone decided that the job would take place at night. Trip said he could get into the gated community without being detected, over the wall. Once inside, Danny would get the Guard's attention, by getting him up to the gate, while Trip got into the station and grabbed the keys. Two Tone would knock the Guard out once he came to see Danny and drag him around to the station, hiding his body. They got a lot of things worked out, but one small thing kept nagging Trip.

"So, how are we gonna knock out the guard?" he asked. He was wondering how he'd knock him out safely, after all he needed to stay knocked out long enough for them to scope the houses, go into the dark ones and get out of there.

"Don't worry, Buddy. You leave that to me." Two Tone told Trip, nodding reassuringly. Trip didn't worry. Two Tone and Danny were solid guys. He trusted them above all. They were his brothers. Two Tone would make sure that everything went according to plan and neither Trip or Danny would get hurt, he'd make sure. Of that, Trip had no doubt.

The men piled into the car. Only the 3 of them were in on this. Two Tone thought it might be dangerous to involve too many to their members, at least until they had gotten the routine down. They were all dressed in black, no skin showing. They all wore gloves and had a cover over their mouths. They parked the car a mile away, making sure they were not on camera. They carried no phones, actually leaving them at home so they couldn't be traced. They stayed to the dark side of the street, keeping low near windows. It was nearly 11:00 pm, and already extremely dark. They saw a car leaving the gate as they approached. Hiding back in the bushes, they waited until the guard was seated in his station, his head slightly lower than the window he sat at.

Trip took a few quick steps and then leapt high into the air, grabbing the top part of the wall that was supposed to enclose the community from the very kind of people about to enter into it. Trip walked along the top edge for a few steps before quietly leaping down onto the other side.

"Fuck me" Two Tone whispered, impressed with Trip's abilities. "Where'da fuck he learn how to do that?" he asked Danny, who just shrugged his shoulders. Success!

Now that Trip was on the other side, he snuck through the bushes, until he was directly across from the Guard and his station. True to his word, the Guard had not detected him at all. He sat in wait for Danny to make his move.

"S'cuse me, Sir?" Trip heard Danny's voice calling out. "S'cuse me, can I ask you to help me, please? I need help!" he called to the Guard. Trip saw the Guard stand and look out over to the front of the gate and put his head out the window.

"What's the matter?" the Guard asked.

"I need your help! Please, I'm hurt!" he told the Guard. He sounded like he was gasping, causing Trip to smile to himself. He may have done some acting in his time, but Danny was great for this. He was smaller than both Trip and Two Tone and his frame made him look a lot younger than his 16 years. The Guard was obviously concerned, leaning further out his window to try and see better. Reluctantly, as he heard Danny's gasps and moans get louder, he stepped out of his station and came over to the front gate. Using a key he opened it up and bent over to see to Danny. Trip's view was obscured by the bushes, but he heard a large *thud!* The large Guard feel to the ground, almost on top of Danny!

"Fuck, dude! He coulda killed me!" Danny whispered, loudly. Two Tone could barely contain his laughter, as he grabbed one arm of the Guard and motioned for Danny to grab the other.

"Drag him over with me, dude and quit whining. This guys a lot beefier than I thought" Two Tone said, pulling hard on the Guard's arm. Danny got up and grabbed the other arm. As the two men dragged him behind his station, Trip got the lock box opened and started grabbing keys from their hooks. His heart racing, Trip was not as careful as he should have been and was dropping as many as he took. He threw keys into the hands of Danny and Two Tone and told them, "Go! Go!"

Off they ran in different directions. Originally, the plan was to grab certain keys and scope the houses out, but these three had not been that sophisticated in the execution as they were in their planning. Trip was trying to calm himself down as he ran around to the side of a house, stopping to catch his breath and regain his bearings. He looked down into his hand and saw 4 keys. Each one had a tiny white string with a round paper attached and a number written on the paper. He held #603, #615, #623 and #625. He looked across the street to see the house number. #588. He held odd numbers, at least he was on the right side! He scoped the house he was hiding against. The cameras were aimed towards the driveway, which he managed to avoid. They had no camera on the corner of the backyard and its fence wasn't that high. *Like it was meant to be!* He thought, confidently. Trip leapt over the fence easily and found himself in a large back yard, dark in the corners and along the left wall. The pool was a large rectangle off to the right side and he was able to run to the very back right hand corner. He stopped for a moment and knelt down in the dark. By his account, he was 8 houses down from his first key. He made quick time of running through the backyards, staying low and in the dark. Thank God for Google Earth! He knew the lay of the land and had very little surprises along the way. He got as far as #601 and stopped. He needed to be sure he was at #603 before scoping it out and maybe making entry. As he ran up the side garden he saw signs of life in the house next door and decided he needed to go on further to scope #615. He was back down into the back garden in a flash, again making good time with his speed. As he came upon the back yard of #615, he could see it was dark. Thankfully, #613 was also dark and he kept low and ran swiftly, hurling himself up and over the garden fence. With that, Trip was into the yard of #615, key in hand! He waited in the dark a moment, making sure he was where he should be. He was able to make it to the garage side of the home. The side door of the garage was locked. Trip walked past the door and took a sneak peek around the corner. The front door was completely well lit. *Shit!* Trip thought. Dressed all in black was great for sneaking around the yard, but not for going straight through the front door! *"FUCK!"* He hissed angrily. He turned back towards the garage door, trying the knob again. He could probably kick it in, but that could set off an alarm, a dog, or God knows what. He needed to be quiet and quick! He was about to run through the back yard and onto the next house, but stopped to try key in the garage door. It worked! He couldn't believe his luck! He turned the knob and stepped into the garage. It was the tidiest garage he had ever seen. It held a new model BMW and numerous shelves and cabinets. The parking spot on the other side was empty and Trip could see a door, hopefully leading into the house! He ran towards it. Unlocked! Another stroke of luck! He was on a roll! *What would Two Tone think about this?* Trip wondered as he easily entered into the house. Piece of cake!

* * *

Things didn't go so well for Two Tone. He also ran into darkness and looked into his hand to see what he held. *FUCK!* He thought. Already this had gone badly. Trip had grabbed the keys without choosing the ones they'd agreed upon. He had only 1 of the key numbers they had discussed. #588. At least it was close. He needed to make his way up past two houses. He looked across the street. He could see Danny leaning against the side of a house, not hidden at all. *FUCK!* He screamed in his head. He watched for a moment wondering if he should help him in some way. He was about to risk a run for Danny when, in complete surprise, Danny ran around the corner of his house, straight towards the front door, used the key and went inside. Easy as you please! *Fuck!* Two Tone thought. *The little guy has balls! Maybe not the brightest, but ballsy for sure!*

Two Tone turned his attention to the house he was at. The front door was lit from above, but he could see the front foyer dark on the inside. No one was home, for sure. He looked down at his key, just to be sure. #588. He turned the numbered paper circle over. SIDE. He stopped. He was standing on a small stone walkway. The side wall had no door, but the stone walkway moved around to the back of the house. Two Tone followed it. Just around the corner, the walkway led to a full patio, a large pool and a large glassed in room. He walked around the pool, past the glass room to the other side of the house and found a doorway, along the back wall. It was dark, as well. Lucky him! He tried the key on the locked door. It opened! *"Fuckin' right!* He thought as he entered the room. *Things were turning around!*

He didn't bother to close the door behind him. One less obstacle to get through on the way, he figured. He took a small flashlight out of his pocket and illuminated the room. A small room housing boots, rain coats, umbrellas and other outerwear. He had a quick look around the room seeing nothing of worth, except another door. He immediately moved across the room and tried the door. Locked. He thought for a moment and realized he had a key. He tried it in the door handle. It wouldn't fit. *FUCK! What the fuck!* He thought. *Why have a key that didn't open the house up?* He turned his attention back to the small room, looking around quickly, scanning for something, anything that might get him inside. It didn't occur to him to search for a hidden key, kept right near the door inside one of the boots.

No, instead he tore the room apart, hoping to find a crow bar type tool, but there was nothing! *Dammit!* He could continue try to get inside #588 or leave and go onto another house. He also needed to remember the Guard. He was knocked out, but not for good. Two Tone's time was being wasted. He had already spent more time than he intended just trying to get in. Danny had probably been inside the house across the street, robbed it and had gone on to the next. Two Tone couldn't have his little brother show him up, not on this job! He had no choice; ego won over logic. He took a run and kicked in the door. It immediately set off an alarm and Two Tone took off running in the other direction.

* * *

Danny was exhilarated! He'd made it into the house in record time. He hadn't seen where Two Tone or Trip had run to, he just heard Trip yell, "Go! Go!" and he grabbed the keys and took off running. He stayed to the right side of the street and had a chance to look down at this keys. He had a few numbers in the mid 600's. *Too far away*, he thought. He saw #587 and looked up to see where he was. The house across the street was #588. *Excellent!* He thought, except he couldn't find a dark hiding spot and from where he was standing, he had no ability to see if the house was dark, or not. *What to do, what to do?* He thought, excitedly. He decided to go for it. He ran towards the front door, tried the key, it turned quite easily and he went directly inside. His heart was racing. His mind was racing. God, he couldn't wait to tell Two Tone about that! What luck!

* * *

Trip found himself going from the garage to standing in a hallway within house #615. At one end, he could see the bannister of a staircase. At the other, it opened up into one large room. As he walked towards the large room, a grand kitchen area came into view on his left. He stopped momentarily and took the area in. It was beautiful. He knew enough and had seen enough to know, this was a beautiful home. He continued onward, into the large room. He saw the biggest couch he had ever seen. It could probably hold at least 9 large guys, easily. *Holy shit!* He thought as he smiled to himself. *These people like to live large!* He gave the room a glance before turning to leave and was stopped dead in his tracks. A family portrait hung on the wall. He couldn't believe his eyes. He looked closer, walking towards the portrait, mesmerized. Was he imagining this? He couldn't look away. He saw *himself* in this family portrait! *What the fuck!* He studied the picture closely. He didn't know the older man or woman, but he definitely knew his own face! His hair was more streamlined, more "barbered", but it was definitely *his face!* *"WHAT THE FUCK!"* He yelled out loud into the dark, quiet beautifully decorated house.

He began looking for any other pictures he could find. The walls had several other pictures and many of them included *him! Him*, at a young age in a swimsuit holding a surf board, *except he'd never surfed! Him,* taken somewhat recently wearing a suit and tie, standing with a bride and groom *he didn't know! Him*, again with the older man and woman.

"What. The. Absolute. FUCK!" He yelled. This was not only starting to anger him, it was starting to creep him out. This…this *guy* was the identical image of *him!* How was that possible? He took a good look around the house and again, noticed the stairwell. He ran towards it and up the stairs. He ran into the first room he came upon. A smaller sized room. It had simple decoration, nothing to help him answer the millions of questions running through his mind. He ran out of the room and continued down the hallway, turning into the next room along. The master bedroom. A beautiful room containing a large king sized bed with lush bedding in soft, light colors. A large tall boy dresser stood to his right and he quickly scanned a piece of mail on top. *Mr. Grant Samuels, LLC* it read. He didn't know the name at all. He grabbed the mail, stuffed it into his pocket and took a look at the much more feminine dresser across the room. It reminded him of a luxury version of one his grandmother had in her room, only hers was beat to hell. A glance across the top of the dresser spied a small velvet ring box, tucked off to one side. He grabbed it and opened it up. A diamond ring sat inside. Like everything else in the house, it was large! He quickly closed it and also stuffed it inside his pocket. He thought about rummaging through the drawers, but decided against it, wanting to explore deeper by going through more of the rooms. He was most interested in finding *his* room. Or, at the least, a room with more things of *his things* in it. He completed

his quest by finding the next room. Now THIS was definitely *his* room! Trip paused a moment, taking it all in. This person had his face, his body! He looked *exactly like him!* He got a shiver as he walked into the room. It somehow felt very familiar. *What the fuck was going on?* He wondered. There were pictures of *him* with people Trip didn't know. Everywhere. At school, at the piano, holding a small Oscar with a huge smile on his face. In every picture, Trip saw himself. "HOW is this possible?" he said out loud, as he stood studying a student card left on the dresser in the room.

"Garret Thomas Samuels" he read. He looked at the picture. No doubt, it was him! The hair wasn't exactly the same, but that was the only difference. Otherwise, he was identical to Trip, not just alike, but *identical*.

Lost in thought, it was the sound of the house alarm from outside that brought him out of his wonderment. He had the presence of mind to grab a few more items from the room and leave quickly, running down the stairs and out the garage door, the same way he came in. The alarm was louder once he stepped outside and he could hear a few dogs barking. He made his way out to the back yard, and he ran for his life, stopping for nothing. When he got nearer to the Guard's station, he was stopped before running right out into the open. He could see the Guard standing, holding a gun on Two Tone and Danny. Both had their hands in the air. *Holy fuck!* He thought. He stepped backwards before being noticed and hid, out of sight. He could hear the Guard telling them to stay where they were, or he'd shoot. *Shoot?* Wondered Trip, his mind racing. *Since when did a Guard like him carry a gun?*

* * *

Danny had managed to grab a few expensive pieces of jewelry, a Rolex watch and a wad of bills from a nightstand before hearing the alarm. It scared the shit out of him! *Would this bring the cops? Did he need to get out of there, or what?* He wondered. He decided to run for it, already pleased with his find. As he got to the front door, he wondered if he should leave as he came in. The alarm was coming from the house across the street. Danny thought he'd be smarter if he ran out the back and took to the shadows. That proved to serve him well, but then he ran straight out into the street, right into the line of fire of the Guard's gun and Two Tone, with his hands held up.

"Stop!" The Guard ordered. "Stay where you are or I'll shoot!" he commanded. He was sweating profusely and gasping for air. Two Tone had hit him pretty hard in the head and the Guard was in a bad way. He was holding his gun on the two young men, trying hard to see clearly. He was shaking as he held them where they stood. He began walking backwards towards his station, keeping his gun aimed towards them. Two Tone realized he was going for the phone, the direct line to the cops. He couldn't let that happen. He couldn't have the cops come here. They knew him well. Too well. He'd go away for sure for this. Three Strikes Law would send his ass straight to jail and he couldn't have that. He looked over at his youngest brother, Danny. He had to make sure Danny was kept safe. Danny looked scared and it tore at Two Tone's heart. In one sudden move, he moved his right arm towards his back, pulled a gun on the Guard and shot twice. One bullet hit the Guard square in the head and he dropped like a stone.

"Run!" Two Tone yelled at Danny and the two took off, through the open gate, grabbing it as they ran and banging it closed behind them. Instantly, they disappeared into the darkness.

* * *

From the side of the house, Trip watched in horror. The brothers were being held at gun point and there was absolutely nothing he could do. He had no weapon, no plan of how to get out of this and no desire to go and stand with them. He stayed hiding, wondering his next move, watching intently. Suddenly, he saw Two Tone reach behind him and pull a gun out of the back of his pants. He had hidden it under his dark clothing. Trip had no idea he had a gun on him. Watching him use it was terrifying, but watching the Guard die instantly as Two Tone's gun shot rang out brought Trip out of his mind set. *He just witnessed a murder. Fuck, he was practically an accomplice to a murder!* It made his blood run cold. He felt his stomach lurch and he ran back into the darkness, throwing up whatever sat in his stomach. He leaned against the wall of the house, hidden in the shadows, breathing heavily, his mind ready to explode. He gathered his thoughts.

What to do now? There was nothing he could do for the Guard. Trip knew he was dead. You don't take a bullet to the head that close and live. The Guard was dead and that was most definitely *not* part of the plan. When he asked Two Tone how he was going to knock the Guard out, never was a gun even mentioned. Never! He was only supposed to be knocked out! Trip wasn't stupid. He knew Two Tone was the leader of a pretty tough gang of guys and figured he'd probably done some really shitty things in his time on the streets, but Trip knew the story of the 3 older brothers and their current residence. He had always thought Two Tone was a lot smarter than to end up like that.

He heard the racket of the gate closing and ran out just in time to see Two Tone and Danny running off. *FUCK!* All 3 of them were supposed to go through that open gate before closing it! That left him stuck on the wrong side. *FUCK!* His adrenaline was now racing and he quickly made like a gazelle towards the brick wall. He jumped straight up and easily reached the top, pulling himself up and over in one swift move. He landed hard on the other side, but didn't pause as he took off. He started running in the same direction, as was the plan, but stopped as he gave it some thought. Those guys were killers. KILLERS! He didn't want to do that *shit!* Trip turned around, ready to bolt off in the opposite direction of the others, when something caught his eye. He bent down, picking it up he could tell it was a large wad of money! Thick elastic bands held it folded over. It must have fallen from Two Tone or Danny's pocket as they took off. He stuffed it into his jacket pocket and ran. He managed to stay in the dark, but lost his way trying to make it home, back to his grandmother's apartment. Fuck going back to Two Tone's and Danny's, fuck that completely! With so much on his mind, he lost his bearings and stopped, hiding in the dark near a large bush. He looked around, trying to get his bearings. This was a much more populated area than they had planned to be in. It may not be gated, but there appeared to be cameras everywhere. He couldn't just go walking down the street. *I've got it!* He thought. Instantly, he pulled up his clothing and contorted his body to appear slightly smaller. He began walking and within a few steps he turned into Two Tone, walking his walk and every once in a while saying something out loud in Two Tone's voice, just in case he was being heard. It was the best he could come up at the moment; an impersonation. Fitting.

* * *

When he entered his Gramma's apartment she was fast asleep in her recliner. He had found her numerous times this way and had noticed the wine bottles that had begun appearing in the house. He also noticed when they left the house empty in the recycle bin. She was drinking a lot these days. He'd never known her to drink in all the years she'd taken care of him, but lately she had been getting wine on a regular basis. Sometimes, he'd startle her when he came home and she'd rouse from her wine filled sleep and mumble about "sacrifices" and "must be in the blood". He rarely paid her any attention and would head straight for his room. He'd hear her stagger off to bed shortly after him.

But, tonight was different. He needed her to wake up and help him. He immediately ran over to her, shaking her arm.

"Gramma! Gramma, wake up!" He said, shaking her. She came awake quickly and was shocked by the sound of his voice.

"What? What?" she asked, her head rolling back and forth. Trip sat her up, patting her on her face, gently.

"Gramma, wake up!" he said. She came to, but she was very drunk. Trip knew she'd probably be of no help. Even so, he needed to tell her. "I gotta leave!" he told her anxiously. "Like, leave and don't come back" he tried explaining.

His Gramma's eyes rolled back and came forward into her eyes a couple of times. She tried straightening her head, but it flopped up and down. Regardless, she managed to speak.

"Leavin?" she slurred. "You're leavin' and good riddance! I shouldda taken the other one…" she mumbled off. "I bet he was bedder 'n *you* were!" she spat at him. Trip figured she was just slurring shit again and turned to

107

head to his room and quickly gather his things, but it suddenly hit him. *"I shouldda taken the other one!" "I bet he was bedder 'n you were!"* Trip's mind went back to the house he'd been in. The photos of *him* everywhere. Did her drunken words now lead to a truth? He shot back to his Gramma and bent down at her knee.

"Who was going to be better than me, Gramma?' he asked her quietly. Her head had fallen back on the recliner and her eyes were closed. He asked her again. "Gramma. Who was better than me?" he shook her arm gently.

"The other one. The other boy. He wouldda been bedder." She answered, almost trance like. Trip took it in, waiting a moment. The other boy? *The OTHER boy!* Was "the other boy" the kid he saw in that house? He felt into his pants pockets and pulled out the student card he had taken, again, shocked to see his face on it. He had to learn more about who Garrett Thomas Samuels was. But, right now was not the time! His grandmother was not going to offer any more information. She had already started snoring, dropping off to sleep once again.

Trip shot to his room, grabbed a gym bag and began stuffing it with clothes. He grabbed a backpack, putting his laptop and all cords, phone accessories, two pairs of shoes and some "must haves" into its pockets. He gave his room one final glance over and left, closing the door. He ran down the hallway, looked over at his Gramma and paused. She was flat out again. He went over to her and hesitated a moment. He wouldn't bother waking her up, but he felt he owed her something. He leaned over, whispered "thanks Gramma" into her face and kissed her on the forehead. He heard sirens, held for a minute trying to judge if they were in the distance or coming towards him. Once he realized they were definitely coming in his direction, he booked it out of there leaving Gramma, Two Tone and Danny behind. The brother he'd always wanted and a younger brother as an added bonus; they'd been his family, his only family for years. Two killers and his gramma. *I gotta do better than that!* He thought as he turned away from his neighborhood and disappeared into the night.

* * *

The police showed up within 5 minutes of Garrett's call from the officer's station. Between the sirens and the house alarm, the gated community had become alive with all manner of people, up and standing like spectators at a golf game, behind the police tape. It was near midnight. Garrett, Grant and Sondra had given a statement to the police and it was close to 1:00 am before they were able to get to their house. An officer escorted them. Nothing seemed out of place to the family of three and they assured the officer that all was fine. Unlike the house nearer to the guard's station, their alarm was not set off. The officer allowed them inside once he had walked through it and made sure there was no one inside. He said good night to them and feeling safe and sound in their home, they locked the door from the awful ending to their night.

It wasn't until Sondra, removing her earrings and necklace and placing them in her vanity, noticed something was missing. She couldn't place it, but she had seen her vanity every day for years and it rarely changed. Something was missing.

Grant checked downstairs to make sure all was secure. He walked through the darkened house, feeling unnerved. For years he had raised his family in this community, without a fear. Not once, not in all these years had there been anything bad happen. Now, that had all been broken. Mike, the officer at the gate had been murdered by thugs who had tried to break into the houses. What a horrible thing to have happened and what a terrible way for their celebration evening to have ended. He hoped to God it wasn't a bad omen. Garrett had worked hard to get the internship and Grant wanted his son to have this opportunity, to reach his full potential. He couldn't have been prouder of this boy. He saw the family picture and stood looking at it for a moment. Garrett had brought such joy to them from the moment he was placed in Sondra's arms. Grant let out a heavy sigh as he turned out the lights downstairs and headed towards the staircase. Poor Mike. He'd have to inquire about whether he had family or if a donation could be made for his funeral arrangements. He'd been wonderful to all the homeowners in this community and had lost his life trying to protect it. A donation was the least he could do.

Garrett closed the door to his room, removed his jacket and threw it onto the desk in the corner. He dropped onto his bed and let out a heavy sigh, his hands rubbing his eyes. It had been such a long day with a roller coaster of emotions. Garrett was trying to process what had happened. He thought about how random things happen; earlier in the day, he'd received the news he'd been hoping would come. This internship will put him in touch with the very people he wanted to become. A music producer; his ability to play and create music was great, but his heart was in the producing. He wanted to bring all the right elements together to produce a piece of musical art.

As a way to celebrate his hard work, his parent's took him out for dinner. How were they supposed to know they would come home to see a dead man? How random was that?

Garrett was also trying hard not to let the vision of Mike's head shot stay on his mind. He'd seen the inside of his head and there was a ton of blood. Awful. He felt bad for the Officer. He was such a nice guy. At Christmas, he dressed up as Santa, decorated the station and had Christmas music playing. He also gave out candy canes to the kids. Poor Mike. Garrett had always liked him.

Feeling unsettled, he sat up, and grabbing his phone from the night stand, checked his social media. As he scrolled through, reading the odd post from a friend, he began to feel very unsettled. As if he wasn't alone in the room. He slowly let his gaze go past the phone screen as the rest of his room came into focus. Keeping his phone still, his eyes swept the room completely. He saw no one, but he felt as if eyes were on him. Quickly, he bolted off the bed into the middle of the room and stood, like a warrior, ready to take on anyone. Holding his stance for a moment he then turned once to be sure he didn't get a surprise attack from behind his back. Nothing. No one. Even still, he couldn't shake it.

After a few more minutes of restlessness and a bathroom visit, Garrett climbed into bed to get some sleep. It was 2:25 am. Another heavy sigh. Closing his eyes, he rolled over onto his side and curled up around a body pillow. To settle his mind, he composed music in his head. It distracted, it engaged and it tired him out. Before long, Garrett was sound asleep and then began to dream.

He is walking beside a river bank, dressed in running clothes. His pace picks up as the walking path leads through the forest. Many people are about, some running, exercising, walking their dogs and enjoying the beautiful day. He realizes he is being paced by someone. They're dressed in the same clothing, they have the same running shoes and from the corner of his eye, Garrett can make out that he's a young black man about his age, his height and size. Garrett picks his pace up, feeling slightly competitive. He was enjoying this! Let's see what this dude can do! Garrett smiled wide as the guy also picked up his pace and kept in step with Garrett. This was awesome! Garrett could see the guy was smiling, too. At the same time, they both picked up the pace, running together, same stride, same step, same running form. As Garrett ran faster, so did his competitor. The pathway was coming to an end, he could go left or right, but he couldn't continue straight. They ran faster, straight towards the fork in the road. As they approached the turn, Garrett made sure to look back and see the face of the dude who just gave him such a thrilling race! He turned, catching the eye of the runner. For a moment, it was as if time stopped. He was staring into the eyes of himself! It was him! Garrett was startled. What the fuck? Suddenly the slow motion moment was gone and the runner took off to the left as Garret turned right.

He awoke with a start, covered in sweat, his heart racing as though he'd done every step of that run. He got up out of bed, changed his shirts and boxers and sat on the edge of his bed.

That was the weirdest thing I've ever dreamt, He thought.

Little did he know.

* * *

The sirens rang out throughout the neighborhood. Six cop cars screamed towards Two Tone and Danny's apartment. They had driven back, lucky to have not been stopped for speeding and bolted inside, locking the doors and windows. At first they thought they had gotten away with it. Everything was silent. They had expected to see Trip make it to the car, as planned, but he never materialized. They didn't really wait for him to show up, instead running to the doors and racing off into the night towards home. No Trip at home, either. *Maybe he'll show up later,* they thought.

Danny started emptying his pockets of the things he'd grabbed from the house. The Rolex was major bling, a large diamond sat at each quarter hour. The rest was gold and black ebony. It was a beautiful watch. Probably worth upwards of $15,000. Two Tone was very pleased.

"But, wait, there's more" Danny bragged as he reached into his pants pocket. Two Tone was already thrilled considering he'd gotten nothing and killed a man! FUCK! He had never done that before, but then, he'd never had a nervous white man holding a gun on him before. From the look in the guard's eyes, Two Tone knew either he or Danny was going end up dead and he couldn't let that happen. He tried to shake it off, figuring the money from the Rolex alone would help and how proud he was of his baby brother, Danny.

Suddenly, Danny started checking all his pockets.

"Fuck! I can't believe it! Where is it?" he screamed, anxiously. He began checking everything in the room, including underneath the clothing they had tossed off when they got through the door. Nothing. He checked where he'd sat down, hoping it had fallen out. Nothing. He then began looking on the floor, getting down on his hands and knees and looking underneath the couch area where he'd sat and moved about. Still, nothing.

"Oh for FUCK'S SAKE'S" Danny roared. There must have been close to $20,000 there in the large wad of cash he grabbed. There was no way of knowing where it had dropped out along his getaway route to the car. *The CAR!* Suddenly, Danny jumped up.

"Gimme your car keys", he demanded from Two Tone, who didn't question his urgency. He tossed the keys to Danny who ran out the door. He took the stairs two at time down and hit the bottom floor quickly. He burst through the door and ran straight over to Two Tone's car, opening it with the remote moments before he reached the door handle. He was inside, his eyes looking stringently around the inside of the car within moments. Every nook and cranny was looked over, but Danny found nothing.

FUCK! He thought. That wad could have been the difference between heading out right now and heading out after pawning the Rolex. With the death of the guard, Danny was sure there would be fallout. All he really wanted was to get the hell away from the whole fucking town. Feeling pissed off with his loss, he slammed the car door setting off the car alarm. No sooner had Danny turned back to the car to try and stop the alarm, more alarms came closer and suddenly he was surrounded by lights and sirens. Danny ran straight into the apartment building and took the stairs a jump at a time until he landed on his floor. He got to the apartment door and was shouting to Two Tone before his hand grabbed the doorknob.

"We gotta go, Two Tone! The cops are all over this place!" he shouted. Two Tone came from down the hallway holding two long shotguns. He tossed one to Danny and told him to get low.

"It's loaded" was all he said to his baby brother.

The building was evacuated. After that, nobody moved for over an hour. The police tried hard to negotiate with Two Tone and Danny, but neither would budge. Their "gang" had not been included in the robbery plan, so they weren't around to help defend the brothers. If they were able to pin the murder of the guard on him, Two Tone would probably go to jail for the rest of his life, leaving Danny alone. He couldn't have that.

Two Tone took the first shot. It caused 15 police men and over 150 bullets to return fire. The brothers tried getting as low as they could, hiding behind furniture and finally holed up in the bathroom. They were both hoping the room had some ability of protection, being an outside room that was long and narrow. Two Tone sat in the tub and Danny crouched on the toilet lid.

They looked at each other, both knowing what the other was thinking. *This is how we're going to die, in the shitter!*

It's funny how brothers can have that real connection. They weren't wrong.

* * *

Trip managed to catch a bus as soon as he had left the apartment which took him to the main terminal in Santa Barbara. Where to go from here? He wanted to be far enough away to be able to be in hiding, but close enough that he could stay updated should he become on the police radar. He looked at the bus schedule and saw "Crescent City, California". That was approximately 500 miles away. *Perfect!* He thought.

"I'll have a ticket to "Crescent City" he asked the pretty girl at the counter. She barely smiled as she typed in his info and printed off his ticket. She handed it to him as he handed her the cash. The first bill he'd removed from the wad he'd found. It was $100.00 bill. He hadn't thought about how much was there, he really hadn't had a chance. When he boarded the bus he took the second last row on the right. He put his backpack and gym bag down in the seat beside him, not wanting anyone to sit there. He dug deep into his pocket and holding the money out of sight, he took off the elastic bands and allowed the bills to unfold. It was well over an inch thick; 100's, 50's. In all, twenty six thousand and fifty dollars. Plus the change from the bus ticket.

Holy fuck! He thought, looking around to see if anyone was watching. This money would help him beyond just getting him out of town. It will make him a new life! *A new life!* Oh, how he'd love a new life right about now! He dug his hand in his pocket and felt the card inside. He pulled it out, studying it again. Garrett Samuels. His mind struggled as to why this guy was his identical twin. It seemed like something out of a sci-fi movie. *The Cyborg That Looked Like Me!* Trip thought and then chuckled. He looked up and out the bus window. The miles were rushing by, further and further away.

When the bus arrived, Trip grabbed the first cab he could find and asked to be taken to the cleanest, but cheapest hotel in town. A cab driver knows shit like that. Trip was taken to a small family run hotel called "Home with the Hancocks". He asked for the smallest room, for at least the next week and he would pay up front. Another 3 bills off the top.

He'd been in the room about a half hour, going through the last 12 hours in his mind. All in all, he'd landed on his feet fairly well. He had managed to get out of the gated community without getting caught, found money his buddy had stolen and was already in a town hundreds of miles away from the crime scene. He suddenly had a thought and turned on the TV to see if anything was being reported. A station broadcasting in the area was reporting on a murder of a guard in a gated community near Santa Barbara. He turned the volume up.

"Police are saying it was an attempt to rob as many of the homes located within the gates, as the thieves could. They first knocked out the guard, but when he came to and confronted the thieves, they shot him in the head and left the area on foot. Police conducted a search of the area, including interviewing neighbors and retrieving camera video of the area. They were able to confirm an identity and found the suspects at home. After an hour long standoff, the suspects started shooting and the police shot back. The suspects were both killed in the shootout. They are identified as 21 year old Derek "Two Tone" Jennings and a 16 year old younger sibling. A number of the items stolen from the houses were retrieved. Police are asking for the community's help. If you know anything about these robberies, please contact them at 305-267-8977."

The news reporter continued on to other stories, but Trip's mind stayed on the last. *"21 year old Derek "Two Tone" Jennings and his 16 year old younger sibling. The suspects were both killed in the shootout."* Trip sighed heavily. The closest thing he ever had to brothers. They were gone. They were killers, but they were gone. At least he didn't have to worry about them coming after him for the money. At least he knew he could spend it freely. To start his life. To live his life.

He took a long hot shower and it relaxed him completely. He got into the bed and immediately felt like he could easily sleep. He turned onto his side, using a spare pillow to put between his knees. It took him only minutes before he was sound asleep and soon after that, he began to dream.

It wasn't a vivid dream for Trip. He barely remembered it, except that he felt like he had been in a running competition. Fuck! He'd spent the whole night running, in one way or another and he didn't feel like he'd stopped. *Sonofabitch!* Stupid fuckin' dream!

Well, all he had right now was time and he had enough money to take his time.

⌁

Chapter 7

SECRETS REVEALED

Hans and Rebeccah moved into the Germany house within a few weeks of Tanya's funeral. She'd had the forethought to have packed up the farm house as much as possible. All Hans needed to do was arrange for a moving van to go in and bring everything up to the new house and leave a forwarding address with the farmer who purchased the property, should any mail for Tanya Nowak arrive. So much had happened so quickly, Hans wanted to be sure that he covered everything. Tanya didn't even get the chance to formally change her name to Baumgartner, there hadn't been time. So, it was possible that Tanya Nowak still had open activities out in the world. Hans would take care of them as they came along. He'd also make sure that he completed all documentation pertaining to Rebeccah and his guardianship of her. They visited the school where they met the principal Frau Grubner. Hans explained the events of the last few weeks and that he would be sure to have Rebeccah in school as soon as he felt she was ready. They then asked to meet with the music director, Frau Brecht. Hans spoke with her briefly explaining Rebeccah's natural talent and repeated their story of recent loss. Looking with sympathy at the beautiful child she agreed that Rebeccah needed to feel comfortable and assured Hans that waiting a bit would be fine. Hans left feeling like he'd done right by Rebeccah, checking in on the school and explaining things to them. He also notified Rebeccah's former school of her move to the new school in Germany. Something Tanya insisted she needed to do.

Frau Brecht also wanted to do right by the young girl. Shortly after meeting Hans and Rebeccah, she had been sent the information for The Morningstar Foundation from Ms. Mueller, Rebeccah's former music teacher and promptly changed the file to read, "single step-father, child is orphaned" but kept the annual income amount the same. With that, the Foundation would be satisfied that Rebeccah continued to meet the criteria and Hans was never made aware of the Foundation's sponsorship of Rebeccah's piano lessons. A secret *not* revealed.

* * *

It was obvious to Hans that Rebeccah was in need of a normal routine again and after another week at home with him, he sent her to school, walking her there and back each day. He took his role as dad with great honor figuring that all that had happened was for a reason. He had become Rebeccah's daddy for a reason. Keeping that in mind and as his main motivator, he began to create a lovely and welcoming home for them.

While Rebeccah was at school, Hans took the time to unpack all the boxes and set up the house keeping in mind the fact that he now shared it with a small female child. He put any of the large leather furniture in a bedroom turned office, replacing the living room furniture with soft textures and earth tone colors. He asked Rebeccah what color she'd like her room. She wanted a red room, with pretty white bedding. Hans painted one wall red and the other three white with red trim. Her bedding was also white, but had large red flowers on it and some black accents. You could almost say they were poppies. He made everything as comfortable and lovely as he could for them and yet at night, after Rebeccah had gone to sleep, he would climb into bed and cry tears for his dead wife and unborn child.

His grief was well hidden from Rebeccah, but it took some time for Hans to start to feel brighter. With no work to go to, he immersed himself in the house and anything that had to do with Rebeccah. He even gifted her with a beautiful baby grand piano which he placed in the front room. At night, she'd play or practice that days' lesson and Hans would sit reading, her always attentive and best audience. He understood Tanya's desire to keep Rebeccah as innocent as possible and would not allow any kind of public display of her piano playing to be videotaped, nor were pictures ever allowed. He agreed that a child being displayed on the internet was not a good thing. Rebeccah was so lovely, so perfect, he didn't want anything spoiling that. Fame too early would definitely spoil her. If she was this good now, imagine the enormity of her talent when she was a mature adult and could then properly handle any fame that came her way, and Hans was sure she'd be famous! No doubt about that!

* * *

After a few months, Rebeccah's routine helped her to acclimate into her new surroundings beautifully. Considering all that had happened to the small girl, she adapted and thrived in her new life. Her hair however, didn't. Since Tanya was no longer around to henna the child's hair into the deep coffee red, it grew out from her roots a soft golden blonde. Hans watched in amazement as a definitive line between old dark red hair and new blonder hair began to move slowly down her head. In an effort to reduce the child any embarrassment, he took her to a hair dresser who cut the child's hair as short as she could, ridding her of the red hair. When he saw her at first, he couldn't believe how completely different she looked. There wasn't much alike between her and her mother and now with her hair so blonde she looked nothing like Tanya. Hans figured she must take after her father's looks or perhaps a distant relative. As a full blonde, Rebeccah was angelic. Her wide green eyes were large on her small face and her rosebud lips would break into such a huge and brilliant smile, it took your breath away. Hans was completely besotted with Rebeccah and more and more felt honored in the role that he'd been placed in.

* * *

One morning, Hans woke up early to the sound of light footsteps walking past his door. He could tell it was Rebeccah and wondered why she was up. He rose from his bed, donning his housecoat and stepped out of his room to find Rebeccah sitting on a chair in the hallway next to a large window, looking up to the sky.

"Good Lord, Rebeccah. What on earth are you doing up at this time? You should be in bed!" As he reached her, he looked up through the window out into the morning sky. Still quite dark, with a faint few clouds, exposed by the moon's light. Off into the sky, a small single bright star could be seen.

Rebeccah yawned and smiled. "I'm chasing the morning star, Daddy!" She said quite confidently.

"You're chasing who?" he asked.

"Is it a who? I thought it was a sun?" she asked him, without answering his question. At this hour of the morning, Hans was certainly not awake enough to discuss stars with her.

"Rebeccah, dear. You haven't explained to me what you're doing here." He told her.

"A friend of my mommy's said I should continue chasing the morning star to find my way home. But, she meant mommy! She meant my mommy!" She told him. She was quite awake now and being very focused on what she said, so that he understood her, but he still didn't. She could see on his face that he didn't.

"Don't worry, I won't be up long. It doesn't shine for very long. I just don't want to miss it, okay?" she pleaded to him. He studied her face for a moment. Those eyes! How could he possibly say no to those eyes? And, what if this was a way for her to feel closer to her mother, then who was he to tell her no. Defeated, he patted her head and headed back to bed, leaving her to her star gazing. What could come of it?

* * *

Once fully settled, Hans decided to take on a part-time teaching job at the local college. Pharmaceutical Dispensary 101. It didn't take up too much of his time and allowed time away from the quiet house and something other than Rebeccah to fill his days with.

Years went by as Hans and Rebeccah grew closer as father and daughter, happily sharing in their love for classical piano music. Rebeccah's musical director trained her classically and she played from memory at an earlier age than Frau Brecht had ever heard of.

At seven years of age, Rebeccah was able to play by ear. At nine years of age, she had conquered many classical pieces and would play with as much ferocity as a grown adult. She attacked the keyboard when the crescendo would build and then dance her fingers along the keys when the music softened. All the while, Rebeccah would sit with her eyes completely closed. She saw the music better that way! It was as if it came to her in colors, many colors. Her musical comprehension far exceeded her age and her ability to play complex classical pieces with ease, was truly remarkable. She was born to play piano and would never have to do anything else. Hans predicted she'd play to thousands one day. How right he was!

And so it went for them. Rebeccah went on to secondary school education and flew through her courses, as well as her piano lessons. At 15 years she had grown into an extremely beautiful young lady, who had grace, humility, generosity of heart and spirit. Rebeccah was always smiling and had a very happy life, thanks to the unconditional love and support of her doting daddy, Hans.

As she was turning 17, Rebeccah periodically complained of bad headaches. Unlike Tanya, Rebeccah had never had a headache in all the years Hans had known her.

She came home one day complaining of a head ache and Hans was alarmed. She looked pale and unwell. She told him she felt sick to her stomach. When she came home the next day complaining of all the same symptoms, Hans was beyond concerned. Instead of waiting to get her into see the family doctor, he raced her to the local Emergency Department to be seen by a Neurologist right away. He was told they would have to wait until the Neurologist on call was paged.

After a two hour wait, they were called in to be seen by Dr. Schuell, a thirty-something young man who looked worn off his feet. Hans pulled the doctor aside before he examined Rebeccah and explained his concern about it being the same thing that had killed her mother years before. Dr. Schuell ordered Tanya's files be sent to him electronically, as quickly as possible and then went into see Rebeccah. He tried a number of motor skill tests on her, looked deeply into her eyes and tested her reflexes. He was paged out of the room briefly and when he returned he informed them that he had received Tanya's files and found cause to keep Rebeccah overnight for some tests.

Hans was worried sick. He reluctantly left his teary eyed daughter in the safe hands of the professionals. He wasn't going to go through the same thing as he'd gone through with Tanya; early detection could save Rebeccah's life! It was gut wrenching for him when he kissed her goodbye. They had told him that there was no need for him to stay. She would be going for some bloodwork and a late night MRI and would be asleep the entire time and when she woke up tomorrow morning, she'd be ready to go home. The results came in a few weeks later when Dr. Schuell called during the day, speaking with Hans.

"I've good news! Rebeccah has no tumors, no brain masses and no genetic work to make us believe that she would." He explained.

Hans let out a huge sigh and then laughed with relief. He physically felt his shoulders drop, his tension had been so great.

"Oh my goodness, what a huge relief!" he said. "What we went through with Tanya was, well, horrendous to say the least. I just couldn't go through that again with Rebeccah" Hans told the doctor.

"No, these things are related genetically and that's not possible."

"Oh, and why is that?" Hans asked confused.

"Rebeccah would have to be Tanya's biological child. And she's not, right?"

A secret revealed.

* * *

The hill and ravine area that took the life of a young mother and daughter many years earlier had begun to become very unstable. There had been several other landslides over the years and this had made it necessary for the local Department of Engineers to come out and have a look at what could be done to shore up the ravine's banks, preventing landslides from jamming up the river.

Surveyors were sent out to assess and a backhoe was carefully maneuvered down to an area to clear away numerous large trees, decades old that have been causing a major blockage along the river's edge. As the backhoe cleared away some of the larger fallen trees, more trees crushed in previous landslides were revealed. The backhoe operator figured more than twenty trees alone on this one site. He struggled to make out what he should move next and came out of the cab to get a better look. He stepped down off of the tread and walked through the thick heavy mud to see what his next move should be. Looking at the area, he went to pull away what looked like a twig and before throwing it, stopped dead and held it tight in his hand. To his horror, he held an almost complete jawbone, teeth intact.

A secret revealed.

* * *

Lucas and Leena had stayed in a long distance relationship for a few years. When her father died and his estate dealt with, Leena left Switzerland and the entire Van Zeeban life behind her and moved to New York and into Lucas's life. They were married two years after, once her citizenship was approved. They were happy, successful and in love. Their life together became so much more than what Luisa had brought them together for and if not for their very dear friend, Robin Hewer, they would have never brought it up again.

Robin however, hadn't given up on the theory that Luisa was in hiding. He had kept the list of names he left Switzerland with and through internet searches was able to eliminate nearly all of the names over the many years.

The friends would get together and reminisce about their early years with Robin often reminding them that there was never any body or name found and that stranger things had been known to happen. At first, it was a bit of fun thinking about how it had all been brilliantly masterminded, but as the years had pressed on, Leena didn't really appreciate it anymore. It was her sister after all, and obviously if nothing had happened after all these years, the case was closed. She was good with that. After one such night of conversation regarding the near decades old case, Leena spoke up.

"I think I'd like to not have to dredge this up anymore, gentlemen. I realize that it was me who started this whole theory with my thinking of spotting her those two times, but honestly, I'm tired of discussing this. Let's just face it, it was a wild goose chase and there is no conspiracy theory. I'm done. Okay?" she asked with pleading eyes. Both men sat astonished, then clamped their mouths shut. Lucas rose from the couch and embraced his wife.

"I'm sorry, honey" he told her. "I didn't realize it was becoming too much for you. We'll stop, won't we, Robin?" he nodded to Robin and he spoke up hesitantly.

"Uh…well, yeah. Sure, we don't need to discuss this anymore. Yes, of course, I'm sure it isn't easy for you." Robin reluctantly admitted. He may not speak about it with Leena in earshot, but there was no way in hell Robin would ever give up on this case. He would go to his deathbed believing that Luisa didn't go over the ravine that night.

"I had better get my ass going. Thanks for the lovely evening, Leena. Great dinner. Sorry for pressing the issue with the case" he apologized again, as he hugged her. He shook hands with Lucas.

"Talk later, okay? I'm working out of Chicago for the next few days, but I'm back in just a few days. I'll call you" he told his friend. They winked at each other, Robin motioned his head towards Leena whose back was turned, and mouthed *"I'm sorry"* to Lucas. He waved his friend off and smiled. Lucas would talk to Leena and all would be set right. She didn't want to have to hear about Luisa anymore and he was going to make sure she didn't have to. It was the least he could do!

* * *

"Hello?" Dr. Schuell repeated into the phone. "Mr. Baumgartner? Are you still there? Anyway, I just wanted to put your mind at ease. Rebeccah's headaches are more likely due to her menstrual cycle."

"What do you mean? What...what ...?" he struggled with what to say. How could Rebeccah *not* be Tanya's child? He'd had the birth certificate, he'd needed it to get guardianship of Rebeccah after Tanya's death. Tanya was listed as Rebeccah's mother. He'd seen it with his own eyes.

"I'm sorry. I'm not explaining it properly. Your wife's tumor was a genetic tumor. Only someone related by blood would have to worry about getting one. And they aren't, right? I mean, I realize your wife was a mother to Rebeccah, but not her *biological mother.*" Dr. Schuell said, as if stating the obvious. Another long pause held the phone. Dr. Schuell waited for Hans to speak wondering if he was hard of hearing.

"Oh, of course! Yes, I just wondered if it wasn't the same thing. Didn't realize they had to be blood related, I apologize for wasting your time." Hans said apologetically, hoping the doctor didn't suspect anything. He wasn't going to take the doctor's word for it, after all, he was so young and the night Rebeccah went into the Emergency Department the doctor looked exhausted.

"Oh no. No problem. The MRI was completely clear. At least you know she has no issues that way. Normal menstrual headaches, I believe. Have her take some pain medications if they happen again. I'll make sure your family doctor has the note on file." The young doctor ended with. Hans put his phone down and sat in his chair, his heart racing.

Not genetically mother and daughter? he thought. *How can that be?* He went over and over what the young doctor had said to him. He suddenly jumped up and ran to his files on Rebeccah and Tanya. All papers pertaining to both of them had been sorted and filed accordingly. That way, should he ever need to provide proof that Rebeccah was in his care rightfully, he'd have it within reach and easy to find. He even had dental records that Tanya had kept, thinking they could prove an established relationship, anything to keep Rebeccah as his daughter.

He pulled out both files and took them to the kitchen table. He opened each file comparing each document to the other.

Mother: Tanya Nowak, Daughter: Rebeccah Nowak

They were listed as mother and daughter on every form. Rebeccah's birth certificate was in both files showing the mother as Tanya Nowak. The father listed was: E. F. Hermann.

Nowhere was there any indication that Tanya and Rebeccah were not mother and daughter. All the appropriate paperwork, all the signed documentation. He knew this! He'd been through this with a fine tooth comb when Tanya first died! Angrily, he shoved all the paperwork back into its respective file and put the file away. He went back downstairs and sat thinking about the doctor's findings. Perhaps they were mistaken? Perhaps, there was something wrong with the tests they ran? Hans could not explain it, but was truly happy to hear that all the tests done on her head were clear and that was the best news. He put the anomaly down to hospital error and nothing more.

The fact that Rebeccah and Tanya looked absolutely nothing alike had been long forgotten by Hans and given time, the conversation with Dr. Schuler would as well.

* * *

When the phone rang in Lucas's New York office, he had just finished going over the findings of a case involving a high profile actress and the underage model she'd been humping. The model's mother had suspected something was up and called asking specifically for Lucas; his discretion meant everything. The underage model was the son of a very distinguished senator. Neither she nor her senator husband wanted their bad name dragged through the mud, however, should a story get out about the high profile actress, say through TMZ then the concerned mother wouldn't be upset. As long as their good name stayed out of it. Lucas smiled to himself, thinking about how people love screwing one another, literally and figuratively.

Leena was calling and he answered, with a laugh in his voice.

"Hello my beautiful Swiss wife! What's up?" he asked, good naturedly.

"Are you sitting down, Lucas?" she asked, quietly. He could tell right away by the tone of her voice, this news was serious.

"What's going on, Leena?" he asked, nervously.

"They've found a jawbone, Lucas" she told him. "After all these years, they've found a jawbone".

"Wait...what? Wait now. What are you talking about? Who found what jawbone?" he asked, not fully comprehending.

"I just got called from the police in Switzerland. They've found a jawbone near to where Luisa's Range Rover went over, in the mud. They've arranged for me to go down to the Swiss embassy and they'll swab my cheek and send it to them and they'll compare our DNA. Lucas, this could be it. This is what we've been waiting for!" she said, full of nervous excitement.

"So, does this mean you want to talk about it again?" Lucas asked, smiling wide. He couldn't forego the opportunity to tease her, especially considering they only just had the conversation about not discussing it anymore.

"Yes!" she said, full of drama. "Imagine. This could answer all the questions we've had. The doppelganger, dead or alive, all of it."

Lucas nodded his head. "You know who we should call?" he asked her. She knew right away and got off the phone so he could.

When Robin answered the phone he was in a bathroom, in the JFK airport having a final call before his final boarding call. Robin hated using the bathroom on the plane. It always made him uncomfortable. It was bad enough the plane was usually a tight fit for him, but the bathrooms were awful. For that reason, he drank very little before a flight and made sure he ate hours before and wouldn't need to until after they land. It was all very intricately timed. It needed to be, as a lead investigative reporter for the major cable station, Robin was anywhere and everywhere. He flew more than he drove.

So, when he answered Lucas's call in the bathroom, he tried making sure Lucas was unaware of his surroundings.

"It's happened my friend" Lucas said, excitedly.

"What has?" Asked Robin, not in the mood to play a guessing game.

"The shit has hit the fan" Lucas said. Robin couldn't help but smile at the irony of his cliché statement.

"Whose shit exactly has hit which fan?" Robin asked, smirking.

"They've found a jawbone. In the mud. In the ravine. In Switzerland." Lucas let it sink in. The phone was silent.

"Holy shit!" Robin answered. It had truly hit the fan!

* * *

The DNA results took a few weeks. The whole time, Robin, Leena and Lucas would ponder over many various outcomes. What was once a sore spot for conversation was now item #1 every time they got together, which was usually most nights if Robin wasn't on assignment.

The call to Leena came in the early morning. The detective calling sounded as surprised as she was to hear the news.

"There was no match. Not at all." He told her.

"So, you're saying it wasn't Luisa's jawbone, correct?" she asked to be certain.

"That's correct. No match between you." He admitted. He wasn't exactly a fountain of information.

"Then do you know whose it is?" she asked, wondering if he would tell her.

"Well," he sighed heavily, "We've found some dental work we're going to follow. We'll see if we can match it to anyone on a missing woman's list. According to our records, Luisa and the Morningstar child were the only bodies that were never recovered from a crash in the area in the last 30 years." He admitted. "We'll call if we have any questions. Thank you, Mrs. Hollomby" the detective offered. He ended the call before she could ask any further questions.

She called Lucas immediately.

"It's not her!" she blurted, breathlessly. It was all she could manage. She couldn't decide whether to laugh or cry, get drunk or vomit. "That means I did see her! It was her!"

Lucas shook his head. If the jawbone wasn't hers, whose was it?

* * *

"No shit!" was Robin's reply. Lucas couldn't decide if he was really astonished or being really cheeky. He figured the latter.

"What? You knew?" Lucas asked him. "Bullshit, Robin. You've been as baffled by this as we have." Lucas pushed his friend. What was he thinking?

"It's the woman at the restaurant. The night of the storm and the landslide. I'm telling you" he said, full of conviction. "It's her. She's been found."

The final secret revealed.

Chapter 8

THE AHA MOMENT

Two years since Rebeccah had started with her headaches, they were now well managed with a mild pain medication. Hans was completely engrossed in the now 20 year old and her gifted piano playing. Rebeccah had graduated school and was into her second year of University studying music, specifically classical piano concertos. She was in her element and Hans, having fully retired from teaching, now devoted everything to making sure Rebeccah could focus solely on her music.

She had been working on an upcoming performance for the University Orchestra and was fully engrossed in the piece she had chosen to perform. Most nights, she was out until late, practicing. When she came home, she'd spend another hour on the piano with Hans sitting by, in awe of her talent.

It was a knock that came to the door late one afternoon that changed everything. Hans almost didn't answer it, except the caller was persistent. Hans answered the door, distracted.

"May I help you?" he answered, insincere. Before him stood a middle-aged man in a suit vest over a blue shirt and a navy pair of pants. He was facing the other way as the door opened and spun around in one movement seeing Hans stood in the doorway.

"Uh…hello!" he said, rather uncomfortably. Hans guessed him to be mid to late 40's and completely lost.

"I'm looking for Tanya" he said and cocked his head. Hans looked at him quizzically. He waited a moment before he answered.

"I'm sorry. She's not here at the moment, may I help you?" Hans asked again, this time more intently.

"Uh….I wonder…is Rebeccah here, perhaps?" asked the man. Now Hans's heart began racing. Who the hell was he? What did he want? How is it he knew of Tanya and Rebeccah? Hans was suspicious of everyone ever since Rebeccah began performing in public. He always remembered Tanya's reaction to strangers taping Rebeccah playing piano at an early age. Hans was forever mindful of that. He had lost his patience with this man who seemed fidgety and unable to stand still.

"I'm sorry, but neither Tanya nor Rebeccah are available at the moment. Perhaps you could leave your name with me and I could inform them you dropped by?" Hans stated, interested in the man's inquiries, especially after his poor wife who was decades dead.

The man seemed to be stunned for a moment. He stood staring at Hans kind of dazed and then a smile broke across his face.

"Forgive me?" he asked. "This has gone so differently in my head. I assumed one of them would be home." He laughed, almost embarrassed. "I suppose introductions are in order. My Name is Ernst Frederic Hermann. I'm Rebeccah's biological father" he told Hans, as he extended his hand.

* * *

The jawbone had been examined by forensics. It was definitely female, of approximately 27 – 33 years of age. One end of the jaw was crushed, making the doctor believe that the woman's head had suffered a severe blow. The jawbone had been found under dozens of broken trees, which worked with that theory.

Thankfully, there had been some extensive dental work done on the lower left portion, a full bridge in fact. It was going to take some hard detective work, going from dentist to dentist to try and find the one who might possibly have done this work. Considering the jawbone had been there for almost 20 years, this was going to take some time.

The chief of police put his best cold case file detective, Karl Braun, on it. Although, it wasn't a cold case, it was exactly the kind of case that Detective

Braun excelled at. The chief knew that Detective Braun would not stop until he found out who this woman was.

He began by running through a database of all dentists and orthodontists throughout Switzerland from 25 – 15 years ago. That might narrow it down to less than 3,000, give or take. Undeterred, Detective Braun, took his listing and began mapping out his plan.

It took all of his fine detective work, his exemplary attention to detail and all the diligent prep work he did, to find the woman's identity. When he did, it was a real "aha" moment.

*   *   *

Hans stood in his doorway with his mouth hanging open, not believing what he had just been told.

"You're…you…are ..uh…I…uh", he stammered. Did he actually hear him correctly?

"Yes, I'm Rebeccah's dad. Well, biological dad, anyway" he motioned towards Hans, humbly.

Hans gathered himself together and moved aside in the doorway. He gestured for the man to come inside.

"Uh…please, come in, come in Mr. …er..Herm" he tried remembering the name.

"It's Hermann. Ernst Frederic Hermann, but please, call me Ernst." He offered his hand again and Hans shook it looking directly at the man and examining his face.

"Hans Baumgartner" he introduced himself to Ernst. "You must forgive me, Ernst. I'm very shocked, of course. I didn't expect to open my door to you today and especially since I was told you were dead." Hans explained as he brought Ernst into the living room and offered him a seat.

Ernst sat, nodding his head. "Tanya said I was dead? I get it, I was a dead beat." He paused a moment. "Again, this all played out so differently in my head" he told Hans. "I just assumed Tanya would answer the door. Stupid of me to assume, I guess."

Yes especially since she's been dead for years, thought Hans.

"So what brings you here then, Ernst?" Hans asked. "I mean, I understand the obvious, but why now?" It was a fair question and Ernst knew it.

Ernst hung his head, ashamed. He looked at his hands, rubbing them together, nervous to spill his confession to this man. "When Tanya and I were together, it wasn't the best situation. *I* wasn't in the best situation. Tanya was great and gave me time to try and adjust and get my life together, but after only a few months, I left her. I didn't tell her where I was going or if I'd be back. I just left." He cleared his throat and raised his head to Hans, looking him directly in the eye. "I needed to grow up. Truly. And, it's taken me all these years to finally do that."

Both men fell silent. Ernst was hoping for Hans's understanding at his confession. Hans was hoping Rebeccah didn't burst through the door anytime soon. He needed to be sure that this man was who he claimed to be. What he wanted was to retrieve the birth certificate he had upstairs. He needed an opportunity to leave the room.

"Excuse me, can I offer you a coffee or tea?" Hans asked.

"A tea would be nice, thank you" Ernest answered. With that Hans jumped up to get the kettle on. While out of eyesight, he shot upstairs and opened the file drawer, finding Rebeccah's file and birth certificate inside. He read the document again. Father: E. F. Hermann. Ernst Fredric Hermann. Damn! *Why aren't you dead?* Hans thought, angrily. He folded the document and brought it downstairs with him and went back into the kitchen, preparing the tea pot and mugs.

Meanwhile, Ernst stayed in the living room looking around. There were many family pictures lining bookshelves and hung in the wall. In one corner, there looked to be a small shrine dedicated to a dark haired woman. Ernst wondered who she was. There were a number of other pictures with the same woman and a red haired child, a toddler. As he was busy looking at the pictures, Hans walked through the doorway carrying a tray with mugs, a teapot, cream and sugar. He placed it on a table and motioned for Ernest to help himself.

Sitting back in his seat, Ernst was pouring his tea when Hans asked, "So, I hope you understand, I must ask if you brought any proof with you to claim you are who you say you are?" Hans said in a gentle tone.

Ernst smiled. Sipping his tea and then placing it on the table, he reached into his coat pocket and pulled out a small photo album and a document. He handed the document to Hans. He unfolded it to find the exact birth certificate that was folded in his own pocket. He nodded his head and handed it back.

"Yes, I have one of those, too. But, I must say, that isn't proof positive. Is that all you brought?" his question died off as Ernst flipped open the photo album of 4x6 prints. The first was of he, and a brown haired woman holding a newborn infant in a hospital bed. Both adults are smiling wide. Ernst looked much younger and thinner. The woman looked tired but exhilarated.

Ernst flipped the next picture of him again holding a chubby little baby with soft curls and a cherubic face. The next picture was the couple and the baby in front of the Christmas tree. When he finished with the last picture, he looked up at Hans's face and was puzzled by the look he had.

Hans was very puzzled. Who were the people shown in the pictures? They weren't anyone Hans knew. They didn't even look remotely familiar. He suddenly thought that he had the wrong family altogether.

"See?" Ernst asked. "They were once my family, long ago." Hans shook his head in the negative and pointed towards the photo album Ernst was holding.

"No, I'm afraid you're mistaken." Hans told him. "They aren't anyone I know."

Ernst looked confused. He flipped open the album again to the first photo and pointed emphatically at it as he said, "This was taken the day Rebeccah was born. That's Tanya right there." He thrust the album towards Hans so he could have a better look, but Hans continued to shake his head, even with a good examining of the woman in the photo.

"No. I'm sorry, you've got the wrong family." Hans turned, pointing to the picture of Tanya in the middle of the shrine. "That is my Tanya. And there, and there with my Rebeccah" he told Ernst, as he pointed from picture to picture around the room.

The two men looked at each other completely dumbfounded, each unable to explain the other's reality.

"Can I ask how you found me?" Hans asked Ernst, motioning for the man to again take his seat and continue drinking his tea.

As Ernst sat, he told Hans, "Before Tanya moved north, she sent my mother a letter explaining her move and giving her the address. She said that if I ever got my act together, she should let me know where she could be found. When my mother died, she left the letter to me in amongst other documents, including Rebeccah's birth certificate." He rubbed his face in frustration. "Finding both of them at the same time made we want to do right by them, find them, maybe explain myself. I went to the address she left and there was no house there anymore. But, the woman on the farm knew where I could find you. She gave me this address." He shrugged his shoulders.

Hans's mind was reeling. This wasn't the first time he had wondered about inconsistencies in Tanya's background and the story she told him. He needed to get Ernst out of his house so he could really think things through. There was no other reason for him to stay, he needed to leave.

"Well, I'm sorry Mr. Hermann, I don't have answers for you. These are obviously not the people you're looking for, so, if you don't mind…I don't mean to be rude but it's getting rather late and I've things to do, so, if you wouldn't mind…" Hans stood and motioned towards the front door.

"Uh, I just wonder, may I please speak to Tanya?" Ernst asked. "Perhaps she knows what's going on?" his hands outstretched.

Hans took in a deep breath and pointed towards the shrine. "She's dead. Nearly 18 years now." It was all he said. Ernst's face fell. Now he was completely baffled.

As Hans turned him towards the door, Ernst mumbled, "How is this possible? The address was in the letter. She sent me here, knew of you and everything." He stopped before reaching the door. "Where are they? Where are *my* Tanya and *my* Rebeccah?"

Hans shook his head, but continued ushering Ernst out the door. "I'm sorry Mr. Hermann, I don't have an answer for you. Good night now, good night" and he closed the door and turned out the front light.

He shot back up the stairs pulling both files on Tanya and Rebeccah again, bringing them back downstairs and into the living room. He rarely drank, but poured himself a glass of wine to calm his nerves. He cleared the table of the mugs and teapot and laid out the documents in their separate piles. He grabbed a note pad to keep a running list.

After looking through all the documents thoroughly again, he sat back more confused than before. He started listing all inconsistencies in Tanya's story he'd experienced in the past.

#1. The neurologist at the hospital saying Tanya and Rebeccah were not blood related.

#2. Ernst was supposed to be dead. That was what she had told him. The birth certificate stated E.F. Hermann. He had ID, he had the same birth certificate. He even had newborn baby pictures, but he had the wrong family. But then, he had the address of the house that was left to Tanya by her late mother. And he said Tanya had sent the letter before she moved. She never mentioned to Hans anything about a letter mailed to anyone's mother. Tanya and Rebeccah were completely alone in the world.

When he looked at what we had written on the pad, he determined that #2, was also #3, 4 & 5.

He sat back closing his eyes, sighing heavily. Remembering a day long ago, before they were married. The trip they took into the city. They were "his girls" that day and he wanted to buy them new dresses and show them off for all to see. Hans smiled to himself recalling the day and then something twigged in his brain. The day ended rather abruptly with a headache. He remembered being at the restaurant with Tanya and Rebeccah and as they were leaving, something caught Tanya's attention. He had thought at the time that it was odd for her to react the way she did to a woman's call and it was after that, she bolted.

Hans went over and over the moment in his mind. It was almost 20 years old and he vaguely remembered it at all except that it was something that made Hans wonder. He was always trying to truly figure her out as she didn't have much of a story and no one to validate her life prior to meeting him.

He still had no answers and as he sat rereading what he wrote it occurred to him that if it was true that Rebeccah and Tanya weren't blood related, then who were they to one another. No genetic relation at all meant, they were…strangers? Did she perhaps adopt? There was no documentation stating so and he'd gone through it all. Everything pointed to them being mother and daughter, everything except…he looked at his list.

How the hell does Tanya end up with Rebeccah if they aren't related and she didn't adopt? His mind tried to follow any logical explanation, and then it hit him. His blood went cold. Could she have taken the child? Taken, without permission? But that would be kidnapping and he didn't believe that Tanya was capable of doing that. It was far too sinister a crime for his sweet Tanya to have done.

He looked over at the picture within the shrine and thought about his beautiful Rebeccah. Again, it struck him how much they did not look alike and after having met Ernst, Rebeccah's supposed father, she didn't bare any likeness to him at all either. But then, he didn't have the same wife and child. *WHAT?*, his mind screamed.

He jumped up from the couch and went straight to the attic. Forget looking over the same documents, somewhere up in the attic were things of Tanya's that Hans either didn't have the heart to part with or, was keeping for Rebeccah. He went straight over to the pile of boxes labeled "Tanya" and ripped the first box open. Just a few personal items. An old jewelry box with her watch in it. Her wedding attire and handbag.

The next box had dishes that Tanya had taken great care to pack away and Hans wasn't sure if they were family heirlooms or what their significance, so he had kept them for Rebeccah to decide what she wanted to do with them.

The third box had some documents regarding the property, a child's blanket and a shoe box. Hans felt defeated, there was nothing here that gave him any clues. He was about to put all the boxes back together when his hand knocked the lid from the shoe box in the last box and it opened up to reveal more documents. Hans couldn't recall which ones these were and sat on the floor to go through them.

The first document was a birth certificate for someone named "Luisa Van Zeeban". Born in Switzerland. He studied it closely wondering who she was and why it was in Tanya's possession. He placed the birth certificate in front of him and picked up the next. It was a marriage license between a "Nicholas Morningstar" and "Luisa Van Zeeban". It was more than 20 years old. Again, who were these people? Hans wondered. He put the license next to the birth certificate and reached for the next document.

It was a brochure. "The Morningstar Foundation" was blazoned across the top with a Poppy being used in each "o" in the name. He wondered why this was in with other, much more important documents. He read the front of the brochure and then opened it up completely. His heart nearly stopped, then it started racing. His eyes darted all over the middle spread, from one face to another, from one paragraph to another. It all made sense, but not quite.

He grabbed the three documents and left the attic, not putting away any of the boxes. When he got downstairs he held the brochure up to the pictures of Rebeccah from years ago as a toddler and then at present. He couldn't believe his eyes.

He brought the brochure into the brighter light and it was then that he saw it. Someone had written "She's been THISCLOSE all along" across Chase Morningstar's face. He started to panic. What had she done? He thought, wildly. He looked again at the other documents. "Nicholas Morningstar. Chase Morningstar. The Morningstar Foundation", the same family name on two of the documents.

He looked at the birth certificate of "Luisa Van Zeeban". She was the same age as Tanya, although different birthdates. Luisa? He thought. Why does that sound familiar to me? He questioned. His mind was scrambled and he took another drink of his wine as he tried to understand what was right before him.

He then remembered what the woman had called out that day Tanya bolted. She had called "Luisa". Hans remembered it now, very clearly. He remembered how Tanya naturally turned as if it was her name being called. He noticed because her own reaction, whoever it was she spotted made her run like a frightened deer. *Luisa!*

He looked at the birth certificate again. Tanya is Luisa. Luisa is Tanya. He was slowly starting to understand. He wasn't sure how she got the name "Tanya", but Luisa Van Zeeban assumed Tanya's identity. But why?

He looked over the brochure again. The Foundation paid for music lessons for underprivileged children all over the world and was dedicated to Chase Morningstar's late young daughter, Poppy. Hans swallowed hard. The brochure had a picture of Poppy in the top right corner, a smiley faced, bright green eyed two or three year old. It was her. There was no mistaking it. She could be an infant or 90 odd years of age, but those eyes were unmistakable. He was looking at the toddler he met in the Pharmacy back in Switzerland. It seemed like a lifetime ago now. What it was, was all a lie. Hans had been led to believe Tanya's story. He believed what she told him, but it was all a lie.

He still had questions and decided to dig deeper. He went to his computer and navigated to the Morningstar Foundation's website. The brochure was probably 20 years old and the website was more up-to-date. He spent the next hour looking through all the information and even watched the video Chase recorded with Poppy as an infant. "Now That You're Here" brought a tear to Hans's eye, thinking how hard it must have been to have lost such a wonderful, beautiful soul from his life.

Hans then searched one name, Poppy Morningstar. Hundreds of articles came up, all recounting the disappearance of the super-star's young daughter along with his secret wife and nanny. How, during a torrential storm, the car they were riding in went down a ravine and they were both killed.

Hans read article after article, but never read where it stated that they recovered their bodies. Ever. Confirming to him what he had already surmised. For some reason, Tanya/Luisa had kidnapped the child and faked their death. Hans still wasn't sure where the names Tanya and Rebeccah came from, but that couldn't be a fluke either?

He then read an article about the murder trial of Chase Morningstar. His wife, Sonya had been murdered in their bed and Chase was charged with the murder. The article then explained that he was exonerated when it was divulged that his wife, Luisa Morningstar (nee Van Zeeban) and former nanny to his child, ordered a hit on Sonya. A paparazzi was charged with the actual murder and sent to jail. The article ended with "Luisa and Poppy were killed in a car accident in Switzerland".

Hans sat back exhausted. Everything lined up. He had been raising Poppy Morningstar, the daughter of mega-music super-star, Chase Morningstar. He sat reading through the Morningstar Foundation website, reading their mission statement and Chase and Dana's belief in sponsoring music lessons.

Rebeccah's voice calling out to him brought him out of his office in a shot, making sure she didn't get to the room and see what he'd been looking at on the computer.

When he saw her, he had his "aha" moment! Rebeccah was home from her practice. Her lessons, her piano lessons. The Foundation had been paying for Rebeccah's music lessons. There was no grandmother's trust fund. Tanya/Luisa had applied for Rebeccah Nowak (now Baumgartner) to be sponsored when she was a child of a single mother, and she was accepted. That's why she had written across Chase's face. His stolen, dead daughter was actually being sponsored by the very Foundation he created in her name. The final insult. The final evil injustice. The final secret revealed.

"What have you been up to?" she asked him, noticing how flushed he looked. "You look like you've been running a race, what's got your heart going so fast?" she asked, concerned. How did he even begin to explain it to her? He decided he would set certain things in motion first. It might help lessen the blow; it might also blow up and leave him with less. No matter what, he had always done what was right and this would be no different.

~

Chapter 9

Haven't We Met?

Tyrone Thomas Townsend (aka Trip) had been in hiding for quite some time. Once things had died down after the murder of the guard, he grabbed the bus back to Santa Barbara and laid low. He wandered out from time to time, but when he did, he went by the name Garrett. He had been doing it for a while and he was *extremely* good at it. How could he not be? He would argue with any actor who would say that his performance of Garrett wasn't a stretch, at all. Looking like someone is easy, acting more so, *behaving* like them is where the art is. Trip understood that.

He had learned so much about Garrett from all his social media sites, including everything he had posted to YouTube, it was really ridiculous how *much* he had learned just from being holed up in his rented hotel room, sometimes in his underwear. Thank God he'd had enough schooling and technology in his life to be able to work a computer to his complete benefit. One of the very first things he did was an internet search of Garrett's high school student card. Loads of information there. Including something very interesting; his birthdate. As first, Trip was pretty freaked out by Garrett's birthdate. How could it be so different? It took him a bit, but he figured out they had actually been born over a few hours of time on New Year's Eve.

He had been studying Garrett Thomas Samuels intently. Not just an online creeper, he had actually visited the places Garrett lived, which was not always easily done. Especially when Garrett chose to live in an apartment building with a Security Guard at the front desk. Thankfully, Trip managed to get away clean, but it caused a lot of questions from the Guard and made Garrett wonder what the hell was going on. When Trip thought about this, it always made him chuckle.

From what he saw and read, Trip actually liked Garrett. He was incredibly smart and after watching a few of his YouTube posts, Trip started wondering;

if it were a different time and a different story, would he approach him and get to know him?

His daydream lasted only a moment before Trip's mind went to how he could become Garrett and possibly live off his life, in some way. Sure, he wasn't into killing and now felt like being part of a "gang" was just giving others the ability to define him and control his destiny. From now on, he worked alone and with an easy target like Garrett Thomas Samuels, who he now knew was his twin brother. How could he possibly pass that up? Too easy, really. Besides, this could have been his life, right?

The more he learned about Garrett's life, the more he resented his Gramma. She was the one who made the choice, she said so herself the night he left. And, she told him that she was resentful of not picking the *"other"* boy. Looking at Garrett's successful life, Trip wondered if she was right. If they were twins, how could they turn out so differently? It began to dawn on Trip that his Gramma's choices, decisions and lifestyle were all thrust upon him. He had no choice but to become who she had exposed him to! Trip was certain, if he'd had the kind of love and money that Garrett had supporting him, he might have shown promise, brilliance and gifted talents. Where was he going to get inspiration like that from his environment? She planted him right in the middle of a gang neighborhood! Trip was pissed at his Gramma. *She shouldda left me where I was in that hospital!* He thought, angrily, Cascades School not even entering his mind.

As he watched Garrett's online posts, persona and public accessibility, Trip thought his life standards could improve 1,000% if he could "be" Garrett Samuels. Many doors could be opened if people thought they were talking to a bright, talented and charismatic young man like Garrett. Trip's conniving mind knew he'd be a fool to travel in the same circles, so Trip figured it was best to be "Garrett Samuels" in places where Garrett Samuels wouldn't frequent. In doing so, he could flash his "business card" and maybe it could take him places? Maybe get him a few freebies; vacations, dinners and drinks. He had never really had trouble getting women, but as Garrett he could really go to the next level of women, those who Trip had thought out of his league.

Really? What could it harm?

* * *

By the end of his internship at KARMA! Labels, Garrett Samuels was a bona fide music producer! One of his supervisors had seen his postings on YouTube and was a big fan. Everything took off from there. The supervisor introduced him to the Director of Production who saw Garrett's productions as "brilliance" for such a young age. He immediately had Garrett involved in productions from television commercials to animated shorts. Those who worked with him were always so impressed with his ability to put music together with literally anything; other music, movies, cartoons, he had a different perspective for all forms of visual art.

He won a full scholarship to university and chose to get his degree at the California Institute of Art University. Only an hour and a half away from Grant and Sondra, but far enough to stay in residence. Garrett adored his parents, but he was looking forward to being out on his own and exploring life and all it had to offer. What Garrett found was, he was a far better student than he was a reckless sophomore. As such, the end of his first year saw a 4.0 grade average and a desire to not live in residence. He began to receive many requests to produce wedding videos. That summer, he produced wedding videos for a handful of couples. He made enough money to cover rent and his living expenses on a single family home located close to campus for the year.

And, learned a valuable lesson.

(But that's another story).

Once on his own in his rental home, he moved all his soundboards, instruments and computerized audio mixing boards into the large basement of the house and started spending all his time there. In the three years he lived there, Garrett rarely took advantage of the beautiful gardens, the pool or, the great neighborhood he lived in. He immersed himself into his work, never feeling tired, never slowing down. His wasn't something he learned, it had always been with him. A God given talent that his parents were in awe of. He'd show them something he was working on and they'd just watch with mouths open, completely captivated by his artistic ability. Neither could recall anything outstanding about his background, except that his young mother had died shortly after he was born. The boy was put up for adoption by the maternal grandmother, who was the only known living relative to the child. Her name did not appear on the legal papers. That information was sealed. As lawyers, Grant and Sondra had made sure the grandmother couldn't show up on their doorstep one day, insisting legal rights. In order to agree to that, the grandmother insisted on all names being withheld and with that, the papers were signed. Garrett's life was handed into the Samuels' hands. When he was three years old, they told him all about his adoption and how all of them were brought together through love. He asked about his mother and was told she was in heaven watching over him. He was sad for his dead mommy, but happy to have Grant and Sondra as his mommy and daddy. He'd never known any other parents and never wanted to. No one, outside of his immediate family knew of the adoption and Garrett was satisfied to leave it a secret. Besides, he looked enough like a combination of Grant and Sondra that people made the assumption they were a natural family. Garrett was tall like his dad, their eyes were the same dark brown and they had the same coloring of skin. He and his mother shared a large, wide smile, the same shaped face and thick dark hair. As far as he was concerned, he was their son regardless of who birthed him.

Garrett's university years were spent honing his talents and perfecting his own creative style. Oftentimes, he'd be on campus and someone would ask him about his current YouTube video, or his thoughts on other projects he might have seen. He was becoming well known. So much so, that people would swear they'd met him before, usually at a party or club. They'd even recall some of the conversation they'd had with him. Garrett would just smile through it, knowing full well they were wrong, but always being polite enough to let it slide. He knew if someone asked him "Haven't we met?" he'd be launched into a memory of theirs he didn't share. He always put it down to the fact that he sometimes appeared in his videos and people had been mistaken that they'd met him. They'd recognized him, but never met him.

After leaving school, KARMA! Labels scooped him up immediately. Actually, he had signed employment documents 6 weeks before he graduated, but it was known he'd work at KARMA! Labels; they had basically told him so after his internship. Garrett's first position was Assistant to the Director of Production. Which meant, he worked on smaller projects that the Director felt he could handle and there wasn't much Garrett couldn't handle. After a while, he was making six figures and had full access to all the company's equipment, far greater quality than he had at home. Since being hired, he'd moved back to the Santa Barbara area and settled into a small ranch style home. He didn't worry about a gated community like his parent's, he wasn't *that* well known or *that* wealthy. He'd consider it in time, but for now he was happily settled in and enjoying life, something he never took for granted.

Working at KARMA! Labels was inspiration overload to Garrett. He stopped posting his videos online, simply because he got paid to do that now! He worked tirelessly on his projects and was nominated for numerous awards, but it was his first Grammy nomination that gave him massive public attention. A music producer of his talent and at such a young age, people were starting to take notice.

Garrett Thomas Samuels was a rising star!

* * *

He sat in the Dr.'s waiting room, thumbing through his phone. The room was quite full and very loud, but he managed to find a seat alone, away from all the other patients, hoping to get called in quickly. He didn't like sick people and wished he'd picked up a mask at the reception desk, but now there was long lineup of registering patients standing between him and those masks.

FUCK! He thought. *If it weren't so important I wouldn't be here.* It has always bothered him that he wasn't like other guys. Hell, if Two Tone and Danny had found out, they'd have really given him a tough time. While he had the money, he figured he'd better get it taken care of.

He turned into the wall beside him and tried to concentrate on his news feed. He managed to get lost on a story of a movie being filmed in the area and were looking for local actors to fill some of the roles, if not, work as an extra. Imagining himself on set, he didn't notice the little boy standing before him, picking his nose. When he pulled his attention away, the child had wiped his findings on the seat next to him, coughed twice and ran towards the crowd. He stared off, looking at the child and his family; a young mother and father with three children all under the age of 5, he guessed. Each child had a snotty nose, a miserable mood and a crying mouth.

The parents looked haggard, as if they hadn't slept in all 5 years. When the father locked eyes with him, he quickly turned his attention back to his phone, but his mind continued on the scene of that family. He forced himself to stay seated and not bolt from the waiting room, but when his name was called he practically ran towards the clerk who called him.

"Tyrone Thomas Townsend" she yelled over the din of the patients. He was before her in seconds, smiling. She couldn't help but smile back, he was so handsome.

"Come this way" she told him, walking him down a hallway and putting him into a clinic room. She asked him to take a seat.

"The Dr. will be with you in a minute, okay?" she offered, as she proceeded to leave and close the door behind her. He was glad to be out of the waiting room. The clinic room was far cleaner and much more private. He was about to start looking at his phone again when a light knock came on the door.

"Come on in" Trip said. The doctor walked through the door and took a seat across from him. He was a tall man with striking silver hair, a relaxed style and an easy smile.

"So, what brings you in to see us, today?" He asked Trip.

Trip took a deep breath and stated directly, "Circumcision". He paused a moment and then added, "Oh and I wonder if you'd also be interested in taking care of something else for me, too?" he asked. He paused for a moment, assessing his audience. As he began speaking, he reached into his jacket pocket and pulled out a large wad of bills, counting out 10 of them and telling his tale, convincingly.

He had the Dr.'s complete attention.

* * *

Trip had come very close to spending almost all of his stolen money from the robbery. It had allowed him to live decently for a while, but he knew he would have to find some kind of work. The article he had read in his news feed gave him the idea to try his hand at acting again. Now, with Garrett being well known it was getting harder to pretend to be him and he found himself trying to hide his looks behind dark sunglasses and different hats. He had also started letting his facial hair grow. It helped a lot and once he felt his look was his own, he put his last of the money towards headshots he used to advertise himself to agencies and agents.

After a few weeks, he got called from an agency looking for new faces. Trip was a very handsome black man and his smile was blinding. The facial hair only added to his sexiness and the camera loved him, but his acting was really only mediocre. Regardless, his looks got him hired, but never in a big way. The movies and roles he got were simply "B" rated and despite his best efforts, he always stayed in that range, never really getting a lot of screen time. More often, most of his scenes were cut and the director would make some ridiculous excuse as to why.

He wasn't raking money in by any means, but Trip was able to make a half-assed living. Even so, he kept up on all things Garrett related. He never knew when he'd want or need to fall back on being Garrett again. He would always keep that little gem in his back pocket, he'd just be much more careful when he used it. With Trip working in the movies, he was sure people would begin to recognize him, now.

* * *

Garrett had been unwell for a few days. Dragging his ass and not able to get rid of his 2 day headache, he found himself sitting in a clinic room waiting to see a doctor. Normally, he would not have taken to this drastic a measure as to go to a clinic to be seen, but Garrett was done. He needed to feel better and get himself back on to work. Being sick was not an option. Sitting quietly, his eyes closed he began to get a strange sensation. It was as if he was having déjà vu. A sense he'd been there before, in that very room, although he never had. He couldn't quite shake it; a feeling as though he'd experienced the same instances before. When it first happened, he was a young boy. He'd told his mother, who laughed and told him about déjà vu. Since then, Garrett decided it was harmless, but it did unnerve him when it happened. It was so crystal clear to him.

He was lost in his thoughts when the Dr. came through the door. He stopped a moment, took one look at his patient and smiled his easy smile. Taking a seat across from Garrett, the Dr. looked down at the chart he held and then looked back up at Garrett, a little confused.

"Haven't we met?" he asked his patient, his head tilted trying to recall when.

Garrett managed to smile back.

Been there, done that.

Chapter 10

ALL THE STARS ALIGN

Ernst Hermann walked into the police station in Zurich, Switzerland, not really certain he had reason to be there. He stood at the desk waiting for someone to take notice of him.

A female officer approached Ernst.

"Can I help you?" she asked.

"I ...uh...I'm not sure" he answered, still looking puzzled. He had driven hours back into Switzerland pondering the whole meeting with Hans and the revelation that the Tanya and Rebeccah he was hoping to find, weren't the ones living in Germany. He came to the realization that perhaps something criminal had taken place, he just wasn't sure what.

"I think I need to report two missing people." He told the officer.

"Oh? How long have they been missing?" she asked grabbing a pen from the desk behind her and getting prepared to take all the information.

"Uh...well, see, that's the problem. I'm not sure how long they've been missing." He answered honestly.

The officer looked at him with a bit of a tired stare. "A person must be missing for at least 48 hours before we can issue an alert" she told him.

"Uh-huh. I ...would say that they've been missing for maybe" shrugging his shoulder "15 to 20 years" he guessed. The officer looked at him questioningly.

"Please can you just take my explanation? Their names are Tanya and Rebeccah Nowak" he started as she began writing.

* * *

Detective Braun had been able to search through close to 200 dentists in a fairly short time. They were easily eliminated as they didn't perform the kind of work that the jawbone displayed. It wasn't much progress but it was a step in the right direction. He had hopes that at some point during the investigation at least one of the dentists could point him in the right direction, recognizing someone's specific work, if that were possible after all these years.

It would take just one lucky break.

* * *

The night of Rebeccah's concert was here! Hans would do something tonight that he had never done. He would video Rebeccah's performance, but only from the back. He now understood why Tanya/Luisa had not wanted the child to be filmed, it would have hit the internet and set it on fire. Chase would have undoubtedly seen it and her ruse would be exposed!

Hans had a specific need for the video. It was all part of his plan to explain to Rebeccah her true identity and how he came to find it out, but he needed to have the video first. After that, he was hoping all the stars would align.

Hans waited for a number of weeks after the concert before he sat Rebeccah down for *the* conversation. He chose a weekend when she had no other obligations, figuring she'd want the full day to herself, once he told her his news. He explained to her that he needed to let her in on something that had been recently brought to his attention. He had all the documentation at the ready, a box of tissues nearby and a glass of wine for each of them.

"You know, I got thinking about your talent, Rebeccah. It's quite unique, you know" he began with. Rebeccah cocked her head to consider his statement.

"I'm not sure if it's as unique as it is just something I understand better than others. It's like a language to me, one I understand a little better than others" she countered, humbly. It made Hans smile. There are some things that the Morningstars can take credit for, but Rebeccah's beautiful outlook was all her own, with possibly a bit of Baumgartner in her, through osmosis!

"Well, I just wonder what side of the family that kind of musical talent came from, don't you?" he asked, hoping she'd play along. She looked at him, her eyes displaying her confusion at his question.

"You said you wanted to talk about something that had recently been brought to your attention" she stated, "does it have anything to do with my family heritage?" she asked. She had never told him because she was afraid to upset him, but she had often wondered who her family was. Where they came from. She knew nothing of her father, except his first initials and last name. She had thought about doing some research to try and find what she could, but she always held back because her dad had always been so wonderful and loving to her; she couldn't bear to break his heart.

"Have you ever wondered?" he asked her directly. She hesitated to answer him, but eventually nodded her head, almost in shame.

"Oh, my darling daughter, don't you concern yourself with my feelings about this. This is all about you and you have every right to know who you are and where you come from." He told her smiling wide, his eyes sparkling. "I've found something absolutely incredible about you, do you want to know what it is?" he asked. She stared at him with her beautiful wide green eyes, not imaging the story he was about to tell her, but grateful for his enthusiasm to do so. No matter what he told her, he was her daddy and no one would ever take his place!

He began with the neurologist's findings, explaining that he figured the hospital had made an error, he was a young doctor, tired as he recalled and probably not on his game. Rebeccah was shocked.

"We aren't related?" she asked, very concerned. "If she wasn't my mother, then who was she?" she asked, right away believing the findings. This made

Hans stop a moment. Something had made the young child aware that Tanya wasn't her mother, Hans was sure of it.

"Well, now let's not get too far ahead of ourselves. There are other things you need to hear first" he explained. He then went on to explain Ernst Hermann's visit just over a month before and the confusion they shared over the two different Tanyas and Rebeccahs.

"But he had the address? Did my mo...Tanya send it to him? And if she didn't, then who did?" she asked, thoroughly fascinated.

"Well, I have a theory, but, let me continue..." he stated, trying to thoroughly cover everything. He explained that once he got Ernst out of the house he went up into the attic to see if he could find anything amongst the older boxes and things of Tanya's that he'd kept.

"I found these" he exclaimed, placing the three pieces of information in front of her. She picked up each one and looked quizzically at each one, tilting her head this way and that when reading a name. When she got to the Morningstar brochure and opened it up, Hans held his breath. She barely got the brochure fully opened up before she gasped.

"Oh my God!" she exclaimed. She bent the brochure down, closer to the light to have a better look at the picture of Poppy Morningstar. She studied it closely, not taking her eyes from it for a long moment. Hans watched her closely.

She finally raised her eyes to his. She shook her head no, then looked back. "This...this, it looks exactly like me as a child." She stammered. Hans nodded.

"What does all this mean, dad?" She asked him. Calling him "dad" got to him and his eyes welled up.

"It means that I was put in charge of a very precious gift for many years and now, I must give the gift back to the person who rightfully deserves it."

He waited for a moment and then continued. "There is still a lot to explain to you, but you can see for yourself, this is you, right?"

She looked back at the brochure then up again at her dad, nodding. "Oh yes, I believe that's me for certain. My hair color was different as a child, but those are my eyes." She answered. She then gave a good look at the brochure, reading the information about the Foundation and seeing the writing across Chase's face.

"She took me?" it dawned on Rebeccah. "She kidnapped me and then what...?" she wondered looking back at her dad. He shrugged.

"My guess is she took you and faked your deaths" he told her. He then took her hand and all the documentation he had and led her to the office in front of the computer. They each took a seat. He showed her all the videos and information he'd come across in his searches. For every question she had, he had the answer, except one.

"So, where are the real Tanya and Rebeccah Nowak, then?" she asked him. He held her stare a moment and shook his head.

"I don't know." He told her honestly. "It's the one answer, I don't have. Perhaps Ernst will find them. I'm not too sure if our Tanya stole the real Tanya's identity or if she did something more...permanent." He admitted. Rebeccah's eyes went wide.

"Seriously?" she asked. "You think she was capable of killing two people?"

"My dear, you have no idea" and showed her the news articles on the murder trial, finding only one picture of Sonya Morningstar. Rebeccah sat astonished in front of the computer. It was all so hard to take in and her dad was carefully watching for her to have had her fill.

She read the two or three articles he had saved for her and sat back in the chair, shaking her head in disbelief at what she had learned.

154

"The final thing I put together was..." he waited to see if she stopped him, but she didn't. "Tanya, your...er...Luisa, anyway she had The Morningstar Foundation paying for your piano lessons for all these years. Essentially, The Foundation your father created because of you has been paying for you to play the piano." It was really then that she made the connection. She was Poppy Morningstar, daughter of the music super-star Chase Morningstar. That was where her musical talent came from. That was why she has such a unique talent, it ran through her veins!

She had been so immersed in classical music for so many years, she really wasn't aware of Chase Morningstar's music. She and Hans must be the only ones because judging from the website, he was known world-wide. It made sense though, why Luisa was so insistent to have as little outside sources of information within the household for as long as she and Poppy were together. Luisa didn't have a television or a computer, not that Poppy could ever remember. Even Hans shied away from watching TV as much as most households. Poppy had used computers through school, but had no reason to ever enquire about Chase Morningstar or even find out who he was.

So, now, with all this information in front of her, she stayed in front of the computer for hours, reading up on and learning all about who she really was and where she really came from. Hans left her to it, bringing her a few meals and cups of tea. By the end of the day, she walked into the living room, exhausted and exhilarated.

"So, what's next?" she asked Hans, dropping into the chair before him. Hans smiled at her, knowing full well she'd be game for what he was about to suggest.

"Well, Miss Poppy Morningstar, I think it's about time you met your father, don't you?" he enquired. She smiled wide at him, a real Morningstar smile. Hans could now see her as Chase and Sonya's child. She was a perfect mixture of the two of them.

He let things sink in for a moment and was about to ask her how she wanted to get started, when she suddenly gasped. "What?" Hans asked, hearing her amazement.

"My name is Poppy Morningstar" She said, at first. "Morningstar, dad. Morningstar! What have I been doing forever since I was a little girl? What was it I was told all those years ago by that elderly woman? Chasing the Morning star will eventually bring you home! Remember, I told you about her?" She stood amazed, her eyes wide, reliving the moment. She had never forgotten the encounter, but at the time, she took the woman's words to mean something completely differently. Finding out now that she wasn't Tanya's child made that conversation so much more poignant to her.

"Looking back now, it means something else completely. I've never been able to figure out who she was, but whoever she was, she seemed to know something about me. She seemed to know I was a Morningstar and maybe she was trying to tell me." She shrugged at Hans. She didn't have the answers, but she hoped to one day.

* * *

Chase Morningstar was working on some guitar chords for a new song he was writing when his wife, Dana walked into the room.

"We need to be at the Foundation office in a half hour" she told him. "They've got it down to ten and want us to pick the final four from those." She explained as she leaned over his shoulders and kissed him on his cheek as he played.

"Great!" he said enthusiastically. "I always get shivers when I see what our work has produced. Who knew that this would be the result for such a horrible time? I like to believe Poppy knows. I think she'd be thrilled to know that she was the inspiration." He told Dana, as he held her arms around his neck. They stayed like that for a moment, the love between them very strong, very deep.

"Well, we now have less than a half hour so, bring your best "Poppy vibes" and let's go and pick the winners. I bet we're going to be blown away by the amount of talent we're about to see!" Dana said as she kissed him again and patted him on the shoulder.

* * *

Detective Braun pulled into the parking lot of the next dentist's office on the list. Dr. M. Soskin was located an hour from Geneva and had been an orthodontist for more than 30 years.

The detective climbed the stairs of the dental office and entered into a large square waiting room. There were four people waiting for their turn in the reclining chair. He walked up to the receptionist and showed her his badge.

"I'd like to speak to Dr. Soskin, for a moment, please. It's important" he told the girl at the desk.

"I'll see if she's available" the girl said, raising a finger and leaving the desk area.

He waited patiently for a moment and the receptionist returned. "She would like you to come to her office, this way" she motioned and took the detective back through the patient rooms and through to an administrative area. At the very back was an office door, closed with Dr. M. Soskin on the door. The receptionist knocked twice softly and then opened it up. She stood back allowing Detective Braun entrance into the room and left closing the door behind her.

Detective Braun was not expecting the young professional looking woman, sitting behind a large oak desk. She stood and came around the desk, offering her hand.

"Dr. Michaela Soskin" she introduced shaking the detective's hand.

"Detective Braun with the Zurich Police. We are trying to identify someone through a jawbone found in a ravine in the northern part of the country."

He started with. Dr. Soskin tilted her head in question. Before she could ask anything, the detective handed her the bag with the jawbone enclosed. She looked at him, turned and took the bag over to her desk, sitting down and pulling out the box. She lifted the lid and saw the jawbone for the first time.

"I'm a bit confused. I had done a search of dentists who would have been practicing approximately 25 years ago. You came up, but." he laughed, motioning his hand towards her "...obviously, you haven't been doing this for that long. Either that or you've found secret youth serum in dentistry, because" he laughed again, embarrassed at what he was trying to say. Dr. Soskin smiled at him, joining in the laugh.

"Oh! No!" she giggled, "I wasn't, but my father was. Dr. Michael Soskin. He hasn't practiced in a few years now but he was definitely around when this was done. And, I can almost say for certain that this is my father's work" she announced proudly.

Detective Braun shook his head in disbelief. Uncanny how this had all unravelled.

* * *

The Morningstar Foundation offices were located on the 30th floor of a Manhattan high rise. Chase and Dana were seated in the main conference room with six of the Foundations main administrators. These were the people who oversaw all the mechanics of running the Foundation. They were good with numbers, excellent at administrating and accounting, but they weren't the ones to make such an auspicious choice as to choose from 10 of the Foundation's recipients to come and see the final stage concert of Chase Morningstar and his band Supernova.

The idea had been suggested during one of their annual general meetings. They knew that Chase would be finishing his final tour within the year and the last performance was going to be a record breaker. The Foundation proposed that they open up a contest to all Morningstar Foundation recipients to send a video of their musical ability along with a letter as to why they should be one of four chosen to win an exclusive VIP Backstage

Pass, which would include special seating for the performance and meeting Chase and Dana after the show. The Morningstars loved the idea and quickly the marketing team put together an online application form on the Foundation's website. The form had been available for 4 months and in that time, over 8, 000 applicants posted videos along with their letters explaining why they should be chosen.

The selection committee had poured through all of the submissions, some easier to approve than others, until finally they had narrowed it down to the last remaining 10. Dana and Chase were anxious to see what their philanthropic endeavors had created!

The applicant's videos were played and then, if necessary their written letter was read aloud. Some chose to narrate their video with their letter, some chose to allow their talent to shine and some were obviously too shy to face a camera and had a loved one send in their request.

The four they chose were extremely gifted musicians, whose abilities were obviously not just something learned, they were God given.

Each story played out to the group, each story gripping in its own way. When the voice of a step-father to an incredibly gifted German pianist told the story of how she was orphaned at 5 years of age and how the step-father took very seriously his role to raise a child with such a unique gift, Chase felt a tug at his heart. The blonde pianist's back was kept to the camera, but you could see she played with a ferocity and drive that was not something learned. It humbled Chase to realize that their Foundation only provided a schooling for something that was already well in place. These people were truly gifted, it ran in their veins! The step-father spoke so eloquently about his step-daughter and told the audience that meeting Chase Morningstar would be life changing for the incredibly talented pianist. This one had to be a winner, Chase was too intrigued by her story. After viewing all the videos, Chase and Dana made their selections and both were very pleased with their final decisions.

"Thank you so much for your hard work on this project" Dana said to all who were seated around the table. "It's incredible to see what our belief in providing music to all children can help create."

"It'll be nice to meet each of these four and shake their hand" Chase said. "Great job everyone" he encouraged. Little did he know how life changing it would be for him!

* * *

"Come quickly!" Hans called to Poppy when she came through the front door. "I don't believe it!" he called, running out of the office, meeting Poppy halfway up the hall and excitedly grabbing her arm and bringing her into the office and sitting her in front of the computer.

"Look!" he pointed at the screen. Poppy was looking at the inbox of his email account. She shrugged her shoulders.

"What am I looking at, dad?" she laughed, "Did you finally figure out how to remove your preview pane?" she laughed again, then something caught her eye. An email from The Morningstar Foundation.

"You contacted them?" she asked looking up at him from the chair, her heart racing. He smiled wide at her and held his hand up, innocent.

"I only did what any proud father would do for his daughter. I gushed about you" he said, almost gushing at the moment. "You won, Poppy! You won!!!" he shouted, laughing and picking her up and spinning her around. He was so thrilled for her, so happy that it had worked out like this.

"It's so perfect for you to meet him like this" he told her, as he hugged her. She leaned back and looked at him and said, "It's like all the stars aligned. All the *Morningstars*, that is!" and they fell into stitches of laughter.

Poppy had a month before she would meet Chase so she spent time getting to know his story and her story, such that it was. She also listened to his music non-stop. Her classical piano would sit quiet as she listened to, or watched videos of her father, Chase Morningstar.

She wasn't really sure what to think at first. Being trained in the classics, Poppy appreciated orchestral music, concertos to rhythm and blues, or rock and roll. Luckily, Chase Morningstar's career was all over the World Wide Web. Numerous websites were dedicated to his music, his work ethic, his philosophy on life. You name it, someone loved him for it.

At first, it was slightly off putting to Poppy and she worried that Chase would be more performer than parent. After all, Hans had been such a loving, caring doting and adoring father; such a humble man, how would she feel if Chase were an egotistical jerk? In trying to know him better she consumed every piece of information she could on him. She must have watched the video of "Now That You're Here" a dozen times, and when Hans came in and watched over her shoulder, she fought back tears at the end seeing her own baby face cooing and yawing, making Chase smile brilliantly. He was her dad then, you could see it. Chase looked at her as a baby the same way Hans had all her life with him. Such love and such caring.

"This will do you good, you know" he told her after the video ended. "He loved you first" he said choking back tears as he turned and left the office.

Poppy couldn't turn to face him, her tears blurring her vision. It was hard to imagine what had been stolen from her when Luisa kidnapped her. It was hard to think of a better outcome than being Hans Baumgartner beloved step-daughter. She was proud of him and when she took his last name at 12 years of age, he hadn't felt prouder. Her making that decision meant the world to Hans. He was definitely one proud papa!

* * *

"Tanya Nowak" Detective Braun said into the phone. "I have a last known address as well as a family history. She had a small daughter, named Rebeccah" he told the person on the other end. He gave the person Tanya's date of birth and other personal information. "Do a search on both names, will you please? Let me know the minute you come up with anything, will you?" he ended the call with a smile. He was thisclose to closing this case. Thisclose. He could practically smell it!

* * *

Robin's phone rang at 3:35 am, waking him from quite a lovely sleep! Damn it! He'd been having difficulty sleeping lately and this had been the first night in a while that he had managed to nod off and stay asleep longer than just a couple of hours.

He reached for the phone and try to focus in on the caller id. Lucas Hollomby. *Shit! This call he had to answered!*

"Hey!" he said roughly when he answered the call. He cleared his throat a few times and became more awake as he heard the excitement in Lucas's voice.

"We have a name, buddy!" He called into the phone. "Did you hear me, Mr. Investigative Reporter? We have a name. Grab your shit Mr. Hewer, we're going on a trip!" he said, laughing enthusiastically into the phone.

After some discussion and plans on flights, a fully awake Robin ended the call and sat back in his bed. He closed his eyes and rested his head against the head board. They finally had a name! Almost 20 years in the waiting and they finally had a name! Robin would bet his life's savings that it was the woman who ate with Luisa the night of the storm. He needed to call his producers and inform them of the new findings.

After all these years! He thought, as he reached for his phone.

Chapter 11

POPPY'S BLOOM

Lucas and Robin landed in Frankfurt, Germany within 18 hours of hearing Tanya's name. For them, it wasn't the scavenger hunt that Ernst Hermann had to undertake. Instead, Tanya Nowak's name was run through a Government database where it was matched to any other woman using that name, filing income tax and claiming a female child. Tanya Nowak came up as filing income tax for the year of her death. Filed by her husband, Hans Baumgartner and listing a young female child, Rebeccah as her only child and heir. The only problem was that Tanya Nowak's jawbone put her death 3 years prior to the Tanya Baumgartner (nee Nowak), same date of birth, who died in Frankfurt Hospital some years later. There was obviously a discrepancy there and when the phone call came to Lucas, it was only because he'd been the lead investigator in the Luisa Van Zeeban/Poppy Morningstar investigation.

Lucas and Robin could easily make it to Mr. Baumgartner's house within minutes of clearing customs, but they had a scheduled meeting to make first. Country protocol and all. If Poppy was there, they'd be bringing home one hell of a huge surprise for Chase Morningstar. He didn't have a clue this was all going on!

* * *

Poppy landed at JFK and managed to retrieve her luggage fairly easily. There was a limo driver holding a sign with R. Baumgartner on it as she came through customs and she was whisked away to a beautiful hotel with incredible accommodations. Before she exited the limo she was told that she would be picked up for the concert promptly at 7:45 pm. Excellent. So far, so good.

* * *

163

Robin and Lucas were scheduled to meet Detective Braun prior to reaching Mr. Baumgartner's home. Once they were together, the three would discuss what the Detective had found and then carry on to the Baumgartner address and hopefully, a decades old mystery would finally be solved. Although, not many were aware of the mystery about to be solved. Especially not Mr. Chase Morningstar!

* * *

He had seen the video and remembered her step-father's touching narrative. She was an amazing pianist with an awe inspiring story. Having lost both parents before the age of 5 years, Rebeccah Baumgartner had certainly overcome tragedy.

When she stood before them at the end of Chase's final performance, she was all smiles, full of energy and vibrancy. It was not lost on Chase or Dana and each thought that this young woman has something very special.

Dana watched as Chase was mesmerized by the final VIP winner. She introduced herself as "Rebeccah Baumgartner" and then pulled Chase in close and whispered something to him. She couldn't hear what she said, but Dana knew her husband very well after all these years together and knew that whatever she said had caused the color to drain from Chase's face. Her lawyer instincts kicked in and she immediately stepped forward to take charge of the situation. She was about to ask a question of the young woman when she heard Chase say, "Poppy?" He was looking almost dazed at the woman and she knew right away she needed to contain this situation.

"Excuse me" She said apologetically to the young blonde woman. "I didn't quite catch what you were saying to Chase." She ended her sentence on hopes that the woman would fill her in on what had transpired.

"Dana, I'm Poppy. Poppy Morningstar" the blonde said quite confidently. Dana said nothing, but looked at Chase who was studying the woman intently. Dana was just about to call her bluff when Chase threw his arms around the young woman, holding her tight.

"Jesus Christ! It really is you, isn't it?!" he said. "That's why I had the dream this morning! Celia was trying to tell me that you were coming! For once, it wasn't a bad omen!" he exclaimed hugging the young woman tightly. Poppy hugged him back with a wide smile, but when Chase's cologne hit her nostrils she gasped and stood back looking at him, tears in her eyes.

"I know that smell, that cologne, I mean, I've known it forever. My dad wears it, too. It's always been such a comforting smell to me. It's because it's yours!" she said, smiling and crying at the same time.

Dana stood back, watching what was happening. She was cynical enough to question it all, but her husband's reaction spoke volumes. Dana could see that to Chase, this young woman really was Poppy. Dana just needed something more concrete than that, like a frigging DNA test. She watched as the two of them embraced, comparing them with her legal eye.

"I'm sorry. I've missed some of this reunion" Dana interrupted. "Do you mind telling me how you came about realizing you were Poppy Morningstar? Forgive me, but as far as we've been concerned, she's been dead for more than 20 years, I believe" she finished, cutting straight to the point. *Gotta love Dana!*

Poppy smirked, understanding Dana's cynicism. "I completely understand your concern, Mrs. Morningstar. I have brought with me all pertinent documentation as well as a willingness to have my DNA tested, at my own expense. This conclusion does not come lightly, I can assure you. I have plenty of proof and will show you at a moment's notice" Poppy said confidently. Dana scrutinized the young woman with her keen eye, while Chase was nearly completely convinced that the person standing before him was his long thought dead daughter, Poppy Morningstar.

"Let's do what we have to in order to confirm or deny this and move on" Chase said, rather aggressively. He grabbed both ladies by the upper arm and along with security, led both of them to the waiting limo. They should have been attending the after party but instead, Chase redirected the limo to the privacy of a secret entrance at the local hospital. With one phone call to Kyle Craven, all the necessary tests were prepared. Chase would know if this young blonde woman was in fact his Poppy, within two hours. In that time, Chase needed to maintain a general calm and try hard to not get his hopes up that this beautiful, incredibly talented pianist was his daughter.

* * *

Lucas and Robin met up with Detective Braun at a local police station. They introduced themselves, shook hands and immediately began discussing the case before them.

"Luisa posing as Tanya died almost 20 years ago at the Frankfurt Hospital. A Brain tumor. No other mention of her. Rebeccah is only mentioned once, a visit to Emergent Care at age 17, complaining of headaches. The neurologist on call was paged and charted." Detective Braun opened his file and brought out the report from the neurologist.

"According to him" he read from the report in his hand "the step-father was extremely concerned that the child's headaches were related to the late mother's brain tumor. However, the mother and daughter are not genetically linked (no blood relation) therefore, no chance of patient having same tumor as step-parent" he stopped reading and dropped the report on top of the file, smirking.

"So, we have proof that Tanya Nowak was not blood related to Rebeccah. We have a jawbone of Tanya's that proves she died essentially twice, three years apart." Lucas listed off.

Detective Braun continued, "Correct. Also, we ran another missing person's search. Guess whose names have come up as missing for possibly 20 or 25 years?" he pulled out another form from the file in front of him. "Approximately a month ago a guy named Ernst Friedrich Hermann filed a missing person's report in a Zurich police station. The report says he's listed as the father on Rebeccah's birth certificate and that he tracked them down through an old address, but when he got to Germany at their new address, he found completely different people with the same names. It was the fact that both Tanyas had the same previous address that caused Mr.

Hermann to file the report. He didn't think it was a coincidence." The detective told him.

"So Tanya and Rebeccah have only just been listed as missing? No wonder they didn't show up in the list we ran. So, we have all we need to go and see what Mr. Baumgartner has to say for himself!" Robin stated, rubbing his hands together. He was trying hard to control his excitement, but he could only imagine what Chase Morningstar was going to think when they brought his daughter and stood her before him.

They left the police station and drove over to Hans's home. All three men stood on the doorstep, each with their own anxiousness. Once the door opened, it couldn't ever be closed again. The secrets, the sinister manipulation that Luisa Van Zeeban set in motion many years previous, would end.

Detective Braun knocked sharply three times. The men could hear movement from within and suddenly the door was answered by a retired gentleman with a very wide smile.

"Hello! Hello!" he said to them as Detective Braun produced his badge for Hans to see. "Oh! Well you finally came, I was wondering when you'd get involved" he told them as he ushered them inside.

"We're here to talk to you about Tanya Nowak and her daughter Rebeccah and what you may know about their disappearance decades ago" Detective Braun started. "We understand you married Tanya Nowak, is that correct?"

Hans was surprised that they started questioning without even making it fully into his home, but he understood their desire to get to the point. It was a mystery 20 odd years in the making.

"Yes, I married Tanya Nowak" he said pointing to a picture of Tanya. All three men turned in unison to look at the picture. All three nodded their head together knowing they were looking at Luisa Van Zeeban.

"Are you aware of your late wife's real identity?" asked Detective Braun.

"I am now!" Hans said, almost laughing. He had the men sit down and he brought out all the documents that had been found in his attic. Instead of answering questions, he told them the whole story of how he came to realize Luisa's duplicitous life.

"So you know you've been raising Poppy Morningstar. And although she's an adult now, we'd like to talk with her and see if she'd go back to the U.S. with us to meet her real father" said Lucas. He was so frigging excited! He was finally going to lay his eyes on the little girl he was sent to find all those years ago!

Robin was pumped as well. This story just got better and better and with an ending of reuniting the world's biggest musical superstar with his long thought dead daughter and all the twists and turns the story had taken, he knew this would make huge news and at least a 2 hour update report. His producers are going to love it!

Hans's smile broke wide across his face. He shook his head. "I'm sorry gentlemen, but you're probably an hour too late. By my watch, Poppy Morningstar has already re-introduced herself to Chase" he said proudly. Lucas and Robin were stunned.

* * *

Chase was not concerned that he was missing the After Party of his final concert and tour. There would be an even bigger party to celebrate if this incredible young woman who claimed to be his dead daughter Poppy, was telling the truth.

Dana wasn't sure what to think. She had been looking at pictures on her phone of Poppy when she was last photographed before she was thought to have died. There was no denying that the young woman sitting across from them resembled Poppy, even had her same green eyes. Dana could also see some of Chase's first wife, Sonya in the girl, but it proved nothing. Dana wanted facts and Poppy promised she would provide them with all they needed to know, but nothing had been provided. She was however, very willing to do the DNA test and didn't hesitate. Dana wondered if she might be psychotic and suddenly worried that she and Chase were being far too trusting of this person.

In complete contrast, Chase didn't need any testing done for him to remember his Poppy. His eyes couldn't get enough of her and he just sat gazing at her and periodically welling up. She was a perfect cross between him and Sonya with Celia's green eyes thrown in for the dramatic effect they produced! Chase was euphoric, his heart beating rapidly. He couldn't believe it!

The hospital was very close so the drive over only allowed for a few quick questions. Where have you been living? Where's Luisa? Who is Baumgartner? Poppy smiled and told them briefly what they wanted to know.

"I will tell you everything and show you everything when we get to the hospital. I think we'll have some time to wait so I can fill you in then" she assured them. There was one thing Dana observed, whoever she was, she was certainly confident in what she knew, confident in herself and very mature for her age.

The limo pulled up to the hospital doors and the three exited, Chase and Dana holding hands. They walked straight through the hospital doors and were greeted by a doctor and a nurse. Introductions were made and Poppy and Chase were led into separate exam rooms. Chase came out a few moments later while Poppy remained in for a while longer. When she finally exited the exam room, Chase asked her, "Everything okay?"

"Yes. They gave me a complete physical and asked me a number of questions. It's okay, they're only doing their job. I wouldn't believe me straight off either and I'd be doing exactly the same thing" she said, wisely. Poppy turned and found a quiet room, walked over and looked in. It was empty. She motioned to Chase and Dana to follow her and she disappeared behind the door. They followed. The room was a small sitting area with two couches, a coffee table and a comfy chair. Poppy took the chair and pulled the coffee table around so she could lay out her papers, just as Hans had showed her. She placed each document with purpose and kept Chase and Dana in suspense as to what it all was.

"You're probably wondering what I'm doing this for. My father, in Germany" she explained "wanted you to see the timeline and path he followed to figure out who I really was. You must understand, for nearly 20 years he had no clue that I wasn't Rebeccah Nowak. No clue. Luisa had all the appropriate papers on us and we were fairly isolated for many years."

"Luisa mastermind the whole thing?" Chase asked, stunned at how much she had manipulated so many lives.

"From what my dad can figure, she acquired the property from the real Tanya Nowak who had a daughter named Rebeccah. We haven't been able to locate her, actually I'm not sure if my dad has tried or not. He got so excited when he figured it out, you would not believe it!" she said proudly. Chase couldn't help but smile, she even got to Dana with her enthusiasm. It wasn't lost on either of them that she kept referring to "Hans" as her "dad/father". Dana wondered if it was bothering Chase. It didn't seem to, he just continued to have that wide million watt smile, beaming away.

"Could it be that the real Tanya and her daughter were the ones in the Range Rover?" Chase asked. Poppy nodded her head in agreement. "Maybe. The father of Rebeccah came to our home several weeks ago and expected to find them, but when he saw our pictures and showed my dad his, the people weren't the same. That was when my dad started getting very suspicious. He searched the house and found these documents hidden in a shoe box" she told them as she handed the marriage license, Luisa's birth certificate and the Foundation brochure.

Both Chase and Dana were amazed. This certainly was intriguing. Who else would be able to obtain these documents if not from the actual source, Luisa? Dana was becoming more and more convinced herself. When they opened up the brochure they both caught their breath. *"she was always THISCLOSE"*. It caused a shiver to run through both of them.

"Are you serious?" Chase said softly. He held the brochure wide open and just kept staring at the writing. His tears began flowing freely and they fell onto the brochure, wetting it with each large tear. Dana put her arms around Chase and said something softly to him and he dropped his head, his shoulders heaving.

Poppy too, welled up. She knew it was going to be an emotional ride for Chase, just as it was for her when Hans told her all he had found out. It was as if being stripped down to your very foundation and being rebuilt. Everything you had known about yourself was a lie, everything you are is unbelievable!

"I'm sorry...dad" Poppy said to Chase, sadly. It made him stop for a moment and look up at her.

"Oh sweetheart, please don't apologize to me. Most of these are tears of joy, only some are for what I've missed out on. Your childhood was stolen from me and when I think that she planned all of this, how evil she was, signing you up for lessons through the foundation! She was right, you were *this close*, right under our noses all along!" he stated, shaking his head and wiping his tears. Dana handed him a tissue.

"Well, it's a good thing she's dead then isn't it?" Dana said, matter-of-factly. They all nodded.

"When did she die?" Chase asked.

"A week after she married my dad" Poppy told them. "She'd been suffering bad headaches, but she wouldn't got to see a doctor. Dad now figures it was because she was afraid of being discovered." Poppy explained. "I would think that she based every decision on whether or not it would hinder or help in keeping us hidden."

"Well, it's not like you were being looked for. Every indication led us to believe that you were both in that vehicle when it slid over the edge." Chase said, understanding how easy it was for Luisa to stay hidden with everyone believing they were dead.

"She also disguised us, colored our hair, mine was red!" Poppy exclaimed making a face. "I love red, but I like being a blonde. I like looking like you and Sonya, my mom" she said rather demurely.

Chase cleared his throat. He wanted to know more about the man who raised her. "So…this Hans Baumgartner, he's a good man?" asking like only a concerned father would. It made both Dana and Poppy smile.

"Yes. Hans is a very lovely father. He really loved Ta…er, Luisa. Really loved her. I feel for him because he only had a week of marriage and then a lifetime of being a widower." She said, sadly. It was obvious to Chase and Dana that Poppy loved her dad very much and determined he must be a genuinely great dad. Chase would take Poppy's word for it.

"Yes, well he also had you as his child for your lifetime. I'm very envious!" Chase said honestly.

"We have a lot of time to make up for! And, I want to know everything. I mean, I've seen you in video and on the internet, but that isn't anything like the real deal" Poppy smiled hugely and Chase matched it with his own.

"Oh dear God!" Dana said, good naturedly. "Could you two smile any wider? You're both like a set of teeth with a face wrapped around it!" They all burst out laughing, Chase and Poppy sounding very much alike. They both stopped, looked at each for a moment catching the likeness and then laughed again.

There was a soft knock on the door and the three went quiet. "Come in", Chase answered and the doctor who had greeted them when they first arrived, entered into the room and closed the door. He was carrying two pieces of paper.

"Sorry to have kept you all waiting for so long", he started, taking his glasses out of his white lab coat pocket. "Now let's see what we have here" he said as he looked down through his reading glasses and went quiet reading whatever it was that was written on the reports.

"Uh, well essentially, I could give you the long version, very medical with long terms, or…" he paused, and then smiled "I could congratulate you on your new bouncing adult daughter." He announced.

Chase, Dana and Poppy all stood up at the same time and hugged together. Like a mother and father welcoming home their child from a long trip, Dana was on one side of Poppy while Chase was on the other cradling her head and kissing it repeatedly. All three were crying, kissing and holding for a while. The doctor looked on and then said, "Okay, well I'm going to let you get on with this reunion. I'll leave these in an envelope at the reception's desk. If you need anything further, my card is with the reports. Congratulations to you all" he said as he smiled at the three and left the room.

As the door closed, Chase picked Poppy up and swung her around, "Whoooweeee!!!!" Chase cried out. "Forget the tour *this* is what we're going to celebrate tonight. C'mon my ladies, one on each arm, if you please." Chase stated as he offered an elbow to each woman and walked them to the limo. Chase couldn't wait to tell the world of Poppy's return and show them what beautiful bloom of a flower she was!

Chapter 12

MORNINGSTAR REUNION

The reunion of Chase and Poppy Morningstar made headlines for weeks. Lucas and Robin returned to the U.S. and immediately informed Chase of their findings. Between what they told him and Poppy's account, everything finally made sense. Chase believed he got the most complete picture of what happened as he could have. Wanting others to know it as well, Robin Hewer was given exclusive access to the story and the Morningstars, and in true form created a fantastic investigative report on the entire story from 25 years previous, up to present day.

Robin was soon dubbed the "Third Morningstar Brother" because his reporting had been so focused for so long. Chase and Charlie thought it was hilarious and sent him a gold Rolex with that engraved on the back. It was one of his most prized possessions.

The first thing Chase did as her dad was to get Poppy's German dad on videophone. He wanted to look into the face of the man that gave him his daughter back. He wanted to let Hans know how much he appreciated everything he had done. Through conversations with Poppy over the course of several days after the reunion, Chase learned how Hans had raised Poppy with unconditional love and support, how he was her #1 fan when it came to her musical talent, and how, when he'd begun to realize that Poppy's background may not be what he'd been told, he got his facts together and then gave all the information to Poppy. He also entered Poppy into the contest to meet Chase at his final concert AND he bought her an Exclusive Pass so that one way or another, she was going to meet her real father. *Now, that's a great dad!* Thought Chase.

The conversation between them was full of equal parts laughing and tears. When the call connected, Hans was suddenly looking at the beaming face of his lovely daughter and her real father. Side by side, he could see the resemblance, no mistaking it.

"Hi Dad? I want you to say hi to…my dad!" Poppy said excitedly to Hans, giggling. Hans was waving and smiling wide, as wide as the two faces he was looking at.

"Hello! Hello! And surprise, Mr. Morningstar!" Hans said, nodding his head and trying hard not to tear up. "I had no idea of her real background, but now so many things make sense. Her musical talent, just to name one!" Hans admitted. Nodding his head emphatically.

"Hello Mr. Baumgartner, I can't thank you enough for being such an outstanding father to Poppy." Chase told Hans.

"Oh, please, please call me Hans" He insisted. Chase smiled and nodded, "and you can call me Chase" he offered.

"You know, I must admit I'm probably the only person in the world who didn't know everything about you. I …I'm more of a classical music man." He tried to explain. When he realized how much news Poppy's death had been back then, he felt embarrassed that he hadn't known, perhaps recognized Poppy. "Luisa had done a good job of hiding the child and changing her looks for a few years. When I met her, Reb..er, Poppy was a red head." Hans told them. Once Hans had shown Poppy what he had found out about her identity and she was accepting of it, he began to call her "Poppy". She wasn't sure she liked it at first, but came to realize that she couldn't hide who she was, nor did she want to.

"I can only imagine how confusing it must have been for you when it all started to unfold!" Chase said to him. "Luisa fooled us all and ruined a lot of people's lives. Including the mother and daughter in the car, three people lost their lives because of her." Chase said. Sonya being one of them, must be up in heaven somewhere, smiling watching this reunion.

175

"It's hard to say whether she was really that sinister or if the brain tumor had something to do with her decisions and manipulations." Hans said in reflection, which made all three of them take pause.

"So, what's next?" Hans asked excitedly, breaking the uncomfortable silence.

"I'm going to stay with my dad and Dana for a while, spend some time getting to know them. I can take time from school, not worried about that." She explained while Hans nodded along.

"Excellent, excellent. Enjoy yourselves! She is such a blessing, Chase. Thank you for the honor of being her dad." He said, respectfully. Chase felt a tug. This guy was the perfect type of person you'd want your daughter to be raised by.

"Hans, if you would like to come over and join us, I'd be hap.." But he was interrupted by Hans.

"No, no. Chase, I'm sorry, I appreciate your offer but I've been more than blessed with the time I've spent with Poppy. This is *your* time. It would be wrong of me to impose on that. I love Poppy very much, enough to know she needs to know you without my interference." He stated honestly.

Chase let out a heavy sigh and couldn't stop the tear in his eye. "You have my undying respect, Mr. Hans Baumgartner" he told Hans and put his hand to his heart while the tear slid down his face. Poppy looked at Chase and did a typical daughter thing. She threw her arm around Chase's shoulder and said, "Awww. Don't cry, dad." And she kissed his cheek which made Chase cry and laugh at the same time. God, he didn't realize how incomplete he had felt for all these years. With Poppy's return, Chase's heart felt whole, his soul felt mended and the light in his life just got brighter.

The three said their goodbyes to one another and vowed to speak again in the next few days. When Hans got off the videophone, he felt a little emptiness, a little less complete and even though he knew she was still his little girl, the light in his life got a little less bright.

Their first days together were consumed with piecing together the whole story. After that, it was learning to understand who the other was. Dana gave them as much space as she thought they needed. There were times when the three of them would spend time together and the dynamic was great.

Poppy was a very mature, independent young woman with a great sense of humor and humility. She had a fun streak and would break into the best giggling fit when something struck her funny. Chase was completely enamored with her. She was sometimes so like Sonya it would take his breath away, but her eyes were all Celia.

Charlie and Georgie flew in from Chicago and they had a wonderful few days together before Chase and Dana hosted quite the celebration in their large New York apartment. The only one missing would be Campbell. He had died six years previous; heart failure. Chase thought it was fitting that Poppy's instrument of choice was a piano. Very Campbell.

Poppy's reintroduction into the Morningstar family and friends also coincided with her 21st birthday. Chase and Dana decided to make it a very respectful event. Chase and Dana passed every decision by Poppy first. A big feast, a few speeches and toasts; a very nice affair.

For her birthday, they surprised Poppy with a black baby grand piano. It was agreed that she could keep it at their home until she had a place of her own in the U.S., which, she had decided was going to be necessary in the very near future. To everyone's surprise, Poppy played a concerto by Bach on her new baby grand. Chase was practically giggling, he was beaming so proudly. Charlie stood beside him and kept poking him with his elbow and then smiling wide, both men recognizing the musically gifted Morningstar gene. When she finished, the party erupted in applause. Charlie grabbed Chase in a huge bear hug and said into his ear, "I'm so happy for you, brother. She's absolutely perfect!" When the brothers pulled away, both were crying.

The Morningstars were, once again complete.

Later that night, Charlie and Georgie pulled Poppy aside and asked for her to follow them. They sat at the kitchen table as Charlie made a pot of coffee. He began talking to Poppy about how thrilled he and Georgie were that she had been alive all along and well taken care of. When the coffee was ready he and Georgie poured a cup and sat down with Poppy.

Charlie reached inside a large brown paper bag, sitting somewhere near Georgie's feet and handed Poppy a large wrapped present. She stared wide eyed at him and gently accepted the gift. She tore the paper off wondering what on earth it could be. Charlie's smile widened as he found himself feeling emotional. He cleared his throat before he spoke.

"You feel up to looking at pictures?" he asked her gently. Georgie, the keeper of all the photos and stories throughout the years, had created a scrapbook full of Morningstar memorabilia for Poppy.

"Yes" she answered her uncle, excitedly nodding her affirmation and with that, Charlie opened the book.

"The Morningstar story begins with this man, George Morningstar, a man before his time, if you ask me", he pointed to a black and white photo of a curly, dark haired man, sitting at a piano with a beautiful young toddler sitting beside him.

"His father and many in his family were lawyers, and he was expected to follow along. Go to law school and then join the Morningstar firm, but he found his calling in music, first the piano, but he was also a fantastic guitar player. Very talented man." Charlie turned the page and revealed more pictures of George. He pointed proudly to a picture of George and Meg taken during a Christmas dinner. They were holding hands and smiling wide at a table of some 20 people. Poppy couldn't help but notice that George was the only white person seated at the table.

"George met Meg when he took piano lessons from her mother. Together they created Celia" as Charlie explained this, he pointed to pictures of Meg and Celia respectively, in the book. He paused, allowing Poppy the time to connect the dots and put it all together. Charlie watched her reactions closely.

"On my seventh birthday, George, my grandfather gave me my first guitar. He promised to teach me how to play it, but within an hour he suffered a stroke. His speech was heavily effected, he had some paralysis, and was in a bad way. He was sent home and my mother and I looked after him. That didn't stop him, though. He was determined to teach me how to play the guitar and although he couldn't speak, he showed me how to place my fingers on the chords. We did this every day after school forever." He said, stopping himself. He fondly remembered the afternoons he and Papa George spent perfecting his finger placement on the neck of the guitar, the proper tone of it, and the most effective way to shift from one chord to another. Papa George was truly gifted, and despite his stroke, he was able to pass along his knowledge to grandson. Charlie enthusiastically pointed to a picture of Celia in full performance on stage. Her sequined dress and head band shining from the flash of the photographer's bulb.

"This beautiful lady was our mother, your grandmother!" he told her. "Her name was Celia Morningstar, and she was an incredible blues singer." He waited for Poppy to take a good look at the photo. A perfect picture of Celia, singing and smiling wide on stage with her mane of hair cascading around her in a firework of tight curls. She looked fabulous.

"Celia" Poppy said softly, a smile gracing her lips, her eyes wide.

"Yes. Celia." Charlie answered her, nodding his head. He allowed some time to pass before he turned the page. The new pages held pictures of Celia with her sons through various life stages.

"This is me with my mom. I think I was about 10 years old. These other pictures are from celebrations with Papa George and my mother. Two generations before you" he explained as he let her study the pictures. She looked at them for what seemed a long while. The pages were filled with Poppy's heritage and she was fascinated with all of it. After looking through a few more pages, she quickly jumped up and hugged both Charlie and Georgie.

"Thank you so much for this gift! You have no idea how much it means to me. I felt like I had lost the chance to ever know the family very well, with all the years I've been gone, but you've given it back to me!" She cried and hugged Georgie tightly.

"I will always treasure it" she told them. They were standing holding hands, tears streaming down their faces when Chase walked into the kitchen area. He stopped dead in his tracks, looking at the three of them in wonderment.

The look on his face made all three burst into laughter, causing Chase to smile, not knowing what he had missed out on. Georgie reached her hand out to Chase and he took it.

"Wanna join in a little family bonding?" Georgie asked, as she drew his attention to the scrapbook. Chase's eyes fell onto a picture of Celia he hadn't seen. Suddenly, Chase was transported back in time. It was hard to believe so many years had passed, so many lives were now gone and yet, The Morningstars prevailed. They were definitely a family of music, regardless of their surroundings. It made Poppy very aware of the talents that had come before her and gave her a feeling of obligation to carry the name and the music forward, for years to come.

Chapter 13

LADY SINGS THE BLUES...FINALLY!

"What's this song?" Poppy asked, suddenly breaking Chase's concentration for his next domino move. He lifted his head to tune into the music playing. They had been going through Chase's music library and playing games on a rainy Sunday afternoon.

"This is a fabulous blues and jazz singer named, Billie Holiday. She's been dead for many years now but, in her time, she was on fire. A great songwriter, too! Very talented lady." He told her, matter-of-factly.

"Billie Holiday" Poppy whispered softly, listening to Billie's voice, her smooth tones and incredible voice as it serenaded throughout the room. The singing style intrigued her, and she asked Chase to turn the volume up. Chase did as she asked and Poppy sat back in her chair and closed her eyes, trying to visualize the woman singing; dark hair and eyes, large smile and suddenly she had a picture of Celia on stage, the one Charlie had shown her in her scrapbook. Her vision then morphed into a different version of herself, with dark hair, dramatic makeup, singing in a club, at a piano. Even though she didn't know the words to the song playing, it seemed as if she was singing it word for word. A shiver ran through her and her eyes flew open; staring at Chase in shock.

Chase wasn't sure what had just happened, but he could tell by the look on her face that she had just seen something that surprised her. "What it is, honey? Are you okay?" he asked, full of concern.

"Yes, yes" she insisted. "I'm not sure what I just saw, whether it was just an imagination or a premonition, but it was so real, so life like. I got a shiver" she told him. Chase sat staring at her for a moment, wondering if he should tell her about the *other* Morningstars' interesting experiences with strange encounters. Premonitions, spiritual guides, reoccurring dreams; all of them had happened at one time or another.

Poppy was still struggling, but according to her *vision*, she knew this song and how to play it on the piano. It confused her and she pondered what she had just seen. *What did it mean?* She wondered. *How did she know these things? This music? This song?* Her mind was trying desperately to recall if she had ever heard the song, or the singer before, but she already knew the answer; a resounding NO! Let's not even mention the singing! Poppy had never thought of singing, it wasn't something she did. Her hands were her gift, not her voice. And yet, in the dream, she sang beautifully. Poppy's focused returned to the game with Chase. He looked at her intently and she felt like he understood her confusion, like he knew for certain of what she was talking about. A vision so real, it could alarm someone. Chase knew all about that.

Poppy had spent years in her childhood having dreams and visions she couldn't explain, until now. It had dawned on her that many of the things that had started happening to her had been seen in limited time, in her dreams.

Looking at Chase's face, she could tell he knew her feelings. Being a Morningstar was turning out to be very interesting indeed!

* * *

Later that night, Poppy lay awake in her bedroom, her mind on her future. Classical music had been her passion from the start, but now she was hearing music that stirred her in a way that classical music never had. In a way, it had been exhilarating for her to experience that feeling. Like hearing music for the first time all over again. She was excited thinking about how she could incorporate her musical knowledge in today's musical industry and have an edge. Her father had an edge. Uncle Charlie had an edge. She needed to find an edge. She needed to rethink her musical ideas and make her own way. She didn't want to do what they had done, she wanted her own sound. But what? She got up and headed towards the kitchen for a glass of water. On her way, she passed the black, baby grand piano positioned next to the large span of windows, exposing the New York City skyline at night. She hadn't grown up around this kind of opulence, not at all. She and Hans lived simply; with fine things, but less social exposure and glamour, that was for sure!

The piano drew her nearer, and she stood before it, closing her housecoat around her, sitting gently on the bench, touching her hands on the keyboard cover. She ran her hands across it, feeling the smooth dark, wood. Oh, how she had loved the feeling. It was one of the things she had loved to do before a performance. She loved to stroke the keyboard cover, then raise it, as if she let the piano know that she owned the keys.

Chase had left his tablet on the top of the piano, with headphones attached, his latest work on hold. Poppy put the headphones on her ears and scrolled through Chase's playlist of music. She chose an old bluesy song she had heard Chase play on Sunday mornings. One, he told her, that reminded him of her grandmother, Celia. As the singer began, acapella, Poppy got shivers. The sound of her voice so pure and deep, without the use of any instrument at all. Deep in her throat, Poppy hummed along. Her hands began to play across the keys as she felt wave after wave hit her. It was slow and rhythmic, caressing her in such a way that she felt lulled along by its movement. She sang along to words she didn't fully know, humming when she had to, and singing out loud when she knew the song, instinctively. When it ended, the player continued into a song Chase had played for her. She allowed herself to completely let the song take her and all her inhibitions were let loose. This music really had a pull over her and she loved it! Just as the song was coming to an end, lights were thrown on, and she blinked into them as Chase and Dana, standing in front of her in complete shock, came into focus.

* * *

They had been in bed for quite some time, when Chase was awakened by the sound of someone's voice, humming low and then breaking out in song, loud and proud, every few moments. He lay there listening for a moment, wondering if he was dreaming, or not. When he heard the singer build to a perfect crescendo, he bolted upright in bed and reached for Dana. She woke up startled, looking to Chase for answers, and with him motioning to be quiet, she listened for whatever it was had roused him from sleep. At first, she wasn't sure what she was listening for, and then she heard it, the quiet playing of the piano as a voice sang along. The voice, in contrast to the piano, was strong. At first, Dana wasn't sure what she was hearing, but it slowly dawned on her and she mouthed to Chase, "Poppy?" as he nodded in affirmation. They both listened for a moment enjoying the raw and quiet performance, before Chase suddenly bolted from the bed and left the room, with Dana following him.

When they entered the living room, the body at the piano bench was backlit with the lights of the New York City skyline. They could only make out the blonde of her hair, as the rest of her was dressed in a dark cotton housecoat. Chase could see she was wearing headphones and figured she had tapped into his music left on the piano after his last working session.

* * *

Poppy was belting out Aretha Franklin's, "Natural Woman" and giving it all she was worth. She didn't know the words exactly, but what she did feel confident on, she sang along to beautifully. Chase and Dana were shocked. When the song was over, Poppy took a breath, and taking a moment to look around, saw Chase and Dana standing in front of her, their mouths wide open. She froze and stopped playing immediately. Lost in the music, she wasn't aware of her audience and knowing they had been watching made her suddenly self-conscious. Chase said nothing, understanding her shyness. It was new for her and instinct took over for both of them. He walked over to her, stroked her hair and bent to kiss her on the head. With a lump in his throat, he turned and walked back towards the bedroom, passing Dana, grabbing her arm gently and bringing her with him. "She's finding herself." Chase whispered to her. "She's finding her true Morningstar soul."

* * *

Kirby Corley had just moved into Chase and Dana's building when she ran into Poppy on the elevator. She couldn't believe her eyes and tried hard not to geek out. She was also a classically trained pianist and had just started a short gig with the New York Orchestra. When she had learned that Chase Morningstar had a daughter who was also a classically trained pianist, she was blown away! Of course, the whole story of Poppy's childhood had been told and Kirby was fascinated by it. Now, she was standing next to her on the elevator in her building and could not believe her eyes! Thank God her aunt had offered her a place to stay while she was in town. Kirby would have never been able to afford such a place. *This is what money does,* thought Kirby. *It puts you in the same circles as people like the Morningstars.* After staring at her for the first few floors, Kirby decided to be bold.

"Hey! I hope I'm not bothering you but, I followed your story and I'm a huge Morningstar fan. And", she went on to explain, "I, too am a classical pianist"

"You are?" Poppy said in astonishment. The girl presented her hand and Poppy shook it, smiling. "I'm Kirby Corley" she said proudly.

"Poppy Morningstar", Poppy replied. Kirby smiled and nodded her head. "How long have you played for" she asked Kirby, who tried desperately to calm herself. *I'm actually talking classical piano with Poppy Morningstar!* Her mind screamed. Kirby managed to sum up her life story in three sentences.

"I began playing when I was five. My grandmother is the organist at her church. She taught me to play." Kirby told Poppy simply. The two women stared at one another for a moment and then Poppy burst out laughing. "And then what? You play with the New York Orchestra? Talk about leaving out a few details" she giggled out. Kirby was very surprised at first, but she slowly began to see the humor in it and joined Poppy in a bad case of the giggles.

"That's like me saying: kidnapped by the nanny. She got me lessons through a foundation. Now, I'm a Morningstar!" Poppy said, nearly collapsing in giggles. Kirby was also enjoying the laugh and the two of them exited the elevator in a burst of hilarity.

They stopped in the front foyer of the building, smiling at one another. It was the first time since moving to New York that Poppy felt a friendship to anyone, outside of her family.

"Why haven't we met before now?" Poppy asked.

"Probably because I've only just started staying here" Kirby answered. Another fit of laughter ensued.

"Wanna hang out?" She asked her. "I've been here for a while and I could do with a friend" Poppy said, honestly. Something about Poppy reminded her of her sister, Jessica. Kirby's heart ached a little, something that she hadn't allowed to happen in many years. She gave it some thought for just a moment and then did something very unlike her.

"Yes…you know what? I do!" she said, excitedly, mentally changing plans in her head. She would have every day to herself until the 6:30 pm pit call, for performance at 8:00 pm. She did have matinee shows on Saturday and Sunday, but for the most part, she was free through the weekday for the next 6 months, at the least. Past that, she hadn't made plans. That was how Kirby liked it. She was a "fly by the seat of her pants" kind of woman and it had allowed her many experiences. Some she would talk about with great flourish, but whenever Poppy asked about her family or childhood, Kirby would give a very vague answer and then abruptly change the subject, or create a convenient distraction.

They spent a lot of time comparing notes on their classical training and being each other's confidant for all things musical, makeup and men! Poppy attended many of Kirby's performance's with the orchestra, supporting her friend and enjoying being on the other side of the stage and piano, for a change. She could see that her new friend had natural talent and was excellent in her skill, but something was missing for Kirby, as far as Poppy was concerned. It wasn't criticism, it was an observation. It may have taken her all over the world, but her profession wasn't feeding Kirby's soul and Poppy knew it. Over a deli breakfast one morning, Poppy raised the point.

"What makes you happy, Kirby?" she asked her, directly. Kirby took a deep breath, sat back in her chair and sighed heavily before answering. Although, not a sunny morning, Kirby wore sunglasses and seemed hungover. A slight smile crossed her mouth as she answered, "Bobby's hug, Bobby's food and Bobby's church". Poppy was taken aback. She had never heard of "Bobby" and she wondered why Kirby had kept him from her. Seeing the confused look on her girlfriend's face, she couldn't help but burst out laughing. She removed her sunglasses, rubbed her face with her hands and sighed.

"Oh Poppy, I wish you could see your face! Hilarious" she said, not containing her amusement at all. Poppy looked even more confused and raised one eyebrow at her and waited for an explanation. Kirby took a very deep breath, not really wanting to have this conversation, however she knew Poppy was owed an explanation. "Bobby" …she paused, dramatically "is my grandmother, my mother's mother. " She then said proudly. "Her name is Roberta Shepherd, but all her friends call her Bobby". She told Poppy. "She's my hero."

As Kirby spoke about her grandmother, her emotions changed. "She makes the most amazing meals, gives the most amazing hugs and her church has been instrumental in my being able to … be here, frankly." Kirby looked at Poppy. It made Poppy's heart sink. She had never seen Kirby so vulnerable and frankly, so close to tears. Kirby replaced her sunglasses offering her friend nothing else. She kept her head down and continued eating her breakfast in complete silence. She let it go for now, but Poppy was determined to get to Kirby's story and try and help her friend with the obvious pain she was carrying.

Chapter 14

ROAD TRIP

After months of staying with Chase and Dana, exploring her new desires musically and getting to know New York better, Poppy began to feel restless. Poppy had spent hours going over the family pictures in the scrapbook in her own time and, after seeing some of the pictures from the touring her father and uncle had done, Poppy came up with an adventurous idea.

"I want to do some travelling. I want to visit clubs, see some bands. I've only really experienced music through the classical world. Some of the music I've heard in the last while, it...it moves me. It makes me feel...sexy." She told Kirby. "I want to explore it." Kirby smiled wide, then nodded her head. Her gig with the New York Orchestra had come to an end and she was days from taking her next job and moving on. Poppy's timing couldn't have been more perfect. Kirby was dreaming of some kind of distraction. When Poppy came to her with this idea, Kirby could only smile.

"I have two words for you, Miss Morningstar." Kirby said, her eyes sparkling. Waiting a moment, keeping Poppy in complete suspense, she sat back throwing both arms in the air, she called out, "ROAD TRIP!"

* * *

"A road trip!" Charlie Morninsgtar laughed. His weekly video chat with his brother, Chase gave him his best smile of the week.

"She'll learn so much on the road, Chase!" he said, excitedly. "Think of what those years on the road did for us!" He said, enthusiastically. Chase had already been laughing at Charlie's exuberance for Poppy's new journey. Charlie made a great point and Chase stopped for moment to take in Charlie's words. Neither said a word, focusing on the moment, when suddenly Charlie spoke up.

"I've just had a great idea!" he told Chase. "I gotta go, but I'll call in a couple of days. Please do me a favor and don't let Poppy go until I speak with her again. Just a couple of days, okay?" Charlie asked, urging Chase.

"Ya, okay. Sure" Chase said, not knowing how on earth he'd hold her back if she wanted to leave straight away. But, he also couldn't say no to Charlie either. *Holy shit, what a bind!* Chase thought.

To his utter delight, Poppy needed to get organized for a few days before her road trip began. He didn't need to try and stall her in any way and on the morning she was ready to leave, Charlie had texted the night before that he would call her at 9:00 am sharp, the next morning.

True to his word, Charlie was calling in on the mega TV in the living room at 9:00 am. Knowing he was calling for Poppy, Chase made sure she was front and center to the TV so Charlie could see her. She waved at him as he and Georgie came on the screen.

"Good morning!" she called to them, smiling wide.

"Good morning, Poppy, Chase and Dana" both Georgie and Charlie answered to their audience. Smiles all around, especially Charlie.

"So, Poppy" Charlie began, "When your dad told me about your desire to travel the blues and jazz clubs of the states, I couldn't help but feel that it's something in our family to go back to our roots to find ourselves again. In saying that, there is something that was done for me to help me feel at home, while I was away and I want to do the same for you" he finished, smiling. "Now, not knowing what kind of driving licence you had, I decided to go smaller in design, but I think it'll serve its purpose well." He told them mysteriously.

It took Chase a minute to figure out what Charlie was talking about and even then, he was 100% sure. *No! Really? He didn't, did he?* Chase wondered, but just as he was pondering the very thought, the TV picture changed to the view of the inside of a Volkswagen camper bus. Not a bus like Charlie toured in, but something the girls could be very comfortable in and sleep in, if need be. Charlie continued to explain that it was outfitted with all the high end features, was well stocked with dry goods, dishes and the like and the fridge had been filled with water, fruit and a few ready made things. He and Georgie had really made sure the girls had all they'd need. After all, who knew better how to take a road trip than Charlie Morningstar?

* * *

When they reached the vehicle, Kirby raised a remote in the air. "Thanks to this little device, we have access to over three million songs. Any genre, any era, any decade for the past 100 or so years. While we're on the road, you play DJ. If you want to hear it, it plays, if not, we move on to the next song. You got it?" She instructed Poppy, as she tossed the remote over the roof to Poppy.

"I got it" Poppy answered, smiling wide.

Together they had mapped out a trip that would take them to 43 of the 50 contiguous states. Poppy wanted to experience a tour of the states and a club atmosphere, much like what George, Celia and Chasing Charlie had performed in many years ago. Kirby wasn't sure she could find exactly what Poppy was looking for, times had changed and clubs like Black and Blue weren't on every street corner. It had taken some research, but Kirby and Chase had come up with several clubs that were as authentic a blues club as Chase could find. After that, Poppy and Kirby were on their own.

Kirby also had a desire to show Poppy other types and genres of music. This girl was very talented and Kirby wanted to open her up to all sorts of musical influences and see what she was moved by. If there was ever going to be a chance to write on a clean slate, now was the time. And so, chalk in hand, Kirby began exposing Poppy to every kind of music there was, sometimes making her dance and sway. Sometimes moving her to tears and sometimes making her see God!

* * *

After many hours of driving, their first stop was in South Carolina. Kirby had driven them to a club called, "The Shades." The act that evening was on within the hour and Kirby needed to eat and some time out of the car, so a cushy bench seat in a booth in the quiet club was welcomed.

During their meal, the place filled in with hungry patrons, looking forward to their meal, and the evening's entertainment. Stage hands began setting up for the band that night, putting together the drum kit, the amps and a keyboard. It took very little time for them to get set up and they began doing a sound check with the equipment. Poppy watched as the stage took shape, the instruments all primed and ready to go.

Her experiences with music had been so completely different. Orchestra's practicing, violins, cellos, every kind of instrument you could imagine warming up and priming. For years, she had been moved by these incredible sounds, but now she found them lacking. She wanted something that stirred her as a woman, and an orchestra of instruments just wasn't cutting it.

After their meal, they ordered a drink, enjoying the intimate club and its welcoming atmosphere. The band took the stage, the front man introducing them as "Wave Lengths". He was a handsome blonde man, tall with wide shoulders, and an easy smile. Immediately, Poppy was intrigued. The band began their first set and throughout, Poppy barely touched her drink. She stayed in the bench seat, but barely. Throughout the bands performance, she swayed and rocked to the music, clapping enthusiastically, calling out as an eager audience participant.

When the band took their first break, Poppy turned to Kirby gushing.

"They're good, aren't they? I'm enjoying this!" She said, smiling wide. She grabbed her drink and finished it all in one go. Kirby was shocked; Poppy was rarely this animated and Kirby was enjoying watching her friend let loose.

Someone had come to the stage and was tapping into it.

"Uh, Hi there. Out there…uh.. Hi." The announcer looked uncomfortably around the room, near to full of happy, drinking patrons and squinted into the stage lights.

"We kinda do a thing here when the stage goes dead between sets, where we offer up the mike to anyone who wants to give it a try. So, if anyone out there wants to entertain us while "Wave Length" is quenching their thirst, please be our guest." The announcer finished by clapping his hands into the microphone and the patrons began whistling and clapping as well. Poppy watched the room carefully and turned to look at Kirby. Kirby raised an eyebrow at her and asked, "Well, you want to get up there? Now's your chance. I've been watching, you just gulped down your first drink in one go! I see how you're itching to get up there. I see how you've barely sat down during the first set." She pointed out.

Poppy couldn't deny her desire to go up on that stage and try entertaining this room with some of the music she had been listening to, not with a concerto. Her mind raced, debating back and forth whether she should stay or go. Kirby only egged her on.

"Isn't this why we're on this road trip?" she asked her, pointing towards the stage. "Isn't this what you're trying to experience?" and with that, Poppy was up off the bench seat and heading towards the stage. She hesitated only briefly before taking the stairs and standing in front of the mike. She smiled shyly and waved to the crowd who whistled and clapped back.

"Uh…Hi." She said, unable to think of more to say. She turned from the microphone and went to stand at the keyboard, positioning its mike in front of her. She took deep, audible breath and began to play. The notes she hit began to wash over her, as if riding along them, they carried her and moved her through the song. It was a new way of approaching music to her and yet, she felt so comfortable playing this way. When she leaned in and began singing, her voice was deep and rich, quite the surprise coming from the petite blonde with green eyes.

The room fell silent as she sang a bluesy love song, popular from a few years back by an artist named, "Daya". She sang and played the hell out of the song, holding the audience completely captive. She sang it with a sexy, raspy tone and her mouth moved sensuously across the microphone, her eyes closed as she sang.

They weren't expecting her talent, they weren't aware of her lineage and they didn't know her name. To them, she was the dead air entertainment before the band's next set, but damn, she was good! She was very good! When she finished the song, the audience erupted, clapping and praising her loudly. They began to shout out for another song, yelling, almost insisting for her to stay on stage. She looked to see Kirby's expression, but the lights blurred her from sight. She looked to the crowd and felt their encouragement. Turning back to the keyboard, she looked down at the keys and placed her hands over them lightly. A calm came over her as she began to sing, her fingers softly caressing the keys. The audience held their breath, her voice a deep resonation moving through the crowd. It not only enticed their hearing, it assuaged the soul. It cut through, to your very core. She sang another popular song, one that spoke of star crossed lovers and their undying love for one another. She sang as though she had lived it, as if she herself was a star crossed lover and as the song came to an end, she modified the popular song with the last two lines sung acapella.

The last note was held for an impressive time and once sung, she pulled away from the microphone, smiled sweetly and turned toward the crowd. Bowing once, she turned and left the stage. All the while, the crowd was in a frenzy. The whistled, they cheered, the called for more songs. They continued with their appreciative response, even as Wave Length took the stage.

"Wow! That was amazing," said the lead singer into the microphone. He nodded toward Poppy as she returned to the booth and asked her, "What's your name sweetheart?"

Poppy hesitated. She nervously looked across the table at Kirby, who had a huge smile, beaming at Poppy. Kirby shrugged her shoulder and raised an eyebrow at Poppy.

Poppy raised her head, trying to call out over the noise of the crowd.

"Poppy" was all she said.

"Poppy? Well, you remember that name everyone. That lady is going places. That was excellent!" He said, as he clapped for her, encouraging the crowd to join in.

"Okay, and how do we follow that?" He asked. "With more great music like this." He turned to his band and with one nod of his head they broke into a rowdy number that kept the crowd cheering.

Kirby and Poppy stayed for one more set and then agreed to find a place to stay for the night before heading off to their next destination. They drove for a few miles and found a luxury hotel, part of the insistence of Chase. He wanted to pay for their accommodations and made sure they stayed in the finest his money could buy. It didn't disappoint.

The women took a suite with two queen beds and when they got to their room, they each claimed their bed, throwing their luggage on the luggage stand at the end of each bed. It wasn't so late for them to consider another drink before bed, so it became Kirby's job to check out the mini bar and choose a drink for them.

"Rum and Coke, it is!" She announced, holding up the cans of coke and the mini bottles of rum. Opening one can, she took a large drink, then opened and poured the mini bottle of rum into the can, and then took another large drink.

"Ahhhhhhh." She sighed as she sat back on the bed with her head resting against the headboard. Poppy watched what she had done and copied her exactly, mixing her own rum and coke. After her first drink, she looked at Kirby whose eyes were closed. She had been so good to Poppy, becoming her closest friend. Poppy felt very grateful for Kirby's friendship. She hadn't really had any chance to form close ties with any woman, so Kirby held the dubious distinction of being her very first best friend.

Looking at her, as she sat on her bed, eyes closed, quickly drinking her rum and coke, Poppy thought it was a great opportunity for her to get some answers from Kirby. "So, tell me about yourself" she said, completely out of the blue as Kirby finished off her first drink and got up to make another.

Kirby stopped to look at Poppy, questioningly. "What?" she asked, as she performed the same routine to make herself her second rum and coke and climbed back onto her bed.

"Well, I realize I've answered every question you've asked me, but you don't tell me much, at all. Seems only right that I know you just as well, don't you think?" she told her.

"Oh, don't be so hard on yourself! I bet you know tons about me, regardless of asking questions. You're very observant" Kirby told her. "Why don't you tell me what you do know, and we'll go from there." She answered, enjoying the game, but not offering anything up. She took another large drink of her rum and coke, smiling at Poppy.

Poppy studied her for a moment and then said, "Well, I know your favorite color is purple!" She said, full of confidence.

Kirby looked completely surprised. "How do you know that?" She asked Poppy, completely surprised.

"Because, you carry your tablet in a purple leather carry case. No one would buy a purple leather anything, unless they LOVED purple!" she surmised. Kirby smiled, but said nothing. Poppy came and sat on Kirby's bed, in front of her and watched as she finished her second rum and coke, and got up from the bed to make her third. Poppy was still nursing her first.

"Okay, that's pretty good" Kirby agreed. As she climbed back onto the bed, resuming her position of sitting up against the headboard. "Yes, my favorite color is purple, you are correct" she said, seeming a little drunk, as she raised her coke can and toasted Poppy taking a very large drink.

Poppy watched her closely. She could see Kirby's eyes getting a little glassy as the rum begin to hit her system. She was drinking her drinks rather quickly, surprising Poppy who had only ever seen her drink at the club, and then she nursed one drink the entire night, probably because she had to drive, Poppy guessed.

"So tell me why purple is your favorite color, then?" She asked Kirby. Kirby studied Poppy's face for a moment as she took a drink, nodding her head as she swallowed. She cleared her voice.

"My grandmother loves reading. When I was a little girl, she shared that with me. She loved books, actual books. This was before everything was digital. She has a huge library in her home, just at the top of a beautiful old staircase. My grandfather built the room for her and it was filled with shelves upon shelves, ceiling to floor. All the shelves were filled with books. All kinds, paperback, hardcover, picture books. She had everything. I used to sit up there and just breathe in the smell of the books. To this day, a book store is one of my favorite places to shop, simply because the smell takes me back to my grandmother's library." She stopped for a moment, taking another large drink from the can. "Sometimes, my grandmother would join me up there and we would talk about some of the books she had read. When I got old enough, she started to loan me some of them. One at a time. She'd encourage me to read the stories she had read, and we really bonded over that." She finished her drink and got up to make another, the rum beginning to affect her. Poppy wondered why she was drinking so much, so quickly.

As she began the routine of mixing her drink, Kirby continued, "One day, when I was about 12 or 13, my grandmother handed me a book to read. She told me it was a favorite of hers and she wanted me to read it. It was called, "The Color Purple" by Alice Walker. I loved it. I read it, probably six times before I gave it back to her. The next Christmas, she gave me my own copy" she told Poppy. With that, she reached into a backpack she carried with her all the time and pulled out a well-worn copy of "The Color Purple". "It goes with me everywhere" she explained to Poppy, as she handed the book to her. Kirby took her place back onto her bed and took a long drink from the can, watching Poppy study the book and read the back cover.

By the time Poppy had finished reading the cover and a few pages inside, Kirby had finished her drink and curled up into the fetal position on the bed, her eyes very heavy.

"I love my grandmother" She said, slurring her words a little as she settled into her pillow. "She's all I have left anymore" she said, as her eyes closed. Within moments, Kirby was asleep, leaving Poppy sitting on her bed staring at her. Now she was even more intrigued with Kirby's story. Why was her grandmother all she left? Where was the rest of her family and how many had there been?

Looking over to her sleeping friend, she wondered what had happened in her life.

She was also surprised to have seen Kirby relax in this way. They had shared a few drinks now and again during the time they had grown as friends, always in good fun. Other than knowing about her Aunt who never seemed to spend time in her New York apartment, Kirby had never fully allowed Poppy into her private family world. This road trip was the first time she and Kirby were spending such dedicated time together and it fascinated Poppy, getting to know her friend better. She had many questions, but they would have to wait; Kirby wasn't sharing anymore tonight.

* * *

The next morning, Poppy woke first, got herself ready and went downstairs for breakfast, leaving Kirby still sleeping. A note next to her backpack told Kirby to meet Poppy downstairs for breakfast, when she was ready. It was another hour and a half before Kirby joined her. Poppy sat drinking coffee and reading "The Color Purple" as Kirby approached her table, wearing sunglasses.

"Argh!" was all she said as she sat down at the table, donning her sunglasses. She motioned to the waitress to bring her a coffee and focused in on Poppy. "Wow, you've read a fair bit already, huh?" She said, as she was poured her first coffee.

"Yes, it's an excellent story. I see why you like it so much. Very sad though, don't you think?" She asked Kirby, who just shrugged her shoulder and drank her coffee.

"It's an epic saga. I like epic sagas. Family sagas with triumphs and tragedies. Families that make it through tough times together and come out stronger than before." She explained.

"That would explain it!" Poppy stated, as she closed the book and put it down on the table.

"Explain what?" Kirby asked, with only half interest, trying hard to not let her hangover show.

"Why you are so willing to help me. A family saga? Like mine? How could you resist?" Poppy explained, smiling wide at Kirby. Kirby did not return the smile, but only nodded her head.

"You're probably right" she agreed. "I can't resist a good family saga and the Morningstars have that in spades! Are you kidding?" she stated. "Someone needs to write your life story, Chase's life story and all the others that came before you. From what you've told me, it would make a great generational saga". Poppy smiled and nodded. Someday, her story would be told. She was sure of it!

* * *

Their road trip continued. The next destination, a club called, "The Prime" was a few hours away. Although Poppy had hoped to continue asking Kirby questions, it was difficult to get her to open up, especially when she'd turn up the music and insist Poppy listen to the song that played at the time. When they reached the club, it was mid-afternoon, too early for it to be open. They decided to find their accommodations for the night and got settled into their room, Kirby taking the bed on the right, a preference Poppy assumed.

Kirby looked into the mini bar and whistled. "Wow, this place has the really good stuff!" she said, reaching in, grabbing a bottle and reading it. "You and I have a date set for later this evening, my sweet" she said, quietly to the bottle. Smiling to herself, she put the bottle back and began organizing her things. It wasn't lost on Poppy, who began to wonder about Kirby's sudden interest in drinking and whether or not it was something to be concerned with. It did seem that anytime she asked questions about her life, she would choose her words carefully, but after a drink or two, she wasn't so choosy. In some ways, this could work to Poppy's advantage to crack Kirby's internal code. So, as long as she wasn't drinking and driving, Poppy didn't mind.

* * *

At dinner time, the women left their room and drove to the club, a few miles away, Otis Redding accompanying their drive. Poppy was appreciating the diverse music collection that Chase and Kirby had put together. She'd had no exposure to this kind of music with Hans. Not that she held resentment about that, it was fine culture and it took her many places and finally brought her back to Chase and the Morningstar family. Her family. But, this music was the background music to the Morningstar's journey. Each one of them had heard this music, loved this music and had been inspired by it. Now, it was her turn. Never too late.

"The Prime" was a more sophisticated club than "The Shades" had been. The music was more jazz than blues, and the performer that night, "Kevin Mac and his Key Players" were excellent. The lead guitarist was Kevin Mac, a 60 something who had played jazz guitar all of his life. When he was in his twenties, he married a woman who knew how to play the piano. They toured together, entertaining audiences with their duet cover stylings of the latest music in the jazz world. When baby girl #1 came along, it didn't slow them down a bit. Once the child was of age, she was set before a piano and off she went. Baby girl #2 followed four years after and fell right into step behind her big sister. Now, 30 odd years later, the three women, all excellent jazz pianists and their guitar playing patriarch toured together, thrilling audiences with their versatility, creativeness and talent.

Poppy and Kirby had a table near the front of the performance. The restaurant area encircled the stage, which sat lower, like the bottom of a bowl. There wasn't a bad seat in the house. The place was filled to capacity and Poppy and Kirby were excited to see what the evening held in store.

Kevin Mac and his Key Players didn't disappoint. The played a solid 90 minutes before taking a break, at which point, the audience applauded them off the stage.

"Is it an open mike?" Kirby asked, watching as the stage sat empty and the audience turned back to their own conversations. Poppy looked through the crowd, wondering if anyone was going to make an announcement, just as at The Shades the night before. There didn't seem to be the same format, and she shook her head to Kirby. "I don't think they offer that here. Might not be something every club does. I'd love to play here though, the stage is fantastic!" she exclaimed, looking down to the three pianos.

"Can I get you a drink, ladies" asked their waiter, stopping by to clear away the two empty glasses.

"No thanks", said Kirby. Poppy shook her head at him, and pointed to the stage.

"Can you tell me please, does this club ever have an open mike night? Or, a night for new talent?" Poppy asked the waiter.

The waiter looked unsure and instead, replied "Let me ask the manager that question" he said, as he held up one finger and walked off towards the kitchen area.

Within a few minutes, the waiter came out from the kitchens followed by a large man in a navy golf shirt with, "The Prime" written above the pocket. His dress pants were stone colored and Poppy realized, he perfectly matched the décor of the room.

"Good evening ladies, everything good for you tonight?" he asked in a friendly manner.

"Yes", both women exclaimed.

"I was wondering if you allow new talent on a particular night, do you have to be booked in, or do you have an open mike night?" Poppy asked, her eyes staring up at the large man. The waiter shifted nervously, still beside his boss and nudged the man gently who gave him an angry stare before answering Poppy.

"We do like to showcase new talent, indeed. But, Gary here tells me you're a Morningstar, is that correct?" he asked her, surprising both women. Poppy suddenly froze, not knowing what to say. She hadn't been recognized for some time and didn't think she would be, having stepped outside of her regular musical environment. Not to mention, she'd been out of the spotlight for a while. She hesitated to answer long enough for Gary, the waiter to add, "I recognized you from your dad, Chase. I'm a huge fan. I've been to dozens of his concerts!" he gushed, showing a large toothy grin, which caused Poppy to smile back. Gary almost melted in his socks.

"Yes, you're right. Chase Morningstar is my father" she smiled, offering her hand to Gary first, and then to his boss. "My name is Poppy" she introduced herself, then turned to Kirby, "and this is my best friend, Kirby" who smiled, shook hands with both men and sat back, wondering if Poppy would get her chance to play on the fantastic stage.

"Uh...you want to play, tonight?" The boss asked, looking around the room as Poppy shrugged her shoulders.

"I...I'm not sure. I certainly don't want to put anyone out. I'm not trying to steal the show. I'm just trying out some new things and wondered if you have a new talent night. It doesn't have to be tonight" she explained. The boss nodded, gave Poppy a thoughtful look and said, "Hang on, let me see what I can do" he told her. She smiled and nodded appreciatively as the boss left their table, with Gary, the waiter in tow.

"What do you think my chances are?" Poppy asked Kirby. She smiled and shook her head, saying, "God knows! I would think he'd have to clear it with Kevin Mac, at the very least. He might come and tell you to come back on another night. Which is fine, we can do that easily" she offered, wanting to be as flexible as need be for Poppy's sake. If she was to find herself through music again, Kirby knew she'd have to be able to adjust to any schedule changes on the fly. "We aren't on any deadline here, so we go with the flow" she said, smiling at Poppy.

Just then, the boss came marching back through the restaurant to their table. He was smiling wide and began speaking before he reached them.

"Did you know Kevin Mac has performed with your Uncle Charlie? He's even performed in his club in Chicago!" he said, excitedly. "He wants to meet you, is that okay?" he asked her, suddenly a bit star struck, himself. Poppy nodded, then looked to Kirby. She too nodded and motioned for Poppy to follow the boss, who was taking her arm and leading her off towards the kitchen.

Ten minutes later, Kevin Mac walked across the stage, carrying his guitar and grabbed the mike.

"Ladies and gentlemen, we have a very special lady here tonight who comes from an incredibly gifted musical family, called, "The Morningstars." The crowd went mad and broke into cheering and applause at the famous family name.

Kevin waited until they settled a bit and then said, "This lady is used to performing as a concert pianist, but tonight she asks for our indulgence as she takes the stage as a new performer in the blues and jazz world." He told the crowd who whistled and cheered. He chose the perfect moment, when the audience had been teased enough and their excitement was reaching a crescendo, and yelled into the microphone, "Ladies and Gentlemen, may I introduce to you, one night only, Miss Poppy Morningstar!"

The applause was thunderous, and this was only her introduction. Poppy suddenly felt very nervous, this was a lot to live up to. What if they thought she wasn't any good? She had been mesmerized by the piano playing of his wife and daughters and wondered if she would be able to match them.

She took the stage and sat at one of the pianos. Kevin Mac sat in the middle of the three, atop his stool, holding his guitar, but not acting as if he would play along with Poppy. She took a moment, looking around her audience and orienting herself before taking a deep breath, then beginning her song.

Kirby was watching from her seat, surprised at how quickly things had come together for Poppy. She saw the audience's response to the Morningstar name and it gave her shivers. They were in for a real treat. Even if Poppy were to improvise, Kirby knew that her talent was so great, that she would have the audience eating out of her hands in no time. This may not be the genre she had started out in, but she definitely took to it naturally, as if it was in her all along.

Kirby wasn't wrong. Poppy sang only one song; her piano playing had the audience spell bound, her voice had them enchanted, the family genes clearly on display. Even Kevin Mac was impressed, and when Poppy played the last note, he quickly stood up, applauding loudly. The crowd also stood, showing their appreciation to her incredible talent. Kirby, also standing, was smiling as she felt tears sting her eyes. Poppy so reminded her of Jessica and as they spent more time together, Jessica kept coming to Kirby's mind. It was so bittersweet

* * *

They left "The Prime", having thanked the boss, Gary the waiter, Kevin Mac and the Key Players and almost the entire audience for their generosity. She was told over and over again how talented she was and that she should be working on an album. Poppy took it all in stride, but had to admit to Kirby how good it felt to know that she was able to play the kind of music that the Morningstars were known for. It was just incredible to feel that connection through the music.

When they returned to their hotel room, Kirby performed the same routine with the mini bottle of rum and can of coke, as before. Again she drank quickly, soon making another for herself long before Poppy was even half way through her first.

This puzzled Poppy. Kirby had nursed one drink all night long, but the minute she got to the hotel room, all bets were off. Something must be behind it.

They were finally alone again with no music or audience to shout over. Poppy hoped to find out more about her friend's life, and began by asking, "So, you have a grandmother, do you have any brothers or sisters? What about your parents?" She asked, surprising Kirby and taking her off guard.

She didn't answer Poppy immediately, wondering where this was leading and unsure if she really wanted to share her story. Usually, she didn't share much, but Poppy seemed intent on staying on the topic.

"My family isn't nearly as exciting as yours, Poppy" she told her, shrugging her shoulders. "I was raised by my mother, had an older sister, named Jessica..." she paused, then with a heavy sigh, stated, "they both died." She finished her drink in one long drink and got up to make herself another.

Poppy was stunned. She had no idea Kirby had lost people so close to her. Now she had to know it all, but Kirby wasn't forthcoming with any further information.

"They died together?" Poppy asked, hoping it would prompt Kirby to continue with the story, but it didn't. Kirby simply nodded and took a drink of her fresh rum and coke, as she climbed back onto her bed. She sat up against the wall, her bum resting on her pillows, almost the same position she had taken the night before in the previous hotel room. Her eyes once again becoming glassy as the alcohol hit her.

"How?" Poppy ventured. Kirby looked over to her friend and held her gaze. Poppy wasn't sure if she had over stepped, but she felt like this was a huge piece of information that had shaped Kirby and as her friend, she felt as if she should know this. Besides, it might be the answer to Kirby's after hour's behavior.

"They died in a car accident" she said, matter-of-factly, taking another long drink from the can. "They were headed home, my mom was driving.

Jessica was a singer in the church choir. She had such a beautiful voice."
She stopped a moment, not looking at Poppy. The alcohol was starting to
take effect, Poppy could tell. Just like the night before; exactly the same.
"The accident took all that away. My beautiful mother and my beautiful
sister." She said, lost in her memories.

"Ever since I came back into his life, Chase thinks accidents happen for a
reason", Poppy said, trying to keep Kirby talking.

"Chase is a very smart man. You're a lucky girl to have such a great dad,
even if you didn't get him as a dad in childhood. Better than nothing." She
told Poppy, as she yawned and stretched before ending with, "I only got a
few years myself." Finishing her third drink in record time, and burping a
number of times, she slid down into her bed. Her eyes were closed as she
let out a heavy sigh, turned onto her side and curled into the fetal position,
fully dressed. Poppy watched her, feeling badly that Kirby had suffered
such loss. Poppy had lost her mother too, having only fleeting memories of
her. Mostly, they came from the pictures Chase had shown her of Sonya.

"Kirby?" Poppy asked, wondering if her friend was out for the night. There
was so much more she wanted to know. Kirby responded with a grunt.
Not tonight, Poppy.

She let out a sigh, grabbed the beloved book Kirby had loaned her and
continued reading, but her mind kept repeating what Kirby had said and
how she had looked at her.

Maybe not tonight, she thought, *but we are in the early days of this road trip
and by the end of it, I am determined to help you as much as you've helped
me, my friend.*

* * *

The road trip carried on in much the same fashion. They would travel
through the day, listening to the music that had been compiled for Poppy.
They would stop for food and bathroom breaks, but would continue to travel
on until the next club came into view. Each night, the club would offer

entertaining music and great food. Most nights, if allowed, Poppy would take the stage, perfecting her music and her singing on a live audience, with only a couple of songs. Sometimes, the band scheduled that night would want her to join them. When that happened, Poppy would outshine the band and leave the audience wanting so much more, just as she wanted. All the while, Kirby would be watching, encouraging and enjoying the entertainment. Poppy really was a Morningstar.

After weeks on the road, both ladies were well into a routine. The days were spent travelling, the evenings were spent in a club and conversation happened only after the women were settled in their room for the night, and briefly at that.

On one particular night, Poppy watched Kirby closely when they returned to their hotel room. Not following her own normal routine, she eyed Kirby's movements in hopes to gain more information from her friend. Kirby marched right over to the mini fridge, prepared herself a drink and rummaged through her backpack at the end of her bed. At one point, she reached in and grabbed something, pulling it just far enough towards her so that she could see it, but out of view of Poppy's ever watchful eyes, at least she thought it was out of Poppy's view. The glint of the handle caught Poppy's attention and she knew Kirby was carrying a gun. This made Poppy feel very uneasy, especially when Kirby's nighttime activities ended in her being so drunk she fell asleep. *What was the gun for?* Poppy wondered. She thought about how to broach the subject with Kirby. Poppy was usually so direct, but instinct told her not to ask just yet. Kirby spoke more freely as the evenings wore on and Poppy learned to hold her questions until just before Kirby nodded off. And so it went. Poppy busied herself with getting ready for bed, while Kirby drank rum and coke, one after the other and slowly became drunk. Poppy started the conversation off lightly.

"It was a good crowd tonight, don't you think?" she asked, coming to sit on the edge of Kirby's bed. Kirby, in her same position as always; back up against the wall, sitting on her pillows, facing the television, said nothing at first. Poppy felt awkward, not something she generally felt around Kirby, but then she smiled a great big smile.

"They absolutely love you, girl!" she said slowly, enjoying telling her friend her observations. "You don't just entertain, you totally carry them out to your own little place. It's like you sing to each and every one of us individually." She paused hoping Poppy understood her. "I see it" she continued, "every night you get up on stage, I see it. I see the audience, their reactions. You're incredible, Poppy. You're gonna be a STAR!" As she said this, she spread her hand and waved it above her head.

"I already am a STAR! Poppy MORNINGSTAR!! Remember?" Poppy said, laughing out loud. Both women fell into fits of giggles.

"Morningstar" Kirby mumbled to herself, quietly thinking for a moment. "You know", Kirby began hesitantly "Lucifer's last name is Morningstar, did you know that?" she asked Poppy, who shook her head wanting to hear more.

"See, Lucifer Morningstar was a fallen rebel archangel. He was cast out of Heaven, fell for something like 7 days" she explained, burped and quietly excused herself, took a drink and continued, "as punishment for leading the revolt of the angels." She stopped and looked at Poppy, smiling.

"I never knew that!" Poppy admitted, shaking her head. "Do you think that means I have the Devil in me too?" She asked, smiling wide, raising an eyebrow.

"I haven't seen it yet, girl! You're all sugar and spice and everything nice! I'm the one with the demons." Kirby admitted, opening a huge door for Poppy. Kirby started to slide down the headboard and under the covers of her bed. Poppy knew she was at that crucial time and went for it.

"Kirby?" she asked quietly.

"Hmmmmm?" Kirby answered softly.

"Why do you carry a gun?" Poppy asked, leaning over her sleeping friend. Kirby's eyes were closed, but her brow furrowed and Poppy could tell she was thinking of an unpleasant thought. She then smiled, a strained, rather evil smile and said, sickly sweet, "Cause if I ever see that bastard again, I'm gonna blow his fuckin' head clean off." With that, Kirby rolled away from Poppy and curled up into the fetal position. Poppy stood up, looking down at her.

Kirby was right, she *was* hiding the devil inside!

* * *

The next morning, the routine continuing, Poppy sat at the breakfast table awaiting Kirby's arrival. Only this morning was going to be different. Kirby was going to spill everything to Poppy and Poppy was going to make damn sure of it! This had gone on long enough, now Poppy was feeling uncomfortable with the whole situation. Kirby's behavior, the gun, all of it needed explaining if Poppy was to continue on with her traveling buddy.

As if on cue, Kirby walked into the dining room, sunglasses in place. She sat down and motioned for a coffee from the waitress.

"Sleep well?" Poppy asked, a hint of sarcasm in her voice. It struck Kirby off guard. Poppy had been very accommodating, very easy going about Kirby's evening ritual. She wondered if Poppy would start to tire of it, thinking she may have to start getting separate rooms, should it become an issue.

Kirby sighed heavily. Sleeping well was not her forte, hence the drinking. Poppy may have seen her fall asleep, but she didn't see her wide awake a few short hours later, tossing and turning through the night. It was a constant struggle, ever since the accident.

"As well as can be expected" she said, taking her first sip of a very hot coffee. From behind her sunglasses, she eyed Poppy carefully. Something was different. Poppy normally greeted her with a smile so wide, the sunglasses barely helped, but not this morning. This morning, she was pissed.

"Everything okay?" Kirby asked, not really ready to deal with a pissed off Poppy before finishing her first coffee and dealing with her hang over, but something was definitely up.

"Perhaps this is none of my business, but if we are going to be friends who take road trips together, who help one another and who share hotel rooms together, then I think it *is my business!*", Poppy emphasized. Before drawing a breath she continued, whispering from across the table. "I saw the gun in your backpack last night" careful to not let others hear her. "When I asked you why you carry it you told me, that if you ever saw "*him*" again, you would blow his head off" she stated, staring at Kirby with an exasperated look.

"I believe I said, "*fuckin'* head *clean* off" Kirby calmly corrected her taking another sip of coffee. Poppy stared at her in amazement.

"Then, you remember telling me?" She asked Kirby.

"Yes, of course" she answered, shrugging her shoulders, as if it were a non-issue.

Now it was Poppy's turn to sigh heavily. She stared at her friend, hoping for an idea as to how to break Kirby open. Her frustration was written clearly across her face and it suddenly pulled on Kirby's heart. She felt badly that this innocent person, who reminded her of Jessica so much, was feeling frustrated by her.

"Okay" Kirby said, looking down at her hands. It would be the first time in 5 years that she spoke of it, but she felt as if she owed it to Poppy to explain. She motioned for another coffee, removed her sunglasses and took a deep breath, about to reveal her devil and demons.

~

Chapter 15

KIRBY'S STORY

From the day she could walk and talk Kirby never stopped. She was a bundle of energy from the get go and her parents and older sister, Jessica enjoyed her happy, bubbly personality. Even at an early age, she was the one to motivate the family into adventures; hiking, camping, a visit to Disneyland in Florida, which was granted when Kirby was 5. She met all the characters; Mickey, Minnie, Goofy, Pluto, Cinderella, Snow White, it didn't end. A week of perfect family fun that would live on in their memories.

She would be forever grateful for that trip, as it was to be their last as a complete family. Her father, an Irishman with a strong sense of integrity and morals had a very weak heart and passed away soon afterwards leaving Kirby's mother devastated and raising her two daughters alone.

Kirby's Grandmother Roberta, known affectionately as "Bobby", moved into a large home, closer to her daughter and granddaughters, helping out whenever she could. Bobby began playing the piano and organ at the church, giving her a social group outside of her female clan. She soon became very well-known and a favorite of the community.

Kirby's sister, Jessica loved to sing and found her passion in the junior choir at school and church. Instantly, her voice was a stand out against all the other children. The musical director at the church noticed it right away and instantly, Jessica took a lead position in the choir. When a Senior Choir member would be unable to attend a performance, Jessica was always the one to be asked to fill in. She didn't have huge aspirations, she enjoyed singing more than anything in the world, next to her belief in God. If her singing could serve God, she would be perfectly happy.

To Kirby, Jessica was an angel. She looked up to her and her performances always made her well up. Kirby wasn't anything like her sister. Jessica's hair was a mass of perfect tubular curls. They fell about her face perfectly, never seeming to be tamed, but never getting in the way. Her eyes were a gorgeous blue/green and very striking. She was humble, innocent and full of talent and poise.

In complete contrast, Kirby had street smarts beyond her years. She had used her talent to take her all over the world. She'd played piano on a cruise line for 8 months and saw most of Europe and the northern countries of Africa and parts of the Ivory Coast. Oh how her perspective had changed after visiting third world countries, or cultures that were different from her own! It opened her eyes to many things and from then on, she accepted all different types of work, as long as piano playing was part of it. From The New York Orchestra to a high school play needing a piano player, to a gig at the local bar, Kirby was out to learn as much as she could. She had been living like this for a while when she and Poppy met up on the elevator.

When Kirby was thirteen the decision was made to move into her grandmother's home. Her grandmother, mother, sister and she made a great team! They would break off into sets of two to accomplish any task. It was generally Kirby and her grandmother doing one thing and her mother and sister off doing another and of course, there was always Sunday service.

On one particular Sunday, Jessica's singing caught the attention of a new parishioner; a man by the name of Blaine Bannister. Blaine was a common man with too much money and whose looks gave him more swagger than skill. He fancied himself a lot of things, but couldn't do many. His biggest dream in life was to be a famous singer, but so far his only accomplishment was a successful karaoke night at a local bar and singing at a cousin's wedding. Neither event went well, but he wasn't aware of that. He was lost in the moment both times and believed he was a singing phenom who hadn't been found yet.

Blaine made his money by wheeling and dealing merchandise which, when looked at closely, could better be described as criminal activities. The local authorities weren't aware of all his illegal dealings; Blaine played his cards very close to his chest. So, his appearance in Jessica's church that Sunday morning raised no alarms for any of the church members other than the fact that he was an obvious new face in the very well established congregation.

He sat, dressed in a stunning black 2 piece suit with matching tie and pocket square, praying and partaking of the word of God respectfully, just as all the other parishioners had. But when Jessica began singing, his attention was captured. Mesmerized by the curly haired beauty on stage and the talent of her voice, he wondered who she was, leaning forward in his pew with every note. She had range, she had presence, she had a true gift and Blaine wanted to know her immediately.

After the service, Blaine found an opportunity and approached Jessica, holding out his hand in introduction. He certainly poured on the charm. Kirby and her mother both elbowed one another, watching from across the pews as the large, extremely handsome man spoke quietly to Jessica. She smiled dazzlingly at whatever he had said with both mother and sister straining to catch anything they could of the intimate conversation.

"Who is he?" Kirby asked her mother.

"I don't know." She answered honestly, shrugging her shoulders. "I've never seen him here before." She watched him with a scrutinizing eye, looking for something that might give away a clue as to who he was and where he came from. Her grandmother was very curious of the handsome man. He certainly had Jessica's attention.

"He's gorgeous!" Kirby said, in a dreamy voice. Her mother poked her with her elbow again, both of them laughing and covering their mouths so as not to draw attention. Just then, Jessica came bounding over to them, a wide smile across her beautiful face with Blaine in tow.

"Momma, grandma and Kirby, I'd like you to meet Mr. Blaine Bannister. Blaine, this is my momma, my grandmother and my sister, Kirby" she said, breathlessly. Jessica had not had many dates. The two choirs kept her busy and her mother's keen eye resulted in Jessica having any fun, who had yet to have a serious boyfriend. Mr. Blaine Bannister showed real promise to all three of Jessica's family, charming them as much as Jessica.

From that moment on, Jessica and Blaine spent every moment they could together. When he visited the house, all the women would be sure to be home, he was such a sweet and charming man! He brought fresh cut flowers for Jessica, trinkets for Roberta and sweet treats for Kirby and her mother. The man never came empty handed and he never left hungry. They knew he was a good man for Jessica. They knew he'd give her a good life and they all gave their blessings to the relationship.

They knew nothing of his secret life; a life where he was referred to as "Blaine the Blade".

His dress suit disguised his true self. He was a work of art underneath his shirt and tie, with tattoos covering most of his body. It was the 9 inch knife tattooed in the center of his shoulders that gave him his "street name", that and the fact that he believed carrying a small concealed knife hooked up to his wrist, that made him a badass; it was his weapon of choice. Many times, he had surprised his victims with a quick jab to the guts, catching them off guard. His normal routine was to stand laughing with his arm around the victims shoulder and in one swoop he would bend to laugh, allowing the blade to fall into his hand and as he rose, laughing harder in the moment, jabbing the knife into his victim. They didn't always die from such a wound, but they could. He got off on the uncertainty of their fate; it was part of the thrill. "Blaine the Blade" was an egomaniacal sick bastard who enjoyed inflicting pain on others, controlling them and out to wreak havoc. He made sure he didn't spill his garbage too close to his home and tended to do his deadly dealings in the bigger cities, outside of the small town he now called home. He didn't want the townspeople to know of his other life, after all, one day he was going to be a singing superstar and he didn't want to tarnish that!

Kirby left for her 8 month cruise job just as Jessica and Blaine met. She returned home at Christmastime that year and was filled with eager anticipation. She had many stories to tell her family; she had seen so many different countries and cultures. The world was a vast and varied place and she was moved by all of it. She hoped the ladies in her life could see the effect it had had on her. She hoped that they had also experienced a wonderful

8 months and she couldn't wait to hear all the news, especially from her sister, who she thought might get engaged over Christmas. Instead she was greeted by an extremely fearful Jessica who confided in her younger sister.

"I want you to promise me you won't say anything to grandma or mom" Jessica made her promise, before telling her what she feared. Kirby nodded in agreement, waiting for her sister to explain.

"I think Blaine is in trouble" she said, whispering. "I mean, I think he may have caused trouble. Very bad trouble." Jessica told her. "I think he might have killed someone" she said, her eyes filling with tears from her confession.

"What?!" Kirby asked, completely shocked. "What are you talking about?" she asked her sister, astounded by what she was told.

Jessica was shaking, her eyes wide. She held onto Kirby's hands tightly as she explained the whole story.

"Blaine has two phones. One for work, one for personal use. I only know the one number, but he is very careful about which phone he speaks on in front of me. His personal phone is one thing, but when he gets a call from work he always excuses himself and walks away." She stopped momentarily, trying to catch her breath and Kirby chose that moment to speak up, but as she tried Jessica held her hand up and stopped her. "No, let me finish. The other night, he took a call and walked away from me talking to whoever had called him. But, when he walked off, he walked into an alcove and it not only amplified him, it amplified the caller too. I heard everything, Kirby. All of it. He was telling someone how he stabbed this Texan guy who had tried to get away without paying him and humiliated him by acting like Blaine was no threat to him. I swear it Kirby. He was talking about killing someone." She was practically whispering at the top of her voice and Kirby could see she was panicked.

"Is that the only thing?" She asked, hoping there was an easy explanation for what her sister overheard.

"No. It isn't. Did you know he's covered in tattoos?" Jessica asked her younger sister, whose eyes grew very wide with that bit of information.

"Of course I didn't know that!" Kirby said in protest. "How would I know that?" she asked, rhetorically.

Jessica nodded her head, still very frightened. "He has, he has tattoos all over him. One is a blade across his shoulders this long" she said, as she held up her fingers several inches apart. "I'm scared, Kirby" She said, near tears. Kirby immediately felt for her sister.

"Have you asked him about them? I mean, surely you asked him about them the first time you saw them right?" Kirby said, as she came to sit beside her sister and rub her back as Jessica began to cry.

"He told me they were mistakes he'd made when he was younger and he wished they were gone. But, I've seen a series of teardrops he has tattooed right here" she motioned to just underneath her armpit on her side. "I've counted them several times, the first time I counted there were five. Recently, I noticed there were nine. Yesterday, there were ten. I read somewhere that teardrop tattoos represent how many people you've killed. That's what they do in prison." She finished while big, fat tears fell down her face.

Kirby wasn't sure what she should think. They had dated for a while and this was the first time Jessica had shared any kind of worry about Blaine with her. She didn't doubt her sister, but found it odd that nothing had been said before.

"Is this just all of a sudden?" Kirby asked her. Maybe she was having cold feet at the thought of Blaine possibly proposing marriage. Perhaps she was nervous and looking for a reason to back out.

"No." was all she said. Kirby studied her beautiful sister's face. She was scared, terrified actually, and Kirby knew it. She put her arm around her sister's shoulder, allowing her a moment to really cry it out. They sat together on Jessica's bed as her sister explained.

"The first few months were really lovely. He was a gentleman, opening doors, careful of what he said, and a Christian man. But then, he changed. He was angry a lot and he began shouting at me. I told him I didn't like it. I actually left a restaurant the other night because of his temper. He told me he was sorry and keeps calling me, trying to make amends. I can't do it, Kirby. I can't. He scares me. I don't want to date him anymore." She told her sister, but Kirby knew she was scared to do it. She wished she had some big burly football playing type male friends that could be there while Jessica broke up with Blaine, but then, Kirby had another idea. A brilliant idea!

* * *

It was Sunday morning service two days before Christmas. Kirby, her mother and grandmother sat in the second pew, proud as punch as the angel voiced Jessica lead the choir in a glorious hymn. She was magnificent! Her voice rang throughout the packed building and the entire congregation applauded excitedly when the hymn ended.

From her position on the altar, Jessica could see Blaine sitting at the back of the church. He stood out. He would make any woman believe he was the perfect gentleman with enough bravado to make him desired and sexy as hell. He really had the look of perfection down, but underneath those clothes and his outer persona was another story.

Jessica caught Kirby's eye and motioned her head towards where Blaine was sitting, Kirby nodded. Both women waited patiently through the service, ready to execute their plan. Her performance over, Jessica left the altar immediately and headed over to where her family sat, forcing Blaine to come to her. He swaggered up and gave a slow smile at Jessica.

"Hey there. You haven't been easy to get a hold of, haven't you got my messages?" he asked, sickly sweet. The hair on Kirby's neck stood up. She could see now what had Jessica so scared. She could see evil in his eyes, where it wasn't before. All of them had been played and Kirby was convinced they were making the right decision.

Before Jessica could answer him, her family surrounded her. She gathered her strength and faced him, standing tall and speaking to him directly.

"I have actually been ignoring your calls, Blaine. I don't wish to see you any more" she told him, raising her voice slightly. It caused some of the choir members who were still standing on the altar to look up and take notice. Suddenly, three large choir members were standing nearer to the family of four women. Blaine took no notice, his anger beginning to take hold.

"What? Are you kidding me? Is this because of the other night? Listen, I already apologized for that. I told you, I've been under a lot of pressure lately." He tried explaining, but Jessica stood firm.

"No Blaine. I don't wish to date you anymore. I've made up my mind. I don't like the way you are when you're angry. I'm scared." She admitted. Kirby was surprised to hear her say that, as was the rest of people who had come to stand closer, making sure no trouble came from this encounter. Suddenly, the church was filled with tension. No one really knew who Blaine was except that he had been dating Jessica and there were those who didn't trust him or his swagger.

"Listen, I need to talk with you alone. Let me explain…" he moved towards her emphasizing his words when he was suddenly surrounded by people. His eyes began to react wildly to being in that position and he constantly looked around him, making sure he was safe on all sides. Like a cornered rabid dog, he lashed out. His handsome face now twisted and contorted, now not so handsome.

"You stupid fuckin' bitch. I LOVED YOU!" He screamed at her, his rage full on. "I was gonna ask you to marry me, BITCH!" he screamed again. In a matter of seconds, he had gone from a stable, sane man to irrational and screaming. Gone was his fake persona regardless of his wardrobe, his true self shone straight through.

Case closed.

As far as Jessica was concerned, she was done with Blaine Bannister.

He was grabbed by the scruff of his collar and dragged out down the side isle of the church and tossed out through the front doors by three of large male choir members. Those were the biggest burliest men that Kirby knew and they reacted exactly as she had thought. There was no way the choir or church members were going to allow their beautiful Jessica to be treated like that! Kirby knew that if she could get Blaine to expose himself at his angriest, that would be all that was needed for Jessica and the family to be safe; the church would guard them and so they did.

That Christmas many church and choir members visited throughout the day and night, filling the house with security and community. It felt great! Kirby welcomed the visitors and kept a keen eye out of any kind of "Blaine" appearances, but he didn't come. Christmas came and went, and nothing happened. New Year's Eve was celebrated and Jessica was beginning to feel more relaxed and safe in the house. Perhaps his tanking business deal was keeping him busy, but whatever the reason, Jessica was grateful. He had been the first man she had ever really had feelings for, perhaps even loved, she wasn't sure. But the minute it didn't feel right in her gut, the moment he scared her with his anger and his temper, she was uncomfortable with him and her feelings changed. *Okay, lesson learned. No more scary guys,* Jessica thought to herself.

* * *

By the end of March, Kirby was rehearsing with the orchestra for a show in Vegas. She had very little time, but managed a few video chats with her ladies. At that time, everyone was fine and doing great. She could focus completely on work for the next few weeks before Easter.

* * *

Jessica prepared herself for the Easter Service. Good Friday was always such a wrenching day to her, the passion of the Christ almost bringing her to tears as the Stations of the Cross were acted out. The choir's choices for hymns that service were also very emotional. Tears were in Jessica's eyes several times as she sang from her heart for her Savior. Gone were her thoughts of Blaine Bannister; he was a distant memory. Since the service before Christmas, she hadn't heard or seen Blaine Bannister and good riddance, as far as she was concerned.

Jessica looked to the congregation and could clearly see her mother, proudly sitting in the second pew. Her mother was her biggest fan. She had sat through every rehearsal, every performance. Every time that Jessica sang, her mother was there, beaming. It was a special moment for her to see her mother's sweet face looking proudly at her, as she sang out in the name of her Lord. She and her mother really did have a very special bond.

* * *

Blaine Bannister was not a man to be fucked with. He was mad. Raging mad. Mad enough to stab someone, to kill someone, and what enraged him the most was when he was humiliated by someone. Someone less than he was and even worse, if in front of others. That, he couldn't tolerate.

Since Jessica broke up with him in such a public manner, he had not been very welcome in the town that he lived. Word travelled fast. This did not please the man with the secret life and penchant for killing. Not at all.

If there was one thing he had learned in his years of crime, waiting it out to make your revenge was always better. The element of surprise. He loved the element of surprise.

And so, he waited. Like a lion waiting for his prey to be distracted, patiently hidden far away in the long grass, he struck when no one was the wiser and he was, conveniently hundreds of miles away. He knew they couldn't pin it on him, and it was so incredibly planned out that he actually wished he could brag; the bastard.

* * *

Easter service had ended, the congregation feeling exhausted at the Preacher's sermon on acceptance and tolerance. The church goers were taken through each of the stations of Christ's journey on the path to his crucifixion and many were brought to tears. Exhausted and spent, the group collectively embraced each other and spent time in reflection, giving each other blessings for the Easter season.

Jessica was, once again surrounded by those that wanted to wish her well and congratulate her on such a stunning performance. For such a small town, they were very lucky to have such a talented vocalist in their choir and they let her know it!

As they left the church that Good Friday morning the rain fell hard, almost in pathos for the mood of the day. Jessica and her mother, exhausted and spent from the morning's service, climbed into their vehicle and headed out of the parking lot towards home. The rain was beating hard on the roof top, and the wipers were at their top speed, having trouble keeping up with the amount of rainfall. Jessica's mother, who was driving suggested they pull over until the heavy rainfall subsided a bit.

"I think it would be safer" she said as she stepped on the brake and put on her right side indicator to pull off the road. Suddenly, the gas pedal stuck full throttle, flat out to the floor without any pressure at all. The vehicle careened forward, surging quickly and directly towards a cement blockade. Within seconds the vehicle was forced into the block, killing both driver and passenger, with the gas pedal stuck to the floor, engine revving on high. Explain that!

At 11: 43 am on Good Friday morning, Kirby's phone rang, and changed her life completely and forever. Gone were two members of her family. Gone were childhood memories and the hopes to relive some of them in adulthood. Gone was everything. Everything but her grandmother and she knew exactly who was responsible!

For years Kirby had bottled up all her emotions and grief at losing her mother and sister on that Good Friday rainy morning.

The police report had stated "driver cause", even though Kirby's mother's foot was found to be nowhere near the gas pedal, but broken into small pieces over the brake pedal. If she'd had the strength to fight the brakes, she would have. Kirby had neither the strength, nor the inclination to argue with the findings.

Now, as she sat before Poppy, telling the full story, her rage built from within. She fought hard to keep it under control, but Poppy could feel her anger, her resentment.

"I haven't seen him and I have no idea where he is, but I know he's responsible. I know it in my heart, and if I ever lay eyes on him again, I will blow his fucking head clean off. I promise you." She stated to Poppy, through gritted teeth. Kirby always kept her promises.

And, Poppy believed her.

Chapter 16

COMING HOME

When they left the hotel restaurant that morning something had changed between them; their relationship grew deeper. As they walked towards the vehicle, Poppy put her arm through Kirby's and they walked together, arm in arm in unison. That's how it would remain, not just for the remainder of the trip, but for the remainder of their lives.

"Where to now? Poppy asked, as she opened the map, looking at all the circled places they had been and those they had highlighted as "yet to visit".

As she buckled herself in her seat, Kirby let out a heavy sigh. She placed her hands on the steering wheel for a moment letting them caress the wheel as she thought through her next suggestion.

"I think I'm going to take you somewhere that isn't circled on that map." Kirby said, as she started the vehicle.

"Oh! A detour from the road trip?" Poppy asked, playfully smiling. "Okay, I'm in!" She said enthusiastically, as she also buckled her seat belt.

From under her dark sunglasses, Kirby smiled for the first time that morning. She felt a lot lighter having getting the story off her chest.

* * *

Their journey took them through some small quaint towns that still held a lot of old world charm, considering they were situated only miles from a big booming metropolis. Poppy thought about the vistas she had seen in Switzerland, Germany and Belgium. A far cry from the American vistas. Everything was a far cry from how Europe did things. With that kind of cosmopolitan knowledge, Poppy had a perspective that helped her to adapt to her surroundings rather quickly. As she sat staring out the window, happy to be a passenger and listening to the music playing, she noticed something she had not heard in the entire time they had been together in the vehicle; Kirby was humming softly along to the song playing. Poppy listened intently. Kirby had good tone, could follow the notes and hummed in key, at least. When she told her story, she had never mentioned her own singing voice, had made out like it was all her sister's gift. *Interesting!* Thought Poppy.

They had been on the road for over an hour when Kirby turned into the laneway of a large two story home, with a foundation covered in river rock stone. The stones where cobbled up the front pillars and gave the whole house a cottage feel. The house was nestled into a line of tall trees, creating a large backdrop of leaves and branches which framed the beautiful little home. Poppy had seen some very lovely homes in her life, especially in the last few years with Chase and Dana in her life, but this house was exceptional. It was a jewel of a home, set in amongst the greenery. The next house closest was nearly 1,000 ft. away, giving the house a wide space to live within.

"Oh, what a beautiful home!" Poppy exclaimed, as she leaned forward looking at the house intently as Kirby drove around to the back. The porch continued around to the back with the same river rock stone on all the walls and pillars. Poppy immediately felt such warmth.

Kirby was tight lipped as they pulled to a stop. She waited a moment before turning off the engine, and then she turned to face Poppy in her seat, still buckled in.

"Okay, full disclosure" Kirby admitted, the keys of the vehicle in her hand, pointing at Poppy. "This is my family home, my grandmother's home. She still lives here, alone. I haven't been here more than a handful of times in the last 5 years." She admitted, shamefully. "But tomorrow, the church that my mom and sister were so much a part of, are going to pay tribute to them." She told Poppy, who sat in silence in the passenger seat, her eyes focusing on Kirby and then the house behind her.

"You've brought me to your home during this time?" Poppy asked, feeling incredibly honored, their friendship etched a little deeper. "Are you sure you want to do this?" she asked Kirby, who nodded her head quickly, her curls accentuating her affirmation. Poppy smiled wide and reached over to hug her friend. Kirby hugged her back and the two women spent a few moments held together before facing the demon before them. They were a force to be reckoned with; the curly haired woman whose mass of curls foretold of her strength, courage and unruly side and the golden haired innocent, who was wise and gifted beyond her years.

They entered the back of the house, Kirby taking the lead and dropping her backpack and suitcase at the back door before heading into the house. Poppy followed her lead and entered into the kitchen area. It was exactly as Poppy had imagined; a large older cooking stove to the one side of a large room, the countertops were all natural granite, and stainless steel. Regardless, the kitchen still held the charm of a warm family kitchen. Poppy imagined many family meals being prepared and eaten in this room, many Christmases celebrated in the open area living room, and more. Four bedrooms, a den, the library and 2 full bathrooms with a mini bathroom on the main floor off the kitchen. It had everything; charm, functionality, modern conveniences, privacy. Poppy could understand Kirby's love for the home and why it would be hard to return after such a tragedy.

Past the kitchen into the living room, Kirby called out for her grandmother, "Gramma! Gramma! Where are you? It's me, Kirby! I'm home!" She yelled, as she moved through several rooms on the main floor. Poppy decided to stay where she was and let Kirby do her search. That way, when she succeeded, Poppy wouldn't be backed up behind her caught off guard.

From a room off the center of the hallway emerged an elderly woman who stepped gracefully into the room, wearing a pale blue cardigan and an ivory skirt with pale blue pants and slippers. She walked with a cane and her once dark hair was now cut with deep silver swatches, giving it a unique look. Kirby's Gramma did not look her 76 years, and Poppy thought her to be a stunning looking woman.

"Gramma! There you are." Kirby said, as she turned and saw her grandmother for the first time. She ran quickly over to the now beaming, wide eyed woman and gently took her into a firm embrace, closing her eyes as she held her.

"It's been too long, child" Kirby's grandmother said to her quietly in her ear. She was always hyper aware of what made Kirby comfortable and what didn't. Not wanting to embarrass her, she was aware of Poppy's presence in the room. She stepped away from her granddaughter and looked her over completely.

"Oh, you are a sight for sore eyes!" She exclaimed, her eyes full of tears as the two fell together in another hug. Poppy fought the lump that formed in her throat, hoping she wouldn't full out cry from the scene she'd just observed.

Once they had both hugged and cried for a few moments, Kirby pulled away to introduce Poppy. "Gramma, I want you to meet my friend Poppy" She paused, purposely not using Poppy's last name.

"Poppy, this is my grandmother, Bobby Shepherd." She said as she motioned to her grandmother, and smiled wide. Poppy had heard so much about this woman in the days that she and Kirby had been on the road. For some reason, she imagined her as being so much larger than the woman she presented. Poppy soon learned the reason. Bobby Shepherd was very much larger than life and Kirby had saved the best of her story for last!

* * *

Kirby showed Poppy to a spare room on the second floor. It was actually two small rooms, with a full queen size bed taking up most of the back alcove, while the front area housed a chest of drawers, a small en suite toilet and sink, and a closet for hanging clothes. Poppy couldn't help but think it was the same, if not more than she had ever had while being on the road. This was the very life Poppy craved. Family, cozy, home.

After getting her things organized, she made her way back to the kitchen area where Kirby and her grandmother were deep in conversation. Poppy approached cautiously.

"No! No, my dear. Come here, come closer. I won't have you feeling shy here. My home, our home" she opened her arms to Kirby and then towards

Poppy, "is your home". She took Poppy by the hand, bringing her into the brighter kitchen lights and studied her for a moment. Poppy returned the inspection.

In Poppy, Bobby saw innocence, brilliance and such smart, intuitive natural talent; she positively shone. Her beautiful golden hair and large, green eyes framed by light, but long lashes. Poppy accentuated little with makeup, but she knew how to make her eyes really stand out with the least amount of work. Bobby thought she looked absolutely enchanting.

Poppy had never had a grandmother. No elder woman had come into her life until she reunited with Chase, and subsequently met Dana. Uncle Charlie's wife Georgie was another woman whose input Poppy often sought, but this elderly woman was something completely different. Her eyes sparkled and as Kirby had described her, "in her heyday, she was full of piss and vinegar". Poppy looked into large hazel eyes, not as dark as Kirby's, but the same shape. Kirby took after Bobby in many ways and Poppy wished she'd had a female relative she could relate to. Just looking at the two women, you knew they were related.

"Gramma, come and have a seat in the living room. I want you to tell Poppy your gun story." She said, nodding her head towards her grandmother. The woman took Poppy's hand and led her over to a large comfy chair, next to the fireplace. She motioned for Poppy to sit, and took the seat across from her. As they sat together, Kirby brought over a tray with a teapot and three china cups and saucer sets. She kneeled before the table between Poppy and Bobby and started pouring tea as Bobby began speaking.

"My father, his name was Robert, I was his first born. He wanted a son so badly, but when I came out kicking and screaming at the top of my lungs, he was satisfied and called me, "Bobby" after him." She laughed a moment, remembering the tall, jolly Scotsman man who taught her everything he knew.

"I was seven years old, the first time I shot a gun, with my father's help, of course. It was a hunting rifle, a 22 caliber rifle. I used it on any pop can, soup can or coffee can within a mile's radius of our house. I was an excellent shot by age eleven and any Fair that came to town were very sorry when I stepped up to the shooting games. I easily won the largest stuffed animals, much to my parents chagrin!" She laughed again, taking a sip of her black, strong tea and placing the cup gently back onto the saucer. Poppy couldn't help but notice how easily she handled the tiny china cup, such confidence and grace all in one!

"It took me many years before my father allowed me to shoot my first shotgun. It was a completely different experience from the rifle. I loved it immediately! It held such force and kicked backed into my shoulder with such power. That's the key to everything when you're not a big person, my dear." She admonished, one finger pointing a Poppy. "Small is only a state of mind" she stated, confidently straightening her spine and holding her head high. "With a decent weapon, even the smallest of person stands a chance! My father used to say; it doesn't matter if the critter is four legged or two, a bloody good shot will take down anything" She stated. Poppy could practically see her grow a half foot before her eyes when she said that.

Poppy had grown up in the years of the terrorist threats across Europe and as a young girl, she remembered being taught by Hans how to prepare for an attack that might separate them during a trip to the city of Brussels, a popular sight for suicide bombings at the time.

"There was a lot of arguments for and against guns in the home when I was a young girl and the Republican Party fought hard alongside the NRA for their second amendments rights. I didn't really think much of it until one night, an intruder entered our home and tied up my mother and me. He thought we were the only ones at home at the time, not knowing my father was working in the shed at the far back of the property. He must have seen this man through the kitchen windows, because before he could do any real damage, or take anything from us, my father burst through the door with the rifle pointing directly at his head." She paused a moment, remembering the memory.

"I remember him entering the kitchen from the back door, and the man literally freezing in his shoes and peed himself, staring down the barrel of a rifle. Oh, my father was not impressed!" she giggled merrily, taking another sip of tea, keeping the girls in suspense of what she was going to say next.

"From that day on, I have always kept a gun in the house. My father taught me how to correctly strip it, clean it and keep it in excellent working condition. And, I do that every single week." She announced proudly. Poppy smiled at Bobby and it caught Bobby's breath. She went to say something and held her tongue, making both Kirby and Poppy wonder what was on the elder woman's mind. Bobby just smiled, keeping her thought to herself. It made her smile, which made both girls smiled too.

"But, that's not the end of it, right Gramma?" Kirby asked, pressing her grandmother for more, who sighed heavily and rolled her eyes.

"Yes my dear, you're right. Three years ago" she continued, turning her attention to Poppy, "I had been asleep in a recliner downstairs in front of my television when I heard something upstairs. I quickly got up and went to the gun chest and got my favorite shot gun. I snuck upstairs in the dark and found a man in my bedroom, going through my jewelry." She told them, Poppy gasping at the thought of the elderly woman carrying a shotgun up the stairs to face an intruder, such bravery!

"I quickly inched up to the doorway of my bedroom, turning quickly with the shotgun locked and loaded on his head." She held the pose, her one eye squinted, focusing on his chest.

"He turned to look at me. He was white as a snow. He had no idea I was in the house. I normally use a sleep timer on the television, and it had turned off while I slept. I caught him completely by surprise!" She laughed, not afraid at all for the danger she might have faced. "You'd better stop your lookin', and get the hell out of here or I'll blow yer fuckin' head clean off" I said."

Poppy looked over at the now chuckling Kirby. Looking at her friend who was obviously enjoying herself, Poppy said, "Hmmmm...sounds reminiscent."

"Hey!" Kirby said, cocking her head towards her grandmother. "She's the original. I get my best material from her." She admitted with a wide smile.

"Do I detect an accent? You sound as if you're from…" Poppy hesitated, pausing a moment, "Scotland, or maybe Britain originally." She exclaimed, sounding confident in her choices.

"Scotland!" Bobby said, with a smile. "I'm from Aberdeen, originally. My father emigrated when I was a wee girl." Proudly sitting up straight, her eyes looking first towards Kirby and then to Poppy. Poppy giggled and then stated, "Oh my God, I would have been praying so hard! Weren't you scared?" Asking Bobby incredulously, who stopped her jovial moment and stared at Poppy wide eyes.

"Why no, Poppy, not at all! God might protect over me, but he can only do so much!" stopping short of explaining herself. Kirby smiled at her grandmother, shaking her head.

"After the accident, Gramma insisted on living in this big house, all by herself. So, I insisted on a security system, but…" She shuffled over to her grandmother's chair and sat beside it, her beloved grandmother stroking her hair, "… she sometimes forgets to turn it on." She smiled up to her grandmother with a weak smile and Bobby leaned over and rested her forehead on Kirby's.

"God forgets to remind me!" Bobby said, playfully.

It brought a lump to Poppy's throat, again. These two women shared so many things; by far the greatest being a great amount of love, respect and adoration for the other. Poppy understood the frustration of her friend for the grandmother who struggled with modern technology. Considering Bobby knew how to strip a shotgun, Poppy was duly impressed.

Bobby gently moved back from her granddaughter and looked deeply into her eyes.

"Tomorrow is a very special and long day on this old lady." She stated with a smile. "I'm off to bed." She exclaimed, kissing Kirby on her forehead, before rising from her seat. Poppy rose at the same time, reaching out to hug the elderly woman. Bobby reached out towards Poppy as well and they embraced for a long moment.

"You have those in your life to guide you through, too" Bobby whispered Poppy's ear. "They mean well, you make sure you listen." She told Poppy, and with another gentle squeeze she was off to her bedroom, waving goodnight to Kirby and Poppy.

The two women looked at each other at her exit and smiled.

"Oh, to have THAT legacy" Poppy exclaimed, as she dropped herself back into her chair.

"I know, right!" admitted Kirby, who sat in the chair that her grandmother had sat in.

"So, tell me something?" Poppy asked, as she tucked her feet underneath her in the chair.

"I thought the car accident happened on Good Friday." She hesitated, her hand gesturing in question. "But, we're in July. Is it a special date?"

Kirby nodded her head and looked to her hands. "My mother and sister were very close. So close, that they shared the same birthday which is tomorrow. The church and choir and all of us decided that it was a more appropriate day to celebrate them. So, every year on their birthday, the church does a special service in their honor." As she said this, Kirby looked away. Poppy wondered what she was thinking. If Kirby were being totally honest, she would have admitted to Poppy that she was ashamed of the fact that she hadn't returned home a lot since the accident, leaving her grandmother alone.

"Well, we'd better get to sleep as well." Poppy said as she rose from the chair, suddenly feeling quite tired herself. She yawned and stretched, reaching for a good night hug from Kirby.

"You're home now, Kirby. Hopefully, you'll sleep well." Poppy told her, secretly hoping it didn't take Kirby the usual three drink limit to get her to sleep tonight.

"Right back at ya!" Kirby said, squeezing Poppy tightly. For almost two months now they had shared a room each night, until tonight. It would be different not sleeping in the same room together. They each hoped the other rested peacefully. Sweet dreams indeed!

* * *

Poppy rose early, showered and entered into the kitchen with a towel wrapped around her head. Only Bobby was in the kitchen, working away on breakfast and coffee, Poppy presumed as she sat down at the island in the center of the room.

"Rise and shine Miss Morningstar" Bobby said, as she turned around and faced Poppy offering her a mug of hot coffee. She had a huge grin on her face which made Poppy grin back.

"You knew?" Poppy asked, slightly astonished.

"Of course I knew! I wasn't always this old and decrepit, you know. Many years ago, I thought Chase Morningstar was the best specimen of male excellence this earth had to offer." She admitted, her eyes sparkling. She danced and swayed about, humming one of Chase's best known songs. Poppy was filled with delight watching Bobby happy and acting silly.

"Gramma!" Kirby's voice brought the room to attention and both Poppy and Bobby stopped and turned towards her, standing in the hallway.

"What do you think Mom and Jessica would say to see you dancing about like that on such a day?" She asked her. Poppy couldn't tell if Kirby was joking or truly upset. Her face was full of question at her grandmother.

"Oh, Kirby, my dear! Your dear sweet mother and sister would never be happy if we were down here all sour and sad. That isn't how they lived.

Today we celebrate their *lives!*" She told her granddaughter as she walked towards her. Giving her a long hug, they shared a few quiet words, kissed each other and entered into the kitchen together, holding hands. Kirby had tears in her eyes as she took a seat next to Poppy, giving her shoulder a rub.

"G'morning." She mumbled as Bobby placed a mug of coffee in front of her. "Thanks, Gramma." Kirby said, as she added a bit of milk and sugar.

"I was just sharing with our guest, of the enormous crush I had on her dad, Chase Morningstar when I was much younger." She told Kirby, expecting a reaction.

"Did you really?" Kirby started with, but then stopped herself. "Wait, what?" She stopped completely, staring at Bobby in disbelief. "You knew!" She said, pointing at her grandmother, who looked sly, turned her back and continued preparing breakfast. Kirby turned to Poppy, winking at her friend. It occurred to Poppy that this was the first time she had seen Kirby not hung over in the morning, since they started on their road trip. No sunglasses, no quiet thunderous headache. She looked rested. She looked good. Her thoughts last night were right; home agreed with her.

"Poppy, I told you my grandmother was a badass. Actually, she's the *original* badass! Yup, full of piss and vinegar." Kirby said as she took her first sip of the hot liquid.

*Hmmm...*Poppy thought, *she's passed it on down the line!*

* * *

The church was filled to capacity. Everyone in town had heard that Kirby had arrived late the night before and within three hours, and thanks to social media, the whole town was there.

Many wanted to wish Kirby well, that the memory of her beautiful mother and sister were forever remembered in their hearts. It gave Kirby a heavy heart and a tear to her eye more than once as members of the choir and congregation came over to give her their best and to tell her how good it was to see her back in town again. To her credit, Kirby smiled all the way through, thanked every last person who stood before her and was gracious to all.

Bobby kept a keen eye on her granddaughter, watching for any sign of being overwhelmed. The flawless elderly woman was used to this celebration. The church had surrounded her with their love and compassion and she was grateful to them for taking such care with her, and the celebration for her daughter and granddaughter. She was concerned about the other granddaughter today and hoped Kirby would be able to appreciate the way in which the church and choir honored her family.

Bobby, Kirby and Poppy sat together in the front, seating reserved for family and special guest. The service began with a hymn, a favorite of Kirby's mother. She sat spellbound by the choir, their voices collectively sounding like one strong voice. At one pivotal point, the hair on the back of Kirby's neck stood up when a crescendo was hit and held. Tears, once again filled her eyes.

The Pastor then came to the altar and spoke of how these women had affected not just the church but their community as well. He spoke of the enormous contribution of talent and time and he spoke of their love of their faith and family. The choir then sang a hymn that Jessica used to solo on. Kirby was holding both Poppy's and her grandmother's hands as they all sang with joy in their hearts. It lifted Kirby as she was enthralled by their voices, their beautiful voices. Kirby had missed these moments, the feeling of love from church and community, the acceptance and support of so many.

As the service ended, the whole congregation stood and held hands, singing together in unison. When the hymn ended, all voices stopped, leaving the church echoing the last note, many were brought to tears. It was a very moving moment, and Kirby felt such love from each choir member and every church member. They had sung their hearts out.

Afterwards, Kirby and Bobby personally thanked everyone and joined many downstairs for coffee, refreshments and reflection. Bobby stood, balancing her coffee mug, a plate of triangle sandwiches and a few desserts, her face light and smiling. Poppy watched her with intrigue. She showed such strength and positivity, such optimism on a day that others would consider difficult.

At 76 years old, Bobby stood straighter than most women half her age with enviable poise. She had been surrounded by the love of the entire community in Kirby's absence, and Poppy could see she'd been in very good and caring hands.

She watched as Kirby walked over to stand beside her grandmother, gently rubbing her back affectionately. Bobby looked up to her granddaughter and the two had a very firm and loving embrace.

"I love you, Gramma." Kirby said quietly to her Grandmother. "I'm sorry I've not been home more often." She told her, softly crying into her grandmother's neck and shoulder.

"There, there my dear." Bobby whispered, stroking her hair. "I understand." She said, sincerely. "Let's get going home, shall we? Will you and that lovely Poppy please take me home now?" She asked Kirby, who nodded immediately. She motioned towards Poppy who had been caught watching them, still captivated by their quiet conversation from across the room. As Poppy made her way towards them, Kirby made a quick announcement thanking everyone for their love and support, it had been a very full day, and they were headed home. The room erupted in blessings and goodbyes. Bobby was swamped once again, and smiling as she managed to say her goodbyes, walking sometimes backwards through the crowd and towards the doors. When the three women got outside, all three felt uplifted, loved and lighter, giving the two younger women a new appreciation for the wealth in the community.

Back at home, the three changed into comfortable clothing and all settled back into the living room, each with a drink in hand. They chatted freely about the celebration and shared some stories of who each spoke to and what was said. The room went quiet for a brief moment, all three women reflecting on the experience they had shared. Bobby broke the silence.

"Well, I hate to ask this question, but I know you can't stay here forever." She prefaced with, taking a deep breath. "When do you leave?" She asked, looking at Kirby.

Kirby smiled softly at her grandmother and jumped up, joining her on the couch, nestling in beside the elder female and holding her hand.

"As much as I want to stay, we need to move on early, tomorrow morning." Kirby explained, snuggling closer.

"Promise me you won't stay away for long?" Bobby asked, her voice quieter. Kirby looked into her grandmother's face. They had had many video chats over the years, had seen one another through telecommunication, but their hands had not touched one another very often in the past 5 years.

"You know my dear, if you don't let go of the resentful, bitterness and anger that you feel, you'll always be running. You'll never fully heal." Bobby told her wisely.

The words rang into Kirby's head. She had stayed away because she was so incredibly angry that her family had died at the hands of this brutal man, there had been no justice and he had paid no price. Kirby couldn't accept that, but her Grandmother had seemed to have found forgiveness.

She had managed to live on, finding solace in her church and community. She had found peace in how they had lived their lives on earth, and made the conscious decision not to focus on their deaths, as Kirby had. Admitting this brought tears to her eyes and made her gasp for air. She put her hands into her face and sobbed, for a moment. Something her grandmother has suspected had not happened in quite some time.

After a moment, she raised her face and sniffed loudly, accepting a tissue her grandmother handed her. Looking up, she realized Poppy had been witness to a large part of her personal drama. She smiled through her tears.

"I guess this makes us *very* best friends now, Poppy" she laughed, finding humor in the situation. "This is the ugly cry" Kirby explained, "meant to be seen by family and forever friends, only." She laughed again, wiping away tears as she did. Poppy leaned forward in her chair, feeling vulnerable herself, but wanting Kirby to know that she was her best friend. She waited a moment wondering if she should share the story, and then, believing in Kirby completely, she continued.

"Have I ever told you about the day my mother died?" She asked Kirby. Thinking about it, Kirby held still for a moment and then shook her head "no". Bobby remembered Poppy's mother's murder and Kirby only really knew of Luisa's influence on Poppy, so she wasn't sure how to respond to Poppy's question.

"When I was very young, not much past two, my real mother Sonya was murdered. When I think back, I recall a day where I saw a lot of police in our home, my father crying and I remember wondering why mommy wasn't holding him while he cried. I don't remember much of my mother; blonde hair, a certain perfume scent, but after that nothing. I understand she suffered post-partum depression and didn't spend a lot of time with me in the early months after my birth. Even so, I resent that I don't remember more. I think I should remember more!" She said, feeling slightly anxious. "But, later on in life, when I thought my mother was Tanya/Luisa, and she died, I felt completely alone. I remember watching her falling to the ground that day and wondering why she didn't get nearer to the couch. Why fall on the floor?" She waited a moment, looking to Kirby.

"When I found out that I was stolen from my real family, I felt a deep resentment towards the woman who I thought was my mom, regardless of the fact that she was dead." She shrugged her shoulder, changed her position and smiled softly at them. "I learned after a while that my anger got me nowhere. Both of my mothers were dead and taking up space in my head." She reached for her wine glass, drained it of its contents and stood up. "In the end, only you can say what goes on in your mind. This guy, the man you say organized their deaths, he's not spending his time thinking of you, I assure you." She said, raising her empty glass towards Kirby. "You can't live to kill someone, Kirby. That's a karma killer, for certain." She told her, turning to put her glass in the kitchen area. "Besides" she continued, facing the two women, before heading off to bed, "Your best revenge to Mr. Bannister is to live your life to the maximum, and in that way, you'll honor your mom, Jessica, your Gramma and this incredible community that surrounded you and your family with love today. That's an absolute gift, my dear." Poppy said, slightly drunk, feeling a little emotional. She walked over to them and kissed each woman on their forehead, telling each of them that she loved them and toddled off to bed.

As promised, they left early the next morning, both feeling much loved by Bobby Shepherd and the feeling was very much reciprocated by both women!

* * *

When they arrived at "Baby Blues", a blues and jazz nightclub recommended by both Chase and Charlie, the women wondered what the night would bring.

Upon entry into the club, both were surprised to see a fairly full room, a great stage area that was occupied by a mediocre blues band. They were greeted by a hostess and shown to a table near to the left of the stage. Poppy's eyes were wide. Kirby had noticed how different she had seemed since staying at her grandmother's. *Perhaps it had been a healing experience for both of them,* Kirby thought.

Kirby ordered a meal, but Poppy asked only for a coffee. Her true drink of choice. She felt electric, almost on fire. As the mediocre blues band finished their set, she wondered what they did for downtime. She waited for the waitress to come back to the table and immediately asked her, "Can you please point me to your Manager?"

The waitress went pale. "Is something wrong with your coffee? Can I get it changed to something else you'd prefer?" she offered. Poppy smiled, understanding the woman's dilemma, and trying to put her at ease.

"It has absolutely nothing to do with the coffee or service. I would like to play piano on stage when the band takes a break." She explained to the girl who was visibly relieved.

"Okay, no problem. He's the tall man, with the full head of blonde hair, standing in the corner of the bar." She pointed out. Poppy followed the waitresses gaze over to the man, who stood off to one side of the bar, watching over his club and his clientele. Poppy observed him for a while, he barely moved, he was studying the room so hard. He looked to be in his early thirties; a slight suntan from a recent weekend outside with friends. But it was his confidence that attracted Poppy and she watched him carefully as he surveyed his space.

Leaving Kirby alone to eat her meal, Poppy told her, "I'm going to go and get this started." Although Kirby wasn't sure exactly what that meant, she knew that if Poppy Morningstar was to have her way, this club was about to get its mind blown. Instinctively, Kirby grabbed her tablet, turned it to video mode, faced it towards the stage and started taping.

* * *

Kerry Cruickshank was spying the room, looking for any trouble makers as well as, making sure the crowd was happy. He couldn't help but feel pissed at the quality of the band he had hired for the week. They were lack luster and mediocre at best, far below the standard of quality "Baby Blues" was known to provide. Their audition was far better than what they produced live. Kerry tried to shrug it off as "it happens", but he hated doing that. The motto "not on my time" kept creeping into his mind.

He was staring forward, lost in thought when a beautiful, blonde walked towards him, with full purpose. Immediately, he was fascinated by her. Her strength of character came through full on and that appealed to him. Her figure was a little thinner than he liked, but her smile could melt an iceberg and as she got nearer, he smiled instinctively back.

"Hello." Poppy said as she stood before him. "I'm Poppy." She said, extending her hand.

"Hello" He said, taking her hand and shaking it warmly. He didn't want to let go. It was soft, sexy and scented; she smelled wonderful. Kerry tried to gain his senses, tried to get back to being present.

"I'm wondering if you'd give me a five minute chance on the piano, while the band takes a break." She asked, Kerry still holding her hand and gently shaking it. Her green eyes had him completely lost and he would have offered her the club in a moment had he not come to, just as she had said "takes a break." He gently released her hand, regained his orientation and looked about the room for witnesses. From what he could tell, no eyes were upon him and he focused his attention back to Poppy.

"You're a singer?" he asked, wondering what she offered as her talent.

"You could say that. I also play a little keyboard. She told him. "Give me five minutes and I'll blow your mind." She stated confidently. He swore he saw her pupils widen and reduce within nanoseconds. He felt slightly bewitched by her and wondered if her powers lived up to the real deal.

"Okay. Sure." He told her, nodding towards the stage. "I'll give you five minutes from…now!" He told her, looking at his watch. With that, she leapt immediately from his sight. Climbing the stairs to the stage, she was stood before a keyboard, placed the microphone to her lips and instructed the lighting crew where to aim the lights.

At first, the crowd paid no attention when she began to play. Voices continued chatting and laughter could be heard from very close by. Her song started softly, but the music she played over rode the voices and quickly, the room began to quiet. She then began to sing, words that uplifted, words that inspired. To most, this was a new song and new music, never heard before.

At first, Poppy wasn't sure what she would play, but she felt on fire. Confident in herself and her music, Poppy took a deep breath and closed her eyes. Her fingers touched the keys and …well, as they say, the rest is history.

* * *

The first recording by Thomas Edson in 1877, singing "Mary Had A Little Lamb" cemented the fact that magical musical moments would forever be recorded. Elvis Presley, The Beatles, The Rolling Stones, Michael Jackson…

the list is endless. Those that changed the world and how it *thinks* musically, recorded for all time.

Poppy Morningstar changed the world and her rise to this distinction began that night at, "Baby Blues". As Kerry Cruickshank watched, a beautiful green eyed blonde took the stage and changed the world, changed *his* world!

* * *

Kirby was mesmerized as Poppy sauntered over to the manager; a tall sandy-blonde haired man, well dressed with a distinct prominence in the room, and had a quick conversation with him before turning quickly and heading towards the stage. It had been the same in almost every club they had entered. She only ever asked for five minutes and with the audiences' insistence, generally took a few more than twenty, keeping the scheduled band from returning to the stage. She wasn't being rude or selfish, half the time, the band themselves were cheering her on. She really was that captivating, her voice that beautiful. Her version of popular songs, be they from the past or recent hits, was so exceptional, so different, you couldn't help but be astonished at the way she made it her own.

Each night Poppy got on stage at a club, Kirby videotaped her on her tablet keeping each of her performances for reference. Poppy's evolution was evident on the tapes, her performances becoming more and more creative, less structured and more free flowing.

Something about tonight felt completely different to Kirby, and she was compelled to make sure she taped the entire evening as soon as she could. The tablet sat at the end of the table, facing the stage, with Kirby safely tucked behind it, slowly sipping a drink out of the camera's shot.

* * *

When she first touched the keys, the colors came slowly, the waves lapping against her, almost as if calm had come over the ocean. But, as Poppy continued to let her fingers play across the keyboard, the waves of blue began rolling in and as her fingers followed what she saw in her mind's eye, she raised her voice, coming up with words as she purged her heart. They touched upon, not only her past, but her present as well. Poppy's eyes were closed as she was guided by the waves that came crashing to her shore. When the explosions suddenly started appearing, she went with them, feeling a comfort she hadn't felt for some time. Her fingers easily flowed through a classical piece, the first few bars similar to a popular song, and then taking the audience back to the future. Poppy was having fun, melding together the many different kinds of music she was raised on. The classical, the ethnic, the contemporary and her family's own history. Once you blended all that, you got a particular kind of music, a very eclectic sound that could grab the fancy of nearly the entire music industry. Poppy Morningstar was creating her own sound, her own genre of music.

By this point, she had become oblivious to her audience, despite their cheering and clapping whenever she flowed from one genre into another. Her transitions were flawless, and her audience was sophisticated enough to know they were hearing incredible talent playing unbelievable music. She finished the performance out with the last few bars of a famous Bach composition. Her fingers touched the last keys and she suddenly came out of her trance. Opening her eyes, she regained her focus, first seeing the microphone, then the piano. *What the hell just happened?* She wondered.

* * *

Kerry stood absolutely in awe. She was right, she did blow his mind! He knew he had just witnessed the early days of a superstar. Her talent was unique; her voice was sultry at times, strong and poignant at others. Her piano playing was "instinctual", was the only word Kerry could come up with. This girl was born with music in her blood, more so, in every cell of her being. She played a piano as if her fingers and the keyboard were one. That much talent in one person doesn't stay contained for long. If he was going to make a move, he'd better do it quickly!

* * *

Chase sat down at his desk and opened up his email. His inbox contained quite a few new emails and he started to go through them.

241

He saw Kirby's email, with the subject line "Poppy's in Bloom!" It grabbed his attention and he opened it immediately. The email had only two words and a video attached. It read: "Open Me!"

He double clicked on the attachment, and it began playing as he sat back in his office chair, arms crossed, watching his large screen monitor.

Suddenly, Kirby's face filled the screen; her hair bouncing around as she smiled showing a full set of very white teeth. Her eyes were dancing about, as behind her, it was obvious that a crowd was enjoying their night in a club somewhere.

"Hi Chase!" She called out as she waved at the camera. "Kirby, here! I am taping this *after the fact*, but Poppy just blew the fucking roof off of "Baby Blues" she said, as she waved her arm behind her towards the club. "And I wanted you to see it, so sit back and enjoy!" She said, as she leaned in toward the camera. The picture suddenly changed over to the same scene, only Kirby was not there. The camera captured most of the crowd, the area in front of the stage sitting lower than the camera angle.

Poppy was walking across the stage, taking a seat at the piano. The crowd was chatting and paying no attention as she began playing. Chase sat motionless for a moment, watching like a father would, feeling nervous for his daughter. But, the crowd got quieter as she played on, and suddenly Chase was sitting up, leaning towards the large screen, completely mesmerized by her. She had the most incredible natural instinct and her ability to piece together contemporary, blues and jazz music with classical pieces that complimented it all was extraordinary. He couldn't move, he hardly breathed as he watched Poppy sway in front of the microphone and sing with her soul exposed and creating such beautiful sounds as her hands crossed the keys. Chase was lost in it all. When it came to the end, he was sitting inches from the screen, his hands covering his mouth and tears in his eyes. His screams were almost masked by the uproar of the crowd on screen.

Downstairs, Dana was working on documentation for the Foundation. Making sure the wording of contractual agreements was easily understood by her clients was important to Dana. The Foundation would not be taken advantage of as long as Dana Rose Morningstar was in the driver's seat!

At first she thought, he might be hurt. His screams were confusing; not necessarily cries of distress. Her heart stopped for a moment as she momentarily assessed his screams and, in the same moment turned from her desk and ran straight for the stairs.

"Chase?" she called, as she ran up the stairs towards his calls. "Chase, are you okay?" she called again as she reached the top of the stairs.

"Oh! Oh! Oh! Dana....Dana, look!" He said as he stood up and pointed to the giant monitor behind him.

"Wait!" he said, as he gathered his senses, pausing her with his raised hand. He pressed a key on his keyboard and the video started again, Kirby's face popping up on the screen. He paused it there, motioned for Dana to take a seat and did the same, placing himself directly in front of the giant monitor again.

"You are witnessing the birth of a star! The birth of a Morningstar!" he said, proudly pressing play. *Wait until she saw this!* He thought.

Chapter 17

SWAN SONG

Kerry Cruickshank stood at the end of the bar, completely stunned at what he had just witnessed. The talent of the beautiful blonde seated at the piano on stage was without a doubt, the most unbelievable thing he had had seen or heard. Everything about her performance had him spellbound. She sat at the microphone and his focus zeroed in on her, her every move.

As she finished, he managed to pull his attention from her and around the crowd as they applauded her and cheered their appreciation. It had all happened so quickly, he wondered if anyone had bothered to get it on video. Damn! He should have thought of that. But, even if he had thought of it, he couldn't have moved to get the video properly if he tried, he was so mesmerized by Poppy's performance.

She stood up from the piano bench and smiled towards the crowd, blinded by the stage lights shining in her eyes. The audience's reaction made her laugh and her smile shone brightly underneath the bright lights. She turned to leave the stage, waving as she left, but she was stopped quickly by a firm hand around her wrist and then her waist. She was gently pushed back into the spotlight as she realized Kerry was holding her, and holding up his arm to quiet the crowd.

"Hey!" He called to them. "Listen up!" He said. He whistled once, very sharp and very loud and the room quieted. "This young lady's name is Poppy, and I hope you all appreciate what you just witnessed here, because one day you'll be paying a ridiculous amount of money to watch her perform live again. That was fantastic!" He said enthusiastically and stepped away from Poppy, clapping towards her as the crowd's applause increased. She stood in the center of the stage, smiling wide and turning pink, which made the audience love her all the more.

Kerry stepped forward, helping guide her towards the stairs. As she stepped down, he caught her arm again and stopped her before she turned for her table.

"Hey, uh…Poppy. Hold up there." He hesitated saying anything when she turned to look directly at him. Her eyes met his and he felt the catch in his breath. Jesus! He usually didn't get tongue tied around women.

"Uh…listen, I'd like to have you back here. Are you in town still for tomorrow night?" He asked her, trying to quickly think of a way to get the band he'd hired for the week to agree. As shitty as they were, he had signed a contract with them.

"Really?" Poppy asked. "I'm not really prepared for a whole night's worth of entertainment. Not of that nature, anyway." She said, gesturing towards the stage and what she just performed.

"Oh, I disagree." Kerry said, smiling down at her. He couldn't help but feel incredibly attracted to her. Perhaps his desire to invite her back wasn't entirely because it was a good business venture. "I don't know what you call that kind of music, or what else you have in your repertoire, but that was all kinds of incredible." He told her honestly.

"Thank you so much for the opportunity." She told him. "I could do maybe a set, perhaps a half hour or so." She said as she contemplated what songs she would feel comfortable to perform.

"You could drag your toes across the keyboard and I bet you'd find a way to make it sound perfect." He said, laughing.

"Can I ask for a bit of practice time on the keys beforehand?" She asked, considering her playlist.

"Sure." He told her easily. "Kitchen staff is here for 3:00 pm. You can have access to the stage and piano from then on. Take the stage at probably, 8:30 pm, play for as long as you want. I'll pay you for a full night" he bargained. Fuck it, he'd cancel the band and pay for them to bugger off.

This was one woman he didn't want to scare off, and she was worth the bargain he offered.

"Oh, I wouldn't ask you to do that, Kerry. Actually, I won't take payment. Just ask that you let me play whatever I want. Is it a deal?" She bargained back. He wasn't sure what to think of her not wanting payment, every new performer wants to get paid. She thrust her hand towards him, and he looked down at it, not taking it straight away.

"Then I insist on feeding you beforehand, or after, whichever you prefer" He said, hoping she'd agree. He'd make sure it was a romantic dinner, even if it would be at the club.

"Throw in dinner for my friend, Kirby and you've got yourself a deal!" She said, happily thrusting her hand in his. Instinctively, he grabbed hold of her hand and began shaking before realizing what he had agreed to, and then he didn't care. This woman's hand was the most sensual hand he had ever touched. Her grip was strong, from years of playing piano, he guessed, but the skin was the softest he'd ever felt.

He reluctantly nodded his agreement and she smiled even wider. "I'll see you tomorrow then." She said, letting go of his hand, and turning towards her table. By the time Kerry's head had stopped spinning from her smile, she was almost back at her table and he was once again, left tongue tied. Damn! Why did that keep happening?

* * *

As Poppy reached the table, Kirby was raising her head from the tablet, her smile as wide as Poppy's. She reached out and grabbed Poppy in a huge hug, turning the girl around and jumping with her in excitement.

"Oh my God, that was incredible!" Kirby said, hugging her friend hard. She broke away from her and held her by the arms. "You were absolutely incredible, Poppy. I can't wait to show you the video." She told her, almost out of breath from excitement. "I've already sent it to Chase!" She told her, taking her seat again. "How do you feel?"

Poppy took a moment to assess. Her heart was beating normally; her mind was full of all sorts of ideas, songs, lyrics, and musical airings. She almost wanted to shoot out of the club and head to the hotel room so she could work on what her mind was racing with. Looking at Kirby's smiling face, brought her back to the table in the club, "Baby Blues".

"I don't know what happened, Kirby. I sat down to the piano and …my mind just went and I went with it." She tried to explain to her friend.

"I feel…exhilarated. I feel …excited." She paused, and then told her "He wants me back."

"What?" Kirby said, a look of confusion on her face.

"Kerry, you know, the owner or manager. He asked me to come back tomorrow night. Play a bit more." She said, smiling and shyly shrugging her shoulders. Kirby eyes showed her surprise.

"Are you kidding?" She asked. "He asked you to come back?" She echoed. Poppy nodded laughing.

"Yes, yes! I can't believe it!" She said, nodding and laughing. "That's okay, right?" She suddenly looked seriously to Kirby, not thinking it might be a problem.

"Of course!" Kirby screamed, as she reached across the table and grasped her friend's hands excitedly. "Of COURSE you're coming back!" she insisted. Kirby was the best friend Poppy could ask for.

* * *

As they settled in their hotel room that night, Poppy watched Kirby closely. She had an important question, a favor really, she wanted to ask her, but wasn't sure how Kirby would react.

Once Kirby was on her bed, sitting and flicking through stations on the TV, Poppy sat on her bed, facing Kirby and asked, "I need a favor."

"Name it." Kirby said, without hesitation, which surprised Poppy, but made her smile. She waited for a moment, closely studying Kirby. There had been so many things they had experienced in the almost three months they had been travelling together. There wasn't anything she wouldn't share with Kirby. But now, Poppy was about to ask her a favor she might not want to do.

"Tomorrow night" Poppy started explaining, "I have an idea about a song I want to do, but I need…" she hesitated, "I need your permission first." Poppy said, her hands clasped in front of her. Kirby turned to look at Poppy, seeing how serious she was being, her eyes taking in her friend's whole demeanor.

"You don't need my permission for anything, Poppy." Kirby told her, not understanding what it was Poppy was asking.

"I want to play the hymn that the church sang for Jessica. You know, the one she was known for." Poppy said, tenderly. Immediately Kirby's smiling face fell and she was drawn back by the request. It made Poppy fear she had taken too much for granted. She held her breath, hoping Kirby would not be offended. In trying to help her understand, Poppy said, "I …think it's a beautiful hymn. I promise to be respectful, but I want to sing it….but…I don't want to sing it alone." She said hesitating with each word, hoping Kirby would be able to read between the lines. She wasn't.

"You want to perform a church hymn?" Kirby repeated. "And who are you going to sing it with?" She asked Poppy, perplexed by her friend's idea.

Poppy looked at her long and hard. *She doesn't see it*, Poppy thought. *She doesn't know at all.*

"You!" Poppy said, shocking Kirby.

"What? No! Poppy! No!" Kirby objected, pulling herself back onto the bed, hugging her knees to her chest. She looked slightly annoyed and Poppy knew she needed to make her friend understand.

"Listen to me, Kirby. Your voice; it's excellent. You have excellent pitch, honestly. And you harmonize beautifully." She stopped, letting that sink in. Kirby looked at her as if she'd lost her mind. Poppy shook her head, understanding what the look on her face meant. "No, honey. You need to trust me on this. I know what I'm talking about. Right? You trust me when it comes to what's good and what isn't, right?" Poppy asked, the two women in a bit of an emotional standoff. It was now or never. They had come this far, both exposing their souls to the other throughout their months long journey. It came down to this request.

The song Poppy requested brought tears to Kirby's eyes just thinking about it. Since losing her sister, Kirby had not allowed herself to get too close to anyone, guarding her heart. Meeting Poppy had changed that. From the get go, she tugged at Kirby's heart, and now she realized why. Poppy Morningstar was placed into Kirby's life to help her grieve her dead family, and fill a void that no one else could. Poppy was as close to a sister as Kirby would ever have again.

With those thoughts racing through Kirby's head she calmed herself. Poppy noticed instantly and sat back, giving Kirby her space. Suddenly, Poppy had an idea. Reaching for Kirby's tablet, she set the video recorder on, put the tablet on the night stand and posed herself on the bed. She took a deep breath and began singing the hymn acapella.

She sang it with a flair that only Poppy could have. Kirby listened, astonished that she could have remembered it, not only the melody but all the words as well, after all she'd only heard it once. When she finished, she reached over and stopped the video from taping. She turned to Kirby and said, "Now it's your turn." Kirby's eyes grew wide as Poppy turned the video towards her. She then admonished, "Now listen, I've sat beside you for all these weeks, listening to all kinds of music from all eras and genres. But, it wasn't until we visited your home that you finally sang along with a song and it was beautiful." Poppy came to sit beside her friend on the bed. "I want you to sing along with my video and we'll tape it, okay? And then we'll listen to it, okay?" Poppy explained. She reached over and faced the tablet towards them on the bed. She hit play and the video she had just taped began to play.

At first, Kirby hesitated, resisting Poppy, but it didn't last long. Soon Kirby was harmonizing alongside Poppy's video. When her voice was strong, Poppy joined in adding a different key to the background, playing with the words and making it so much more. When they finished, Kirby sat quiet for a moment, with Poppy giving her some time.

After a long pause, Kirby looked to Poppy and said, quietly "Again." Poppy simply nodded her head, pressed the replay button on the tablet and the video began to play once again. Immediately, Kirby started harmonizing, this time, with more confidence, her voice rising strong. She closed her eyes as the words stung her heart, a tear streaming down her face. When they finished, they were seated in front of one another, both had tears, both moved beyond words. They instinctively hugged one another, each grateful for the others friendship, each realizing that the friendship they shared was a true blessing.

* * *

The next afternoon, Poppy and Kirby were at the piano in "Baby Blues" ready to rehearse for the evening's performance. Kirby's stomach was all in knots and she began to question why she had agreed to perform with Poppy. She had never been a singer, it was always Jessica and although Poppy seemed convinced she had a good voice, Kirby was now doubting her judgment.

Poppy explained to Kirby that she would begin the hymn with a few musical bars, she would start singing and Kirby was to join in just where she had last night with Poppy's video. Kirby nodded her head but said nothing, her eyes wide. She looked around the club to see who would be listening to them. There was two cooks in the kitchen, a woman behind the bar stocking the fridges and ice buckets, and Kerry Cruickshank, seated at the side of the bar near the back. He could barely be seen, but Kirby was almost certain his sight wasn't blocked and he more than likely had Poppy in clear view.

Kirby could tell when a man was smitten and Kerry Cruickshank was all kinds of smitten!

No matter what kind of piano, it sounded it's most beautiful when Poppy's hands played it. She brought the most creative sounds from it and Kirby wondered if any other had made it sound so beautiful. There were loads of musicians that were multi-talented, but there was only one Poppy Morningstar and she had a gift with music and the piano, specifically. Kirby was so lost in her composition, she was surprised when Poppy began to sing. She had taken liberty with the hymn and made it her own. Kirby was in awe. When it finally became her turn to start singing, she felt slightly self-conscious, but Poppy opened her eyes and stared straight into Kirby's eyes, giving her the strength and courage she knew her friend needed. Kirby's harmonizing rose, louder and stronger until the empty club was echoing their voices. The women sang together beautifully and Poppy ended the hymn with another short musical composition. When it ended, the women were both thrilled with their rehearsal and were about to begin again, but they were interrupted with small applause. Their focus was broken as they looked up realizing the staff present, including Kerry were all standing around the club, clapping.

"I guess that rests the question as to whether or not you can do this, huh?" Poppy said, giggling. She stood up from the piano bench, grabbed Kirby's hand and both bowed to their small audience, laughing with delight.

Kerry approached them as they thanked the kitchen staff with a wave. He sauntered up to the edge of the stage, leaning his arm on it as he smiled up at the women.

"I don't know what you call that, but it was beautiful. I didn't know you were a duet!" he told them, his smile getting wider as his eyes rested on Poppy and held them there. It made Poppy blush, but Kirby who had noticed Kerry's stare, wanted to straighten him out on one point.

"Uh…I'm not…" Kirby began, but Poppy quickly interrupted her.

251

"She has…uh…reservations about her singing." Poppy admitted to Kerry, rolling her eyes at him. He shook his head at Kirby.

"You have absolutely nothing to worry about. That was perfect, as if you've been singing all your life." He told her, waving his arm around the room. "Did you hear them?" he asked Kirby. She blushed, then smiled then blushed again. She really was out of her element, but it felt good. For the first time in five years, Kirby felt very good.

"Well, I'd be very careful when dealing with Miss Poppy Morningstar!" she called over her shoulder towards Poppy. This caught Kerry's attention and he stood up straight, his head cocked to one side.

"Morningstar? Like…THE Poppy Morningstar? Chase Morningstar's daughter?" He asked, rapidly as she gave a quick flash look to Kirby, then smiled at Kerry rolling her eyes. She nodded her head, then brought her finger to her lips.

"Shhhhhhhhhh." She hushed him, bending towards him so no one else could hear. "It's our little secret, okay?" She asked him, her eyes dancing like her smile. He stared at her and got lost in her face, so much that he found himself nodding without realizing it.

"I'll keep your secret. If…you agree to have a date with me. I mean, a proper date. Not in the club." He turned his body towards the club and looked around. "I'd like to take you on a proper date, somewhere we can eat a nice dinner and have some privacy. Would you agree to that?" he asked her, holding out his hand.

"We leave for home tomorrow. Tonight is actually my swan song, my last show of the tour, if you will." She told him, not accepting his hand. He took her hand in his and gently pulled her closer to him.

"The minute you get home and get settled, you call me. I'll fly out to you, wherever you want." He told her boldly. Poppy was slightly taken aback. Her reaction told him so. She gently pulled from him and stepped back, unsure of what to say. She studied him for a moment. His had an easy smile, friendly eyes and great hair and that was just off the top of her head. She had noticed him immediately yesterday as they had entered. He drew attention. He was more than 6 feet tall, she was sure. Taller than Chase and much taller than Hans. His hair was a bit shaggy with blonde streaks running through it. He'd definitely seen many days in the sun, despite owning and operating "Baby Blues". She figured he was in his early to mid-thirties, he looked young and tanned and full of energy and he looked very seriously at her.

"I'm sorry. I must come across as pushy. It's just that…" He hesitated, "A woman like you doesn't come along every day. I've lived enough to know to appreciate that." He paused, smiled and looked down, almost in shame. "It's been a long time since I felt so intrigued by someone. You intrigue me." He told her honestly. This made her feel much better. She leaned towards him again, extended her hand and shook his when he offered it.

"Dinner date when I'm settled, and in return, you don't mention my last name tonight. You can only introduce me as Poppy. Do we have a deal?" She asked, shaking his hand once, firmly.

"Deal" He shook her hand back, then smiled like a teenage boy. "Gonna give me your number?" he asked her, reaching for his phone from his inside jacket pocket.

Poppy laughed at his enthusiasm and sat on the stage. She took his phone and entered herself as a contact, then handed it back to him. For a moment they locked eyes and both felt a surge go through them. Poppy had no reservations about the feelings that had started growing within her, feelings of sexual interest, excitement and intrigue.

"I give it to you in good faith." She told him.

"I promise to remember that." He told her softly. They continued to keep each other's gaze until Kirby's throat clearing brought them both back to the present.

"Uh…excuse me? Can we have one or two or thirty more rehearsals please? Some of us aren't used to this center stage, lights on me, kinda crap and require more time feeling comfortable with this whole performance thing." Kirby asked, as she leaned against the piano.

Suddenly, Kerry turned and walked towards the kitchen as Poppy jumped up and was back on track. She sat on the bench and began playing freely, almost adding music to Kerry's exit. He sauntered into the kitchens with such a huge shit eating grin that one of the cooks stopped dead in his tracks as he watched his boss practically float through the kitchen. Usually the smells coming from the kitchen caused the boss to come drifting back to see what's cooking, but tonight, the cook wasn't sure what was causing the boss to float, but from the look of it, he was on cloud nine!

* * *

Kerry's introduction of Poppy was short and simple, just as he had agreed to. No last name. Not that it mattered. "Poppy" would be all they needed to know. Kerry was sure that, given time, Poppy would become a one name icon; an incredible woman that many could look up to, and a musician that many would admire.

However, for tonight, she was simply, "Poppy, here to entertain you." Kerry said, and stepped away from the microphone. The lights hit the piano bench in a flash and Poppy began playing. She blended many different songs into a variety, making some classical blues and others, a bluesy classic. Her musicality kept the audience enthralled, every once in a while she would sing a few lines of a song, and the crowd would begin clapping, showing their appreciation at how she blended it seamlessly together. She played her intro for nearly 15 minutes, leaving everyone in the club in a trance. She was spellbinding, utterly amazing in her ability. The club was on a stupendous high and she hadn't even begun!

For the next 30 minutes, Poppy took them all on a joyous ride through classical and contemporary blues, all melded into a beautiful mixture. No one was sure of what was coming next and it excited them. It grew within the room, until finally, Poppy took a moment and looked over to the table where Kirby was sitting, taping the entire performance with her tablet.

"Kirby, would you please join me?" She asked, nodding to her friend. Kirby hesitated for just a moment and then gained her confidence, pushing herself from her seat and headed towards the stage. Poppy smiled into the microphone.

"Ladies and gentlemen, may I introduce to you, my dearest friend and closest confident, Kirby." The audience erupted in applause for her and her stomach lurched and went wild both at the same time. If there was anyone worth doing this for, it was Poppy. She trusted her and it had been a long time since Kirby trusted anyone.

She cleared her throat and positioned herself in front of the solo microphone, next to the piano.

Poppy waited for Kirby to give her a visual clue when she was ready. Almost on cue, Kirby looked to Poppy and nodded her head slightly and Poppy began to play her introductory composition. It was such a compliment to the hymn, the audience had no idea they were hearing a new piece created in only the last few days. Poppy played from her heart, knowing her own creation so well no notes were written, no notes required. She played from memory, from the ebbs and flows of colors that could sometimes explode across her mind creating a detour into a classical trend, only being brought back when the waves began to lap against the shore again; a true celebration of music from many genres.

And then she began to sing.

The words of the hymn so wrenching. A question to God about a soul's existence, a reason for a purpose on earth. Kirby's voice joined in, harmonizing and Poppy complimented them both with her playing, bringing an incredible song to the audience. No one moved during the performance, some hardly breathed in. All were held within the vortex of the music and singing coming from the two, very talented women on stage. When Poppy hit the last note on the piano key, there was a singular moment of silence and then the crowd exploded into applause, cheers and excited shouts. In total, there were probably 300 people who were lucky enough to be in "Baby Blues" that night to witness the moment. It would become famous, nearly overnight via social media. There were two or three videos taken that night, all from different angles, but it didn't matter from what angle it was taken from, it all amounted to the same thing; instant exposure through social media and pure gold.

Chapter 18

POPPY AND KERRY

It didn't take long. Once back home in New York, Poppy found herself thinking about Kerry Cruickshank more and more. With all the taping that had been done over the weeks Poppy was away, she studied the two nights at Baby Blues the most. The performances there were different from others she had done along the way. Poppy had reinvented herself in those two nights. Looking back, she wondered if it was her visit to Kirby's grandmother's house that had caused her to discover her new genre, but to anyone else watching it was clear what effect the Baby Blues manager had on her. She was in love.

Despite Poppy going straight into the recording studio, she contacted Kerry almost immediately and from that moment on, they were always in touch, either Skyping, face timing or flying out to see one another when time permitted. After a year of hard work and determination, Poppy released her first CD, "Nightscape" straight to the online music world and it was a huge overnight hit. Her raw performance videos from her road trip had been uploaded to the internet and were viewed millions of times over by hungry music lovers who thought Poppy Morningstar was a musical genius. Her following grew exponentially and you couldn't go anywhere that wasn't playing her music, her videos or broadcasting news about her in one form or another. Poppy had become a major musical influence all of her own and her life would never be the same.

After a year of flying back and forth for some precious time alone, Kerry decided it was time to get serious with Miss Poppy Morningstar and after an extended long weekend in New York City, Kerry Cruickshank proposed to Poppy Morningstar right outside Rockefeller Centre with many tourists and city dwellers taking out their phones to capture the moment. The news went viral immediately, with pictures showing Kerry down on one knee,

Poppy leaning over slightly, her hand covering her mouth. It was a complete surprise to her! The headlines read: Poppy's Proposal!

* * *

Considering the magnitude of her audience and following, her wedding by margins, was very small. Hans was flown in and both Hans and Chase walked Poppy down the aisle and gave her away. She looked stunning in her beautiful white dress made exclusively for her by New York's latest hot bridal designer, Guy LaRoche. Poppy had brought Guy some ideas and from them, he was able to create a one-of-a-kind wedding dress that was exquisite. The wedding pictures made all the fashion magazines, every prime-time news show and almost every internet posting had something about Poppy's wedding. Poppy was used to the publicity and all the fuss by this point, but Kerry was not and it took him a while to get used to how much his new wife was wanted by the public. It made it difficult for them to find their alone time, but Kerry was determined. He loved Poppy Morningstar with all of his heart and if he could only have her to himself a few hours a day, or a few days a week, then so be it. Kerry wasn't deterred. Yet.

* * *

The first three years was wedded bliss. Both had hectic schedules, but once they were back in each other's arms, they would fall into bed and explore the other with every part of their being. They became famous for not showing up to events, especially if it was held on the first day of their being reunited after a lengthy period of time. All of those closest to Poppy and Kerry knew that if they were together, there was a high likelihood they would show up much later than anticipated or not at all. Amongst those, only a few were ever put out by this, understanding that their relationship was one with long lengths of time apart and passionate times when they were together.

Kerry continued to manage Baby Blues, but spread out to locations in Nevada and Chicago. He was constantly in one hotel room or another for those first three years, and when he was in his own bed, it was rare that Poppy was beside him. Her music took her all over the world; interviews here, special appearances there. In between, she had a recording studio built in the couple's Connecticut home and when she wanted to create new music, she'd hole herself up in the studio and lock the rest of the world out. She was consumed by her music and Kerry was lost in his clubs. The only other thing that held a higher priority was each other. Each night they were apart they would end their evening with a face chat, telling the other about their day, how much they missed one another and how they couldn't wait to be together. Then, Poppy would say, "Goodnight my love" and Kerry would reply, "Sweet dreams, baby" and the call would end. It was the one moment in an otherwise hectic day that would ground them and they never missed doing it.

On the eve of their 3rd wedding anniversary, neither was at home. Poppy was in Los Angeles attending the Grammys, of which she was nominated for 6 awards, including Artist of the Year and Album of the Year. She was preparing for the evening's awards when her cell phone rang and she answered it.

"Hey" she said softly, recognizing her husband's number.

"Hey!" he said enthusiastically! "What's up?" He asked her right away, detecting sadness in her voice.

"I miss you!" she complained to him. "How much longer are they going to need you in Vegas? I need you here!" she told him, throwing herself down in a chair. Poppy rarely had time for temper tantrums and emotional outbursts, but Kerry was unable to attend the awards with her that night and she wasn't happy about it. She wanted him by her side as she won or lost the awards she was nominated for. She wanted his body next to her to congratulate her or take her in his arms later and make her feel better, regardless of what award she lost. She always felt better in Kerry's arms.

"I know, baby" he said, consolingly. "I wish I could get there, but there are problems with some of the building permits and I need to stay by in case things fall through. I promise I'll try and make it up to you" he told her, hoping she'd understand. "Isn't Kirby good company?" he asked, wanting to change the subject. He seemed a little distracted to Poppy and she was hurt by his lack of attention to her big night.

"Yes, Kirby's great company. As always", she answered. Kirby had stayed by her side and been with her since their return from the road trip. She was Poppy's personal escort when Kerry was unable to. If Kerry wasn't by her side, then Kirby was.

"But, this is important, Kerry. And I know we've always been understanding with one another's careers, but this…this one's…." her voice trailed off as there came a knock at the door. She looked up at it, wondering who it could be and continued talking as she went to answer it. "This one's a biggie to miss, Mr. Cruick…" she stopped dead as she opened the door and saw him standing there! Her squeal of delight was heard by the entire hotel floor as she threw herself into his arms and kissed him full on the lips. They fell back against the closed door and broke out laughing, then kissed again.

"What happened?" she asked, incredulously.

He straightened himself up and grabbed her hand bringing her to a full stand, still laughing. He brought his hands to her waist and pulled her against him, taking in her scent.

"I told the lawyer to deal with it" he said "I needed to be with my Grammy Award winning, wife!" He smiled down at her. She smacked his arm playfully.

"Don't jinx me!" She said, half joking. "I haven't won anything, yet!"

God, she looked so lovely. He held her back from him and took a good long look. She was already dressed for the show; a sleek satin dress in midnight blue with diamonds dripping from her ears and wrist. Her neck was bare and it was the sexiest thing Kerry had seen in a long time. He took his fingers and stroked her collarbone, mesmerized by her.

"I'm sorry I put you through that, Poppy" he admitted. "I wasn't sure if things were going to be okay and I was worried, but I told them if things weren't settled by the time the last flight could get me here, I was gone anyway, so it motivated them to get it done." He said, smiling. Poppy smiled back and drew him into a long languishing kiss. When they finally came up for air, Kerry was slightly light headed.

"God, you make my head spin!" he told her, squeezing her tightly. "Now!" he smacked her ass, "You'd better let me get going and get into a shower. My tux is on its way up" he swung her around and left her twirling as he walked straight into the bathroom. Poppy smiled to herself, still feeling his arms around her. She sighed happily. Kerry was the best. He'd never let her down. Yet.

* * *

The Grammy's were spectacular! There were music stars from every genre all humming with excitement at the prospect of being named Grammy's best. Poppy and Kerry stood out from all others. Her genre was her own and nothing like her music had ever been created or celebrated before. It was a very special night for Poppy and she was thrilled to have Kerry by her side, holding her hand and showing his support.

By the end of the evening, Poppy held 5 of the 6 awards she was nominated in. She absolutely glowed and Kerry was so proud of her accomplishment. She remembered to thank him in each speech, as well as both fathers, Chase and Hans and the Morningstar family for the gift of music that ran in her veins.

At the after party, Kerry wanted to make a brief appearance and then get back to the hotel and be alone with her, but Poppy was interested in meeting a few of the producers that had won that evening, in particular; Mr. Garrett Samuels. Garrett had produced a number of the winning compositions from tonight's show and Poppy had been very impressed. It was hard to find a producer who had vision and the financial backing to allow the artist free reign, but word around the industry was that Mr. Garrett Samuels was one of them.

As Kerry's hand grasped Poppy's to leave, she spotted Garrett Samuels across the room and pulled Kerry with her, dragging him through the dance floor and right past the bar. As if it were meant to be, just as Poppy reached the other side of the room, Garrett Samuels spotted Poppy and walked straight over to her, followed by a pretty blonde in a gold lament dress.

"Hi, I've been hoping we'd run into one another at some point. Congratulations on winning just about everything! We should work together on a project one day" Garrett said, smiling wide and showing brilliant white teeth. His smile took Poppy's breath away. He was the most handsome man she had ever seen. Regardless of her love for Kerry, she would have been lying to herself not to admit that Garrett Samuels had an electrifying effect on her. She reached her hand out and they shook. Pure vibrations. Poppy was speechless for a moment and just as she was about to say something, flashes started going off as photos were taken of the two music Phenom's meeting for the first time. "I'd love to" was all she could manage.

"Grammy's Golden Couple!" It made all the papers. The photo showed Grammy Award winning Producer, Garrett Samuels, a very handsome black man in a black tuxedo shaking hands with the Grammy Award winning, very beautiful blonde haired, green eyed Poppy Morningstar. The juxtaposition of them alone was striking, but given the circumstances, social media had a field day with it, much to Kerry's chagrin.

* * *

At six years married they were still going strong, only now neither of them was able to be at their home in Connecticut for any long period of time and rarely together. Poppy would stay long enough to record her next album then spend the next 15 months touring the world. Most nights they'd face chat with each other and promise to be together in a number of weeks, until something would come up. They were still very much in love, but also very much in demand. Both understood, although Kerry would usually be the first to grab a flight to wherever Poppy was playing and stay a few days before flying back to whichever club needed him most. The house stood empty for many long months at a time.

After a lengthy stay in Vegas, Kerry headed home for a few days. On his first night, he walked around the house looking at each room as if it were the first time he was seeing it. He missed Poppy. He imagined them sitting together on their large overstuffed couch, with her feet resting on him and laughing at something he had said. It had been a long time since the house had seen that happy picture.

He entered their bedroom and stood in the doorway. A familiar room, but empty as the rest of the house. The large carved wood headboard they'd found online from an overseas company made the bed look small against it. The dark wood, carved with intricate artistry was massive and took four men to install. Poppy and he had fallen in love with the piece as soon as they had seen it. Poppy had said it reminded her of an exotic island getaway, Kerry just thought it was an excellent piece of workmanship. It seemed a shame it adorned a lonely bed.

Kerry took out his phone as he climbed upon the bed and lay against the pillows. He dialed Poppy's number and held the phone in front of his face so when she answered, he was there.

"Hey!" she said excitedly when she answered.

"Hey!" he said back. "Guess where I am?" It was a game they played. Both had stayed in so many hotels over the years, they were able to recognize the hotel merely by seeing a small portion of the décor.

"Hmmmmmm" she answered, pondering for a moment. "I can't see the pillows. Show me something as a hint." She asked him. He obliged by holding the phone up towards the headboard and further out so he still remained in the view.

"Awwww! No fair!" she squealed. "You're home!"

"Yes I am" he answered her. "But, you're not. Now who's not fair?" he stated.

She looked sadly at the phone as he positioned it in front of his face again.

"I miss you, baby" he told her. "Isn't it time you came home and we tried to make some babies?"

"I miss you, too" she told him. "And I would love to come home and try and make babies with you, but I'm in the middle of this tour. Another two months and I'm yours for a while, how about that?" She tried consoling him, but it wasn't working, he sighed heavily.

"I'm just getting tired of us not being together." He admitted.

"I know. But I'm not the only one in this marriage who travels" she answered with a knowing smile. He nodded, agreeing with her.

"I'm here for just a few days, then headed to Chicago for the blues festival." He told her, emphasizing her last comment.

"So, you're only lonely for tonight then?" she said, tilting her head at him and raising her one eyebrow above her spectacular green eye.

"No! I'll be lonely tomorrow and the next day, too!" he laughed, just a little. He really was lonely and did miss her very much. They had never lived a normal married life like others did. They'd never discussed having children, never spent more than a couple of weeks together and then they'd be apart for much longer. Their careers really became the priority and even though they tried hard, their marriage suffered from it.

"Goodnight my love" She said, blowing him a kiss.

"Air sex. I love it" he mused at the blown kiss. "Sweet dreams, baby!" he said as he ended the call and threw the phone across the bed. Someday, Poppy would be in bed next to him and it had better be soon!

* * *

Another two years later and Kerry was tired. He didn't want a long distance relationship anymore. He didn't want to share his wife with the world and only find out about where she was or how she was doing by either the news or a quick face chat that usually ended with him throwing the phone down on whatever bed he found himself that night. After his stay at home those three days, he had never made it back to the house. He found it so sad to go there when Poppy wasn't home and she was never home. She had even recorded her last album as a live tour, so she hadn't been home long enough for their paths to cross. The world loved Poppy Morningstar, but only Kerry loved her for her. The world loved the musician, the singer, the songstress. He loved the woman.

Kerry began to feel resentful of her life and career. He started wanting her to be beside him at night and wake up to her in the morning. Their phone calls often ended in him venting his frustrations to her, but Poppy was of a single mind. She needed to finish the tour, or album or whatever musical project she was working on at the time.

As they entered their 10th year of marriage, neither Kerry nor Poppy was paying much attention to it. Kerry's attention was completely in Vegas where a new hotel, not far from Baby Blues Vegas was located, was now taking most of his clientele with their big name acts, large stage and even larger theatre. It was tough to compete with the kind of money they paid to their musical talent. Kerry had never had a business failure, but he was facing one now.

Poppy had been approached by the Academy Award winning composer, Jonathan McArthur about collaborating on a soundtrack for the latest blockbuster that was to hit the screens just as the summer was starting. "Last One Standing" was expected to be a huge and if Poppy Morningstar's name was associated with it, there was no doubt it would be even bigger. She was literally incommunicado for several weeks as she holed up and worked on creating a musical masterpiece. Even Kerry had a difficult time reaching her; their late night phone calls relegated to one or two a week now.

Poppy's talents and creativity paid off as she and Jonathan were nominated for Best Original Soundtrack for Last One Standing. She was thrilled! This was a huge accomplishment for a musician to win an award for their work on a movie and Poppy was so proud. The morning the nominations were announced, she received calls from Chase and Dana and even Uncle Charlie and Aunt Georgie, but not from Kerry.

They did manage to speak a few days later, but Poppy could hear in his voice that he was disinterested in her news. She told him the date of the awards and asked if he could make sure he'd be there. He told her he'd try but couldn't promise. He blamed the Vegas club for being such a pain in the ass and got off the phone quickly. No, Goodnight my love, no sweet dreams, baby.

The day of the Academy Awards came and even though Poppy was nervous and anxious. She was hoping Kerry would walk through the door at any moment, just as he did all those years ago for her first Grammy awards.

She fidgeted and fussed, pacing her hotel room and checking her watch. When the phone rang, she raced to answer it without even looking at the number.

"Kerry?" she asked into the phone.

"Uh..no. Sorry honey, it's just me" Kirby answered her. "What's up? Is he not coming?" she asked. Lately, it had been noticeable to everyone that the happy couple were anything but.

"Oh. Hi there" Poppy said flatly. "I don't think he can make it. I really thought, given the fact that it's the Oscars that he'd try, but it's getting too late now. The limo will be here in 15 minutes to take me to the show." She explained.

Kirby wanted to blast Kerry bigtime. This was possibly going to be the biggest night of her life and he couldn't be bothered to show up. What an ass!

"Damn! Why didn't you tell me, I would've been there in a flash!" Kirby said, trying to console Poppy. She had been busy exploring more of the world through her classical talent, adding her voice to some of Poppy's music and visiting Bobby, whenever she could!

"I know. I was just hoping he'd make an effort" Poppy said, sounding dejected.

"Okay, well screw him. You need to put a big beautiful smile on your face and go out and win that award and not think about this now until tomorrow. Deal with it then." Kirby told her sternly. The next time she saw Kerry she was going to ring his neck! She felt awful for Poppy, who was now all alone at the award ceremony.

"Okay, I will" she admitted. Kirby was right and she knew it. There wasn't going to be a surprise showing this time and she had worked very hard, earning this nomination. No one could take that away from her. She straightened her shoulders and stood up waiting for the limo to arrive.

She walked the red carpet alone, posing for numerous cameras, but not talking to any reporters. They were calling her name, but she was quickly rushed in passed their questions. She was seated in the fifth row, middle from the front and a "seat warmer" was placed next to her. With no escort, the seat beside her was filled with someone she didn't know, so the show looked well attended. It mattered only to the TV audience, but was an old trick producers used to fill the crowd. Poppy sat quiet, wishing the show was already over.

Last One Standing was doing well having picked up 3 Oscars of the 8 categories it was nominated in. Poppy sat through an hour and a half before they reached the "Best Original Soundtrack" category. Her category. Poppy sat still and composed. She took a deep breath, held it and exhaled in a four beat process. She had done this for many years when she'd felt nervous or anxious. It helped calm her down.

The renowned composer and last year's Oscar winner for Best Original Soundtrack, Jesus De Luca walked across the stage, carrying the envelope with this year's winner inside. He paused in front of the microphone, took a moment and then smiled broadly as he read the teleprompter, announcing this year's nominees in the same category.

Poppy's heart was racing, regardless of her breathing technique. She watched as each nominee in the category was showcased, finally playing her soundtrack while showing a few montages from the movie "Last One Standing".

"And, the Oscar goes to..." Jesus paused, struggling to open the envelope. When he finally opened it he raised his arms and shouted, "Poppy Morningstar and Jonathan McArthur for Last One Standing!" The audience erupted! It was completely surreal to Poppy and with no one around her to bring her out of her spell, Poppy sat there for a moment, frozen in place. Jonathan McArthur, who sat two rows behind her, jumped up, kissed his wife exuberantly and raced out of his seat, grabbing Poppy from her's. He hugged her momentarily before turning her towards the stage and gently pushing her forward. She felt in a daze, things moving slowly in front of her.

Jonathan gave her the privilege of speaking first. She looked at him with wide eyes, stepped towards the microphone and spoke slowly, choosing her words carefully.

"I…uh…want to thank the Academy for this honour. My partner in crime on this project, Jonathan McArthur who could inspire a dry river to shed tears and was an incredible partner on this project. The cast and crew who gave this film life and the producers for putting together such and incredible team. Thank you to Chase and Hans, my two dads who were instrumental in my love for music and the musical blood that runs through my veins! Thank you so very much!" She raised her Oscar in the air and stepped away, allowing Jonathan his chance. He thanked numerous people by name, the production company heads and his wife and family or so Poppy thought. She was still in a daze.

When the music began, Jesus Du Luca walked her off stage and congratulated her numerous times before leaving her to walk off towards the bar. Jonathan came and hugged her, saying how grateful he was for her work and told her he would love to work with her again! He left her backstage after another bone breaking hug and a kiss on her forehead.

Left alone backstage, her heart was racing and her mind was going a mile a minute. She'd won! She was holding an Oscar and he was heavy. She had never expected him to be so heavy. She looked him over and was amazed at how beautiful he was! Immediately, she went to her clutch and grabbed her phone. She wanted to phone Kerry and share it with him. She wasn't angry with him anymore, she understood. They had both become obsessed with their careers and she now realized that it may have caused a bit of a drift between them, but he was her love and she wanted to show him how well she'd done. She dialed his number.

"Hey!" he answered after a few rings.

"Did you watch it?" she asked, almost out of breath. "I won it, Kerry! I won!" she said excitedly, moving her phone to show him the golden statue.

"Yeah, I saw. That's so exciting!" he told her, smiling. He didn't mean it, though. He noticed she hadn't mentioned him in her acceptance speech.

"I know, right?" she said. "I can't believe it. God, I wish you were here. I miss you so much" she said, looking longingly into the phone. "Listen, I have to go and get interviewed, but I need to see you, to be with you. I know it's been crazy, but once this is done, I'm heading home. Think you could take some time off and meet me there? I miss you so much" she asked. She could make things all better now that the movie was done and the awards season was over. She could make it right again between them. Maybe they could start a family.

"Uh…yeah, sure" was all he said.

"Okay well, goodnight my love" she ended with her famous line.

"Congratulations Poppy" was his return reply and he ended the call.

Poppy looked at her phone as the line went dead. Things weren't great between them, she knew that, but she also knew that she could now focus on their marriage. She could devote the time to her marriage and be the supportive wife. She could do that. She would do that. They deserved it.

* * *

In a hotel room off the Vegas strip, Kerry threw the phone down on the bed.

"God, haven't you told her, yet?" the naked redhead asked, as she stretched seductively on the hotel room couch. Kerry admired all she was offering.

"No, I haven't told her yet. I couldn't tell her tonight. Not right after winning an Oscar. That wouldn't be cool" he said, trying hard not to sound pissed off at her. As if he'd tell Poppy about his extra-marital affair with one of the dancers from a show on the strip. It had been going on for some time.

"And I don't plan to just yet, either so you'd better be a good girl and be patient. You know who she is? Only the most famous musician of our time! I can't just blurt out that I've been screwing you!" he said, not choosing his words carefully. This made the redhead equally as pissed off. She had considered herself a lot more than just an available screw, now and again. Not able to hide her anger, she grabbed her clothing, ignored his apologies and stormed out the door. She had been a good girl, had followed all his requests for secrecy and had even lied to her family about who she'd been seeing. If all she was going to be classified as was a "screw", then she would. *Screw* him, that is.

* * *

Robin Hewer had been up late watching the Academy Awards in hopes of seeing Poppy Morningstar take home her first Oscar and she didn't disappoint! He was thrilled for her and planned on calling Chase in the morning to congratulate him and have a quick chat. They hadn't spoken for some time, although any news regarding Poppy went through Robin first, as per the family's request. He was still top dog in the investigative reporting when it came to the Morningstars and he liked it that way!

When his phone rang, he had half a mind to ignore it and just get straight to bed, but the reporter in him couldn't let it be and despite being up later than he normally would, he answered the phone.

"Do you still hold all the cards on Morningstar reports?" the woman's voice asked. "Cause if so, I have a story for you. And it's not from an anonymous source, it's straight from the horse's mouth!"

Robin suddenly became very awake.

Chapter 19

FACE FORWARD

"MORNINGSTAR'S MARRIAGE MELTS DOWN!"

Headlines were everywhere. Paparazzi gathered at every location that Poppy had been seen in the last few days, but no one had spotted her. Kerry and the redhead were splashed all over the front page, breaking news and every social media post and a lot of very angry tweets, posts and emails were sent his way. Once word was out, some creep went through hotel surveillance cameras and found video of the two of them in some very unflattering situations and sold them all for a hefty profit. No one was on Kerry's side. Not the media, not the family and certainly not Poppy's fans. He had become a pariah in a very short period of time and to make sure he was kicked in the nuts enough, his Baby Blues Vegas club tanked a week later. His reputation was shit.

Poppy cried for days. She had been brought back to Chase and Dana's New York apartment almost immediately after the Oscars, hardly having a moment to enjoy her win. She spent her days mending her broken heart by playing piano and looking out the window for extended periods of time. At times, she was very logical and recognized that both she and Kerry were to blame for the failure of their marriage. You can't be married and travel like the two of them did, it just doesn't work. Someone always gets lonely.

At other times, she'd be angry as hell that he'd done this to her. The news ate it up and spit it out like it was suddenly the best of reality TV. She hated how people who didn't even know her, speculated about her married life and what it must be like to be married to a Morningstar. How could anyone speculate on that? They had made it work for almost ten years, regardless of the physical distance between them, why had it failed now? Poppy couldn't understand Kerry's betrayal. It was true that their sex life took a real beating due to their careers, but they both understood that

271

and would do their best to make up for it when they could. Perhaps she was asking too much of a man to put his sexual needs lower on the list of priorities. Perhaps she needed to realize that her music really was her life and a man would always take second place to that.

Kirby was a great help. She would take Poppy out, far beyond the cityscape to hiking trails where no paparazzi would find them and let Poppy scream her guts out to no one in particular. Sometimes, she'd just cry quietly while they walked the trails. Whatever Poppy felt, it usually came out of her once they got out into nature. In time, Poppy began to see the truth of the matter. Their 10 years together was far from a real marriage and as their individual careers grew, each of them put less and less priority on the marriage than they did for their work. But, Poppy had never betrayed Kerry, had never even looked at another man in the entire decade they were married. For that, Kerry was all to blame. She had been totally faithful and he hadn't. So, for Poppy, there was no forgiving that. Kerry Cruickshank was now a past chapter in her life and she knew she couldn't lick her wounds forever. The best medicine was to get back at it, back to her music which never betrayed her!

After one particularly long hike, Poppy climbed into Kirby's SUV and let out a heavy sigh.

"Well, that's done now", Poppy said.

"Huh? What's done?" Kirby asked, trying to navigate the SUV out onto the main road.

"Me, being a crybaby." Poppy answered, smiling. It had been a while since Kirby had seen Poppy's smile, a few weeks, at least. "I'm done crying over my marriage. I'm done with feeling like this. I'm just done. Now, I'm going to write about it!" She said, her eyes twinkling. Kirby smiled back at Poppy. It was good to have her friend back. The weepy, crying Poppy was not someone Kirby was used to. Poppy had shown such resilience, strength and courage since Kirby had met her, it surprised Kirby how badly Poppy had taken Kerry's betrayal. Not that she didn't have the right, of course she did. Kirby was actually surprised at the restraint Poppy had shown.

If it had been Kirby who had been betrayed, she'd have had a trophy of the man's dick and testicles hanging in a shadow box in her bedroom, as a way of letting any other man who enters her life know what happens to someone who betrays her. And, she'd have used a dull knife to perform the procedure! But, not Poppy Morningstar. Oh sure, she'd cried and screamed until her voice was hoarse, but there was no desire to seek revenge, no want to hurt him back equally as bad.

"So?" Kirby asked Poppy on their drive home. "You and Kerry split things 50/50 and he goes one way and you go another?" She didn't want to pry, but she'd spent a lot of time with Poppy since Kerry's betrayal and couldn't recall her discussing any kind of prenuptial agreement or dividing of property. Frankly, she never really understood her best friend's marriage, nor how it lasted 10 years. She figured that the distance would be a huge disadvantage, but they seemed to make it work, at first. As far as Kirby was concerned, she loved Poppy, but it was no way to have a marriage.

Poppy sighed and stared out the window as they drove along. She hadn't thought about dividing the property up. She hadn't spent any time at the Connecticut house in over a year. Now, with the realization that Kerry's girlfriend might have been laying in their bed a time or two made Poppy not want to go back there, whatsoever. She would arrange for a mover to go in and pack up her things and deliver them to a storage shelter in New York. Chase and Dana welcomed her staying with them and she would often be working or touring; there was never much time for her to be at home. *Why have a permanent home if I'm not going to be there?* She figured. She would stay with Chase and Dana for now. She could use Chase's studio to create her new songs and when the CD dropped, she'd be ready to tour with it. No sense in hunting out a home if she wasn't going to be there.

As she stared out the window, it took all of 5 minutes for Poppy to decide the whole deal. She'd take a few items that were sentimental to her, things that Kerry would have no interest in and she'd walk away. Poppy Morningstar didn't need someone else's money, she had plenty enough of her own! And thanks to the pre-nuptial agreement that Chase, Hans and Uncle Charlie insisted on her having, she'd walk away with all of her earnings. It was part of their agreement, if either one were to stray, the other gets to walk away!

Within a week, all her belongings and those few items she cherished had been gathered up, packed and stored in a storage container, not far from Chase and Dana's. If there was anything Poppy needed, she could easily get access to it. Kerry didn't challenge her on anything, he had enough on his plate with his public persona taking a real nose dive and his Vegas club foreclosing. He understood he'd fucked up; even though he was done with the marriage, he should have just ended it. The minute he slept with whatshername, he reneged on the whole deal, in more ways than just the pre-nup. She couldn't look at him. She couldn't speak to him. She was made to think they had a relationship that transcended distance and time apart. She really did. He really should have just ended it, clean.

Poppy hadn't laid eyes on Kerry since before the Oscars, other than their face chat that night, right after her win. Robin Hewer had been informed and he contacted Chase who had done everything to try and protect Poppy, but no matter what Chase tried to do, it couldn't save her broken heart. Thankfully, she'd been given some privacy and the ability to act out without hungry paparazzi trying to get the best shot of the "Miserable Morningstar".

It had now been almost 3 months since the betrayal had hit the news and Poppy was ready to purge all of it. She locked the door to Chase's studio, sat at the piano and did her therapy; she wrote songs. For weeks, Poppy Morningstar stayed in the studio. Alone. Some days, it was all she could do to get herself fed, she was so consumed with her writing. Once it started, it was like a torrent that wouldn't stop. 15 songs, each one a different and unique testament to her experience and growth over the decade she had been with Kerry. When she looked back she realized that her career took off just as her relationship with Kerry had started. The person she was then is not the person she was now. She knew she had Kerry to thank for a lot of that, she couldn't deny it. Love wasn't a switch she could turn on and off, no matter how hard she tried. She kept herself secluded while she wrote and came to peace with things. She would always love Kerry. He had supported her during her early years, understanding her drive and focus, giving her encouragement to be herself and confirming the fans will love her, and he wasn't wrong. He was rarely wrong when it came to his business, which was why his Vegas business not being successful was shocking, and his straying from their marriage, was also so shocking. She just didn't see it coming.

Song after song, each one better than the last. It took her four short months to come up with "Face Forward", her new CD. Once again, Poppy Morningstar had found a niche. Poppy's unique piano playing was at a new level on "Face Forward", like she'd been a caterpillar in a cocoon for months and then a rebirth as a beautiful butterfly. "Face Forward" also featured her profile in black and white, with a blindfold over her eyes. A secret nod to her belief in having blind faith in what she had passion for. "Face Forward" was another passionate project and it brought Poppy world-wide acclaim. A ten year marriage became a record breaking 10 for 10 win at the Grammy's that year. Poppy attended the event alone. It didn't go unnoticed.

Chapter 20

PRECISION TOUCH

Garrett Samuels sat in his living room, reading. Engrossed in a film script he had become very fond of, he barely noticed the 105" TV monitor on the wall. The script of "Precision Touch" had been sent to him 5 years ago and he had loved it from the moment he turned the first page. Normally, Garrett worked on music, but his heart tugged at this true story of a young soldier, Connor McClure, who forever changed the way prosthetics were built, after losing both arms in an explosion during his second tour of duty. Not being satisfied with that, the young soldier, turned inventor then focused his mind to space and came up with a new all-in-one space suit made of a material that could breathe for the astronaut. It was lightweight, could self-calibrate and had no need for large bulky gloves, boots or helmet. It was all attached together.

It took him 7 years before NASA was interested in Connor's space suit and he was smart enough and patient enough to wait it out. He knew they'd come around and they did, as soon as they heard that Russia was calling him. He worked closely with NASA and because of his ingenuity, became one of the first 5 astronauts to try the suit on a trip to the moon, and the first amputee astronaut to travel in space! The suits worked perfectly and the mission was a huge success. They were returned to earth safely and Connor McClure retired a few years later, living out his life quietly in suburban America. No one knew his name, past the mailman and a few neighbors. A quiet, brilliant mind that revolutionized the world with a simple precision touch. Garrett Samuels wanted the world to know this incredible man and his fantastic story.

The script had numerous hand written entries, almost as if each page held a journal of how it would be told. This story resonated something in him and even though he was a music producer, he was driven to get this movie made.

As he made notes through the script and dog eared certain pages, his eyes were drawn to his 105" TV as it showed a close-up of a beautiful green eyed, blonde haired woman. Even with the sound off, he knew her to be Poppy Morningstar. He clearly remembered shaking her hand several years before and the unexpected effect it had on him.

Now, they were interviewing her and Garrett Samuels was transported back to an evening a long time ago; a Grammy Awards when both of them were new to the industry and big winners that night. The moment in time captured forever by a quick thinking photographer and the media labelling them "Grammy's Golden Couple". He recalled their handshake and the jolt of pure electricity that ran through his hand. It literally made his eyes water for a moment. He knew of her work, had followed her for a while and looked for her that night at the Grammy Awards in hopes to be able to tell her how much he admired her. He only had a moment and all he could remember was her green eyes, her shiny, beautiful blonde hair and how blown away he had been by her obvious talent. Every project she was involved with was exemplary in its process and product. Poppy Morningstar truly shone and he really was a huge fan. Except, he'd felt like such a knob after their first meeting. Now, with her face smiling, 105" large on his living room wall and a decade of work later, Garrett Samuels felt the jolt of electricity he felt that night shaking her hand, just seeing her face. Her work was unique and he realized that Poppy Morningstar was the genius musical mind that he wanted to work with on "Precision Touch". Garrett increased the volume on the TV and watched mesmerized, as she spoke about the end of her "Face Forward" tour. He was in the audience the night she won the Oscar, had heard of her marital problems after that, was thrilled to see her sweep the Grammys and had kept her on his radar for a long time. All of her CD's were in his collection and definitely make his top ten favorites. Poppy Morningstar had been on Garrett Samuels' radar for many years. He reached for his phone. Things were about to change.

* * *

The "Face Forward" tour was ending and Poppy was hoping for some downtime. She had worked solid for many months since her divorce, created an award winning CD, toured the world and was needing to curl up somewhere and sleep for a week or two. She sat, wiping away her onstage makeup, staring at her bare face in the mirror. Another concert behind her. Years behind her. Would she ever have time to sit back and relax? Taking a deep breath, she took a moment and stared down at her hands and the cotton balls of removed makeup she held. Her hands. They had a mind of their own once they hit the keys. Everything she had experienced in life were due to her hands. Her gaze broke from her hands to her face in the mirror. She let out a sigh. Where to go from here?

She was right in the middle of wondering just that, when her phone buzzed. As she reached to answer it, she tossed the used make up covered cotton balls in the garbage. A smile rose to her lips as she answered her phone and listened to the caller.

* * *

They worked like a fine tuned machine. They understood each other's drive, matched the other's work ethic and when they put their minds to it, created a true work of art. Once "Precision Touch" had been produced, cast, shot and edited it was Garrett's baby to present to Poppy and together they were to create its soundtrack. It was their complete obsession for over a year. Each day they would step into the studio, and through collaboration, a deep respect for the other's talents and a pure passion for the movie, they came up with two main songs and a written soundtrack. She and Kirby sang one of the songs, a twenty-something, Scottish heart throb named Zander MacMurray sang the title song. He was perfect, having been hand-picked by Poppy and Garrett. Not only did he nail the song and make it his own, he drew in the younger crowd because of it. The song drew them to the movie like ants to a picnic. It was more than they had imagined, it was historical. It would always be Garrett's favorite project. Always. The story of Connor McClure needed to be told, the experience of being a movie producer and notoriety it would bring him was such a thrill, but for what it had brought him the moment he made the call was truly immeasurable. He was so thrilled when she answered his call and said yes to his request and proposal to work on his new project. She said yes, right away, making his vision of the movie really come true. He knew Poppy Morningstar would add her magical touch! He remembered the electricity he felt when they met, but he never expected her to absolutely steal his heart.

Garrett had fallen in love with Poppy. He was pissed at himself for it. *Poppy Morningstar isn't looking for a relationship*, he thought. Especially after her much publicized divorce, but he truly couldn't help himself. She was quite simply, amazing. He'd worked with many different artists over the years, some great, some fantastic and some he'd never work with again. Poppy was the best artist he'd ever worked with and regardless of the project, even if his love went unrequited, Garrett Samuels always wanted to be friends with Poppy Morningstar. It was rare to find someone who fit in so well with who he was and what he did for a living, and Garrett knew it.

He had given it a lot of thought. Day in and out, he fought his heart and stayed completely business with Poppy, regardless of their situation and success. Many times he watched her closely as she created the complimentary music to adorn his movie.

Before "Precision Touch" neared release, Poppy and Garrett's soundtrack hit social media. They'd agreed to a minimal amount of publicity, visiting only a few cities that the movie premiered in. It was an interview they gave to an L.A. Late Show that started everything. The show's host had interviewed them separately years before and was easily chatting with them during the interview, very at ease. Knowing her audience would want to know, she asked about their next project and if they would consider working together again? Both stared at each other, pure electricity flowing between them; a quiet understanding shared.

Suddenly, turning the subject around, Garrett answered, "I'm headed to a paradise island with some friends. It's a yearly "Guys weekend away" beginning tomorrow" he explained with a huge smile spreading across his face and giving a nod of his head.

The Late Show host gave Garrett a huge smile back and said, "Ohhhh. That sounds wonderful, tell us more."

Garrett explained, "It's a vacation I look forward to each year with a very small group of friends, who all stayed in touch over the years. Every year we find a remote and fascinating place to go, to do some incredible deep sea diving and hide from the rest of the world. We'll be incommunicado for a full 7 days." He told them. "And that's intentional and necessary." Both Poppy and the Morning Show host laughed.

"Wish I had thought of doing something like that" the host said. Turning to Poppy, she asked, "And, what are your plans?"

Poppy smiled and looked to Garrett. "I'll probably go back to the studio for a bit. I've found a muse, I believe."

Hmmmm, I'll bet you have, thought the Late Show host. She'd have to be deaf, dumb and blind not to see what was happening between them and she knew her audience would see it, too.

* * *

He stepped out of the shower and toweled himself off, stopping to appreciate himself in the mirror; he loved what he saw! He'd worked hard to have the physique he had and no one appreciated it more than him.

He had left the TV on in the living room with the volume on high so he could hear it. He liked the Late Show and thought the female host was hot, also his brother was going to be on and he insisted on watching when his brother was on TV. There was always things to learn and watching his brother practically melt on camera when he looked at the gorgeous Poppy Morningstar, was a fortuitous moment. Suddenly, an idea came to him, more so, an opportunity.

It was time for Trip to make his move. He leaned into the mirror stroking his facial hair.

One last time, he thought to himself as he reached for his razor.

* * *

After the interview, Poppy and Garrett shared a limo ride to their respective homes. As the vehicle drew up to Poppy's building, Garrett looked over at her and reached for her hand. She immediately reached out to his. They sat for a moment, completely silent, looking at one another.

"I didn't know you were headed out of town." Poppy said, quietly.

"Yeah, it gets planned a year in advance." He told her, almost apologetically. She realized that it sounded that way and immediately felt badly. Her hands covered her face.

"Oh, I'm so sorry" she started, "You don't have to explain it to me. Please…" she said as she dropped her hands, but continued to look down. They had worked so closely together for all those months, but now she was suddenly unable to look at him without sputtering and stumbling over her words. He made her heart race, quite frankly.

He stopped mid-sentence and stared at her intently, debating about asking her if he could join her inside, deciding reluctantly to hold back. His hesitation confused her and she moved quickly so as not to be embarrassed. *Maybe he doesn't feel like I do*, she thought. Better to get out of there than make a fool of yourself. Before Garrett could speak, hoping to ease her mind, she had leaned over, quick as a flash and kissed his cheek, squeezed his hand and left him sitting with the scent of her perfume, the feel of her hand still lingering and the sight of her walking away from the limo. He sat, transfixed for a moment. *God, I hope I don't regret that decision*, he thought as the limo pulled away.

* * *

Garrett arrived home to a dark and lonely house. The same home he'd bought when he first started at KARMA! Labels. His friends and co-workers ribbed him about living in the area, an older area with many things that catered to the elderly. Not much had changed in his neighborhood over the years and Garrett was happy with that, he didn't spend too much time there. If he had to be brutally honest, there wasn't a home that could change how he felt. He was lonely. He longed for a wife and children; a family of his own and he wanted to be surrounded by love. He turned on the two lights for the living room and kitchen area, leaving as little light as possible.

He threw his suit jacket and laptop onto his couch and went to the fridge, grabbing a cold beer and popping the cap off easily. He quickly drank from the ice cold bottle, finishing half in a few gulps. Being a proactive personality, he had packed and prepared himself for his week away and could enjoy his night, instead of stressing over projects and keeping in touch while away. Garrett Samuels knew his job exceptionally well. At 4:00 pm that afternoon all emails, phone calls, concerns and considerations had been addressed. At 4:00 pm, Mr. Garrett Samuels' status became "ON VACATION" and he completely gave in to that.

* * *

Lying in bed, Garrett was having a difficult time getting to sleep. He daren't think of Poppy or he'd never get any rest. He decided to concentrate on what his next project would be. He had numerous musicians that wanted to work with him and another movie script being handed to him and yet, all he could think about was a beautiful pair of green eyes. He came to a very sound decision.

* * *

Poppy awoke to her door buzzing incessantly. It was after midnight! She was able to see who it was through her phone, so she grabbed it to see who it was. Garrett's smiling face greeted her. As soon as she saw it was him, she sat up in bed immediately and reached for the light.

"Hey!" he said, smiling wide.

"What's up? Are you okay?" she asked, half asleep. "I thought you'd be fast asleep and dreaming of paradise by now" She told him.

"I wish. I'm outside, can I come up??" he asked her.

"Sure, I'll buzz you in", she answered, wondering what was wrong. He was smiling, so whatever it was, couldn't be so bad. She pressed the "Open" icon on her phone which allowed entrance to anyone outside.

It didn't take him long before he was at the door and as she opened it, he swiftly took her up into an embrace, planted her against the wall and started kissing her deeply. Although she was taken by surprise, she didn't try to move away, in fact, she fell deeply into the kiss, holding him tightly as his hands, moved down from her head, to her waist and around to her bum. He broke away just long enough to look her in the eyes.

"I was laying there in bed and all I could think of was you." He told her and then kissed her deeply again. He moved to her neck, giving it little kisses as he told her softly, "I can't go away for a whole week without being with you. I thought I'd die!"

"Drama King" she teased him, enjoying his touches, his kisses, his everything. He smelled so good, so fresh and clean. He always smelled good. She had noticed that while they had worked together. He'd walk past her and she would breathe in deeply, enjoying his scent. Now was no different.

He brought his face up towards hers again. He slowly bent his head down and continued to kiss her as he picked her up and carried her down the hallway, looking for her bedroom. She nudged the door open with her foot and he carried her over to the bed and gently laid her down. He stood above her, looking at her beautiful body, only slightly covered by a flimsy nightshirt. He could see her nipples through the shirt and it drove him mad. He started there, pulling the night shirt up and over her head as his mouth landed firmly upon her right nipple. It responded to his mouth immediately and Poppy let out a slight moan. He continued to suckle her nipple as his hands began their own exploration. Her other breast, which was full and had a hard nipple all its own was massaged and handled just as his mouth moved and he began kissing her down her body. Her hips began writhing, moving in an undulating motion, driving his desire through the roof. It was all he could to maintain himself on the way over to her place, he needed to try and keep himself in check or this could be all over very quickly. He continued kissing down her body until he reached her pussy. He licked his finger and began worrying her bud, making her moan even more. He could feel her juices running and lightly teased the bud with the end of his tongue. Her back arched with his movement, almost begging for his touch more. He instinctively indulged her, now sucking on the bud and pushing his tongue inside her. Her taste was exquisite. She was exquisite and his raging penis began throbbing, needing its own release. Making sure she was ready for him, he pushed his finger into her further and felt the contraction of her pussy. He shot up quickly, undressed with lightning speed and lay back down on top of her, moving her legs apart with his body as he entered her slowly. She raised her hips up to take the full length of him and they began moving rhythmically, together. His thrusts met her thrusts, his heart beat was racing and he could feel his excitement growing. His hands explored her body gently, always making sure the sounds she made were from pleasure. He pushed his hands underneath her and grabbing her by her ass, he thrust into her, holding onto her ass as he began moving quicker. She met him thrust for thrust; their passion building, their breath quickening. Poppy's mind and body were soaring and she knew she was very close to climaxing. As her orgasm grew, she held onto him tightly, digging her nails into his back as she exploded with passion. Her mind became a kaleidoscope of colour and imagery that blinded her, She could feel his thrusts getting stronger and he then pushed into her hard as he also exploded, his orgasm making him shake and roar. As he finished he fell on top of her, both of them completely spent, both of them, completely satiated.

After a moment, she began giggling.

"I don't believe we even said "Hello" at the door, did we?" she laughed as he rolled off her and onto his side, giving his eye a hard rub as he did. He even made that look great.

He lay on his back smiling wide, his hand gently stroking her arm. He didn't say a word, just closed his eyes and continued to smile. She rolled onto her side looking at him, then closing her eyes, she went quiet. They rested for a little while.

When she awoke, he was up out of bed, standing in her bathroom in front of the sink. He was naked and she took that moment to study his fantastic physique. His skin was a dark brown and had a shine to it. *Beautiful skin*, she thought. His shoulders were quite wide and his back was very muscular. He had the most amazing ass, very sculptured and perfectly shaped. When he turned to his side, she could see his penis, now flaccid, but still impressive. She loved the look of a naked man. Kerry had been endowed, but not like this man! The head alone was quite bulbous and gave the impression that he'd be ready to go at a moment's notice. Poppy smiled to herself. It didn't seem to be a detriment last night.

Not. At. All.

She stretched, languishing in their lovemaking and was about to call him back to bed, when he was already on top of her and half dressed. He kissed her deeply and she held onto him, hoping for more.

"I hate to leave you, especially like this. But, my flight leaves very soon and I have to get myself to the airport. But, I promise you", he said as he kissed her again, "I will be thinking of you over and over and over again." With that, he pulled away from her, pulled on his shirt, grabbed his jacket and kissed her on the forehead before leaving. "I'll call you the minute I get back" he said, and then left. Poppy laid back down into her bed, hearing the door close as he left. She curled up onto the side he'd been laying on and smiled to herself, smelling his scent, where he'd been. She may never wash that pillowcase again!

* * *

The bar was dark when Trip entered. It had taken him a while to find a place still open after midnight, but he was on a high and looking to celebrate. He went straight to the bar, ordered himself a drink and sat at a table closest to the dance floor, so he could check out the floor action. There weren't very many people there, just a few couples; a large guy by himself off in the corner and two girls who looked as though they were trying to find someone to go home with. A sad night, really. Trip was up for some fun, but it didn't look as though he was going to find it. Just his luck! He figured he'd have a couple of stiff drinks, maybe get a buzz on and leave. So much for the big night!

He'd finished his third drink and feeling quite buzzed, decided to leave when the large guy from the corner came over to his table. He stood there looking at Trip, not saying a word.

"Uh….can I help you, friend?" Trip asked him. He wasn't sure if the guy was drunk, or dangerous or both.

"You Garrett Samuels, ain't you?" the large man asked.

It took Trip a moment to respond. He smiled wide, "Yes, Yes I am. And you are…?" he asked, holding out his hand. The large man reached out and shook Trip's hand, almost crushing it. Trip could tell the man had also been drinking and by the looks of him, he'd had a fair bit.

"I'm BB" the large man said, exposing perfectly white teeth and a mile wide grin. Trip thought how the man needed to smile more, he looked far less menacing. He was quite a handsome guy, but had taken some obvious blows to his face and nose. The scars weren't recent either which made Trip wonder was his deal was and how he knew of Garrett.

"I'm a rap artist." And, there it was! Trip smiled at the guy, knowingly. "I'm looking for someone to make me rich, give me a label to record with, but I ain't had any luck." BB told him. There was something about this man that intrigued Trip, as if he was pretending to be something he wasn't. *How ironic*, Trip thought and motioned for the man to sit and join him.

"What'cha drinking there, BB?" Trip asked, as he motioned for the bartender.

"Sippin' some whiskey" BB told Trip. The bartender took their order and Trip turned his smile to BB.

"So, a rap artist, huh? Have you recorded anything?" Trip asked, giving BB his best Garrett.

"Naw, them fuckers don't know what they're talking 'bout" said BB, nearly spitting his words. "I ain't written anything so I thought I'd do my first album from raps I know, until I come up with some of my own." He explained. He had started emulating certain rappers and their unique way of speaking, thinking it helped to make him look cool. It didn't.

Oh Fuck, Is this guy for real? What a loser. Trip thought. Garrett probably wouldn't touch him. Trip wasn't sure what the process was and he really didn't care. He was almost sorry now that he'd asked the guy to join him. BB may look menacing, but Trip figured he was harmless. Harmless, stupid and no longer intriguing.

"Do you ever make it to New York?" Trip asked BB, expecting him to answer in the negative.

"Uh, yeah, sure…I can make it to New York." BB answered, surprising Trip who knew now he needed to go through with pretending to be Garrett with this guy. He reached into the jacket pocket and drew out a business card.

"You come and see me in a few weeks in New York. I'll get you a label." He told BB, whose eyes grew wide as he hesitantly took the business card he was being handed. He glanced at it in disbelief, reading it a few times over.

"You shittin me?" BB asked, his voice raised in question.

"No" Trip answered, shaking his head. "I'm heading out of town for a few weeks. Get yer ass to my offices after that and we'll talk." Trip lied, draining his final drink as he stood to leave. BB tried to protest and called out to the bartender, but Trip wanted to get out of there and away from him.

"No, no. I can't stay any longer." He told BB who finally accepted Trip's insistence and shook his hand hard.

"You a good man, Mr. Samuels. And, don't you worry, I'll get my ass to NYC. Don't you worry!" BB called out after Trip as he tossed a few dollars onto the table and walked out of the bar.

Oh, I won't worry, thought Trip. *I'll never see your ass again!*

But, you know what they say?

Never say never!

* * *

Garrett lay on a lounge chair, under a palm tree with a book resting on his chest. To those around him, he looked peaceful, but he was anything but. He was being driven mad, his brain not giving him any peace whatsoever. He wait a year for this vacation, flew thousands of miles to get there, spent a ton of money on the best of everything and all he could think about was Poppy. Even his small group of friends weren't enough of a distraction.

She was perfect. Absolutely perfect for him. He was sure of it. She liked all the same things he did, they worked so well together in every area, and there was such electricity between them, he could still feel her touch. He could feel himself starting to get aroused and that was the last thing he needed with all his buddies lying around the pool area. He needed to stop obsessing over her and her gorgeous body. He needed to think of something else, someone else.

As a waiter passed by, he ordered a round of shots for the boys. They weren't going out in the water today, rather staying poolside. Time to get their drink on and get this woman off his mind, until he could do something about it.

* * *

Poppy stayed in L.A. for the week. She was enjoying the sunshine and warm temperatures, but mostly she secretly hoped that she would see Garrett when he returned from his trip and they could travel back to New York together. Ever since he surprised her the night before he left, she'd done nothing but think about him. She relived that night many times and hoped he had, as well. She was sure he had. She hoped he had. The worst was nighttime. She could smell him on her sheets still, and stayed on that spot the whole week.

288

Lying in bed, in the wee hours of the morning, she heard a ping to her phone. Someone was texting at 5:00 am. At first she ignored it, but came awake immediately when she realized that it could be Garrett! She grabbed for her phone and looked at her messages. Sure enough it was Garrett!

Sun 5:02 am

Hey! Just landed at LAX. Are you in L.A.?

Poppy sat up as she typed into her phone.

Sun 5:03 am

Welcome Home! Yes, still in L.A.

Poppy waited for a reply to hers, but it didn't come. She wondered if he'd head straight over or if he'd make arrangements with her once he'd gotten home and unpacked. It didn't matter at all, because he contacted her immediately as he landed. That means he'd been thinking of her. That means she'd been right! She smiled to herself and decided she was far too awake to sleep and jumped up out of bed and into a quick shower.

She had just stepped out and was drying off when she heard her phone. Wrapping her hair into a towel she ran to answer it. She saw Garrett's smiling face!

"I'm downstairs" he said to her. "I'd love to see you."

"Yes, certainly" she said. "I'm buzzing you in." She pressed the security button to allow Garrett access while she tossed her phone down and ran into the bathroom. She removed her towel from her hair and quickly grabbed a satin bathrobe and began to tie it up, wondering if she was wasting her time. That brought a smile to her face!

The knock on the door was timid, as if he didn't wish to wake the whole building. Poppy answered the door and smiled at Garrett who was smiling wide and looking exhausted.

"I'm sorry, but I just couldn't wait" he said as he entered her place. He let her shut the door and then he took her up in a sweep of his arm and just before kissing her, said "To kiss you." He stood holding her in a lock tight grip, his solid strong arms keeping her, but she wasn't trying to get away. She returned his kiss and moaned deeply while he began gently kissing down her neck. Her satin bathrobe fell open and exposed her naked body. It shocked Garrett for a moment and he stepped back. Thinking he wanted to see more, Poppy opened her bathrobe wide, allowing Garrett to see all of her and he took all of her in. Slowly his eyes scanned her from head to toe. He was dreaming of this all week, had been utterly and completely distracted; his friends had noticed and put it all down to a woman. Oh, they were so right! This incredible woman who was giving herself to him, wanting him to take her. He stepped towards her quickly and took her into another embrace. Garrett was truly exhausted and on a great high all at the same time. He didn't want to rush through this, he wanted to take his time, take in every moment. As he was kissing her, he started to slowly drop the robe from her, leaving her completely naked beneath his touch. Her waist was so tiny, he thought for sure he could wrap his arms around her twice. His hands explored her back as he pushed her into him, feeling her breasts against his chest. This aroused him and Poppy knew right away! She took his hand and led him to the bedroom where she laid herself out onto the bed for him. Garrett never took his eyes off of her, as he quickly undressed and climbed onto the bed. He gently laid beside her and had her turn onto her side facing him. He brushed the hair from her face and traced his fingers down the side of her face, gently touching her lips, her chin, her neck; slowly moving down to her breast. He traced her nipple as he leaned over and kissed her, his finger toying with her nipple and then softly, he caressed her breast. His mouth followed his hand downward and took to her nipple; his tongue playing with it and sucking it hard. He guided her backwards and had her lay on the bed. He looked darker, she thought as he rose above her and placed himself over her, now kissing her neck. They both instinctively slid together, as if they were made to fit together. It took Poppy's breath away, finding his gentler approach much more arousing and there was no complaining about the first time they made love!

Garrett certainly did take his time, exploring her body completely and bringing her to orgasm twice before he allowed himself the pleasure. When he finally did reach climax, it was with such force, he collapsed on top of Poppy with his full weight, causing her to call out in surprise. His fingers gripped the bedsheets and he drove into her as the orgasm reached its fulfillment, Poppy rose her hips up to give him the most incredible sensation and contracted her inner muscles making Garrett's penis throb from the feeling. Garrett lay on top of Poppy for a few minutes, his heart racing and pounding hard. Poppy could feel it. While he stayed still, Poppy's body became alive and she put her arms around Garrett and hugged him hard, squeezing him closer to her. She loved how hard he felt, his muscles tight and toned. She began kissing his head, his ear, his shoulder, wherever she could reach, trapped underneath him.

He roused slowly; his sexual afterglow more intoxicating than anything he'd ever experienced. *My God*, he thought. *That was incredible!* He smiled lazily, pushed himself up and rolled over onto his side. Poppy curled up next to him as his arm went around her, holding her close. His exhaustion set in and he could now feel himself falling into a deep sleep. Just before he dozed off, he thought he heard her say, "Will we always have sex when you come through the door?" He didn't know why, but it made him smile. He moaned in appreciation and was asleep.

Poppy woke up later in the morning to the sound of her shower running. She rolled over to find that Garrett was not in bed beside her. She dragged herself over to where he had been and lay there taking in his scent. A hint of coconut lingered, probably from the sunscreen, she figured. It made her think of the tropics and paradise. She lay there for moment as her gaze slowly fell onto the dark form standing in her shower. His body was hidden behind the glazed glass, she could only see the upper half of his head and his feet. She watched him closely, remembering their love making. He was the real deal. A brilliant mind, a gentle soul, a great laugh and a wonderful, giving lover. The first time they'd made love, he was more aggressive and filled with desire. She had felt ravaged. It was fantastic! But last night, he took his time; she was left completely spent. He'd tended to her every need, every desire and brought her to climax multiple times. He was, in her mind, absolute perfection.

She heard the shower shut off and saw the doors open, one strong arm reaching out for the towel hanging on the wall. Garrett stepped out of the shower, using the towel to rub his head madly. His body was truly impressive and she found herself staring at him again, admiring every inch of him. She sat up in bed, correcting her perspective and then studied Garrett closely as he toweled off.

She felt almost devilish the way she looked at him. She allowed herself to drink him all in. Once again, marvelling at what an exquisite male specimen he was. From top to bottom and everything in between.

But, suddenly she stopped and her head tilted to one side.

What the...?

* * *

New York was fantastic! Trip loved everything about it – it made him feel alive. TOTALLY alive! It was his first time and he found the streets crawling with people at all hours of the day and night. The amount of entertainment one was exposed to within a square city blocked was mind blowing! It was the capital of everything entertainment and Trip was feeling electric to be deep in the thick of it. He had flown out on a red eye after he was called to an audition, landed at just after 2:00 am and spent a few hours walking New York and loving it. Finally feeling tired, he found a room at a Holiday Inn not far from the audition address and grabbed some much needed sleep. When he awoke, he still had a few hours' time and was rehearsing an audition piece he'd prepared over in his mind as he got himself ready. For the first time in a long time he felt great. Things were finally going his way!

Taking a glance in the mirror, Trip stepped closer looking himself over. He looked deep into his own eyes and paused. Suddenly, he was covered in goosebumps. There was no cold breeze, no open door, nowhere a chill could have come from, but even so, Trip felt a real chill.

He got himself dressed, still feeling slightly cold. He grabbed the jacket he'd brought along, the same one he'd worn weeks ago when he'd gone out to the bar as Garrett for the last time, a handful of Garrett's business cards still in the jacket's pocket. *Maybe it was good luck!* He thought as he patted the pocket and walked towards the door.

He smiled as he reached for the door handle. His grandmother would have told him "that chill you got was someone walking over your grave, boy!"

She was such a superstitious thing!

* * *

Poppy was still struggling with something she just couldn't explain. How was it that the man she'd recently started a very passionate relationship with was circumcised one week and not be the next? It was on the tip of her tongue numerous times when she and Garrett had spoken, but she just couldn't bring herself to ask. For one, she didn't want to look stupid, what if she had not seen what she thought she saw? And two, what if it embarrassed him? She didn't want that, at all. Easier for her to mark it up to a mistake and move on, but it stayed with her, pushed firmly to the back of her mind.

Poppy had been having a terrible few weeks. Each morning, she'd wake up feeling wretched and covered in sweat. Recently, she had been dreaming very vividly and her heart was racing. As she recalled the dream, her stomach began to turn. She waited only a moment before she leapt to the bathroom, throwing up her dinner from the night before. For a moment she stayed crouching in front of the toilet, hoping her stomach would settle down. When she began to feel better, she stood very slowly. Turning on the bathroom faucet, she rinsed her mouth and looked at herself in the mirror, her reality staring her back in the face, and she knew it immediately.

Oh dear God, she thought, *I'm pregnant!*

* * *

Garrett had been working non-stop in the weeks since he and Poppy flew back to New York. They had seen each other when time allowed. She seemed somewhat distant lately and he wondered if she was having second thoughts. Garrett was making sure to keep in touch with her, as much as possible; texts, face time, dinner a couple of times and of course flowers delivered unexpectedly.

This past week had been a busy one. It was now Friday afternoon and he was looking forward to a weekend with Poppy. She had been staying with Chase and Dana and it had been difficult to have some alone time with his green eyed beauty. Garrett had just finished signing off on a record deal and called his assistant in to take the legal documents over to counsel's office.

"You have someone waiting for you in the lobby" his assistant told him.

Garrett looked confused. "I wasn't expecting anyone. Who is it?" he asked. The assistant shook her head.

"I don't know. He didn't have an appointment, but he had your card and said you had told him to come and see you. He calls himself "BB" she said making air quotes.

Garrett ran through his mind, trying to recall meeting someone named "BB". He even checked through his phone to see if he had made notes on the guy, but found nothing. Being convinced he hadn't met him, he instructed the assistant to get rid of him. The assistant figured it would go that way. It was understood that she would let Mr. Samuels know, but if you didn't have an appointment, you rarely got in. Rarely.

The assistant left Garrett's office, carrying all the documentation he had signed. He paused for a moment thinking he might get out of the office early. He began to pack away his desk when he heard shouting coming from the outer office. He waited a moment, wondering if it would escalate, and then heard a man getting verbally abusive.

Garrett raced towards his office door and yanked it open quickly. A very large man, dressed in all black leather and wearing a black fedora and lots of gold chains was pushing past his assistant and gunning straight for him. Garrett put his hands up to stop the large man from entering his office.

"Hey, there buddy. Slow down, now" he cautioned him. "If you want to meet with me you have to go through the proper channels. There's a way we do things around here" he told him, hoping to calm the large man down.

"I already did the proper channels!" He shouted. "Remember our drink together? Remember you told me to come visit you in New York a few weeks ago? You said you'd help me get a record deal!" He was obviously not calming down. In fact, he was getting angrier as he spoke.

Garrett kept his hands up, staring at the man, who his assistant had said was, "BB". He didn't look familiar to Garrett at all. He looked the man square in the eye and shrugged his shoulders.

"I really don't know what to tell you, buddy" he started to explain, but BB wasn't having it. He exploded!

"YOU FUCK! I KNEW you was lying to me! You hand me your business card, feed me some bullshit and to get my ass to New York and then do THIS to me?" As he started to move towards Garrett, BB felt a hand on the back of his neck and another on his arm.

"Let's go, buddy" the large security officer said, taking a strong hold of BB and turning him around and out of Garrett's face. By now, a crowd had gathered near to Garrett's office as his employees had heard the man's anger escalate.

BB became enraged, trying hard to get away from the Security officer.

"Quit fuckin' calling me THAT! My name is BB. B-FUCKING-B!" He managed to spin himself around and shove his finger out, pointing to Garrett. "And BB is going to KILL your ass!" he screamed. "You remember, this'll be the last fucking face you see, you lying FUCK!" he swore as the Security Officer was joined by another who managed to get BB dragged out of the area and out of the building.

His employees were left absolutely stunned, looking at him and wondering what the hell just happened.

And, so was Garrett Samuels.

* * *

Trip had given his all at the audition and it showed. The casting directors were very keen on him. They had told his agent to keep him in town for a week longer, they were going to get working on a contract. Trip's agent called him immediately. He had done it! He had snagged the leading role in a new series of action movies; 4 at least. Filming was to start in a few weeks, on location in Bora Bora. It was finally happening!

He was walking on absolute air! Now, he'd have his own fine clothing, just like Garrett did! No need to have to stay at a shitty hotel; he'd have his own homes in New York and L.A., just like Garrett did! Now, he would start traveling by limo, just like Garrett did! Still wrapped up in his thoughts, his world came back to reality when he got to the subway. Until he had money, he'd still need to get around by cab or subway, just like everyone else did! He pulled up the collar to his overcoat, left the building and stepped out into the rain. Even the weather wasn't going to get him down. He was smiling as he dashed down the street to the subway entrance, down the stairs and onto the platform, waiting with his hands in his overcoat pocket.

* * *

BB was an evil, angry man. He had spent years taking his anger out on people; some unsuspecting, some able to see the smile in his eyes before they took their last breath. He had been many different people and personas over the years, but "BB" was, by far his favorite. He was able to mimic some of the best rap artists, but he could never quite come up with his own rap. Actually, he could never quite live up to anything he tried to be and it infuriated him. The final push for him was the humiliation he'd received when he went to the offices of Garrett Samuels, by his own invitation. He even had his business card! But, it had made no difference; Garrett Samuels acted as though he didn't know him and had BB dragged out of the building by Security, humiliating him! BB was now out for revenge! He was now in attack mode.

He was quite prepared to wait his time out and attack when everyone had all but forgotten his verbal threats, but an opportunity had just walked past him and was too good to pass up.

He held himself still, not moving an inch so as not to draw any attention. He was good at that; hiding in plain sight, even for his size. He watched the man, so completely unaware of the fact that he was being strongly observed. Only when the man put his hands in his pockets and then turned around smiling at him directly, did he make his move, grabbing the man by his arms keeping them to his sides and thereby, trapping his hands in his pockets.

"You're nuthin' but a fuckin' asshole! You're a liar! You say to me to come and see you, but you lie when I show up! You nuthin' but a fuckin' asshole" he repeated. He was much stronger than the man he had caught unawares and after reaching into his overcoat pocket and stealing his wallet, he quickly turned his prey towards the subway tracks, screaming at him, "You're a dead man!" as he thrust him outwards with a hard jerk and let go of him. The man fell onto the tracks, as his attacker disappeared from sight. There were a few bystanders who had seen what happened and tried desperately to warn the subway train coming quickly around the corner, but it was not able to stop. It cut the man's body in two at the waist, but it didn't matter. He died instantly when his head and neck hit the steel track.

* * *

Poppy had been in the studio when her phone began to light up. She managed to grab it on the last ring.

"Hello?" she answered, not recognizing the number.

"Poppy?" a woman's voice asked. "Poppy, this is Sondra Samuels", she told her, her voice cracking. "Can you tell us what happened?" she managed to say before she lost her composure. Poppy could hear her sobbing and wondered what on earth was going on?

"Mrs. Samuels" Poppy said trying to calm her down. "What is it? Can you tell me what's wrong?"

"It's Garrett", she said, between sobs. "He's dead!" she wailed. "He was hit in the subway. The police just called. They've identified him".

Poppy's heart lurched. What? This made no sense. She had just spoken to him a half hour ago. He said he was exhausted; he was going to finish up some work, have a shower and go to bed. Why would he have gone out, again? And, why take the subway? Garrett had his own driver!

"Mrs. Samuels" Poppy said, trying to maintain her own composure. "When did this happen?" Poppy asked her. Her mind was racing.

"About two hours ago" she said, still crying. "But, we only just got the call!" she wailed.

"Well, that's impossible!" Poppy told her, trying to reassure her. "I just spoke to Garrett not a half hour ago. He's in his apartment in Manhattan. He's fine, Mrs. Samuels, I can assure you" Poppy told her. She hoped to God she wasn't wrong, but if it had supposedly happened two hours ago, then Garrett was hopefully just climbing into bed.

"Have you tried calling him?" She asked Garrett's mom. The silence on the other end of the phone made Poppy realize that Garrett's mother was not understanding what she had tried telling her.

"Poppy. I told you, the police say he's dead" she stated, sounding pissy. Poppy felt badly and apologized, but she knew she had to get off the phone and prove herself right.

"Mrs. Samuels, I did hear you. My apologies. I just need to contact the police station and I'll find out what's going on", she lied. "I'll call you right back as soon as I find out what happened, okay?" she said, reassuringly to the poor, distraught woman.

"Please do, Poppy. I need to know what happened to my only son!" she said, as she began to sob heavily, again.

Poppy ended the conversation and immediately called Garrett's number.

"Awww, honey. I know we'd said we'd talk later, but can't we chat tomorrow. I'm just dead." Was the first thing out of Garrett's mouth when he answered the phone.

Poor choice of words.

* * *

Garrett sat in his pajama bottoms and housecoat on his couch. Poppy was beside him and two New York City police investigators were sitting with them, asking questions. It was 5:30 am and Garrett had gotten very little sleep. No sooner had Poppy explained his mother's strange phone call to him, than his phone began going crazy. Everyone was trying to contact him. He received texts from every colleague at work, a few major stars he'd worked with and of course, his mother. That was the only call he answered. The relief in his mother's voice was instant and she began crying all over again. She became angry with the police officer's mistake and made Garrett promise that he'd reprimand them for scaring his parents so badly.

"They ought to be ashamed of themselves! How dare they wrongly identify someone and then contact the next of kin. Your father or I could have had a heart attack!" she admonished. Garrett eased her mind, swearing he'd let the police know what she said and left her with a heartfelt, "I'm fine. Don't worry, now. I love you both, very much".

Now, the police investigators sat stone faced at Garrett, while he dealt with his mother. They hadn't given up too many details, mainly asking Garrett all the questions.

"Do you have any idea why this man was carrying your business cards?" the first investigator asked. "It was the only identification we found."

Garrett was completely blindsided. They had only told him that a man was killed on the subway tonight and had some identification stating he was Garrett Samuels. "I honestly have no idea" he answered, bewildered by it all. The investigators assessed Garrett for a moment, reading his facial expressions for any sign of a lie.

"Mr. Samuels, do you have any siblings? Any brothers?" the investigator asked him. Garret shook his head no.

"I'm an only child" he told them, straight faced. The investigators both looked slightly perplexed by that.

"You sure about that?" asked the mustached one.

It was now Garrett's turn to look perplexed. "Yes, of course I am" he answered, looking slightly pissed at the question.

Both investigators looked at one another, then back at Garrett. Garrett was starting to feel annoyed at being treated like he was a fool. How would he not know about siblings? What a stupid question!

"You see, the thing is, Mr. Samuels. This man looks exactly like you." They told him. Garret was confused.

"What, like he was pretending to be me?" he asked them, not fully understanding.

"Yes, we believe he was. But more so, because he could!" the mustached one told him. "He's your spitting image, like ..." the officer paused, "... a twin. He's like your twin!" he admitted. Garret was still not completely aware of what they were saying. How can someone look *identically* like him? Was he wearing makeup, or something? A mask?

The investigators knew he wasn't getting it. It was obvious to them; Garrett knew nothing about who this guy was. The one investigator reached inside his coat and pulled out his phone.

"These are some pictures we took at the scene. You can see the man's face wasn't damaged in the accident. Although, he had a nasty gash to the head when he fell, his features are intact. You can see for yourself." The officer explained as he handed his phone to Garrett.

Garrett and Poppy leaned into one another, looking at the officer's phone in awe. The man was in a grotesque position and was covered in blood, but the one thing you could plainly see was his face. He most definitely looked exactly like Garrett. They both stared in awe at the photos. How could this be? Poppy raised her head to the officers.

"How are you going to find out who he is? It's obvious he's an imposter who's had surgery to make himself look like Garrett." Poppy said to them, fully convinced that this person had no relation to Garrett. The officer did not flinch at the comment. Instead, they sat there looking at Garret's face, full of expression.

He studied the pictures closely, looking for some way of explaining how this was possible. Surgery? Maybe, but whoever the surgeon was, he was absolutely perfect, right down to the ears. If Garrett didn't know any better, he would have thought it was him, too. No wonder they made that mistake, especially if the guy was carrying his identification. But, who was he? How did he get his business cards? Garrett still had many questions.

"Our lab is taking samples of the victim now and we're hoping it will identify him." The officer told him. "We aren't any further ahead and we appreciate your taking the time to talk with us. We'll be keeping in touch" he said as he stood.

"Thank you, Officer" Garrett said, standing. The officers smiled towards Poppy and turned to leave, but the mustached one turned back to Garrett.

"Would you be willing to give us a DNA sample, Mr. Samuels?" he asked, inquisitively.

The question confused Garrett. "Why?" he asked. "I mean, I wouldn't have a problem with it, but I can't understand what you think I have to do with any of this" he told them, directly.

"Oh, I don't think you do." The officer said confidently, as he smiled and turned to leave. "We'll be in touch, Mr. Samuels" he said as walked out of the living room towards the front door, his officer buddy in tow.

Garrett stood watching the men leave and took a big, deep breath. Poppy leaned over, giving him a warm hug. He held her close, enjoying her being there with him, helping him try to make sense of what was going on. But, she was as baffled as he was. He kissed Poppy on her forehead and reached for his phone.

"There's only one person I trust to investigate this thing." He told her, going through his contact list. Finding the number he hit the send button and held the phone to his ear.

* * *

Lucas Hollomby was as perplexed as Garrett was, but after decades in the investigation business, he'd heard just about every strange thing you could imagine. So, the fact that the police had the dead body of someone pretending to be Garrett Samuels didn't surprise him, but seeing the man was another thing all together. He was essentially cut in two after being hit by a subway, but there was no denying it; this man was a perfect look-a-like to Garrett. Lucas spent a few minutes examining the face, looking for surgical scars of any kind, but could find no telltale signs. If this was done by surgery, the Dr. was a complete genius. He had no idea how to explain it and that never sat well with Lucas. Everything could be explained. Everything.

After leaving the morgue, Lucas made his way to his office in New York City. His offices took up the entire 11th floor and had a clear view of the Hudson River. Entering into his office, he threw his coat onto one of the two dark leather chairs sitting in front of his desk. He sat in his desk chair and leaned way back, stroking his hands through his hair. His mind was working overtime on what he'd just seen. It wasn't just that the guy looked like him, he was the same size, build, approximate age, hair, hair line, mouth, and nose. There wasn't a thing he could spot that was different from Garrett. How could that be? On cue, his phone rang. It was Garrett.

"Hey! How's it going?" asked Garrett.

"Good, thanks. I just got back from the morgue" Lucas told him. "Listen, I have something I need to discuss with you, are you available?" He asked Garrett.

"Yes, I'm at my apartment. Did you want to stop by?" He asked the investigator.

"Right away" he replied as he got up from his chair and was off again. He grabbed his coat and headed for the elevators.

The first car that opened had a load of furniture and two movers who apologized to Lucas and closed the doors before Lucas could enter. Luckily a second elevator stopped and he got on, noticing the car was fairly full. Probably because the movers were using the other car. *Fuck!* He thought, he should be in a more stately building, but he loved the view. On the 3rd floor the car stopped and a mother and set of twin girls got on. Both were dressed in bright red coats, their hair in large curly pigtails and white socks with black paten shoes. They were giggly and adorable and the whole elevator car smiled at them; a lovely moment in a busy day. The car came to a stop on the main floor and the doors opened. The twin girls and their mother were the first to head out as the rest of the passengers each left, on their way, except Lucas. He was stopped, dead in his tracks as he watched the giggly red coats skip away beside their mother, each holding her hand.

As if the answer was right in front of him.

* * *

When Lucas was let into Garrett's home, he was also greeted by Poppy Morningstar. Although, a very pleasant surprise, he had not expected her to be there and hadn't planned on having Garrett having company. He hesitated before taking a seat.

"I have to admit, I wasn't expecting anyone else to be here, Garrett. I have some very confidential information and some very personal questions I need to ask" he spoke matter-of-factly, but before he continued, Garrett was already waving his hands.

"Poppy's cool. You know her and her family better than I do. It was Chase who told me about you a while ago and after Poppy told me what you've done for her and the Morningstars, I wasn't going to turn to anyone else. You can speak freely and ask away." Garrett assured him. Lucas looked him in the eye, paused a moment, then nodded. They all took a seat and Lucas began.

"I've seen your imposter." He told him as he wrung his hands for a moment, thinking of how to tell Garrett. "Uh…it's uncanny, Garrett. He's your exact image. He could very easily pass for you and probably had no trouble doing it." He told them.

"But, how is that possible? Surgery?" Garrett asked, astonished at what he was hearing.

"No. I looked for any scars, you know, tell-tale, like behind the ears and near the hairline. There's nothing. Absolutely nothing. But, it's isn't that…"he paused again, hesitant to suggest it so quickly, "it's like he's your twin."

"Well, that can't be true. I'm an only child" Garrett said. Poppy and Garrett both looked at Lucas with eyes wide. That was the same thing the New York officers had told him.

"What if you weren't?" Lucas asked him, raising his eyebrow. Garrett's head shook immediately, not buying it.

"No. That's not possible. My parents would have known something like that and would have told me something like that. Do you realize what you're saying? What?" By this time Garrett had stood up and was pacing back and forth in front of Poppy and Lucas.

Lucas pulled out his phone and asked Garrett for his place of birth and birthdate. Garrett gave him the information, wondering what he expected to find. Lucas quickly searched hospitals in the area of his birth place and then requested access to birth records from the month and year. Lucas was on his phone for at least 20 minutes, keeping them updated of what he'd found until finally he showed them his screen.

"So, I have a record here of a baby boy born on Dec. 31, 2018 after 11:00 pm and the same mother having another boy on Jan 1, 2019 at 12:37 Am." he stated, showing them the results.

"But, what does that prove?" Garrett asked, almost angrily. He wasn't very impressed with Lucas Hollomby, so far and was wondering if he'd made a mistake in asking him to investigate this.

"Listen to me. There is no way that man lying down in the morgue is not related to you, in some way. I realize what you believe is the truth and what you've been told is the truth, but I've worked too long in the business to not believe what the facts and my own eyes tell me." He told Garrett, directly. "I suggest you do a DNA test and see what comes back, then go from there. I've made arrangements for that to happen immediately."

Garrett looked to Poppy. She wasn't sure of what to think, but she trusted Lucas completely and if he said the DNA test was necessary, then she agreed Garrett should do it. She nodded her head at him in agreement with Lucas. Garret sighed heavily, his jawline tight. He went over to the closet and grabbed his coat.

"Alright then, let's get this done" he told them, putting his shoes on and grabbing the doorknob. Poppy could tell he wasn't completely on board, he may even be doing it for her sake, so as not to embarrass her in front of a family friend, but she had to believe Lucas was onto something. If this imposter was such an uncanny match, then he must be related. If that were true, there was a whole other story that needed to be told. She wondered if they would ever get to the bottom of it.

* * *

Lucas pulled some strings to get the test done within an hour. Garrett had given his DNA over for testing against the imposter's. Expecting nothing from it, Garrett questioned Lucas on next steps, but Lucas wasn't giving anything up until the results came back within the hour. So, they waited in the private office of the doctor friend that Lucas had called upon. Poppy and Garrett were very recognizable faces in New York and didn't need that kind of media blitz.

There was a soft knock on the door and Lucas called out, "Come in."

The Doctor entered the room, a middle aged man with a cheery face and Dr. Moulin written on his white lab coat. He carried a pen in one hand and papers in the other. He came around to the open side of the desk and took his seat, pulling the chair up to the edge.

"Well, I have the results of the DNA testing on the John Doe in the morgue. Mr. Samuels, he is your identical twin" he stated, handing the papers he held over to Garrett.

Garrett could barely speak, let alone take the papers from the doctor. His mind was racing. An identical twin? How could that be possible? He was always told Grant and Sondra Samuels adopted him as an only child. They had never said anything about him being a twin. They had always been very open about his adoption, giving him as much information as they could.

Lucas took the papers from the doctor and looked them over. There was no mistaking it. He was an exact match. Identical. *See? Everything has an explanation*, Lucas thought. His internet search was also correct in finding Garrett's birth record and his twin's birth record, but everything else was on lock down. He'd have to do some deeper digging to get to the bottom of the story. Maybe pull a few more strings, he'd helped a few influential people in his time and they were always happy to help him out, if they could.

Lucas thanked Dr. Moulin and got Poppy and Garrett out of there before any news got out about it. Lucas needed to get on this or the media would break it and Garrett would have no way of stopping it. If there was one thing Lucas had learned from Robin Hewer, it was how the media worked.

The trio headed back to Garrett's apartment in two separate cars, all the while Lucas was making phone calls to his office and around the city. By the time they each reached the apartment building, Lucas had pieced a lot of the story together, except one. Garrett's parents would have to answer that.

* * *

Garret was exhausted. It was hard to believe what Lucas was telling him and yet, he couldn't deny the facts to be true. Lucas' office had been able to get a high court Judge to sign a court order to open the adoption file, then had it faxed over to the hospital, who upon receipt had to send the file immediately to Lucas' office and they sent it to his phone the minute it was received.

It identified Garrett's biological mother as 19 year old, Vella Townsend. She died within 24 hours of her sons' births and custody of the boys was given to the maternal grandmother, Angel Townsend, who then decided to adopt one of the boys out. The child born Dec 31st was given to Grant and Sondra Samuels at 5 days old. However, there was no record of the other boy being adopted and the chart made no mention of him except that the maternal grandmother left the hospital with the boy.

Lucas was able to find the mother's birth certificate. Vella Townsend's mother was listed as "Angel Townsend". She had died three years previously. So, all at once, Garrett had found unknown blood relatives and lost them. It was a lot for him to take in. And, what did his parents know? He didn't look forward to that conversation.

"I would think they weren't aware of your brother's existence. It was a closed adoption, which was rare for that time. They were told there was one baby available for adoption. From what I could find, it was the grandmother who insisted the records be closed. Her death and then Tyrone Townsend's death meant there was no family left, except you and you had right to have the file opened." Lucas told Garrett. He could see on his face how hard it was fathom.

A twin! He had a twin! Garrett thought. He stood up, again pacing back and forth, his mind racing. So often he'd been mistaken to have met someone. So often. He put it down to coincidence or mistake, but as if a cloud had lifted, he eyes widened and he said to Poppy and Lucas, "It all makes sense, now."

"Haven't we met?" Yes, they probably had. They had probably met his twin.

He. Had A. Twin.

* * *

Poppy sat quietly, studying the papers that the doctor had given them. Lucas had also given them some of the documentation and notes he had taken at the morgue. They were hand written and listed measurements and details of the body. Poppy read through them, noting how each one was identical to Garrett. Unbelievable! Garrett had a twin he didn't even know about. If she wasn't holding the documentation, she wouldn't believe it herself. She was about to hand the papers over to Garrett when she saw something that made her blood run cold. Her mind raced back to a night weeks ago; the first night Garrett had surprised her before his trip, the first time they'd made love. A sudden nausea came over her. She excused herself for a moment and ran to the bathroom just in time to vomit.

A cold shiver ran through her as she looked in the mirror, rinsing her mouth. She leaned against the counter and waited a moment gathering her thoughts and trying to settle herself. Her mind was going over it and over it, but try as she might, she had to face the obvious.

She'd been duped.

Chapter 21

THE BROTHER AND THE BABY

It was a hard conversation to start with, but Garrett knew to take it gently. After the complete shock of finding he was a twin, he needed to know if Grant and Sondra knew. He flew to LA as soon as he could, contacting his parents on the way instructing them to speak to no one from the press and to lay low until he got there. After the horror of thinking he had died, they were not going to ask any questions, but do as he asked, until he could explain.

"What? A twin?" Sondra Samuels screamed, as she gasped. "We knew nothing of another baby or we would have gladly taken both of you!" She said, her hand raised and tears in her eyes. The thought of having two Garrett's was overwhelming and she was saddened they didn't get the chance to also give him a wonderful life. Instead, this unknown man was reduced to pretending he *was* Garrett. What kind of a life had he'd had?

Garrett stood in the open kitchen area of their home, looking at the very picture that Trip had found that night, many years ago. He wondered what it would have been like to live his brother's life. What if the other twin had been given to his parents? These thoughts plagued him as he realized the difference between being raised by affluent parents in comparison to a hard working grandmother. He felt guilty that he was the one chosen to be given away. Obviously, his brother didn't have the same advantages that he'd had.

Grant Samuels called his firm to see if there was any more information he could find for his son. He was impressed with the documents Lucas Hollomby had managed to obtain, but the twin's health records would certainly be beneficial to Garrett. The proof was in the DNA test and any Court or Judge in the land would rule in Garrett's favor, as the only living next of kin. With that, Garrett was granted copies of all Trip's health records along with all the belongings left at his residence in LA and in the hotel room in New York. The health records were faxed to Grant's personal fax number and handed to Garrett immediately. Garrett scoured them and got a lot of information. It was still shocking to see how much alike they were, medically. Neither had ever broken any bones, neither had been sick other than a cold or the flu and neither had any major surgeries, although Garrett noted his twin had a couple of minor procedures done.

Hmmm, he thought. *Not exactly identical.*

* * *

It had been 3 weeks since Trip's death and the realization of his existence to the Samuels family. Poppy remained in New York, while Garrett returned to California to speak with his parents. She had wanted to go with him, but was still trying to complete her latest CD and Garrett had insisted he was fine to do it alone. In afterthought, she knew that was the right decision. Garrett needed to share this with his parents, without her being there. This was a private family matter.

And, at this point, Poppy wasn't considered family.

* * *

Working on her music was generally a fantastic, focus driven activity for Poppy. She could immerse herself in her project and forget the outside world, but not this time. Even though she was getting the work done, Poppy was very distracted. She'd had time to dwell on the reality she faced. She tried very hard to ignore it all, but there was no denying it. She was a victim of Tyrone Thomas Townsend's. He had raped her. But, was it rape? She was a consenting adult when she thought it was Garrett, but now, knowing it wasn't Garrett, she felt completely violated. She knew after seeing the report from Lucas that Tyrone had been the one to visit her the night before Garrett's holiday. Which also gave her another dilemma. A much more worrying one.

Knowing Garrett had just been dealt a huge blow, Poppy couldn't bring herself to tell him about the pregnancy, let alone the rape. What good would it do to explain to him how his unknown twin brother, posing as him, took her to bed before he ever had and she was a willing partner? All the understanding in the world would never erase that, she was sure.

However, she couldn't hide the pregnancy for long. At some point it would be obvious, so how to tell Garrett and what would he think? She could admit to herself that she loved the man, but could she admit it to him? He hadn't said those words to her, not yet. And, would he want a baby? If not, what was she prepared to do?

Poppy's mind wouldn't rest. While sitting in her studio, her music playing around her, she suddenly stopped the music and picked up the phone and placed her call.

"Hey!" Kirby said excitedly when she answered. "How's the CD coming along? I've been dying to call you, but didn't want to interrupt the creative process!"

"Are you sitting down?" Poppy asked her.

"I am now." Kirby said. "What's going on?"

"More shit than I care to admit" Poppy said, honestly.

And, she meant it.

311

Chapter 22

THE NIGHT THE STARS COME OUT

With Garrett in California, Poppy's pregnancy remained a secret for a few weeks more. Whenever they would video chat, Poppy was sure to keep the view of her face only. Garrett was doing well, considering all he had gone through. It did Poppy good to see him like that. She knew how hard it had been on him, but he seemed to have taken it all in and dealt with it. He really was an amazing man.

At night, when she was lying in bed, she'd rub her slightly rounded belly and pray that it was Garrett's child. Sometimes, Poppy would cry, worried that this was all going to end up being a big mistake. Her biggest worry was her child was the product of Tyrone and not Garrett. She didn't know Tyrone, but she didn't need to, either. For any man to do what he did, think like he did and act upon his deception in such a way; who'd want a baby from that kind of man? And how was she going to ever know? The brothers were identical twins, so no physical attributes would give it away. She could have the baby's DNA tested, but how would she explain it without giving away the real reason and would it even identify the father if they were identical? And so, she lived with the worry that she was going to give birth to the wrong man's baby.

Poppy finished her work on her new CD and returned to California. She intended to go straight to her home there, but Garrett pleaded that she stay with him. They'd been on different coasts for over a month and Garrett had missed her. He even suggested he pick her up from the airport, but she insisted that she grab a cab and meet him at his place. She didn't want to be in the middle of the airport when Garrett realized she was pregnant.

As the cab drove into her driveway, Poppy's heart began to race. *There was no going back now*, she thought as she got out of the cab. No sooner had she grabbed her coat and bag in her hands to exit the vehicle, the door flew open and Garrett's smiling face was there. He grabbed her hand and pulled her out of the car, straight into a massive hug. She was unable to move, he even had her arms pinned and was holding her in one long emotional grip. They stayed like that for a little while, until the cabbie cleared his throat. He had taken Poppy's luggage from the trunk and was waiting for payment before he could leave for his next passenger.

Garrett quickly stepped back from Poppy to pay the driver and grab the luggage. Poppy was thankful for the opportunity to get herself inside, before Garrett could see her fully. She had dressed loosely, mostly for comfort on the flight, but it wouldn't be long before she and Garrett were alone and she'd have to tell him before then.

He came into the house, smiling wide. He put the luggage down in the front hall and closed the door behind him. When he opened his arms wide to Poppy, she couldn't resist. Their hug this time was all encompassing. He kissed her face, he smelled her hair, brushed her lips lightly before kissing her mouth in a very long and intimate kiss. It actually made her dizzy. When the kiss ended, he continued to hold her in his embrace, staring into her eyes.

"You have no idea how much I've missed you" he said, quietly.

"I've missed you, too" she admitted.

"Please, let's not ever be apart like that again?" he asked, seriously. She looked at him and could tell he meant it. She nuzzled into him and he tightened his embrace.

"We need to talk" she said to him, realizing now was the time. She couldn't hold it back anymore and even though they hadn't ever mentioned the word "love" to one another, she knew what she felt in her heart. She wanted him to know. She led him by the hand, into his living room and dropped herself onto the couch. He followed, now a little apprehensive.

"Is there something wrong, Poppy?" he asked, wondering. She certainly seemed welcoming to him and her kiss didn't give away anything. He sat beside her, reaching for her hand and holding it in his. "What is it, baby?" he asked gently.

Baby, she thought. *That's it, exactly.* She smiled at his choice of wording and it eased his mind. If she was smiling, it couldn't be that bad, could it? She gripped his hand harder and she told him.

"I'm pregnant, Garrett." She smiled again and bit her lip, nervously. At first, he didn't know what to say. His smile froze on his face and it unnerved her. *Oh no*, she thought. Before she could say another word, his smile grew wider, he stood up, pulling her to her feet and threw his arms around her. As he held her he rocked her back and forth, saying nothing. At first, she was unable to fully assess his reaction, until she pulled back from him and saw the tears in his eyes.

"Poppy, you are the very best thing to ever happen to me. Thank you so much for this incredible news." He told her sincerely. She immediately felt incredible relief and threw herself back into his arms, tears forming in her own eyes.

"We're gonna have a baby" he said to her, laughing and holding her. "We're gonna have a baby" he shouted as he leaned back, laughing louder. Poppy threw her head back, "WE'RE GONNA HAVE A BABY", they shouted together.

Best news ever!

* * *

It didn't take Garrett long to get organized. Poppy had been on his mind a lot while they were apart. She had been so incredibly strong for him during the entire nightmare of the last while, making herself available to him at a moment's notice and helping him come to terms with it all, even while she worked on her latest project. When he'd lie awake at night, he thought about how much he wanted Poppy to be in his life, forever. He was planning to propose to her as soon as she stepped off the plane, but she wasn't open to him meeting her at the airport. Besides, thinking it over he realized it would cause a lot of unwanted attention. Trashing that plan he, decided he would wait until he had her in his arms at home. Her announcement of the baby certainly wasn't in the planning and he got lost in the moment for a little while. He and Poppy were cuddled up together on the couch when he realized, he still had a plan in place. Now, it was going to be even more special.

When the knock came at the door, Poppy sat up, wondering who it could be. Garrett excused himself and made his way to the front foyer. Poppy listened intently to see if she could make out who it was. She could hear Garrett's deep voice, but couldn't hear anything of what was being said. Before long, she heard him say, "Thanks so much" and the door closed.

"Can I get you a drink, Poppy?" he asked her. "I'm just going to get myself one."

"I'll just have water, please" she asked him. Since becoming pregnant her tolerance of juices or sodas were non-existent. The only thing that seemed to keep her stomach calm was water. She could hear him in his kitchen and stood up to go and join him, just as he called out to her "I'll be right there. You stay on the couch, I won't be long"

Poppy stopped mid step and shrugged her shoulders, sitting back down on the couch. She grabbed the TV remote and turned on the TV, getting comfortable. It wasn't long before her eyes were getting heavy and by the time Garrett returned with her water, she was fully asleep. He smiled when he saw her. He was looking very forward to seeing her, asleep on the couch in his home from now on. He grabbed a cashmere throw from the chair next to him and covered her with it, set her water on the table in front of her and sat down beside her. When she felt him next to her, she sleepily cuddled up beside him, her head resting on his shoulder.

He waited patiently while she slept. It wasn't easy. Garrett had a whole evening planned and was anxious to get on with it, but he didn't have the heart to wake her; the mother of his child. He smiled to himself with the thought. In a few short months, they would be parents. He couldn't wait to tell his parents the news. Especially with the anguish they had recently been through, good news like this would be unbelievably welcome.

His day had been spent planning and preparing to pop the question. He had called her favorite restaurant and asked the chef for a special favor; a proposal dinner for the incomparable Poppy Morningstar. No chef would have refused such an offer! He was honored and got to work. He was sending it over and all Garrett had to do was put it in the oven for 45 minutes at 350 degrees. He could do that.

She awoke in perfect time and immediately smelled dinner. Suddenly, she was ravenous and stretched out of her cashmere cocoon,

"Oh, what is that smell? It's fantastic!" she asked, her nose in the air taking a deep breath in.

"It's your dinner" he told her, slowly standing up and stretching himself. He brought his arm down around her and led her into the kitchen. She was till sleepy and allowed him to guide her to her seat, pulling out the chair and offering her a seat. As she sat down, she looked at her plate. A ring box sat open with the most perfect emerald cut, white gold ring Poppy had ever seen. She had never thought that she'd ever want to marry again after Kerry, but then she met Garrett. She turned in her chair and saw Garrett on his knee, in front of her. He reached for the ring box and took it out of its place holder. He gently took her hand while he held the ring close by.

"Poppy?" he asked, suddenly very anxious. "Will you do me the honor of being my wife?" He had so much he wanted to say, so much he had planned to say, but when the time came, he could only ask the question.

Poppy was astonished. "You love me?" she asked him. He hadn't told her. She would admit, he'd certainly showed her, especially his reaction today to her pregnancy, but she hadn't expected this, so soon. She looked at his face, his wonderful smiling face.

"Yes, Poppy. I've been an idiot for not telling you before now. I do love you. I love you very much. I have for a while now, I just figured with everything going on, it probably wasn't the best time. Now that you're here, all I want to do is be with you" he told her, sincerely. He was still on his knees, presenting her with the ring. She pushed her finger through the ring and her arms went around his shoulders as she answered "yes!"

He picked her up and spun her around, nearly knocking their dinner table over. Their celebration was interrupted by the timer buzzing, signifying dinner was ready. Garrett again seated Poppy and proceeded to present her with the most delicious dinner.

Over dinner many decisions were made about their upcoming nuptials. Having been married before, Poppy was open to whatever Garrett wanted, but her preference would have been to keep it small. Thankfully, Garrett felt exactly the same way.

After filling themselves, they made their way back to the couch and once again got under the cashmere blanket. She began thinking about all of the organization she was going to have to get done; a wedding, the arrival of a baby and of course, she was always working on music. She decided to call Kirby. She was thinking of adding her voice to some of the tracks she'd been working on anyway and once she found out about the wedding, Poppy would welcome any advice she'd offer. Kirby still played classical piano, but had also started singing as backup for some artists. And, she stilled stayed at her aunt's place when in NYC.

"Uh, do we want photos taken? Maybe a video made?" Poppy asked, thinking to herself.

"As long as *I* don't have to make another fucking wedding video, that's fine with me" he chuckled to himself.

"And, why is that Mr. Samuels?" she asked him, playfully.

He took a deep breath and groaned which made Poppy sit up and look him straight in the eye waiting for his answer.

"You're going to laugh" he said, coyly smiling and hanging his head. Her curiosity was now piqued and she couldn't resist.

"Oh, I promise I won't" she swore as she held up her hand, smiling the whole time. He hesitated for a moment, but knew she deserved an explanation. He dropped his head onto the back of the couch, rolling it from side to side and groaned again, smiling.

"C'mon, honey. I promise" she told him, with pleading eyes.

He sighed heavily. Her eyes killed him. He had no hope if their baby was born with her eyes. He smiled and sat back as he began to tell her his reason.

"I was in University at the time. My production videos on the internet were creating a lot of buzz and I became fairly well known by some of the staff and students. I was asked to create a wedding video for a good friend, a classmate and his fiancé. I agreed because I thought it was a chance to really introduce a whole new kind of wedding video, you know? A different perspective, an avant garde piece that would be more than just a video of a wedding day. I had some great ideas for different shots and at first, they were totally into it. I even presented a story board to them with music pieces I thought would work beautifully", he paused as Poppy's eyes widened and she mouthed "storyboard" with questioning eyes at him, "Yes, I said a storyboard." He answered, his eyes rolling as he nodded his head. "Anyway, I did a ton of work beforehand, but when the day of the wedding came, I was brought back down to earth by the bride, who demanded that I do everything to her specifications. I hated it. The entire thing. The happier I made the bride the further away from a Garrett Samuels production it became. Which I suppose is how it should be, but who wanted another boring wedding video? I promise you, if I had been able to create my vision, it would have won an Oscar" He told her with a smile. Poppy smiled back and gently snuggled back into him, waiting for him to continue.

"By the time I was in attendance to the first wedding that summer, I had signed myself up for 5 or 6 more. And it was no different for any of them. I learned pretty fast that my vision wasn't theirs, they just wanted a wedding video and that I would never be satisfied by doing things at other people's demands. That's not what I do!" He finished, hoping it didn't sound as pitiful a reason to Poppy as it did to him, just then. "I know" he said to her "kinda pretentious of me. Pretty ridiculous reason."

"It's not ridiculous, I get it. You're a craftsman at what you do, not someone to just film it. I bet most people haven't got near the visual concepts you have. You're always 4 to 5 steps ahead of everyone else in your ability to extend a story, the music, whatever element it is your working with." She paused, hoping her words helped. She really did understand. People like Garrett and her weren't wired like others. Their creative abilities took them to the next level.

Garrett chuckled low in his chest. The feeling vibrated through his chest and resonated into Poppy's. Even his laughter sent musical vibrations through her. She snuggled in closer, the blanket getting tucked under her feet.

"We aren't like others, Garrett" she said out loud.

"No, we are not" he admitted, smiling. "And now we've taken all of our gifted DNA and joined it together to create...who?" Garrett said. They sat, both lost in the thoughts of the new life growing inside Poppy's belly.

Stroking her hair gently, Garrett wondered out loud, "That first night we were together, was that when it happened, do you think?" Before the question had left his mouth, Poppy had stiffened slightly. She didn't expect the question and didn't want to show any of her worry to him.

"Possibly" she mumbled, shifting her positioning, not wanting to continue the conversation. Garrett, not aware of her body language, put his head back on the couch and sighed heavily.

"God that was pure magic. Especially after not being able to get you off my mind that entire week" he laughed out loud, as he thought back to his trip. "The boys were ribbing me the whole time after they saw us on the Late Show. They said they could tell I was in love, even then." He chuckled to himself. "I didn't know it then, but on my way home, I couldn't help myself. I couldn't stay away from you anymore. I wanted you to be mine!" he said, kissing her head. "All of this is the perfect ending to all of the upset that's happened. A huge secret has been revealed and we all lived, thankfully. Tyrone can no longer fuck with my life and that's a huge relief. Now we can all move forward without the fear of anything coming back to haunt us."

The nagging, sinking feeling that Poppy had been able to push aside for the past few weeks returned immediately with his words. Suddenly, her stomach lurched and she sat up quickly, before running out of the room towards the bathroom.

Garrett thought it was the pregnancy.

Poppy thought it was the guilt.

* * *

They were married within a month. Small and quiet, family only. Chase gave her away and Kirby stood by her side. Hans was able to watch via video streaming, his health too delicate to travel. There was no cake, barely a reception, no honeymoon and definitely nothing recorded. Neither needed, nor wanted the publicity, not for this, anyway. They had a few months of quiet life, travelling between New York and L.A. and planning for the birth of their first child, due in February.

Poppy's CD drop for "Generations" had been put off until after the baby was born. Her music was still in demand and with Precision Touch being released in theaters just before Christmas, it did Poppy no harm to hold off on the release. She could afford the time to be at home with Garrett and relax into married life. But, the quiet would not last long.

By January, they had been nominated for an Oscar for their soundtrack on "Precision Touch" and stayed in L.A. for the ceremonies. By then, Poppy was nearing the end of her pregnancy and she felt incredible. Pregnancy certainly agreed with her. She had experienced morning sickness for a short period of time, but by her fourth month she was not experiencing any sickness, at all. Once she could eat, she ate well. She put aside her worries about the baby and surrounded herself with positivity and tried to enjoy her pregnancy, as much as she could.

The fun they shared with attending the Academy Awards was exactly what they needed. There was excitement in the air with "Precision Touch" being nominated in 13 categories, including Best Original Soundtrack and Best Original Song. They had spent the awards season accepting a few and losing a few, but both were keen on the Academy Award for this movie. "Precision Touch" was where they met and fell in love. It would always be special to them.

Poppy had a special dress created for her. A deep, blue halter dress that didn't hide her baby belly. She and Garrett stood on the red carpet, enjoying the attention, enjoying the cameras flashing and the fun of it all. Poppy's face hurt from smiling and she couldn't wait to sit down for the two to three hours it took to get through the awards. Her baby was quite active and she was uncomfortable as she sat, waiting for the night to unfold.

When they announced the winner in the Original Score category "And the Oscar goes to…Poppy Morningstar and Garrett Samuels for Precision Touch" Poppy threw herself into a standing position, clapping her hands vigorously and reaching out to Garrett. They shared a hug and kiss before he led her by the hand to the stage.

The whole audience, not just those in attendance in the theater, instantly fell for the couple, so obviously in love. Poppy, her beautiful blue dress, rosy complexion in full baby bloom and smiling from ear to ear was helped up the stairs and onto the stage by her husband, Garrett who, quite simply beamed.

In years to come, their speeches may not be remembered word for word, but no one would ever forget the incredible love they shared, how much they cared for one another and the joy they felt for the many wonderful things they had created.

They will also always and forever be remembered for Poppy's water breaking in front of all the world, live and on camera; that and the look of surprise and laughter she and Garrett shared as they realized that Oscar wasn't the only little guy they were being blessed with that night!

Chapter 23

REDMOND MORNINGSTAR SAMUELS

Redmond Morningstar Samuels was born the next afternoon at 3:55 pm. Poppy had done well, a beautiful birth by any standards and both mother and baby were fine. Garrett was exhausted. Never had any project he worked on exhausted him more than the birth of his child. He was thrilled with his son! He was so beautiful! A perfect blend of Poppy and himself. As a newborn, it was hard to tell who he took after most. His coloring was a deep honey. His eyes were a lighter blue, but it was too early to tell if they would stay that way. He had a full head of hair, more a mane than anything. Even the nurses at the hospital wondered how his hair had come out looking like it had. He was one of the most beautiful babies they had ever seen; they all said it. And they weren't lying. Redmond Morningstar Samuels really was a beautiful baby.

And his mother prayed it was from inside and out.

* * *

She never stopped working, far from it. As a matter of fact, Poppy Morningstar worked very hard, wrote constantly and spent many hours in the studio. She was happy as a mother and Redmond became a huge source of inspiration for her. She wrote songs about the love of a mother, the hope for her child and the realization of loving someone so much, more than you ever loved yourself. Redmond and Garrett brought such happiness to Poppy, she was almost able to push her worries away.

Almost.

She had so much pride for her lovely little family. Their pictures were splashed all over magazines and televisions everywhere as THE couple in the entertainment industry. Poppy's heritage made her music royalty and

Redmond and Garrett, her Princes. It was her quiet moments, when her fears would come forward; those moments that she dreaded most.

Poppy watched Redmond closely. If he was with other children, she watched his behavior. Was he a nice boy? Did he treat his friends nicely?

Because she didn't know who Redmond took after.

Because she didn't know, for certain, who Redmond's father was.

And, try as she might, it plagued her.

* * *

Trip's murder remained unresolved. After Lucas Hollomby took over the full investigation for Garrett he was able to ascertain that it was the "rapper" BB that was the main suspect. Garrett had only remembered his encounter with BB long after the fact, giving the murderous man the chance to get away. Despite an FBI manhunt, he had disappeared; no one had seen or heard from him since. Lucas Hollomby was still on his trail, thinking he'd been hiding somewhere in South America or the Caribbean Islands.

During his investigation, Lucas continued to uncover information about Trip's impersonations of Garrett. As far as he could tell, Trip had been pretending he was Garrett in both New York and California in the last few years. Garrett was still taken aback by this news. Poppy wasn't.

* * *

Poppy spent her days between elation and deep concern. Being Redmond's mother and Garrett's wife was pure bliss. Redmond's wonderment of the world around him gave Poppy so many new perspectives, her music began to take on a life of its own. She would spend her days with Redmond and her nights in the studio turning her day into music, into a musical story. Garrett would sit and listen in awe every evening as she played whatever new sound she had created. But not matter how much happiness there was in her heart, her head would go to dark places when she'd see signs of Trip in Redmond's actions. The only dark spot in and otherwise bright life.

She witnessed a 4 year old Redmond chasing a cat that had wandered into their backyard. He wasn't just a curious child, he was relentless with it, going after it endlessly until it got tired with his antics and promptly left. And then, he had a truly epic tantrum afterward. This concerned her.

When he was 6 years old, Redmond was sent to the Head Principal's office for emptying a full tube of toothpaste into the running shoes of his gym teacher. He told them it was on a dare from his schoolmates. Poppy wasn't sure.

By 8 years old, Redmond had been caught in trouble from his private school so many times, she and Garrett had to have a talk with him and with the Head Principal. Their talk with him was stern, restrictive and enforced. If he didn't stop his behavior, he'd have no luxuries at home and no freedom outside.

Poppy was beside herself. How is it that she could create magical music, but she couldn't keep her son from acting out? She was at her wits end. She and Garrett were discussing therapy and possibly boarding school…but, then it happened. Poppy found her answer and Redmond found his way!

And, sometimes wonderful things are born of tragedy.

* * *

Poppy had been working in her studio, rerecording some of the tracks on her CD "Generations". She had asked her father Chase and her Uncle Charlie to each record guitar tracks for it and they had. Of all her musical creations, this one was her proudest. Garrett had produced it and that was the cherry on the top; a true family project.

She was at her piano when she heard the vibration. At first, she wasn't sure what it was, engrossed in her music. The buzzing was insistent and made her look up to see her phone lighting up and humming against the piano.

It was her Uncle Charlie. Right away she was concerned. Chase and Dana were out visiting them in Chicago and were due to come home in another week. She had not expected to hear from them at all during that time.

"Hey Uncle Charlie, how are things?" She asked.

"Uh, not great, Poppy. Your dad is in hospital here. He's had a heart attack, dear. He's okay, but not out of danger, quite yet. I think you need to come here." He told her solemnly. She gasped at the news, her hand to her mouth.

"Okay, I'll…uh, start making arrangements. I'll let you know when we land." She told him. "Until then, please tell him we love him. And love to all of you. I'll get there as soon as I can. Thanks for the call, Uncle Charlie". She got off her phone and immediately called Garrett.

He was in the studio at the office, working on his latest project. He was happy to hear from his wife and Poppy could hear it in his voice.

"Hey! How's your day going" he asked her. The pause on the other end of the line told him something was up.

Within minutes the flight was booked.

* * *

Redmond walked into the music room of his great Uncle Charlie's home in Chicago, looking around the walls in awe. It was his first visit to their home, although he and his mom video chatted with them a few times a year. Redmond loved his Grampa Chase, and his Grampa's brother, his great uncle Charlie was an older, quieter version. Redmond thought he looked really edgy and cool in some of the photos that adorned the room. They were mostly of musicians, some on stage, others posing with other musicians. Redmond recognized only one or two of the people in the photos and studied them closely, interested in the thousand stories they told.

Charlie was stretched out on his recliner, napping after spending the morning at the hospital. Redmond was careful to be very quiet while he looked around the room. He knew Uncle Charlie was tired and didn't want to disturb him, but he loved this room. He was fascinated by all the pictures. They were his heritage, his family. There were pictures in this room that went back more than 100 years, Uncle Charlie's home was like a time machine.

Charlie raised an eye open, seeing Redmond bending over looking at a picture of his great-grandmother, Celia. Redmond studied the picture closely. He'd been told she was a fantastic blues singer. Both his grandfather and great-uncle had told him stories of her, both clearly in awe of her strength and talent. Redmond wished he could have heard her sing. Apparently, she was amazing. He had heard his mother sing and figured she must have taken after Celia.

He moved onto a picture of a family of seven. At closer inspection, he realized that only three of them were related; Celia, Charlie and Chase. His grandfather looked to be about 7 or 8 years old, same age as Redmond was now. He had no idea how old Charlie would have been.

"I was in my early twenties" Charlie answered, as if reading Redmond's mind.

Redmond was surprised at Charlie's voice and jumped back at first. Charlie's laughter at scaring the boy gave him away and within moments, Redmond was by the side of his chair smiling.

"Hi Uncle Charlie" he said in a whisper.

"Hi, my favorite, great nephew. And, I do mean GREAT!" he said, as he reached a hand out to pat the boy's arm. He smiled at Redmond, the wide Morningstar smile that Redmond had spotted on many of those in the pictures that surrounded them. Charlie pulled himself up, sitting upright in the chair and looked Redmond in the eye.

"Your mom tells me that you're not happy in school." It was a nice way for Charlie to bring the subject up. "What's wrong, Big Red, you bored?"

He loved the "Big Red" nickname Charlie had given him and it immediately put Redmond at ease. Charlie had an easy going way with kids and they usually responded well. It made Redmond feel like he lived up to his coolness in the pictures he'd seen.

Redmond was teased a lot in school for many things, including his name and great uncle Charlie was right, he was also bored. Between the teasing and the boredom, Big Red was struggling. Uncle Charlie had always seen the spark in his eye and knew that the boy just needed to find his niche. Charlie believed all Morningstars were gifted individuals and once they were introduced to their "gift" there was no stopping them. It had happened with Celia, himself, Chase and Poppy. Charlie figured it was only a matter of time before Redmond would find himself and when he did, look out!

Redmond didn't answer his great uncle immediately. Instead he turned towards the numerous guitars that were displayed along the far wall of the room. Charlie watched him as he studied each one. He wondered if Chase had ever had Redmond hold a guitar. He didn't want to over step as the great uncle, but with Chase in the hospital, it was all hands on deck. Charlie had to do his family duty and show this child the magic he could make. Maybe, just maybe through this, Redmond would find his niche.

"You ever play one, Big Red?" Charlie asked him. Redmond spun around quickly and shook his head, his eyes wide. Charlie nodded, knowingly. Sometimes, the answer was right in front of you the whole time.

He motioned to Redmond, "bring Meg to me, will you, please?" he asked the child, thinking he was probably the same age when it all started for him. *Funny how life repeats itself,* Charlie thought to himself.

Knowing the whole story of Meg; Uncle Charlie's guitar, given to him on his 7th birthday, Redmond immediately reached for the neck of the starburst Gibson Les Paul. She was beautiful. Charlie had kept her in immaculate condition, even having her restrung just a year previous. As rare as it was for them to get together anymore, when Chase came to town, he brought his guitar and they would play. Sometimes, Dana and Georgie would sit and listen, but most times, the girls left the musical brothers alone, giving them the chance to connect again, through music. After all, neither of them were getting any younger. Chase was near 80 and Charlie would be 95 on his next birthday.

Redmond handed Meg to Charlie and watched as Charlie gently placed the strap around his shoulder and placed his hand on the neck.

"Any interest?" he asked simply, as he played a quick blues riff. Even at his age, he still played the guitar like it was an extension of his hand. Although he was mesmerized by Uncle Charlie's ability, Redmond shrugged his shoulders.

His parents had tried to get him interested in music at an early age, but Redmond showed no inclination. Any kind of keyboard you could imagine sat in his home, just asking for the inquisitive chubby fingers of a curious child, but Redmond would walk past them all, never drawn to press down on the keys and hear their tune.

Ever since he could recall, Redmond remembered music in his house. His parents both worked creating music and his grandparents and great-grandparents were all known for their musical abilities. Now, he was the latest Morningstar/Samuels in the family. The truth was, he was acting out because he believed he didn't have any kind of musical calling. He just didn't feel it. He watched both of his parents create fantastic musical pieces, but it didn't move him. It didn't speak to him.

Not yet, anyway.

As Redmond stood watching Charlie play the guitar, he became interested in how his fingers worked the neck and strings. His hands moved up and down the neck creating an unbelievable sound and he did it all with his eyes closed. He had seen Grampa Chase play guitar as well and had heard adults describe him as "gifted". Redmond agreed, both were definitely gifted men. He also watched his mother's ability to play piano, as if she were in a trance. She was gifted, too. Redmond wanted to be gifted.

"Well? You wanna play?" Charlie asked him, again. He hesitated a moment and then, Redmond nodded his head which made Charlie smile. "Go grab your grampa's guitar, the blue one beside Meg's stand" Charlie told the lad. Without hesitation, Redmond ran towards the guitar, had it in his hand and the strap over his shoulder, neck in hand and stood before Charlie, his smile brilliant and wide. Charlie nodded, smiling back. For a moment, Charlie was taken back to a time when a 7 year old Chase was given his Grampa George's guitar.

"Now, you play back what I play, okay? Here we go" Charlie stated.

It only took a few chords for Redmond to begin to love the feel of the guitar in his hands, the strings underneath his fingertips and how, when he manipulated them with his feelings, and stroked the strings with his other hand, it made incredible sound.

Not only sound, but vibration. Redmond could feel the vibrations running through his fingertips, into his hands, down his forearm and up into his shoulders. Once it hit his head, it created a huge burst sensation that made him close his eyes. He saw a kaleidoscope of colours and burst of bright white.

And with that, another Morningstar burst into a super nova.

Chapter 24

KARMA WAS WATCHING!

When there was no media announcement of Garrett Samuel's murder in a subway, BB took notice. Garrett Samuels was still alive and BB had thrown some other stupid fuck onto the subway tracks, but who? When he was safely far enough away from the subway he rifled through the wallet he had stolen. *Who the fuck was Tyrone Townsend?* He wondered angrily.

After many years of letting the story die down, BB crawled back out from under his hiding spot in Columbia, made his way to New York and began to look into who this Tyrone was and how the fuck he was going to get at Garrett Samuels now? Especially since Garrett was an Oscar winning producer, married to an Oscar winning musical phenom and member of the Morningstar family.

Hooking up with some of his old contacts, BB was able to pay a very unscrupulous cop thousands of dollars for a safe file transfer of the electronic police report on the murder. Another contact helped him look at the files and glean through the numerous reports it had. He read an entry from an officer first on the scene after the body was found, "Identification found on body - Garrett Samuels". *What the fuck?* He thought. Weeding through another report, the officer who had interviewed Garrett Samuels and had written: "only child."

So, Samuels didn't die that day, but the Tyrone guy had his ID and looked exactly like him? BB wondered. It took him another 4 reports before he found something that answered it all. Someone, a police officer or investigator had written in large letters, "TWINS" and circled it several times with their pen. So, Garrett Samuels had a twin. Reading further, he found out that Garrett had no idea about the existence of that twin and that he'd been adopted by a couple of lawyers in Chicago.

No wonder one brother didn't know him, but the other did. No wonder, when he went to Garrett Samuels' offices, Mr. Fuckin' Samuels didn't know him. He hadn't shared a drink with Garrett Samuels, the brilliant music producer, it was his twin, Tyrone! BB thought. BB knew now he'd been played by the twin that night at the bar and it gave him satisfaction to know he'd killed his ass for duping him, but that still didn't give Garrett Samuels the justification to humiliate him like he did that day. No one humiliated BB and lived. No one.

Now BB needed to start research on his new plan. He'd been waiting long enough. It was time for him to finish what was started years ago and now long forgotten by the Samuels. His best weapon was his patience. He'd get this done when they were the most unsuspecting, when they were at their most vulnerable. Nothing gave him more joy than knowing his victims were taken by surprise, but at the last moment they realized who had taken their life. He liked to see the realization hit their eyes just as their life slipped away and with age, he had become even more vindictive with a real taste for brutality. He not only planned on murdering Garrett Samuels, he was going to take his whole family out, too. A wonderful Christmas present to himself. After all, Santa never gave him anything.

Christmas was not a special time for BB. He hadn't celebrated Christmas for many years, except that one year. He'd attended church on Christmas Eve and fallen in love with an angel, but she rejected him and embarrassed him. He hated being humiliated by others and she had humiliated him in front of the entire congregation. For that, he had to kill her, regardless of who else was killed. Actually, especially because of who else he managed to kill. He had hated her mother, too. How convenient that they always travelled together when they went to church. Two for the price of one, so to speak.

* * *

The Samuels' L.A. home had gotten quiet after a fun and boisterous Christmas Eve celebration. Many guests had shown up for a catered affair and most came with gifts in hand. By early in the evening the Christmas tree was overwhelmed. Kirby had come to stay with them for Christmas, having lost her grandmother Bobby the year before. Kirby's aunt was not in the country for Christmas, so Poppy made sure to open her home to Kirby. Chase and Dana were not able to travel. Chase's health wouldn't allow it, but they were all going to head to New York in a few weeks to spend time with her parents. It had been all planned. Now, they merely waited for a good night's rest and the jolly old elf to come! Going to sleep that night, Poppy smiled to herself. She always loved the excitement in the house on Christmas Eve.

* * *

Christmas in L.A. was different than Christmas in the East. It goes darker a lot earlier and soon kid's eyes look to the skies for Santa. BB didn't believe in fuckin' Santa and didn't give a shit about kids. The early darkness allowed perfect cover and the fact that the house was alive with guests only helped him to get indoors without anyone being any the wiser. He'd been tipped off that the evening would be catered and that was all he needed to know. He got in just behind the catering truck and made excuses that he was the Catering Manager, needing to oversee the event. He was dressed in a Chef's jacket and looked the part. The Security Guard didn't question it and BB was let through.

Fuckin' idiot, he thought, smiling to himself. As he drove along the road, he saw extreme houses, with extreme cars dripping extreme money. It made him angry.

If Garrett Samuels had just listened to him that day, had given him a chance, a LABEL for fuck's sake, he'd own one of these mother-fuckin' houses! Hell, he'd own THREE! He raged, inside. As he drove along, he slammed the steering wheel several times, shouting *FUCK! FUCK! FUCK!* Just the rally cry he needed to perform multiple murders.

He managed to get himself calmed down enough to find a parking spot that wouldn't cause alarm. A driveway next to a pool house at the back of a lot. It was a few minutes' walk, but he waited patiently once he got there to see the caterers unloading their truck. When he had a clear chance, he grabbed a tray of covered vegetables from the inside of the truck and walked it straight into the front door without anyone noticing.

The house was large and decorated with numerous trees, holly boughs and twinkle lights. He watched where all the other waiters were heading and followed them easily into the kitchen area, placing the tray down on a counter before turning and heading out of the kitchen. He took a right outside of the kitchen and stopped at the first door he found, turning the knob and opening the door easily. It was an unoccupied bathroom. Stepping inside, he removed the white chef's jacket he had worn, opened the cupboard under the sink and having folded the jacket as small as he could, he hid it in the very back. It was completely veiled and wouldn't draw any attention. BB would come back and retrieve the jacket, once they were all dead. He then moved his gun from the back of his pants to a holster by his side. His plan now was to find a place to hide inside the house until the celebrations died down and things got quiet. Deathly quiet.

He left the bathroom and managed to see a staircase ahead that took him out of the view of anyone on the main floor. Up he went, easily avoiding everyone else and went off to find a hiding spot. The upstairs was very quiet and there was many rooms that branched up off of a large main landing. He checked the rooms and chose to slip inside one that contained no obvious sign of being occupied. Although the house was full of celebrants, by his count only a handful of the rooms were being used. The house would clear out and then he could make his move.

He wanted to kill them all.

On Christmas Eve.

That would be a Christmas present to himself.

A great time of year to settle the score.

This most wonderful time of the year.

* * *

Kirby awoke quickly. A strange sensation washing over her. She had woken from a deep sleep abruptly, with a shiver running through her. She sat up in bed listening intently, all her senses were on high alert. Holding her breath, she held herself still, not moving a muscle. Something wasn't right. She could feel it.

WAS SOMEONE IN THE HOUSE? Her mind screamed!

That couldn't be possible! Surely, Garrett and Poppy had a security system and the neighbourhood was a gated community. She tried to find reason for the feeling she just couldn't shake. *Was it Redmond?* She waited, wondering if she could tell. She heard no doors open, no telltale signs of Poppy or Garrett moving around.

Feeling completely unnerved and not able to justify why, she rose up out of her bed and reached for her gun; the same gun Poppy had spotted years before in her backpack. She was a confident shooter. She didn't want to miss and had no intention of doing so.

Kirby quietly walked over to the bedroom door and very slowly turned the knob. She was able to open it up enough to see along the hallway, but she couldn't see the stairs. She slipped into the hallway and took position in an alcove and waited. Her heart was thumping loud in her chest and yet, she had imagined this moment for a very long time and she felt sure of herself. She thought back to a time she'd made a promise to herself and she held that resolve now. *If someone is in this house to hurt us, I'm going to blow his fucking head clean off!*

Kirby could literally smell him. Her senses were that in tune. She felt like a predator, awaiting her prey. She could sense the footsteps and his presence in the hallway, coming towards her. Not a sound had been made, and yet Kirby knew he was maybe 10 steps away. She held her gun rigid wanting him to get closer before she made her move.

* * *

Garrett and Poppy lay in bed, snuggled together after some Christmas Eve lovemaking. Christmas was always a special time for them and they made the most of every chance to relax and spend time with each other and Redmond. Garrett had just begun snoring lightly and Poppy was slowly drifting off, when she began to dream.

She saw the elderly woman immediately and smiled, now finally remembering her from years before.

"You, it's YOU! Poppy said, excitedly. "I remember you now. You've been helping me, haven't you?" she asked, feeling exuberant at finally being able to converse properly with her. Before Poppy could say anymore, the elderly lady held up her hand to her.

"You must wake up, Poppy! Your baby is in danger! Your family is in danger!"

It was blunt and direct and as real as anything Poppy had experienced. It brought her completely out of her dream with a gasp, sitting straight up. She looked over to the end of the bed and saw Garrett holding a gun, motioning for Poppy to come to him. When she got close enough, he whispered quietly into her ear, "Go through the shared door to get Redmond and lock yourself in his bathroom." He looked into her eyes, nodding to her and she nodded back. Garrett knew how to use a gun and since Tyrone's murder he took no chances. Even if BB wasn't coming for him, who knows how many other maniacs were out there seeking revenge or some sort of prestige and publicity. Many people had been made infamous by killing someone famous and to some, fame and infamy were the same thing.

Garrett watched Poppy go through the shared door into their son's room and scoop Redmond up into the bathroom, closing the door. He followed behind them, closing the shared door just enough for him to see into the room. He stood ready, his gun in hand and his heart pounding. No one was going to fuck with his family and get away with it, he was going to make sure of that.

* * *

BB slowly made his way out of the spare bedroom and began to make his way down the hallway. While he waited for the festivities to die down, he had time to plan out his attack. He'd decided he'd stick to the rooms on the same side his room was on. He'd brought a silencer with him and hoped he could take out Poppy and Garrett first. Then it was just the kid and the friend. Easily done. Perfect that all the staff who usually worked in the home were all off for Christmas. If he played his cards right, he could get these killings done, spend time ripping off as much as he could and get his ass out of the country before anyone was aware. The murders were no longer going to satisfy him, he wanted to be able to live an affluent life afterwards as well and who better to pay for that than Garrett Samuels.

The first two rooms were of no concern to him; one, another empty guest room and the other a storage room. It only fueled his murderous rage that the storage closet was the size of most people's living room. *It was time he had this kind of money!*

He prepared himself, believing the next two rooms were family bedrooms and his main targets. He took a deep breath and moved forward. He couldn't wait to see the blood spew from their heads. The life go out of their eyes. Poppy wouldn't know him, but maybe Garrett would remember. He wanted to make sure he didn't just get so excited he killed him before letting him see his face. *You fucking humiliated the wrong dude, asshole!*

* * *

Redmond lay in bed, not able to sleep. He was far too excited! It was Christmas Eve and he'd always loved Christmas. It was so fun and it meant time spent with his mom and dad, all to himself. And this year, Aunt Kirby was joining them. What more could he want, but the love and attention of these 3 amazing people for the next few days. His thoughts were filled with the games they'd play, when the shared door to his parent's room opened. At first, it frightened him, the door was used a lot when he was a small boy, but not in recent years. He soon he made out his mother's face, holding her finger to her lips. *Shhh!* She motioned, a big smile on her face. He smiled widely at her, his arms lifted to her in hopes she would lift him up and cuddle him as she had done many times over the years. She scooped him up quickly and moved swiftly into his own bathroom, where she closed and locked the door. She then held him closely and whispered in his ear stories of how Santa was coming and how she needed him to be very quiet in case Santa detected him awake and left without placing his gifts under the tree. Silently, mother and child waited.

* * *

Kirby stayed hidden in the darkness of the alcove, unbeknownst to the intruder. It was going to be by his error, not hers. She was so ready to do this, to end this rage within her. Regardless of who was at the end of her gun, they had no right being there and she would stop their invasion, period. She held the gun, locked and loaded.

* * *

As he reached for the door knob to the third room along the hallway, he smiled to himself. What a Christmas present he would give himself, vindication! Once inside, he could make out the decorations of a child's room. He could see sports posters, dinosaurs and a few models of cars and space ships. Judging by the décor, this was the boy's room. *Hmmmm,* he thought. He turned towards the bed and tried to focus on the rumpled sheets. *Was a body in there?* He screwed the silencer end on the gun shaft. He didn't plan to take the kid out first, but so be it. This should be easy.

* * *

She had seen him enter Redmond's room. *Dear God!,* her blood ran cold. She needed to get in there quickly, but she was fearful that rushing in might cause the intruder to react hastily and kill Redmond in the process. She needed to keep her cool. She got to Redmond›s door and quickly peered around to see the man with his back to her, putting the gun into the bed sheets. He then pushed the gun around, moving the sheets. There was no one in the bed. He quickly turned to one of two doors in his room.

* * *

He was confused. *Which door was which? Why two doors? If he wasn't in his bed, where was he? If one door was his bathroom, where did the other lead? SHIT!* He thought to himself. *Last thing I need is to be chasing some fucking kid all over the house.* So, now he had a choice. Which door to choose? Maybe one was a closet and the kid was hiding in there? That sounded good to him. So, the other was the bathroom and he could very well be in there. That sounded good to him, too. Either way, it was a win-win for him.

* * *

Kirby waited a moment, wondering if he could hear her heartbeat. It was literally pounding in her chest. She didn't let it stop her and as he moved closer towards one of the doors, she entered into the room behind him and took position. As he reached the door knob and tried to open the door, an audible gasp was heard from inside. He noticed and so did Kirby. It was now or never. He raised the gun towards the door and took aim. Without a second thought, Kirby swiftly took aim and shot quickly. One single shot.

* * *

The police investigation had concluded that BB, aka Blaine Bannister, aka Blaine the Blade had been responsible for Tyrone Thomas Townsend's death and was still under suspicion in the death of Jessica Corley and her mother.

Blaine Bannister was now lying dead upstairs between Redmond's bedroom and bathroom. Thankfully, Redmond's mother had protected him from seeing anything too horrific.

Because, Kirby had kept true to her promise.

She blew his fucking head clean off!

Chapter 25

GOODBYE CHARLIE

He had died on his 102nd birthday. Quite the feat, he'd have thought! There were so many that turned up for his funeral, monitors had been placed outside the bar he had owned for decades and his niece gave the eulogy. She spoke of Charlie Morningstar's commitment to "the band" and how he was truly a gifted artist. She spoke of her father Chase's love for his older brother. By the time she had finished, there were very few with a dry eye. Happy to give her wonderful uncle the funeral he would have wanted, the funeral he truly deserved, Poppy sighed heavily as she took her seat. Chase, never fully recovered after his heart attack a few years back, was only able to attend view live feed as well, Hans in Germany, who was also ailing, drying his eyes the whole time for Poppy's loss. It was tough on her two fathers, but especially Chase. His heart will be broken and she wondered if he was strong enough to endure it. Thankfully, Dana was still quite vibrant and would probably outlive all of them.

Poppy had tried hard to push her own worries behind her, but it plagued her more often now than it used to. *As Redmond got older, who would he take after?* So far, he'd shown no "gift" as far as Poppy could see, although he did spend a lot of time in his room. He was still a mystery to her. She had watched him over the years, hoping for some sort of sign, some sort of answer to her silent worry. *Whose son was he? Would Tyrone's DNA poison the Morningstar blood? Would he be a Morningstar without a musical gene, the first in a long time?*

Poppy's mind was never at peace. She wondered if she would ever know the truth, for certain. As she stood in the main room of "Black and Blue" the bar her Uncle Charlie had once owned and entertained in for years, she clasped her hands together and prayed to her beloved late uncle.

"Oh Uncle Charlie, I know you understand my anguish. You probably understand everything now you're up there." She said, smiling to herself. "Please, please send me peace of mind. Some kind of sign that would help me know the truth." She spoke, tears in her eyes. She stood quiet for a moment and allowed her tears to flow as she closed her eyes, picturing his face and hoping he heard her.

* * *

The funeral and celebration of his life had ended. Only a few people remained, eating up the last of the food, having a last conversation with Poppy and Garrett and basically enjoying the quiet after a hectic afternoon. Garrett was surprised to see his own friends, the ones he used to vacation with yearly, paying their respects. They remembered the vacation when he professed his love for *the* Poppy Morningstar, and even more so when he married her. Every one of them was a Morningstar fan; some knowing Celia's music, others having followed old blues, more recently Chase's influence on music through the past two decades. All of Garrett's friends came and he was grateful.

They sat at a large round table, bottles of beer and glasses of hard liquor in front of them and raised their glasses numerous times to the Morningstars that had entertained multitudes of fans and gone before them. It caused Poppy to choke up. *These guys are really lovely,* she thought. Nice to know her husband had such upstanding friends.

During the course of conversation, the subject of Tyrone came up. Immediately, Poppy was uneasy with the subject. She folded her arms into herself and quietly looked away.

"So you can tell us all now, dude. What the hell was with all of that?" Due to the police investigation at the time, Garrett hadn't shared everything with them, but now, all was out in the open.

"So, you were his only next of kin?" he was asked. He nodded.

"I was given all of his belongings from two residences and all of my maternal grandmother's belongings, including $15,000 in life insurance." He told them, taking a drink of his beer.

"Oh, burn to the twin, Tyrone!" one of his friends stated. Garrett just shrugged his shoulders. "It's not that I don't feel sorry for him. I do. I think he got burned bigtime and if he'd have reached out to me and been decent, I would have helped him in any and every way I could, but he didn't and he put me in danger and ultimately my family in danger." Garrett stated frankly. "I owe him nothing."

No one could deny him that and many nodded in agreement.

"Ya, but are you sure?" another asked. The room fell silent. "Are you sure you're the only next of kin? What about children?" Garrett's friend questioned, innocently. He couldn't have known what he was asking and it only mattered to Poppy, but her heart stood still. It was the one question she always feared. What if Tyrone had fathered a child? Her child? As her mind was racing, Poppy felt her stomach drop. *It was always going to be this way,* she thought.

"No, no, no" Garrett laughed, waving his hand. "I know the truth!" he declared, not telling them right away. His friends booed him and teased him until he finally told them.

Okay, Okay" he said, holding his hands up and laughing. "Tyrone Thomas Townsend and I were not *identical* twins." He told them, taking a slow drink of his beer as everyone cheered him on to tell them the rest of the story.

"My father was able to appeal to the courts for access to all records, as I was the only living next of kin. This meant I also got health records from all his years past. And, I counted two ways we are not identical" he announced.

"Number 1. He was circumcised when he was in his early twenties. I" he announced proudly, "am not!" This caused many groans from his buddies and a blush from Poppy, which only made things worse. Even Poppy couldn't help but smile at the fun these guys put Garrett through.

"Number 2. He'd had a vasectomy when he was 22, and took multiple tests to ensure it worked. Seems he didn't want children and I can only assume he paid someone to do it. If he had children, it was before then and the records show no history of children to that point" he told the group. "I'm pretty confident with the investigation and what was in those records." With that, he smiled his wide smile, winked and drank the last of his beer, putting the empty bottle down on the table with great finesse to more hoots and cheers from those around the table.

Poppy couldn't move. Her heart skipped a beat, she was sure! Had Garrett really just said that? Tyrone had a vasectomy at 22? Which meant, Tyrone couldn't possibly be the father to Redmond. The weight of years of worry immediately lifted off Poppy's shoulders. She tried hard to hide her tears, but the relief she felt was overwhelming. Needing to come up with a good cover to hide her emotion, she stood up and held her drink up.

"To my Uncle Charlie. May you and Georgie be happy in heaven, making great music with all the other Morningstars that have gone on before you. And, may we Morningstars who remain down here continue on exploring and recreating through our musical journey and keep the world entertained with our gifts. Thank you for *all* your gifts, tutelage, your guidance and your gentle and quiet strength. Rest in peace, Charlie" as her voice broke and the tears flowed, she raised her glass to the air and the group around the table did the same. "Rest in peace, Charlie" they repeated together. Poppy took a deep breath and downed her glass.

Uncle Charlie's final gift to her. *Bless you Uncle Charlie!*.

* * *

At the reading of Charlie Morningstar's will, Redmond stood in the back corner, remembering the day he'd first spent with his great uncle Charlie, years before. From that day forward, Uncle Charlie and Redmond would video chat twice weekly without either of his parents knowing. Redmond even managed to sneak a guitar into his home and he and Uncle Charlie would work together, improving Redmond's skills each time they chatted.

When Redmond's Grampa Chase was well enough to take part, they'd video conference together, all 3 of them; Chase, Charlie and Redmond.

Great-great-Grampa George Morningstar was the patriarch to start it all; he loved to play piano and taught his grandson Charlie how to play guitar, regardless of having suffered a stroke. Now his descendants continued that line and carried it on through the generations. Now his great-great grandson, Redmond was walking in his and Charlie's footsteps.

* * *

As the few family and friends who were contacted for the reading of Charlie's will gathered, Poppy and Garret sat near the front. Poppy looked around for Redmond, but he refused to sit with them up front. *Teenage boys were so difficult*, Poppy thought.

"Finally" the lawyer read "I leave my entire guitar collection including and most importantly, my one guitar love, Meg, to my GREAT nephew Redmond "Big Red" Morningstar Samuels. The lawyer cleared his throat before he continued reading.

"Big Red, if you treat her well, she will teach you much. And may you make beautiful and magical Morningstar music together". The lawyer stopped, looking up at the people sitting before him and blushed slightly.

Poppy stood and turned to look at her son, Redmond. He was smiling as wide as he could. *Practically giddy*, Poppy thought. *Meg?* She questioned to herself. *What does Redmond have to do with Meg and Uncle Charlie?*

She watched her son intently as she walked over to him, her look of surprise on her face, hard to hide.

"Meg?" She asked when she got closer to him. She cocked her head to one side and he knew by her look that she needed answers. As she was questioning him, his dad, Garrett was approaching him carrying Meg and holding the beautiful guitar out to him.

343

Redmond took Meg in his hands, threw her strap over his shoulder and told his mother, "I've decided I'm going into the family business." And, with a wide and beautiful Morningstar smile, Redmond proceeded to play a beautiful and unique rendition of Amazing Grace, for his great Uncle Charlie. His teacher.

Poppy stopped herself and took in the moment. Music ran in his blood, another generation who had the musical gene. Five generations and counting. Redmond would also carry the gene on, no...the *gift* on and Redmond *was gifted*, there was no disputing that! He played the guitar as if he'd always held one. Poppy and Garrett stood side by side, arms around one another, both had tears in their eyes. Music would continue on with their child. Their wonderful child.

Their gifted and musical child.

The Morningstar story will never, truly end.

Epilogue

Alabama 1911 - 1912

When she was found, she was in the fetal positon, shivering and half naked. Her dress had been pulled up to her neck and it was apparent to her family that she had been sexually abused; her thighs and buttocks were covered in blood. The 13 year old girl had been brutally raped.

Her father raced her home to her mother who shushed her brothers and father away and spent over an hour cleaning her up. She had cried in pain and her mother had given her a drink of whiskey to calm her down and let her rest. The mother knew her young daughter was a full woman and had started her bleeding just four months previous and it worried her. If the monster's seed had planted, how could they live with that? She tried her best not to worry over it, but it stayed with her, like a bad gut feeling.

When her daughter finally awoke, she was there beside her, making sure she had what she needed and concerned the attack would haunt her.

"How you feelin', child?" her mother asked quietly.

"Thirsty" she answered. Her mother stood and poured her a cup of water and brought it to her. "There now, drink this." She said, feeling her eyes well up to watch her young daughter, beaten and raped at only 13, surviving her attack.

She helped her daughter sit up as she took the cup and drank, readily. As she handed the cup back to her mother, they looked each other in the eye. The held each other's gaze as the young girl began to wail and threw herself into her mother's arms. Her heart broke and she took her only daughter into her protective embrace and rocked her. She had no words to give to her, no words of comfort to say and even if she did, she couldn't vocalize them at that moment; she was so heartbroken.

* * *

Her father sat outside, rocking in his chair, his shotgun across his knees. He knew who had attacked his daughter and he knew he wanted to kill him, but he didn't want to hang for it. If he did anything, regardless of what he was defending, the community would not be in his favour and not only he, but his sons and probably his entire family would be in danger for their lives. He had to be smart about it. He had to be willing to wait and see if God took care of it and if not, he would.

He swore he would.

* * *

He waited for any word to be out. He read the papers, front page to back, sat in the local bar and asked "any good stories?" to a few of the locals, even checked police reports that sometimes came across his desk, but heard nothing. This disappointed him. He liked it when the town was in an uproar over his sickening preoccupation. He controlled the town with fear and he liked that. Especially since, he was so very well known. Little did they all know that the very person who was creating fear in the community, was the very person they trusted to lead it. He was one sick fuck of a waste of skin and he reveled in his secret identity. Mayor of the town for 7 years, serial rapist for 6 of them.

He never chose to attack in the white sections. He always preferred the black areas. No one would suspect the Mayor of the town of rape, let alone of raping 5 black girls. He was a town favorite; known for his love of community and his fellow man. His quick smile, blonde hair and green eyes made any woman swoon, but that wasn't really where his sexual interests were. An avid walker, who knew every square inch of the town, he'd walked every block of it. People were used to seeing him out and about. But, not like he did when he was on the prowl. Oh no, then he made sure he wasn't seen

346

or known. He could never be caught. Ever. And so, his horrific pattern continued.

The girl he had attacked this time was tough. He had not expected her to fight so hard and in his efforts to subdue her, he had been careless in almost every sense. He did his best to never ejaculate inside them, for fear he might get them pregnant, but this one had fought so hard that once he knocked her out, he just went at her with little regard for anything else. His rage had taken over and he carried out his crime with vengeance. Besides, who would believe her anyway?

Now, with his urges somewhat satisfied, he spent his time trying to find out anything he could, without it being suspicious. It took him 3 days before he'd heard from his police chief that there had been another rape of a very young teenage black girl. The father and her older brothers were on the hunt for who might have done it.

"The family know?" The Mayor asked.

"I believe they found her. She was hit pretty hard and left for dead. They aren't certain it's the same guy because of how brutal the attack was. The other ones weren't this bad, I guess" the Police Chief told the Mayor. *No, they weren't,* he thought to himself. He had really been enraged by the amount of fight in her and quickly, he started getting aroused just thinking of it.

He excused himself from the conversation and left to go satisfy his arousal in the bathroom. He really was a sick fuck.

* * *

It wasn't long before the mother knew her daughter was pregnant. Her body had changed, her monthly bleeding had stopped and she had been retching each morning for the past few weeks. Try as she might, she couldn't deny it and she had to find a way to tell her husband. If they found the man who did it, she prayed her husband wouldn't take to killing him. All dreams of moving away were now replaced with revenge. The revenge for the brutal rape of their daughter.

* * *

It had only been a few months since his last urge overtook him. Normally, he was able to be satiated for many months, but he was finding himself more and more aroused at the thought of raping again. He would disguise himself in heavy dark clothing and black gloves and boot polish on his face. Sometimes he wore a black balaclava his father had brought back from a trip to England. He had his attack down, except for that last rape. He promised himself he'd have to do better this time. He couldn't be stupid enough to ever get caught. Ever.

His next victim was also a young black girl. Similar looking to the last one, but a little younger. Maybe a year or two. He had spotted her also leaving church about a month ago and immediately his fantasies began.

He watched her walking route from home to the church and back. Her route went near a steep ravine that was pitch black. He could hear the river rushing below on the cold wintery night. Another perfect place! He had decided he was a genius for plotting this one so well!

He could see her from his hiding spot, his heart racing with excitement and his groin beginning to throb. He tried keeping calm so his breath wouldn't give him away on the cold night. There was one dark patch of roadway and once she had walked a little bit past him he took that opportunity to make his move. He quietly sneaked up from behind her and grabbed her, his hand covering her mouth. She struggled hard, but he held her in an iron grip, his hand crushing her mouth. When she wriggled her head back and forth, his hand slipped and she chomped down as hard as she could onto his hand. His rage went through the roof, along with his pain. He punched her in the head, hitting her hard. She let go of his hand and he quickly grabbed her head and snapped her neck. She fell instantly to the ground. Dead.

His adrenaline was pumping and he was having a hard time catching his breath. Even though he was hidden in the dark, he was worried about being seen and grabbed her and dragged her off toward the ravine. He was at his height of euphoria and decided to rape her, none-the-less. So what if she was dead?

After he was done, he dragged her closer to the ravine. He positioned her on the edge and went to push her off, down into the narrow gorge and into the raging river below. As he stood to position himself, he was unaware of the ice beneath his feet. He raised his foot to give the girl a good kick and send her on her way, but his foot missed its mark and kicked out farther than he hoped, caused him to lose his balance. His other foot, sitting on a patch of slick ice was all the inertia his body needed to send him flying down to the ground, slamming him hard and knocking the wind out of him. Desperately, he panicked and rolled over and over, trying to catch a breath. Thinking he was nowhere near the edge, he managed to pull himself up, still unable to breathe. He was a good 5 feet from the girl's body and still trying to catch his breath when he took two steps towards her to finish the job and proceeded to step right off the edge. He fell down the ravine head first, hitting a tree. It killed him instantly, but didn't stop his body from continuing down until it hit the water hard, taking him away. Never to be found, never to be caught.

Ever.

Just the way he wanted.

Karma had served him well.

* * *

News of the missing Mayor coincided with the end of the brutal and vicious rapes in the community and only a few were able to put the pieces together.

The father knew as did his sons, but they were satisfied that he was missing and figured someone else's family got to him before they did. They focused their attention now on their own kin.

* * *

It was no longer easy to hide her pregnancy and her parents discussed how they would deal with it. Neither wanted their beautiful daughter to have to endure the shame of carrying a baby, so young and unmarried, never mind the result of a rape. But, their daughter held her head high. She seemed very determined to carry the baby to full term and took very good care of herself, eating well and making sure she did all the right things to ensure the best health of the baby. Her mother and father were torn between their feeling of hatred and rage against her attacker and the love and pride for their daughter and how she was dealing with her circumstances.

She had just finished an exam by the town doctor, when her mother asked her, "Do you want to keep the baby?" It was a fair question and she and her husband had discussed the options. The baby would be mixed and not easily accepted into either race. Although, they were willing to love the child, they knew their community might not. The best idea would be to move before the child was born and perhaps find a community that wouldn't judge them or their grandbaby. It was worth a chance.

"I want what's best for this baby" her daughter answered. "Don't worry 'bout me. No matter what, I want this baby to survive" she told her mother, the words of the elderly woman in her mind. "If something should happen to me and you can't keep the baby, then please, find her a good home. Make sure she is safe" she begged her mother. Thinking her words were unusual, her mother said nothing, but it haunted her. Her own mother had spoken of a familial ability to speak to the dead and know what the future would bring. Her own mother had once been guided by dead kin. She wondered if her daughter also had that gift, if she knew what was coming and was forewarning her.

The daughter went into labour too early, the birth of the child coming weeks sooner than expected. It was extremely difficult. To start with, their daughter was so young and small framed that the baby got stuck trying to come out. This caused their daughter to sustained long and endured labour, with no success. The baby was in trouble, but then, so was the mother. The town doctor was called and between her mother and the town doctor, they did the best they could. The young girl was never fit enough to birth such a baby and her body was shattered by the delivery. She hemorrhaged and lost a lot of blood. She was able to hold her new born daughter for a few minutes before her life ended, but she knew she'd be there to guide her and her kin forever more. Whenever they needed her, she'd be there for them. And, she'd pass this gift on to the coming generations.

Her parents could not accept the baby created in evil who killed their daughter. Although they tried their best, they could not accept the baby as their kin, but the mother kept her promise to her daughter. They put the baby up for adoption. She was sent to an orphanage close to Chicago, where she stayed for a little over a year, until one day when Vera and Carson Preston walked into the orphanage.

Vera Preston took one look at the honey skinned, green eyed, beautiful little girl, with the mane of hair and fell in love. If she couldn't have that little girl, she didn't want any other. Even though Carson Preston didn't want a mixed race child, he did it for the happiness of his wife and happiness in his marriage. Maybe he could learn to be happy. Maybe.

Shortly thereafter, matriarch of the Morningstar family, Meg Preston was brought home. It would take George Morningstar's knock on the front door, more than a decade later to begin the Morningstar story.

So it begins.

And, so it continues.

The End.

About the Author

This project began as a story developed from the lyrics of a Ray Charles song, during a long car ride. DJ Sherratt had no idea what would transpire personally for her during its creation. Life got in the way and now, in 2020 the trilogy is complete.

DJ Sherratt lives in London, Ontario and continues to work in the health care industry. She and her husband, Mark celebrated 25 years of wedded bliss in 2020 and her beloved dog, Rosa still insists on sitting as close to mum's laptop as she will allow. DJ likes nothing more than giving her readers captivating narrative; a place to escape to when life needs to stop!

Visit my website at: djsherratt.wixsite.com/dj-sherratt

Printed in the United States
By Bookmasters